Nicola Marsh is a multi-award-winni[ng] ... than losing herself ... a previous life, she ... raising two dashing heroes, whipping up delish meals, cheering on her footy team and writing—her dream job. And she chats on social media. A lot. Come say hi! Instagram, Twitter, Facebook—she's there! Also find her at nicolamarsh.com.

Kelli Ireland spent a decade as a name on a door in corporate America. Unexpectedly liberated by fate's sense of humour, she chose to *carpe* the *diem* and pursue her passion for writing. A fan of happily-ever-afters, she found she loved being the puppet master for the most unlikely couples. Seeing them through the best and worst of each other while helping them survive the joys and disasters of falling in love? Best. Thing. Ever. Visit Kelli's website at kelliireland.com.

If you liked *Under His Skin* and *Wicked Heat*
why not try
King's Ransom by Jackie Ashenden
Good Girl by Christy McKellen

Discover more at millsandboon.co.uk

UNDER HIS SKIN

NICOLA MARSH

WICKED HEAT

KELLI IRELAND

MILLS & BOON

First Published in Great Britain 2019
by Mills & Boon, an imprint of HarperCollins*Publishers*
1 London Bridge Street, London, SE1 9GF

Under His Skin © 2019 Nicola Marsh

Wicked Heat © 2019 Denise Tompkins

ISBN: 978-0-263-27378-6

MIX
Paper from
responsible sources
FSC™ C007454

This book is produced from independently certified FSC™ paper
to ensure responsible forest management.
For more information visit www.harpercollins.co.uk/green.

Printed and bound in Spain
by CPI, Barcelona

UNDER HIS SKIN

NICOLA MARSH

MILLS & BOON

For my very own tradesman, Martin,
who brings a smile to my face every day. Muah!

CHAPTER ONE

LOGAN SHOULDERED OPEN the heavy glass door to the trendy café in inner Melbourne and froze.

He didn't belong in this artsy-fartsy place.

Hipsters with wispy beards, rimmed glasses and tight clothes jostled for position alongside whip-smart professionals in designer suits, studying their mobile phones with the usual self-absorption. Garish art reminiscent of a kindergartener's finger-painting dotted the walls, while muted jazz added to the cacophony of the baristas' raised voices shouting out names for take-out double decaf soy lattes and spicy chais with extra cream.

His skin prickled with discomfort as he pushed up his rolled shirt sleeves and stepped inside. The comforting aromas of coffee, cinnamon and toasted sandwiches did little to ease his wariness as he scanned the packed tables.

He couldn't see her.

It didn't surprise him that Hope McWilliams would be late. She'd sounded hoity-toity on the phone and it had nothing to do with her posh British accent. An annoying mix of aloof and condescending, she'd insisted he be the one to quote the renovations to her music studio and not one of his subordinates. He could've blown her off. He should've. But his foreman had injured his back last week, meaning Logan needed to stick around town for another month before Rick was back on deck.

It pissed him off, being confined to this city when he'd rather be on the road. He'd built his construction company into one of the best in Australia and he'd done it by travelling the length and breadth of the country, ensuring his clients were happy with his sub-contractors. He trusted his team but he'd learned through sheer hard work and determination that being the boss didn't entail delegation; he needed to take full responsibility for every job too.

A woman standing in the far corner of the café caught his attention; more precisely, her exaggerated arm-wave, making her look like a seaman waving in a fighter jet on a carrier. A quick glance over his shoulder confirmed she must be beckoning him and he strode towards her through the ridiculously tiny tables. The closer he got, the more he could see: tall, slim, blonde, pretty. But it was the goofy kaftan thingy she wore that captured his attention most: pale pink, covered in music notes. Bizarre.

He stopped short of her table and stuck out his hand. 'Logan Holmes.'

'Hope McWilliams.' She shook his hand tentatively, as if she didn't want to get dirty.

That irked. It had been a few years since he'd been

on the tools alongside his workers and he hated how narrow-minded people labelled men who worked with their hands as ignorant, grubby tradies. They took one look at steel-capped boots, shorts and a fluorescent work vest and immediately thought 'Neanderthal'.

He didn't like her supercilious stare either so he responded with a smirk. 'Taking the music theme to extremes, huh?'

Her tight smile slipped as she sat and gestured at the seat opposite, a stupid, tiny wrought-iron thing that barely held his weight. 'I'm a music teacher. It pays to advertise.'

Okay, so the ice princess had a sense of humour. He liked that. He could work with that.

'From your email and our discussion on the phone, you're looking to expand your current space into a custom-built recording studio?'

One imperious eyebrow rose, instantly adding to her air of superiority. 'You don't waste any time, do you?'

'I'm here to give you a quote.'

'We could have a coffee first?'

This time when she smiled, he almost reeled back. When she relaxed, her heart-shaped face transformed from severe to breath-taking. He'd tried not to notice her beauty when he'd first seen her, because that was another assumption some people made: that all tradesmen were lecherous creeps who wolf-whistled at any woman walking past a work site. So he'd practised showing no reaction other than politeness with women from the time he'd first picked up a hammer as an eager eighteen-year-old apprentice.

But with Hope staring at him with those wide green-grey eyes and her full lips parted in a genuine smile, his famed poker face slipped and he couldn't help but gawk.

'Coffee to go would be great.' He stood, eager to get away from the disarming blonde. 'I'll get it.'

He'd taken a step before belatedly realising he hadn't asked her what she wanted. 'What would you like?'

'A soy chai decaf, regular.'

Figured. He hated fancy fake coffee blends almost as much as pretentious cafés like this.

'I'll meet you out the front,' she said, reaching for her wallet on the table.

'This one's on me.' He held up his hand and walked away before she could argue.

His flaky father might not have given him much growing up but he'd instilled in him old-fashioned values about how to treat a woman, such as paying for meals or beverages, being respectful and active listening. Pity his old man hadn't practised what he preached after he'd married.

It took a surprisingly quick five minutes for the barista to make their coffees and as he wound his way through the tables towards the door he spotted Hope waiting for him outside. It gave him time to study her and this time he reacted to more than her pretty face. His cock hardened as he realised that ugly kaftan ended mid-thigh, exposing glorious long legs, which were surprisingly tanned given her pale English skin. Smooth. Lean, with a hint of muscle, testament to a subtle strength, perfect for wrapping around him…

Fuck, what the hell was wrong with him? He didn't ogle prospective clients, especially ones who made him feel inferior with a single glance.

Scowling, he bumped the door with his hip and backed out, carefully balancing the takeout cups. He didn't think she'd be impressed if one drop of chai froth bubbled up onto the rim. He could smell the awful spicy blend and it tickled his nose.

'Here you go.' He sounded gruff and cleared his throat when she turned and flashed him another one of those smiles that made him stare.

'Thanks.' She took a sip, followed by a soft appreciative moan that made him want to shove her up against the nearest wall and see if he could coax a few more out of her.

Instead, he took a gulp of his straight black and burned his throat.

'My place isn't far from here. Shall we go look at it now?'

What the fuck? Why had she insisted they meet here and not at her studio if it wasn't far?

Another thing he hated alongside frou-frou coffees, artsy cafés and glitzy inner cities: game-playing.

'If you're wondering why we didn't meet there, it's because I wanted to get a feel for you first.' She laughed, a little self-consciously. 'Not literally, of course, but websites and recommendations can be misleading and I wanted to see if you were the right man for the job before I showed you what I want done.'

He refrained from pointing out the obvious—they hadn't really talked much yet so how did she know he was right for the job?—because her tone had taken on a husky edge and for an irrational moment he wondered what she really wanted done.

It wouldn't be the first time horny women had confronted him on jobs before. First as a naïve nineteen-year-old, when he'd rocked up to a new house to check the kitchen cupboard installation and the home owner's new girlfriend had greeted him at the door in a loosely belted robe which she'd proceeded to undo when he stepped inside. He'd bolted.

The second time he'd been a fully qualified carpenter on his first job, building a pergola for a rich couple in South Yarra. He'd been on a ladder in the back yard when the wife had stepped out of the pool house, naked, and invited him to take a swim. He'd been deferent and polite, but building that pergola had been the hardest job ever because she'd been a stunner with a body to match. Thankfully, he'd never forgotten his first boss's advice—'Don't screw where you glue'—and it had served him well.

So what was it about this woman that had him forgetting liquid nails and contemplating nailing her?

'It would've been easier to meet at your place,' he said, sounding rude as he fell into step beside her. He tempered it with 'So what is it you want done exactly?'

Her startled gaze flew to his and he bit back a chuckle. He hadn't meant to sound remotely flirtatious but he needed to regain the upper hand, to show her that he jumped to nobody's tune, so he'd lowered his voice, knowing she could misinterpret it. The fact she had meant one of two things: she was smart or she felt the unexpected buzz of sexual attraction too.

When he returned her stare, deliberately guileless, she tilted her nose in the air and picked up the pace. 'I'll show you when we get there.'

'I'll bet,' he muttered, so softly she couldn't hear, unable to stop a smug grin breaking through.

Not many women challenged him. Because he moved around a lot he dated sporadically, but never longer than a few weeks.

He never, ever, wanted to leave a woman waiting for him to come back, the way his mother had constantly, tragically, waited for his father.

'Don't you love Melbourne?' She reverted to distant and cool as she gestured at the graffiti-covered walls they strolled past. 'So many hidden gems like this.'

Personally, he didn't get the appeal of the laneways that criss-crossed the city. Some Einstein had thought spraying a bunch of ugly murals and opening up dive bars, hole-in-the-wall cafés and boutiques with crazy clothes would spruce up the place.

'It's messy,' he said, taking another gulp of coffee and ignoring her glare that read 'you're a Philistine'.

She didn't speak after that so he filled the silence by whistling his football club's song. That was one thing he did love about this city: Aussie Rules, and the North Melbourne Football Club in particular. He attended every game he could because for those all too brief few hours when the elite athletes kicked an oval ball around the field he remembered the one and only thing he had ever bonded over with his dad.

Stupid, he knew, but he didn't hate easily. It was a wasted emotion. So he preferred to remember the good times rather than the bad. Eating pies and drinking soda while cheering for a long fifty-metre goal on the run rather than sitting at the kitchen window in their shitty two-bedroom weatherboard in the middle of outback Victoria, waiting for his dad to come home. Something Stephen Holmes had rarely done.

'My place is just around the corner.'

He stopped whistling as they rounded the final block, wishing he hadn't been thinking about his dad. It always made him tetchy and he needed to focus on giving the princess a quote then heading over the West Gate Bridge to Williamstown to oversee a new project.

'Here we are.' She threw her arms wide and he found himself glancing at a hint of cleavage before dragging his gaze towards the glass-fronted shop, the window filled with music memorabilia and an ornately scrolled *Hope and Harmony* etched across the top.

'I take it the harmony angle refers to your music and not a twin?'

'I'm an only child,' she snapped, her curt response belied by a hint of sadness.

Great, he'd touched a nerve. This got better and better.

'This is prime real estate.' He pointed to the park opposite, flanked by apartments. 'Inner city with the feel of suburbia.'

'I like it.' She shrugged, as though the fact a twenty-something woman could afford to teach music from an expensive place like this meant nothing. The fact that she wanted a quote on renovations meant she didn't rent, she owned it, making it all the more startling.

Yeah, Hope McWilliams intrigued him, so the sooner he focussed on the job at hand the better.

'The quote will work better if you show me around.'

He expected her to bristle again so her chuckle disarmed him. 'The renovations I want done are out the back.'

She unlocked the door and punched in an alarm code before locking the door behind them. 'Follow me.'

As they moved further into the shop, he couldn't help but stare. The regular, square shop front opened into a hexagonal room that housed a grand piano, a cello and a drum kit. The wooden floorboards glowed, the walls were covered in framed sheet music and light poured into the room via an expansive skylight. His immediate impression was one of peace, and not many places made him feel peaceful these days.

'You teach those instruments?'

'No, I like the way they look in the room.' She

rolled her eyes and he barked out a laugh. Sarcasm. He liked that.

Her nose crinkled. 'Sorry. It's just that I'm tired of teaching and I want to do something more, hence the need for renovations.'

She opened the double wooden doors at the back, revealing darkness. 'What I need you to build is through here.'

When she flicked a light switch, Logan gaped. If the hexagonal room was unique, this one was truly odd. Sandstone floor, three roughly concreted walls and one brick, scattered with mediaeval light sconces and a glass-domed ceiling with more cracks than a plumber's convention.

'I need this converted into a soundproof recording studio.' She faced him, hands on hips, a worried frown slashing her perfectly shaped brows. 'Is it doable?'

'Anything's doable.'

And there it was, the unmistakable flare of excitement in her eyes.

He hadn't imagined it earlier.

She was into him.

Considering he hadn't got laid since he'd arrived in Melbourne three weeks ago, ruffling the princess to the point of unravelling could be fun.

CHAPTER TWO

HOPE SILENTLY CURSED her fair English skin as heat surged to her cheeks.

Damn this man for making her feel more flustered than she had in years.

No man rattled her, not any more. She'd only been foolish enough to fall for a guy once before and the lessons learned seven years ago courtesy of her first—and only—love ensured she didn't sweat the small stuff. What she'd endured with Willem, and the resultant fallout, had hardened her to the point of complete and utter cynicism.

Sure, she dated. She hadn't completely given up hope of finding a genuine guy. But her in-built self-protective mechanism ensured that whenever a guy got too close she found herself picking faults, picking fights or being picky in general, doing whatever it took to sabotage the relationship. Not a great trait for finding any kind of lasting happiness; then again, Willem's deliberate destruction of her naïve love meant she didn't believe in anything long-term so it didn't fuss her.

No man perturbed her; she didn't let them get close enough. Yet Logan bloody Holmes, with his broad shoulders, smouldering blue eyes and cheeky grin, had made her discombobulated since the moment he'd strode into her favourite café as if he owned the place.

She'd first learned the phrase 'sex on legs' when she'd been fourteen, after smuggling a bag of illicit romance novels into her room. Nothing got past Mrs Folsod, the housekeeper, a woman who Hope assumed to have been an off-the-books operative for MI6 because the battle-axe had been that good at snooping and ferreting out secrets. But those fabulously eye-opening books had made it past the old bat and Hope had devoured them, savouring every saucy page. She'd learned a lot from those glorious books: the art of self-pleasuring, how raunchy sex could be beyond the boring sex-ed classes at the snobby private school she had attended and many intriguing terms, including the one that described Logan perfectly—sex on legs.

Muscly legs too, from what she'd glimpsed beneath his denim. The fabric outlined a sensational butt too. As for those forearms...corded with muscle, tanned, with a fine dusting of dark-blond hair the same colour as that on his head.

It looked as though he hadn't had a haircut in a while, the shaggy surfer style suiting him, drawing attention to those cut cheekbones and jaw, accentuating the unique blue of his eyes. They reminded her of a Yorkshire sky on a perfect summer's day, which was crazy, considering she hadn't been home in five years.

'Hope?' He snapped his fingers in front of her face and she wrenched her attention back to him.

He'd said 'anything's doable' in a tone so loaded with innuendo she'd clenched her thighs, like she had thirteen years earlier reading that first racy novel.

Sure her cheeks must be a fiery beacon to her embarrassment, she mustered a disinterested expression. 'I want to know if you can turn this space into a state-of-the-art recording studio.'

When he grinned, she knew she hadn't succeeded in fooling him and she almost sagged in relief when he stopped staring at her with those too-knowing eyes and glanced around the room.

'This is one quirky space.' He pointed to the cracked glass ceiling. 'Looks like a few birds ended up with a headache up there.'

'It was like that when I bought it.'

'How long ago was that?'

'About a month after I arrived in Australia, five years ago.'

'Yet you still sound like the Queen.'

She laughed at his lame impression of a British accent. 'I love living here but I can't quite manage a "no worries, mate" yet.'

'Takes practice.' He winked and that heat in her cheeks spread to every inch of her yearning body.

God, it was embarrassing how long since she'd last had sex. One year? Two? She'd given up counting around the time she'd had her third putrid date via an online app one of her students swore by.

Her unintentional celibacy had to be the reason she wanted to push this rugged, sexy Aussie down onto the floor and mount him.

'Are you okay?'

To make matters worse, he took a step closer, bringing him within touching distance. He smelled good too, like cut grass on a rainy day. Earthy. Wholesome. It made her wonder what he would taste like…

Crap. Thinking about those old novels wasn't good.

'I'm fine, it's a tad hot in here.' She refrained from fanning her cheeks, just.

'Really?' His gaze locked on hers and she knew without a doubt he was toying with her. 'I guess it's better than the initial chill.'

The corners of his mouth quirked into a cute smirk; he wasn't talking about the ambient temperature.

'I'm reserved when I first meet people,' she said, annoyed by the compulsion to justify herself but needing to get this guy onside because he was the best for her needs. The needs of her studio, that was, and the first step to really proving herself in the music industry. Her story, and she was sticking to it. 'I can come across a little cold.'

'Brr…try freezing.' He mimicked a shiver and rubbed his arms, drawing her attention to his fine biceps and pecs straining beneath the simple white cotton of a button-down shirt.

Seriously rattled by the urge to keep ogling him, she gritted her teeth. 'Do you want this job or not, Mr Holmes?'

'Uh-oh, the thermostat got turned down again.' His teeth fake-chattered and she bit back a laugh. 'And for what it's worth I don't give a fuck about this job. I run one of the top specialised construction companies in the country. I don't advertise because word of mouth recommendations will keep me busy with potential business for the next few decades.'

He took another step closer and she held her breath. 'So let's get one thing straight. The real question here is whether I *choose* to do your job and whether you can afford me.'

Nobody spoke to Hope like this, ever. From the moment she'd been born into the illustrious Mc-Williams family, everyone around her had kissed her aristocratic ass. She'd thought it the norm until she'd grown older and wiser, around the age of seven, when one of the maids' daughters had called her a stuck-up prig. She'd been shocked to be disliked for the first time in her life and hadn't liked it. Her parents had deferred to her and the domestic staff had too; even her teachers had been politely fawning.

The problem with everyone pandering to her meant she could never fully trust when someone liked her for herself. And she'd made a monumental mistake in her personal life because of it.

She couldn't tell the difference between suck-ups and sincerity. So she really admired those who didn't kowtow to her. Like Logan.

'Sorry if I offended you.' She offered the same smile she'd used to great effect over the years when wheedling exactly what she wanted out of her parents. 'I revert to my English roots all too quickly when I'm bamboozled.'

'I have that effect on you?'

Damn, in her efforts to calm him she'd slipped up and said too much. 'I meant the upcoming renovations and my eagerness to get them done quickly.'

She gestured at the walls to emphasise her point but by the glint in his eyes he knew her excuse was BS.

'Right, the renovations,' he drawled, sticking his hands into his pockets and following her line of vision around the room. 'Here's what I see. You'll need a complete revamp of the space. New roofing for a start. If you want to keep the glass dome, it'll need to be double-glazed. But if you want this to be completely soundproof I'd ditch the glass. The flooring will be an easy fix and the walls not too hard either.'

She could listen to him talk all day, his deep voice with the broad Australian accent as intoxicating as the rest of him. His eyes lit up as he explained the renovations, demonstrating true passion for his work.

How would he look indulging in other passions?

When she caught him staring at her oddly again, she quickly cleared her throat. 'How much?'

'I'll outline all the proposed changes and costing in a formal quote I'll email to you later, but from what I can see, including materials and labour, you're looking at a ballpark figure of around sixty grand.'

Hope tried to hide her surprise and failed. She wasn't a complete novice and had obtained quotes from two other companies, both coming in at about half of Logan's. But a fellow music teacher who also played violin in a major touring orchestra had recommended him to her. Apparently Logan's company had constructed their rehearsal spaces to a standard higher than that of anything in which her friend had practised around the world and Hope had known then that she had to have him. Renovate, that was. That clarification was important for her howling libido that hadn't quit since she'd first laid eyes on him.

'Done.'

His eyebrows shot up and his lips thinned, as if he was clamping them together with all his might to prevent from blurting that she was crazy for accepting his first offer.

'I'll settle for nothing less than the best and I know what I want.' She stepped into his personal space, almost toe to toe, done with him toying with her. Time to regain the upper hand. 'And I want you.'

CHAPTER THREE

LOGAN KNEW HOPE was referring to him doing her precious bloody renovations when she said 'I want you' but it took a second or two for his eager cock to catch up with his logic.

He'd been rock-hard since he'd set foot in this room and she'd become animated, like one of those wind-up ballerinas in his mum's old jewellery box that whirled when wound up.

He'd tried to get a rise out of her several times, to tease her into lightening up, to see what was beneath that frosty exterior.

He hadn't expected her to turn the tables on him.

She stood too close, some exotic flowery fragrance reminiscent of newly budded roses teasing him to bury his nose in her neck and inhale. Close enough he could feel the heat radiating off her, as if she'd been standing next to a radiator too long. Her cheeks were flushed, her lips parted and tiny jade flecks glowed in her eyes.

For a second he almost lost it. He imagined backing her up against the nearest wall, flipping up that short kaftan, tearing off her panties and burying himself in deep. Or having her kneel before him, that prim and proper mouth wrapped around him, sucking him off...

'I accept your offer. When can you start?'

Logan blinked, his X-rated fantasy instantly obliterated by her coolly polite question.

Of course he had to accept the job now, even after throwing out that ludicrously inflated price. He'd done it to see her baulk and had looked forward to bargaining with her. She had a hidden fire beneath the frost and it had come out several times already when she'd returned his quips. He sure as hell hadn't expected her to agree to it so fast.

But he couldn't recant now, not without appearing unprofessional, so he nodded. 'I'll do the preliminaries and get my team set. We can start Monday if that suits?'

She grimaced. 'Monday is my busiest teaching day and I don't want my students disrupted. Can you start Tuesday?'

Usually he called the shots on where and when his crew worked but residual guilt over the exorbitant quote for a fairly routine job made Logan nod. 'Sure, but you'll need to reschedule the following Monday, because a job of this magnitude may require two weeks to complete. Plus we need to factor in unforeseen hold-ups like bad weather.'

'Understood.' She twisted a strand of hair that had come loose from her elaborate topknot, gnawing on her lip absentmindedly. 'I knew there'd be some dis-

ruption but maybe I'm better off closing and changing all my appointments for the next fortnight.'

He nodded. 'It would make life easier on us. We
take occupational health and safety very seriously
and having people around during renovations is a
hazard we'd rather avoid.'

'Okay.'

He eyed her suspiciously, wondering why she
sounded so meek, as though the ice princess had
melted into a submissive little snowman.

'I really need this to work,' she murmured as she
headed back towards the room with the instruments,
winding that strand of hair tighter around her finger. 'It has to.'

Intrigued by her glimpse of vulnerability, he followed, stopping only to turn out the lights and close
the double doors. He found her slumped on the piano
stool, eyeing him with open speculation.

'I have it on good authority you're the best at what
you do.'

While he didn't need the validation these days,
it was always nice to get praise. 'My company only
takes on a limited number of boutique jobs, meaning
we focus on one at a time per city, ensuring quality
and attention to detail.' He shrugged. 'When you're
the best, word gets around.'

'So I heard.' She pinned him with an astute stare.
'And you charge accordingly, so it seems.'

'That's right. Supply and demand.'

Though in this case he was quadrupling his profit
margins because he'd been a smart-ass trying to get

a rise out of her and it didn't sit well with him. Too late to back down now.

When she continued to stare at him as if she could see right through his BS, he distracted her by pointing at the instruments. 'You play and teach all these?'

'Yes. Viola and double bass too.'

'Wow, talented.' The only thing he played was the fool. 'My music tastes extend to good old country and western, that's it.'

'I'm an indie girl myself, hence the recording studio dream.' She pointed at the closed doors, managing to surprise him once again with her eclectic taste in music.

'I picked you for classical.'

The corners of her mouth drooped. 'I'm not some cliché. The indie scene is huge in Melbourne, which is why I want to record my own songs and then branch out into recording other artists.'

Damn, he'd trod on a minefield without meaning to. 'Sounds admirable.'

'Are you mocking me?'

Fuck, she really was testy about her music. 'Not at all.' He held up his hands. 'Hey, the only musical talent I have is playing the washboard back in Rally-Doo and even then I was only ever mediocre.'

Her forehead crinkled in confusion. 'Washboard? Rally-Doo?'

'It's a tiny town near Swan Hill, in the middle of nowhere, really, where I grew up.'

Even saying the name made him clear his throat like he'd done as a kid when the summer dust grew so thick it clogged in his nose and the back of his mouth. 'As for the washboard, how can you call yourself a musician if you don't know the finer points of dragging a metal brush against a piece of corrugated iron, redolent of the old washboards used in years gone by?'

Her forehead cleared and a small smile played about her mouth. Good. He much preferred her like this rather than in the maudlin mood that had been hanging over her the last few minutes. 'You Aussies are inventive, I'll give you that.'

'That we are.'

They locked gazes and in that moment something in the air between them shifted and shimmered, a hint of the forbidden, straining to drag them together.

Logan should resist. He never got involved with clients. But there was something about this woman that begged to see how far he could delve into this subtle attraction.

'Maybe if you're lucky, I'll play you some time?'

Her eyes widened at his innuendo as he mock-slapped his head. 'Sorry, play *for* you some time.'

She continued to stare at him with those big, expressive eyes and he waited to see if she'd change the subject or spar for the sheer hell of it.

'Playing any kind of instrument takes concentration, you know.' She patted the space on the stool next to her and he found his feet moving towards her. 'Precision. Timing. Talent.'

He sat and her smile was pure devilry. 'But the most important is practice. Hours and hours of practice. Listening to your instrument. Feeling your instrument. Stroking your instrument. Caressing your instrument—'

He kissed her. He couldn't fucking help it. All that talk of feeling and stroking and caressing had got to him.

Her mouth opened to him and her tongue sought his, teasing his, taunting, demanding to give whatever he could. And fuck, did he want to give her everything and then some.

She clutched at him, her hands pawing his chest, and when her fingers slid between the buttons of his shirt and grazed his chest he felt as if he'd stuck a sander into a tub full of water.

She moaned as he palmed her ass and dragged her onto his lap, grinding her against the fly of his jeans, leaving her in no doubt how far he wanted this to go.

When she started to writhe against him, as if she wanted to get closer, he slid his hands under her kaftan, encountering the soft, smooth skin of her thighs, then slid higher to her…bare ass.

Hot damn. The prim princess went commando.

'Fuck, you're full of surprises,' he said, squeezing the perfect handful of ass.

'I'm not who you think I am,' she murmured, nipping his ear with a sharp bite that bordered on pain, until her tongue darted out and licked it all better. The touch of her tongue lapping at his earlobe sent a jolt straight to his rock-hard cock.

Eager to feel her wetness, he slipped a hand over

her hip and between their bodies, when the blast of a trumpet made him jump.

'Shit, that's the entry bell, which means my next student is here,' she said, scrambling off him and tugging down her kaftan. 'You have to go.'

He stared at her standing in front of him, wild-eyed, flushed and dishevelled, and thought he'd never seen anything sexier.

'Hey, calm down—'

'Don't you dare tell me what to do.' Her lips pursed in disapproval as he watched the woman who'd been willing and wanton on his lap a moment ago morph from warmth to cold disdain.

'Fine.'

But it wasn't, and as he stood and readjusted himself so he could actually walk out he shot her a curious glance. How could someone change like that so quickly? He was an open book. Upfront to the point of bluntness, people knew what to expect from him. It pissed him off when people said one thing and did another, or vice versa.

When she turned her back on him and started flipping through a music book, he said, 'For the record, you came onto me.'

She spun around to face him, that spark back in her eyes. 'Go. Please.'

She almost whimpered the last word and rather than push the issue he took pity on her. She had a student waiting and, by the way she vacillated between poised and uncertain, she needed time to pull herself together.

'I'll email you the formalised quote.' He headed for the door leading to the front of the shop and paused. 'And I'll be here Tuesday morning to get the boys set up.'

She gave a brief nod, her gaze riveted to his mouth. Yeah, this one was full of contradictions. Fire and ice. Unexpectedly scorching one minute, frigidly chilling the next. The contrast only served to pique his interest further.

'Unless you want to see me sooner?'

He could've sworn the corners of her mouth twitched before she shooed him away. 'Go.'

CHAPTER FOUR

HOPE WENT THROUGH the motions of teaching piano to an uninterested, average student. The reluctant teen hadn't practised since their last session so it made the forty-five minutes even more torturous than usual. Parents who pushed their kids into learning instruments when they'd rather be skateboarding had a lot to answer for.

She should know. Her parents had pushed her into horse riding and polo and chess when she would've much rather been jamming with the local kids in the village. Sure, they'd encouraged her interest in piano and violin but had been horrified when she'd mentioned the D-word. Apparently drums weren't the preferred instrument for an aristocratic McWilliams' child.

So she'd learned in secret, using some of her generous allowance to pay a teacher in the village, an ageing rocker who still toured on occasion. Harry Remme had been more attentive to her music career than her folks and posh music teachers put together. He'd introduced her to a world beyond Mozart and

Chopin, to a world filled with guitar riffs, drum solos and the deep bass rhythms that she felt all the way down to her soul.

She'd been hooked.

From that moment she'd known what she wanted to do: create the kind of music that changed people's lives, the way Harry's music had changed hers.

Harry's band hadn't conformed. They hadn't done covers. They'd written original material, recorded it in a tiny studio outside of London and distributed it online to whoever was lucky enough to hear it. She'd spent countless hours listening to their quirky songs and loving every minute of it. Harry had fostered her love of unusual music while teaching her everything he could about the drums. She'd been thrilled to be accepted into a premier international music college in Paris once she finished school but what she'd learned at that prestigious place hadn't come close to fuelling her creativity the way Harry's music had.

It broke her heart that eventually he'd betrayed her like everyone else in her life.

She'd never recovered from his deception so close on the heels of Willem breaking her heart but she'd always be indebted to him for encouraging her to break free of her parents' expectations and choose her own path. If she'd done what her mother and father had wanted she'd be married to some uppity earl named Charles Butterworth with a brood of kids by now, a nanny, housekeeper and chauffeur, living down the road from her parents in a palatial country house.

They'd humoured her love of music by accepting she'd attend the college in Paris, never imagining she'd follow her dream all the way to Australia. They'd threatened to disown her, to cut her off. She hadn't cared.

They'd lied to her like everyone else.

She benefited from her granny's trust fund, meaning she never had financial worries. Sure, things might be different if she didn't have that safety net, but she doubted it. Nothing would stop her from pursuing her dream.

Not even some six-four gorgeous guy who kissed like a pro and who'd almost made her come by groping her ass.

Heat flushed her cheeks at the memory of how turned on she'd been. If that student hadn't arrived she would've screwed him on the piano stool.

Never in a million years would she have expected him to discover her dirty little secret: that she didn't wear underwear most days.

Being so daring was her one concession whilst living a well-ordered life. It made her feel a little bad when her entire life she'd been so very good. A way of cutting free from the constraints of her past. A way to prove, albeit to herself, that she held all the power and was in control of her own destiny.

The more refined guys she usually dated had been repulsed by her lack of constraint. Logan had been turned on big time, the focus being on *big*.

He'd felt huge through his jeans and she'd been so

close to riding that bad boy. She needed the release so badly…

The throb between her legs became insistent so Hope did the only thing possible: she locked up, picked up her mobile and headed for the bathroom.

It didn't take her long to find what she needed: the picture of Logan on his company's website.

The photo didn't do him justice. Neither did the suit. She preferred how he'd looked today: a little rough around the edges with his scruffy dark-blond hair skimming his collar, his shirt sleeves rolled up, that denim hugging his ass and those eyes so penetratingly blue she could've sworn he could see right through her.

She leaned against the hand basin and stared into those eyes, remembering how he'd looked at her the moment before he'd kissed her. As if he wanted to ravage her.

She'd enjoyed taunting him, had liked how he stood up to her and gave as good as he got.

Her gaze drifted to his mouth as her hand drifted lower, her fingers seeking her clit. She was so wet, thanks to him.

She stared at his lips and remembered the feel of his tongue in her mouth, skilled and sure, and imagined what it could do where her middle finger zeroed in on now. Her pulse raced, the lightness in her chest making her feel as if she were floating as she circled her clit over and over, her excitement escalating too quickly. She didn't care. She needed a release and, with the man who'd wound her up gone, she needed it now.

Breathless, she started panting a little. Her eyes drifted shut for a moment as she imagined Logan's fingers touching her, Logan's tongue licking her, Logan's dick inside her... She tensed and came on a soft moan, sagging against the basin.

When she opened her eyes, he was still there, staring at her from that photo, looking way too smug and self-controlled.

He'd got her so wound up that she'd just masturbated away from home for the first time.

Time to ruffle him as much as he'd ruffled her.

CHAPTER FIVE

LOGAN HAD DOUBLE-CHECKED the quote twice before firing it off to Hope an hour ago.

Considering he'd already fucked up by kissing her, he didn't want there to be any potential problems with this job.

Not that he expected any, as she'd been as into that unexpected make-out session as he had, but it still didn't sit right that he'd crossed the line with a client.

'Hey, bozo, what's happening?' Rick, his foreman, slapped him on the back as he slid onto a bar stool opposite. 'You know I can't drink when I'm on pain meds so why the hell did you ask me to meet you at a pub?'

'To torture you, of course.' Logan raised his schooner in a cheer. 'What are you having? Lemonade? Cola? Soda water?'

'Fuck you.' Rick flipped him the bird. 'Get me a light beer. That way I'll only get half-pissed when it mixes with the meds.'

'Dickhead.' Logan headed for the bar and ordered Rick a lemon, lime and bitters, glad he'd invited his old mate here tonight. He needed the distraction. Sitting here rehashing what he'd done with Hope wouldn't help anybody, least of all himself.

When he placed the drink in front of Rick on the small round table between them, his friend groaned. 'You're not my mother. Get me a real drink.'

'No can do, mate. You're the best foreman in the country and I need you on deck sooner rather than later, so let the meds do their work and that means sticking to soda for you.'

Rick grunted, took a sip and wrinkled his nose. 'Fucking lolly water.'

'Bottoms up.' Logan took a gulp of his beer and ignored Rick's woebegone expression.

'So what do you think of the new job I emailed you?'

Rick gave a thumbs-up. 'Looks good. We've done a few of those recording studios now. You must be getting a reputation.'

A bad one, if Hope ever blabbed to anyone about that kiss.

'They're lucrative, that's for sure.' Rick took another sip and made a gagging sound. 'Though the quote seemed high. Is there a problem?'

Logan shook his head. 'The owner was being a bit of a smart-ass so I upped the ante, expecting she'd cave. She didn't, so now we're going to make a healthy profit.'

'Uh-oh.' Rick's eyes narrowed. 'You've got the hots for her.'

'Don't be a dumb-ass,' Logan said, unable to meet

his mate's eyes and opting for looking into his beer glass instead.

'You do like her!' Rick made an odd triumphant, crowing sound. 'You always like the ones with the smart mouths because they challenge you, so if you charged her that much she must've really got to you.'

'Maybe a little,' he admitted begrudgingly, unable to stop the grin spreading across his face. 'She's a fire-cracker all right. Ice princess one minute, fiery the next.'

Rick imitated playing a violin. 'Look at you, all smitten kitten.'

'Bullshit.' Logan downed the rest of his beer. 'Don't mind me while I go get another alcoholic beverage.'

Rick flipped him the bird again and Logan laughed. He liked the company's Melbourne jobs for this reason: he got to hang out with his best mate. They'd known each other for twelve years, after he'd met Rick on the first day of his apprenticeship in the city. He'd been a naïve eighteen-year-old who loved building stuff; Rick had been a thirty-year-old electrician on the same job. They'd been mates ever since. Logan trusted Rick when he didn't trust many people in this world.

When his construction company had started taking off, he'd offered Rick the job of head foreman on all jobs in Melbourne. It gave him peace of mind, knowing Rick had his back when Logan travelled the country doing quotes. He had a good, reliable work team in each major city but Rick was the only guy who would never screw him over.

'Seriously, mate, how's the back?'

Rick screwed up his nose, held up his hand and wavered it side to side. 'The anti-inflammatories did the trick in the first week and I'm weaning myself off the pain meds now. I'm seeing Madame Lash, the torturous physio, three times a week, and Doc wants to review at the end of the week.'

'Cut the cookie-cutter medical spiel.' Logan rested his forearms on the table and leaned forward. 'How are you feeling?'

'Shitty from being cooped up at home and not on the job site but otherwise okay. The back really is improving.'

Logan nodded. 'Good to hear.'

'So tell me more about this client.' Rick slipped his mobile out of his pocket and scrolled through his emails. 'Hope McWilliams. Fancy-schmancy name.'

For a fancy-schmancy woman. Logan had never met anyone like her. Sure, he mingled with the rich on occasion. Being a successful CEO of a major construction company ensured he got invited to all the right parties, particularly when he had so many satisfied customers. People talked and he hadn't been bullshitting Hope when he had said he didn't have to advertise. But even the refined women he met in those circles weren't like Hope. Those women looked at him as if he was a curiosity, as if he was a wild pet they needed to tame. Hope hadn't looked at him like that. When she'd dropped her frosty exterior and thawed, Hope had looked at him as though she'd wanted to devour him whole.

'She owns a piece of prime real estate on the

outskirts of inner-city Melbourne, so she's loaded. Didn't baulk at my asking price either.'

'I'm not interested in her bank balance, doofus.' Rick rolled his eyes. 'What's she like?'

Logan searched for the right word to describe Hope, coming up with a lame 'Interesting.'

'You're pathetic.' Rick took another sip of his drink and mock-barfed. 'I can't drink this shit, it's too sweet. I'm going home to have a beer.'

'Hey, you can't—'

'Take a chill pill, dude. I'm messing with you.' Rick stood slowly, unkinked his back and winced. 'But I am heading home. I'm just as keen to get back to work as you are to have me there, so it's exercise time for me. Keep me posted on the McWilliams job, okay?'

'Sure. I'll email you updates—'

'And for fuck's sake, don't screw the crew.' Rick made a gun with his thumb and forefinger and shot him.

'She doesn't work for me.'

'But she's a client so close enough.' Rick slapped him on the back. 'I'm serious, bro. Tread carefully, okay?'

'Yes, Mum,' Logan muttered, knowing he had no intention of adhering to his friend's advice.

As Rick shuffled towards the door, the screen of Logan's phone lit up with a text from Hope.

Need 2 C U 2nite 2 discuss quote. Please.

'That's weird,' Logan muttered, staring at the message. It looked as though she'd added 'please' as an afterthought, as if she doubted he'd want to see her.

He knew what he should do. Make an excuse. Blow her off. Because seeing her tonight, hot on the heels of their unexpected make-out session earlier, could be playing with fire.

Then again, since when had he backed away from a challenge?

I'm at Golden Treble, Nth Melb. Can U come now?

As his thumb hit the send button he realised how that last sentence read. He hadn't meant it as an innuendo but, considering how they'd bantered earlier, she might mistake it for such.

Her response pinged.

I'm coming.

And she really would be, in the not too distant future, if he had any say in it.

CHAPTER SIX

HOPE LOVED THE vibe of inner Melbourne and its surrounding suburbs: Carlton, with its lush parks and Little Italy on Lygon Street; Albert Park, with its lake and accompanying restaurants; and Brunswick, the bohemian capital of the city jam-packed with alternative boutiques, bars and comedy clubs. But she rarely ventured into North Melbourne and discovered she'd been missing out. Trendy eateries lined Curzon Street but as she followed the instructions of her trusty satnav she found herself in the back streets where a small, grungy pub sat on a corner.

It figured Logan would ask her to meet him here.

He had a thing for throwing her off-guard. Maybe he wanted her to feel out of place. Maybe he'd already labelled her as some rich bitch wanting to slum it. Neither could be further from the truth because as she found a parking spot not far from the front door and entered the pub an immediate sense of coming home enveloped her.

This place reminded her exactly of the small pubs Harry used to play in.

Dark wood panelling adorned the walls roughly three quarters of the way up, with a deep crimson paint finishing the walls to the roof. A small elevated stage was tucked into one corner, a cluster of tiny tables in another, with the mahogany bar dominating the back wall. A few tall tables and bar stools were tucked away behind the stage and that was where she spotted Logan nursing a beer and fending off a buxom bar girl. Not that she blamed the woman. If she had DDs like that she'd be deliberately resting them on Logan's arm as she cleared the table too.

Unfortunately, her average Bs would barely make a dent in his biceps so she'd have to settle for wowing him with her scintillating wit.

That, and the fact he already knew she didn't wear underwear.

A tingling swept up the back of her neck at the memory of his hands on her, the slight rasp of his fingers against her bare ass... She'd been so turned on it wouldn't have taken much more rubbing against his crotch for her to come. It was why she'd had to take the edge off in the studio's bathroom. But it hadn't been enough, not nearly enough, and she'd asked to meet him for the simple fact she wanted to have sex tonight.

She'd never done this before, so brazenly approach a guy with the sole intention of screwing him. She didn't care that he was a direct adjunct to achieving her dream. She didn't care it might muddy their semi-working relationship. All she cared about was getting off with him tonight.

As she wound her way towards him, her soles stuck to the navy carpeted floor. Yeah, pubs like this were the same the world over. Despite regular cleaning, the spillage of many pints of beer over the years took its toll. She inhaled, savouring the smell of bar snacks predominantly featuring fried onions, and the yeasty aroma of beer.

Harry had been a stout man. She'd tried the stuff once and almost vomited. She'd stuck to her G and Ts after that. He'd never baulked at her under-age drinking; not that she'd had more than one drink and only after she'd turned seventeen. He hadn't lectured. He'd supported her, nurtured her talent and had been the father she'd never had.

Until he too had betrayed her trust.

He'd died during her final year at the music college in the middle of her exams. She would've attended his funeral if he hadn't shattered their relationship a year earlier.

She'd never forget the day she had discovered the one person she'd thought she could trust was just as duplicitous as the rest of the people in her life.

Harry had been her go-to person when her first love had gone pear-shaped. She'd cried buckets over Willem, had poured her heart out to Harry, confiding in him in a way she'd never felt comfortable doing with her emotionally repressed parents. Yet a scant month later he'd crapped all over her regardless. He'd stolen more than her songs from her. He'd taken her ability to trust and turned her into a hardened cynic.

Everybody lied. It was a fact of life, a human

frailty. She should've been immune to it, growing up with parents who stretched the truth whenever it suited them; with so-called friends at boarding school who only told her what she wanted to hear in order to suck up; with her only serious boyfriend, Willem.

But she'd expected better of Harry. He'd been her idol, her friend, her confidante and he'd screwed her over regardless.

Hope blinked several times to dispel the moisture from her eyes and continued traversing the pub. A few old men sat at the bar, locals probably, from the way they bantered with the barman. Logan caught sight of her and stood. He didn't wave. He didn't smile. He just stared at her, jaw set, gaze steady, and she felt that damn jolt again arrowing between her legs.

She'd made the right decision in coming here.

She needed one night.

One night of fast and furious sex to dispel this weird fascination for him.

Then she could return to furthering her goal in setting up the best indie record label this city had ever heard.

She strode towards him, intent on appearing poised, when in fact the closer she got the more her confidence fled and her legs wobbled like just-set jelly. The empty sensation in her stomach intensified when she reached him and a slow, knowing smile spread across his face, as if he could see into her horny soul.

'You wanted to see me?' He pulled out a bar stool for her and she slid onto it, relieved to have it holding her up rather than her traitorous legs.

'Yes, thank you for agreeing to meet me.' She sounded so stilted, so formal, his grin widened.

'Every time you open your mouth I feel like I'm being addressed by royalty,' he said, leaning in to murmur in her ear. 'Except when you kissed me, of course.'

'*You* kissed *me*,' she said, intent on reprimanding him when in fact her voice came out breathy.

'So I did.' He chuckled and straightened, and she immediately wished he'd return to whispering in her ear. 'Got to say, Princess, you surprised me.'

'The underwear thing?'

'Yeah. That.' His eyes darkened to indigo as his jaw clenched. 'Pretty fucking hot.'

His husky tone rippled over her like a caress and she squeezed her thighs together. It did little for the ache only he could assuage.

Here went nothing. 'That's actually why I wanted to see you.'

His eyebrows shot up but he remained silent, meaning she'd have to spell it out.

'I…um… I want to finish what we started in the studio.'

The words tumbled out in a rush and she held her breath. Mortification tightened her stomach and a tingling swept up the back of her neck. Fantasising about riding him was one thing, articulating it quite another.

His lips curved with amusement—he knew exactly how uncomfortable she was—and she clamped down on the urge to bolt.

'You mean the quote?'

He was being deliberately obtuse. She could see it in the teasing glint in his eyes, and hear it in his taunting drawl.

'I've approved the quote and already wired a deposit so, no, I don't mean the quote and you damn well know it,' she said, ending on a huff. 'Do you need me to spell it out for you?'

'Yeah.' He stepped in close again and trailed a fingertip down her forearm. 'I want to hear you say it.'

Her breath hitched when he reached her wrist and circled her pulse point, over and over, slow and concentric, before moving on to her palm and doing the same thing. Her skin prickled all over, like tiny zapping stings from touching one of those weird static electricity balls.

He lifted her palm to his mouth and pressed an open-mouthed kissed to it. 'You want me to fuck you.'

She nodded and mimicked him, her voice barely above a whisper. 'I want you to fuck me,' she said, and bit her bottom lip to stop from moaning as his tongue darted out to give her palm a little lick before he released her hand.

'Good, because I can't stop thinking about it either,' he said, resuming his seat. 'I like a woman who speaks her mind. Game-playing gives me the shits.'

She laughed at his typically blunt Aussie response. 'So you're up for it?'

He shot a glance at his groin and she did the same, delighted to see that sizeable bulge. 'I've been up since I felt you up.'

Laughter burst from her lips again. It was rare for a guy to amuse her this much. She usually found the half-assed flirting guys used as foreplay rather tedious. With Logan, his words were getting her as hot as his touch. 'So how do we do this?'

'The polite way would be for us to have a drink, talk a little, before going back to my place or yours.'

'And the impolite way?'

He took a moment to answer, his smouldering gaze dropping to her mouth. 'I take you out the back and fuck you up against one of those artistic alley walls you love so much.'

Hope's mother had lectured her from a young age that gaping wasn't ladylike but she couldn't help it. No man had ever spoken to her like this—and she liked it, a lot.

Apart from her habit of going commando, she'd never done anything remotely adventurous sexually. She liked the act itself and if she got off with the guy she considered it a bonus. Willem had been a considerate lover but bland. He'd never gone down on her but expected she blow him regularly. His selfishness right there should've alerted her to his asshole ways. And the six guys she'd screwed since had been vanilla all the way. None of them had wanted her so badly they did it up against a wall, let alone in public.

Resisting the urge to squirm, she eyeballed him. 'I'm not thirsty and I think we're all talked out.'

His eyes widened in surprise, with a healthy dose of respect for her brazenness thrown in. 'Are you saying...?'

'Time for you to show me exactly how impolite you can be.' She stood and grabbed his hand before she could second-guess this crazy impulse. Her heart jackhammered at the thought of having sex in public, a potent mix of excitement and panic at the thought of being discovered. But she couldn't walk away from him now, not when she craved him so badly she almost trembled.

He scrambled to his feet so fast they collided and she would've stumbled if he hadn't steadied her, bringing her flush against that gloriously muscular chest. She rested her palm against it, over his heart, feeling the racing thud matching hers.

His eyes blazed a scorching indigo. 'You strike me as a hearts and flowers kind of girl. You sure you want this?'

Her palm slid up to rest on his shoulder, an anchor for the out-of-control lust slamming through her. 'I thank you for being a gentleman and giving me an out, but I've never been surer of anything. I want you. Inside me. Touching me. I want...it all.'

Saying it made her want to writhe against him and she gritted her teeth against the urge to squirm.

Doubt clouded his eyes as he gave a little shake of his head. 'You deserve satin sheets, not a graffiti-covered wall at your back.'

'I deserve…this.' She slid her free hand beneath their bodies and cupped him, vindicated when he groaned.

No one told her what she wanted, not any more. Taking back control of her life involved more than moving a million miles from home five years ago. Her independence stretched to knowing exactly what she wanted.

Right now, she wanted Logan.

After what seemed like an eternity he nodded and tightened his grip on her hand. 'Let's go.'

CHAPTER SEVEN

LOGAN DIDN'T BREAK stride as he wound his way through the pub towards the back exit.

He should stop this madness, despite her bold assertion. But he had as much hope of reining in his rampant libido as he did of staying put in one city: absolutely none.

He'd had his fair share of women, some who'd worn their sexuality more overtly than Hope. But he'd never had any of them articulate so precisely what they wanted.

'I want you. Inside me. Touching me. I want... it all.'

Fuck, her cultured voice reverberated through his head.

She wanted it all? He'd give it to her.

He understood. She wanted one fast fuck with a guy who was opposite to her. The princess slumming it with the fabled bad boy. Her walk on the wild side. Opposites attracting and all that crap.

He'd been intent on shocking her, throwing out that comment about alley sex as a challenge.

He'd never expected her to accept.

When they reached the door that opened out into the alley, he gave her one last chance to back out.

'Once we go out there, it's game on,' he said, tugging her flush against him and grinding himself into her pelvis.

Defiant, she tilted her head back and their gazes locked. Her eyes glowed in the dim light cast from a single globe hanging from the ceiling and he saw her desire matched his.

'Bring it on,' she said, pushing him at the same time so that his butt hit the door and he backed through it.

Having her take control was a huge fucking turn-on and he grinned for the hell of it when she shoved him a tad hard against the wall and the back of his head clunked.

'Shit, I'm sorry,' she said, her stricken expression making him laugh.

'Babe, I'm fine.' He knocked on the top of his head. 'This one's as hard as the one in my pants.'

Her face cleared and she managed a rueful chuckle. 'I'm so bad at this.'

'No you're not. You're refined and cultured and not used to being corrupted by a horny tradesman with one thing on his mind.'

Her eyebrow arched. 'And what's that?'

'Fucking you.'

She slammed her mouth against his and his head clunked the wall again. He didn't care. The pain barely registered when she had her tongue in his mouth and her hand on his zipper.

'Not here. More private,' he said against the corner of her mouth, guiding her towards a sheltered nook he'd first discovered as a horny teen during his first year in Melbourne.

'You've done this before,' she said flatly, some of the fire draining out of her eyes.

'I've made out with a girl here once, when I was nineteen.'

She took a moment to respond and when she did he knew it'd be a zinger by the quirk of her lips. 'Practice for the real thing now.'

He laughed. 'Something like that.'

Her smile faded as she slid her hands up his chest to rest on his shoulders. 'I have no idea what's gotten into me but I need this, you, so badly.'

There was a hint of wistful forlornness in her voice, as if wanting him confused her.

Join the club, lady. No woman had ever got under his skin so fast.

Taking her hand, he did a quick visual check of the area. Empty, apart from used kegs stacked neatly at the alley's dead-end, creating the perfect nook he remembered. Back then, he'd wanted to go all the way with his date but she'd been a reluctant virgin. This time, he had a confident woman in his arms who had demanded what she wanted.

He tugged on her hand and eased her into the nook. As soon as they were shielded from the possibility of prying eyes from a late-night stroller at the other end of the alley, she was on him. Hands pawing, mouth devouring, leg hooked around his waist as if she wanted to climb him.

He grabbed her ass and lifted her, pinning her against the wall while her legs wrapped around him. She whimpered as he kneaded her ass and kissed his way down her neck, nipping at the tender skin and following it with a lap of his tongue. With every bite and lick she rocked against him, her breathing short and choppy.

'Oh, yeah, so good,' she murmured as he found her nipple through the thin material of her kaftan and playfully bit it.

She arched, her head flung back against the wall, eyes closed, the column of her neck smooth and pale in the wan moonlight. He'd never seen anything so beautiful, so erotic.

Gently easing one of her legs down, he backed away slightly. Her eyes flew open. Clouded and dazed, she stared at him, disoriented.

'Why did you stop?'

'Because I want to be inside you when you come.'

Approval glittered in her eyes as he lowered her to her feet, unzipped and made fast work of a condom from his wallet.

'I knew you'd be big,' she murmured, the tip of her tongue darting out to moisten her lower lip as she stared at his cock. 'You felt huge back at the studio.'

'Wait til you feel me inside you,' he said, taking his cock in his hand and rubbing the tip against her clit.

'Ooh…' she sighed when he prised her thighs apart and slid his cock through her wet folds.

'So good,' she whispered, biting her bottom lip as he angled his pelvis to align with hers and nudged her entrance.

'You're so fucking wet.' He slid in slowly, using every ounce of his shredded willpower to take this slowly when he wanted to pound into her.

As if reading his mind, she said, 'I need to come. Now.'

Logan didn't have to be asked twice. He lifted her thigh so she hooked a leg around his waist, opening her wider as he slid in to the hilt. She gasped as he slid out and did it again, savouring the feel of her tight pussy squeezing him.

'More,' she demanded, soft and breathy, so he obliged. Sliding out and driving in, over and over, knowing this wasn't the place to prolong things but wishing he could.

She started panting and writhing so he slipped a hand between them and pressed his thumb to her clit.

'Yes. Now. Please…' Her head started rolling side to side as he circled her clit, the beginnings of his own orgasm clawing at him, tightening his balls, pooling in his lower spine.

'Yes, yes, yes…'

He covered her mouth as she came apart, swallowing her cry of release as he thrust one last time and followed her into an orgasm that rocked him to his core.

Logan had no idea how long it took his mind and muscles to work in sync again but as he eased away to look Hope in the eyes he knew one thing.

One fast and furious fuck with this woman wouldn't be enough.

CHAPTER EIGHT

HOPE CLUNG TO Logan's hand as they re-entered the pub's back door. She needed the support, considering her legs hadn't recovered from that pounding he'd given her in the back alley.

Even now, after she'd come down off the high of that earth-shattering orgasm, she felt wobbly and a tad off-centre.

She'd never had sex in a public place before, had never contemplated it, but this crazy out-of-control yearning to have Logan had made her lose her mind.

And for the first time in her life she didn't care.

Despite moving to the other side of the world to escape her parents' overt disapproval, inside she was still the model daughter doing everything right for fear of being judged and found lacking. She never did anything outrageous and, discounting her penchant for not wearing underwear, she was conservative to her core.

So what she'd just done with Logan left her reeling, but in a good way.

He hadn't spoken since they'd disengaged but the

fact he'd taken her hand meant he hadn't intended to ditch her as soon as the deed was done. Not that she'd blame him if he did. She'd made it more than clear what this was: a quick screw to satisfy an urge and thankfully, he'd obliged. They'd part ways inside the pub and she'd see him Tuesday morning when he arrived with his crew. No problems.

As they entered the main public bar, she heard the haunting strains of a guitar being strummed. Her feet slowed as the soft melody washed over her. Original. Untainted by commercialism.

Craning her neck, she spotted the sole guitarist perched on a stool, one leg outstretched, the other resting on a rung. He wore denim and a flannel shirt, and sported a buzz cut and five rings in his right ear, the only unconventional thing about him. When he started to sing, the hairs on her arms snapped to attention.

'What's wrong?' Logan stared at her, confusion creasing his brow.

When she flashed a beatific smile, the creases deepened. 'That guy is amazing.'

Logan gave a little shake of his head, as if he didn't understand what the big deal was about. 'Do you want to have a drink and listen to him for a while?'

'I'd love to.' Her feet were already moving towards the elevated table and bar stools they'd vacated not that long ago.

'What'll you have?'

'G and T, please,' she said, her attention riveted to the tiny makeshift stage and the guitarist.

His lyrics were average but that voice... Goose bumps peppered her skin and she rubbed her arms. He was exactly the type of talent she wanted to foster with her indie label.

Lost in the lush timbre and captivated by his masterful strumming, she jumped when Logan touched her on the arm. 'Here you go.'

'Thanks,' she murmured, unable to tear her eyes away from the guitarist.

'You're giving me a complex, you know,' Logan said, clinking his beer bottle against her glass. 'I thought what happened out in that alley was pretty fucking great but now you can't take your eyes off that dude playing a lame-ass song nobody's ever heard of.'

She bit back a grin at the hint of vulnerability in his tone. 'You're a musical neophyte if you think that guy is lame.'

'He is. Give me good old country and western any day.'

'Each to their own.' Hope smiled and patted his forearm. 'Don't be jealous. I'm only interested in him for his music. And you're right; what happened outside was pretty damn fantastic.'

'Good to hear,' he said, clearing his throat to ease the gruffness. 'So, my musically talented friend, what's so great about this guy?'

'We're friends?'

He rolled his eyes and she chuckled. 'There's

something unique about his voice. And his song writing isn't bad. Throw in the fact he plays a mean guitar and he's the kind of talent I'm after when I launch my recording label.'

His eyebrows shot up. 'You think this guy's going to be a star?'

'It's not about being a star. It's about being heard…' She trailed off, remembering using the same words to convince her parents why she had to follow her dream.

They'd scoffed and berated and lectured, completely clueless that her passion for music stemmed from more than teaching, that she too ultimately wanted to be heard.

Not for fame or stardom, but for the simple fact that if one person got as much pleasure from listening to her music as she had from Harry's, she'd feel vindicated.

Harry had understood. It was why he'd fostered her talent and love of music. Or maybe that had been more about his desire to plagiarise her songs than any real interest in furthering her musical career. Bastard.

'There's a story in there somewhere, right?'

She nodded. 'I'm classically trained. Attended the best music conservatory in Paris. My folks expected me to return to England and take up a position in a world-class orchestra they would've used contacts to get me into.'

'You didn't want that?' His intense stare unnerved her. Why didn't he down his beer and leave? If she'd found the rugged tradesman sexy, this softer, intuitive guy had the power to make her unravel.

'No, I wanted freedom. To be my own person. To make my own choices. To follow my own dreams.'

'I can understand that.' Tension bracketed his mouth and he swiped a hand over his face, but not before she glimpsed pain. 'So this recording studio you're setting up is the real deal?'

Rather than bristling at his suggestion she was doing nothing more than dabbling, she took a sip of her drink. 'Yeah, it's real. I want to record my songs and songs like this guy is playing. Not for the masses, but for the simple listening pleasure for people who enjoy the indie scene.'

He tilted his head, studying her as though he couldn't figure her out. 'You've already proven you're not stereotypical, but what made you change from the classics to this?'

He wrinkled his nose and gestured at the guitarist, who'd moved onto a soulful ballad of loss and heartbreak. The lyrics spoke of untold sadness and she could identify. She'd been despondent once, to the point of losing her appetite and her focus. She'd trusted Willem, incredibly starry-eyed and optimistic in the throes of first love, and he'd upended her well-ordered life.

He'd deliberately targeted her, not that she'd known it at the time, and made her fall in love. It had been a magical, whirlwind three months that had come crashing down when she'd discovered the truth.

That he'd never loved her; that he'd used her as a means to an end; that she was expendable.

Music had been her saviour. It hadn't been the first time she'd turned to music for comfort but in those weeks following the break-up with Willem it had provided her with the impetus to get out of bed in the morning. She'd written songs, listened to her favourites on repeat for hours and spent days watching Harry jam with his band, when she hadn't been moaning about her imploded relationship, that was.

Harry had known what Willem had meant to her, had known what those songs she'd written soon after represented. Yet he'd betrayed her regardless.

Her eyelids grew hot, her throat scratchy, as she quashed the memory of lost love and shattered friendship. Tears burned the backs of her eyes and she blinked. This wasn't good and she had to give Logan something so he'd stop studying her so intently.

'There was a guy...'

His lips compressed and his eyes narrowed slightly, and for a moment Hope wanted to laugh at the thought of a guy she barely knew being jealous. It was nothing more than a typical male reaction, needing to be dominant and front and centre in her mind.

'Harry was like a dad to me.' She bit her bottom lip to clamp down on the urge to bawl. 'When my parents said no to me learning drums, Harry taught me on the sly. He was an old rocker who lived in a village near us and his band toured the country playing at pubs like this.'

She swallowed, willing the urge to cry to subside.

'He got me hooked on the indie movement, the kind of music that doesn't conform, the kind of music that can change things.' She thumped a fist over her heart. 'In here. It's magic.'

She'd been so caught up in the euphoria and the way Harry had brought music to life that she hadn't seen him for what he was—a clever liar—until it had been too late.

Even now, all these years later, she couldn't fathom how he'd been able to do that to her. How he could have taken four of her original songs and passed them off as his own.

She'd been young, naïve and starting in an industry that terrified as much as enthralled. She'd trusted him implicitly, especially after the balls-up of her relationship with Willem, another narcissistic liar.

Those songs after the break-up with Willem had been good. Heck, she could say objectively they were brilliant. Harry had thought so too, enough to steal them and obliterate her trust in people once and for all.

'It may sound corny but music doesn't just inspire me, it's my life,' she said, her voice wavering with emotion and she hurriedly cleared her throat.

Logan stared at her, wide-eyed, the silence filled with the guitarist's crooning. He leaned forward to whisper in her ear, 'You have no idea how turned on I am right now by your passion.'

It was just the distraction she needed from her mawkish thoughts and this time, when she nibbled on her bottom lip, it was to stop herself from nibbling on him.

'I love what I do,' she said with a bashful shrug. 'Not many people understand the dream. They see me as some rich bitch dabbling in music because I can. They don't take me seriously because I have the money to back me if I fail.'

His eyes blazed with fierceness. 'Don't let the dickheads drag you down. You have a dream. You go for it.'

His unexpected protectiveness made her want to snuggle into his arms, so she defused the situation. No good could come of wanting to get closer. 'And I will, if your company is as good as you proclaim at getting the job done right.'

'I'm the best.' He winked, as if sensing her need to lighten the mood. 'As I'm sure you can attest to.'

'We're not talking about your construction skills any more, are we?'

'There can be a tool belt involved next time if you want.'

She arched an eyebrow, deliberately provocative. 'There's going to be a next time?'

'Only if you're lucky,' he murmured, trailing a fingertip down her bare arm, leaving a trail of goose bumps.

Their eyes locked and in that moment, with the heat from their earlier encounter still pulsating through her body, the guitarist's soft melody filling her with yearning, and Logan's teasing touch, she really wanted to get lucky again.

CHAPTER NINE

LOGAN HAD PICKED up the phone to call Hope over the weekend because the passion she'd shown at the pub four nights ago intrigued him.

Not solely because of the alley sex, which had been beyond hot, but because he'd never seen a woman so into her work. She'd practically glowed when she'd talked about her music. This, after he'd watched her listen to that guitarist, transfixed, eyes wide, mouth open, like she couldn't get enough. He hadn't been lying when he'd told her it was a turn-on. Seeing her so completely in the moment, after the sensational sex, ensured he'd been hard every time he thought about it. Which had been too often over the weekend.

When they'd parted at the pub, he'd sensed her withdrawal. She'd been cool and aloof, shaking his hand after he'd walked her to her car. *Shaking* his fucking hand, as if he was some inconsequential acquaintance. Considering the way she'd come onto him in the first place, then later shared all that stuff about her music, he'd expected more.

He'd got bupkis.

After the way they'd hooked up he'd expected her to call, and when she didn't he wanted to. Three times. More. So he'd settled for a text, a brief greeting with a 'How are you?' kind of thing. She'd responded with a terse 'Fine, see you Tuesday', which had put him firmly back in his place.

It surprised him, her ability to have sex like a man. Then again, what did he really know about her? She'd been cool initially, had morphed to hot, then reverted to cool again. Maybe this was a game she played with all guys? More to the point, why did he care?

He had to be thinking with his dick. The sex had been phenomenal so he wanted more of it; it stood to reason. But he couldn't ignore his insistent voice of reason that made him remember how much he'd enjoyed seeing her light up while listening to that dude in the pub, meaning she intrigued him beyond the sex.

Dawn streaked the Melbourne sky as he pulled up outside *Hope and Harmony*. His team was arriving at seven so he'd made sure he got there at six. Stepping from his ute, he shrugged into a suit jacket and adjusted his tie. He hated getting dressed up, preferring the good old days when he'd been on the tools, wearing shorts, a T-shirt and a high-visibility safety vest. But he always arrived on the first day of any job in a suit, intent on being the model CEO instilling confidence in the clients, and this job would be no different.

However, as he knocked softly on the glass door and glimpsed Hope moving through the shadows at the back of the shop, he knew he was kidding himself. The instant hardening of his cock and the accelerated heart beat meant that seeing her again after what they'd done in that alley behind the pub ensured this job was different.

She unlocked the door and let him in, locking it behind him. 'Did you have to get here at the crack of dawn?'

Even bleary-eyed and frowning, with her hair caught up in a messy ponytail and a raspy voice that wouldn't win any singer of the year contests, she was gorgeous with that just-tumbled-out-of-bed look that had him hankering to take her back there.

'Not a morning person, I see,' he said, resisting the urge to kiss her cheek as the faintest waft of her rose fragrance tickled his nose.

'I'm a muso. We keep late hours. What do you think?' She continued grumbling under her breath as she stalked ahead of him, doing some weird stretching thing with her arms and shoulders. 'Coffee's on if you want some.'

'Would love a cup.' He followed her, checking out her ass. She wore grey yoga pants and a matching hoodie. But what captured his attention was the VPL. A visible panty line meant she didn't go commando all the time. Or was she trying to send him some unspoken signal that what had happened between them had been strictly a one-off?

'Help yourself,' she muttered as they entered a small kitchenette and she pointed to a state-of-the-art coffee machine tucked into the corner of the narrow bench top. 'I need to inhale this caffeine otherwise I'm not fit to be around humans.'

She sat at a table for two, picked up a mug and cradled it between her hands. She lifted it to her face and inhaled the steam first before taking a slurp. 'Ah...so good...'

Logan gritted his teeth and turned away before she spotted his boner, her appreciative moan for coffee eliciting a clear memory of how appreciative she'd sounded when he'd made her come.

He poured himself a large coffee and joined her at the table. The thing was tiny and their knees jostled, before she surreptitiously slid her chair back a fraction. That subtle movement away from him confirmed it. She wanted to re-establish distance between them despite going at him behind the pub. Fine, he could do cool and aloof too, and as they sipped in silence he inwardly cursed his stupid expectations that in arriving early they might get back on solid ground.

When she'd emptied the mug, she set it down and eyeballed him. 'Right, now that the caffeine has jump-started my brain, what are you doing here so early?'

He couldn't admit the truth—that a part of him had hoped to take the edge off his usual morning boner—so he settled for 'I always scope out a job on the first day before the tradies arrive.'

'Bollocks,' she said, the English version of 'bullshit' making him grin. 'And why are you wearing a suit?'

Damn, he liked how she wasn't backward in coming forward. Most women he'd been involved with casually would hedge around questions and play stupid mind games that made him lose his shit. Hope was different, but he'd already figured that out considering the way they'd fucked in an alley.

'I'm the boss.' He flicked an imaginary fleck of lint from his lapel in mock fastidiousness. 'It pays to make a good impression with the clients.'

'You've already done that,' she murmured, meeting his eyes without qualm, the jade flecks glowing with unexpected fervour.

'Do tell.'

He threw it out there as a challenge, wanting her to articulate how good they'd been together up against that alley wall, and how badly she wanted to do it again, like he did. Instead, her gaze slid away and he quelled his disappointment with a gulp of coffee.

'Are we still on track for the job to be finished in two weeks?' She reverted to coolly distant and he wanted to rattle her out of her deliberate temerity so much his teeth ached.

But he settled for an equally sedate 'Absolutely. My men are the best and when we give timelines we stick to them.'

She toyed with a crumb on the table top, her forefinger pushing it around. 'Will you be here every day?'

'No.'

Fuck this; he never played games and he wasn't about to start now. His hand snaked across the table and covered hers. She jumped and her startled gaze flew to his. 'Unless you want me to be.'

Her tongue darted out to moisten her bottom lip and his cock twitched. He glimpsed excitement in her eyes before she snatched her hand out from under his. 'No, that's fine, I was just wondering.'

Now it was his turn to call bullshit. 'What's up with you?'

She focussed on the cupboard above his right shoulder. 'Nothing.'

'Okay, have it your way.'

Disappointed, he stood and headed for the sink, where he dumped the rest of his coffee and rinsed the mug before placing it upside down on the rack to drain.

'Hey.' Her hand touched his waist and he resisted the urge to spin around, lift her onto the sink and bury himself in her. 'I'm sorry for being an idiot.'

'Maybe you can't help being one,' he said, turning to find a smile playing about her mouth.

'At the risk of sounding like the idiot you think I am, I don't do well with unexpected outcomes. I'm a planner. I have clear goals and lists. Having sex with you disrupted my plans and my sleep and now seeing you again today makes me flounder and I don't like feeling out of control—'

He slanted his mouth across hers, a soft, tender kiss when he wanted to devour her. But she needed the reassurance and he wasn't an emotionless dickhead who took advantage of a situation.

Because he didn't know her well enough, he'd

had no idea her aloofness was the result of confusion. He'd pegged her for a reserved ice princess at the start and assumed she'd reverted to type. If he hadn't been able to get her out of his head all weekend, maybe she'd been the same.

She made a soft mewling sound and slipped her arms up around his neck, angling her mouth to give him better access. She tasted of coffee with a hint of vanilla. Delicious and enticing and addictive.

When she pressed against him he claimed her mouth with deeper precision, his hands drifting to her ass, loving the way the globes filled his palms.

She eased away too soon. 'I have a room, a miniature recording studio off the main teaching area.' Her eyes glittered with intent. 'It's soundproof,' she added.

Not that it mattered. While it was only the two of them here, he had every intention of making her scream.

'You know I didn't come here early just for this,' he said, taking her hand when she offered it. 'I wanted to make sure everything was okay between us after what happened at the pub.'

'Liar. You wanted to get laid as badly as I do.' Mischief twinkled in her eyes. 'But don't sweat it. We'll be respectable by the time your crew arrives.'

Grateful for her bluntness, he made a grand show of glancing at his watch. 'So that means I have forty-five minutes to allow you to disrespect me?'

'And I intend on making every one of those minutes count.' She squeezed his hand and led him out of the kitchenette.

He'd meant it when he'd said he hadn't come here early for sex—though the thought had crossed his mind several times since waking with a boner and knowing he'd be seeing her shortly—but having her clearly articulate she wanted to fuck made him glad he'd arrived before his tradesmen, as she led him past the grand piano and into a tiny room that could barely fit them.

'This is snug,' he said when she nudged him to one side in order to close the door.

'That's the whole idea.' She grabbed the lone chair and turned it around before guiding him to sit. 'All the better to be closer to you.'

'What are you, the big, bad wolf?'

'Yeah, and I'm going to gobble you all in one go.'

She knelt at his feet and reached for his zipper. He imagined her mouth wrapped around him, those lips moving over his cock, sucking him…

'Wait.' He stilled her hand and tugged her up until she straddled his lap. 'Don't get me wrong, I love a blow job like the next bloke, but I've fantasised about being inside you all weekend so that's what I want.'

Her lips parted and her tongue darted out to moisten her bottom lip as she gave a brief nod. 'Okay.'

He liked this about her—no fuss, no need for extraneous explanations—as she stood and shimmied out of her yoga pants, taking purple panties with them, leaving him a glorious view of her neatly trimmed pussy at eye level. The alley sex had been hot but he liked this way too, being able to see her. As if sensing his need, she unzipped the hoodie and slipped it off, revealing small, pert breasts with perfect pink nipples. No bra. Nice.

'You're beautiful,' he said, reaching for her.

She waggled her finger at him. 'I want to see you too.' She pointed at his fly. 'Unzip.'

Glad she didn't want him to go through the whole rigmarole of taking off his tie, shirt and jacket too, he unzipped, pushed his trousers and jocks down a fraction and slid his hand in to free his cock. It sprang to attention and she moaned.

'Wow.' She reached out to touch the tip of his cock and it jumped as he used every last ounce of self-restraint not to haul her down and impale her.

He slipped his wallet from his back pocket, grabbed a condom and had the foil torn in record time. She watched as he pinched the tip between his thumb and forefinger and rolled it on. He'd got about halfway when he saw her hand drift towards her pussy. Fuck, watching him was turning her on and she was going to touch herself.

'I did this the other day, after our first kiss,' she said, her hand sliding lower with a torturous slowness. 'I was so turned on I masturbated in the bathroom here, imagining you doing this.'

Blown away by her admission, and so fucking turned on his balls ached, he slowed down the rolling action, mesmerised as her middle finger slid between her folds. His throat tightened as her finger moved, in and out, and he slid the condom the rest of the way, desperate to be inside her.

'You are something else.' His voice sounded half-way between a rasp and a growl as he reached for her and she spread her legs either side of his thighs. She lowered herself onto him, inch by exquisite inch, pleasuring herself all the while. When he reached for her she swatted him away.

'Interlace your fingers behind your head,' she said, her voice husky, her eyes wide green pools he could easily drown in.

Liking her take-charge attitude, he did as he was told and she smiled, a purely provocative curve of her lips that made him want to yell with the joy of having this sexy, wanton woman issuing orders.

'Now, sit back and relax as we enjoy the ride.' For emphasis, she picked up the pace, sliding up and down as her fingers played with her clit, so fuck-ing hot.

He went into sensory overload, watching her tits bounce in his face, her fingering her clit and her pussy, sliding up and down his cock. He wanted to taste her so badly, to feel her, but as he leaned for-ward she pushed him back with her free hand and continued to ride him until the first ripples of or-gasm built.

She bounced harder as her finger moved faster, her pussy clenching him as she came on a cry that made him want to shout in victory. He followed a second later, his back spasming with the force of it, his mind effectively wiped.

She leaned forward, resting her forehead against his, as he unlocked his fingers and slid his arms around her waist.

He couldn't get over the contrasts of this woman and wondered if that was the main attraction...

Followed by a more sobering thought. So far, she'd been the one calling all the shots. Which either made him a dumb schmuck being led around by his dick or a guy so smitten he was happy with whatever scraps she tossed his way.

They needed to talk.

Starting now.

CHAPTER TEN

HOPE HAD NOWHERE to run this time.

The guitarist at the pub had been a good distraction after the alley sex to fend off any possible awkwardness but this time she couldn't flee, considering this was her place and his crew would be arriving in half an hour to start work on her dream.

And he had a look in his eyes as she re-dressed and he took care of business, as if he wanted to ask her questions she had no intention of answering. So she deflected as usual, using a mechanism honed from years of practice when avoiding any kind of deeper connection with a guy.

'Want to hear a song I wrote over the weekend?'

He hesitated before nodding. 'Sure.'

She padded into the music room and sat at the piano. Immediately her muscles relaxed and her shoulders unkinked, the tension of their post-sex interlude draining away to leave a welcome calm in its wake. When she rested her fingers on the keys, she entered her happy place, the smoothness of the ivory lulling her. It had always been like this, from the first moment she had sat at her parents' Steinway, like magic had enveloped her and swept her away to a better world.

Her parents hadn't understood when she'd tried to explain it. They'd labelled her imaginative and dismissed her feelings as fanciful. It made it all the more special somehow that only she could experience this kind of euphoria.

Her fingers drifted over the keys, plucking at middle C, B and D, setting the tone for her voice. She knew he wouldn't understand the meaning behind the words, just as her parents hadn't understood all those years ago, but she needed to sing now, needed to get grounded in a world frighteningly topsy-turvy.

Thanks to Logan.

She'd never been so captivated by a man before.

Since the moment they'd met last week he'd filled her every waking thought, and her sleepless ones too. She hadn't been this hung up over a guy since Willem and that thought alone should've sent her running, doing her usual sabotaging trick before anything could develop.

That was what the frantic alley sex had really been about: showing him she was bold, in control and good for a quickie only. That kind of overt come-on turned some guys off; she should know, she'd done it before. But with Logan her deep-seated desire to push him away hadn't worked. If anything it had intensified her fascination for him, so to distract herself over the weekend she'd composed this song.

The notes filled her and burst out of her mouth,

pure and melodic. Lyrics filled with wonder, excitement and the newness of hedonistic pleasure. She sang without pause, without fault and when her hands struck the final chords before drifting into silence she let the calmness wrap her.

Her eyes had drifted shut at some point and when she opened them Logan stood before her, leaning against the piano, looking like a model in that slick suit. He stared at her in open-mouthed shock and she crashed back to earth in a big way.

Embarrassment flooded her; her skin prickled, making her want to itch. What had she been thinking, revealing so much of herself to him? If she'd been uncomfortable standing naked in front of him in that room before, it had nothing on the mortification sweeping over her now.

'That was…incredible.' He gave a little shake of his head, as if trying to wake up. 'You're better than half the pop stars rocking the charts today.'

'Thanks.' She resisted the urge to press her palms to her flushed cheeks. 'Music is my go-to place.'

He nodded, as if he understood, but she could tell by his dazed expression he didn't. 'The pub's mine.'

She laughed, interlocked her fingers and stretched her arms overhead. 'We all have our different escape mechanisms.'

When she lowered her arms, he was studying her with a quizzical slash between his brows. 'Is that what you needed to do over the weekend? Escape?'

Crap. She'd left herself wide open for that one.

He was far too intuitive. She needed to distance herself, pronto.

'It's what I do most weekends. Song-write. Tinker.' Feigning indifference, she stood and busied herself dusting off the keys. 'I'm really living it up, in case you didn't notice.'

'Hey, you're more adventurous than you think.' He touched her arm and just like that her synapses short-circuited again and she imagined him touching her all over. 'Are we going to talk about the sex?'

Hell, no. She squeezed her thighs together to guard against the instant throb elicited by him even saying the damn word.

'What's there to talk about?'

The corners of his kissable mouth quirked. 'The fact we like doing it? The fact we're explosive together? The fact I want to keep doing it for however long I'm in Melbourne?'

Of course Logan was transient. She'd found a guy to give her the mind-blowing pleasure she craved and he'd be moving on. Figured.

She should be glad, as any kind of relationship wasn't part of her grand plans. Short-term, sizzling sex with a hot guy was doable. So why the tiny zing of disappointment?

'How long are you staying around?'

'Probably a month, max. I don't stay in one place long, preferring to do quotes in person for jobs around the country.' His response sounded rote and determination darkened his eyes. 'I'm not a long-term guy, if that's what you're asking.'

'I'm not asking anything of the sort,' she said, clipped and frosty, sounding as if she actually cared about his wanderings. She didn't. She liked the sex; she didn't have to like the guy.

Liar, her conscience screamed. She already liked him beyond his obvious talents. She wouldn't be talking to him now if she didn't. She would've dismissed him, employing her icy persona she used to great effect when distancing herself from men who wanted more than she was willing to give.

She hated Willem for hurting her to the point she could never let any guy get too close. He'd really done a number on her and she'd been clueless until the end. He'd pursued her and wooed her with a relentlessness that should've alerted her to the fact that everything about him, from his five-hundred-dollar Italian leather shoes to his designer suits, was fake. She'd loved him, she'd depended on him and he'd abused her trust regardless, leaving her a duped fool. She never, ever wanted to feel like that again.

'You sound pissed off,' he said.

'I'm not,' she snapped, and he chuckled and held up his hands, as if he had nothing to hide.

'All I'm saying is I'm probably in town for another few weeks, so if you want to keep hanging out that's fine with me.'

She snorted, hating the traitorous lurch of her gut that said she'd like nothing better. 'Is that what men are calling sex these days? *Hanging out?*' She made air quotes with her fingers. 'Because I'm okay with admitting the sex is great and I would like to continue, if that's suitable.'

Damn, she sounded so stilted and formal, the exact opposite of how she felt around him when he got *that* look in his eyes. The one that made her feel wanton and wicked, like a sex goddess capable of anything.

For someone who hadn't had a lot of sex over the years—and what she'd had had been lacklustre at best—there was something about Logan that set her alight with a simple glance.

'It's certainly suitable,' he said, the corners of his mouth twitching.

'Stop mocking me.' She huffed out a breath that served to make him laugh.

'You're full of contrasts,' he said, tapping her on the nose like a benevolent uncle. 'Fire and ice. I like it.'

'Most people don't,' she said, masking her wistfulness with an abrupt cough. 'Okay, so we're dating while you're in town?'

'Yeah.'

'Monogamous?'

Anger pinched his mouth. 'Yeah.'

'Hey, just checking.' She turned away to stack sheet music before he could see the importance of his answer written all over her face.

She'd had a fling before, with an up-and-coming indie band's lead roadie. She'd fallen headlong into lust before realising she wasn't the only woman he'd been plugging his lead into. She wouldn't make the same mistake again.

'I won't jerk you around, Hope.'

He laid a hand on her shoulder and spun her around. 'I'm a stand-up guy. I know what I want and I call it. No bullshitting. And, while I'm in Melbourne, I want you.'

An insane urge to blubber swept over her so she kissed him, plastering herself so hard against him that his butt hit the piano keys in a resounding clash of mismatched notes. He laughed and gently eased away, holding her at arm's length.

'While I'm happy to do you every which way wherever and whenever you want, I don't think banging on your precious piano is a good idea.'

She smiled, relieved they'd moved past the awkwardness of their conversation. She loved his sense of humour. She didn't laugh often enough and she knew it.

'I'm not very good at this…' She trailed off, feeling as if she owed him some semblance of truth for her swiftly changing behaviour but regretting bringing it up the moment he pinned her with that astute stare he did so well. 'That's why I back off sometimes. I get spooked and embarrassed and—'

'You're a sensual, empowered woman embracing her sexuality. Don't ever be embarrassed by that.' He cupped her chin so she had to meet his eyes. 'You should be proud.'

'See, this is what I mean.' She shoved his hand away. 'I'm no good at this. At you understanding me.

At you being kind. Ah, fuck…' She rarely swore and it only served to make her feel further discombobulated. 'I'm not even a vamp, though you might think so with the commando thing. But that's more about me doing something completely out of character than any great plan to seduce guys. I just feel…out of my depth around you.'

His expression softened and she wanted to bawl again. 'Do you have any idea how rare it is to have a straight-talking woman articulate exactly what's going on in her head?'

He tapped the side of her temple. 'Contrary to popular belief, us guys have no clue as to what goes on in there. We wing it and hope for the best that we don't make complete asses of ourselves.'

He winked. 'So thanks for letting me know what's going on in your think tank but seriously, don't over-analyse this. We're two people insanely attracted to each other who are having fun. That's it.'

'Okay,' she said, nodding, but she couldn't help a wistful sigh escaping her mouth a second before he claimed it.

She liked fun. She needed fun.

But what if, for the first time in her well-ordered life, she wanted more?

CHAPTER ELEVEN

'WHAT BUG CRAWLED up your ass?' Mike, the lead electrician on Hope's job, nudged Logan in the back with the blunt end of a screwdriver. 'You're never this moody.'

'Leave it alone, dickhead,' Logan growled, snapping his fingers at two apprentices who were dilly-dallying over measurements. 'Get a move on.'

'Shit, you're in one foul mood, boss, and it ain't pretty.' Mike jerked a thumb towards the open door. 'Hopefully, the foreman can get you to lighten the hell up.'

Logan scowled and glared at the door where Rick stood, sporting a giant shit-eating grin as if he knew exactly what had precipitated his mood. He strode over to his mate and jabbed him in the shoulder so he had no choice but to back up. Once they were outside, Logan slammed the door. 'What the hell are you doing here? You're supposed to be resting up.'

Rick's grin broadened at his overt rudeness. 'I came straight from a physio session; thought I'd check the job out.'

'You're not supposed to be here, so fuck off.'

Rick mock-winced and held up his hands. 'What's up with you?'

'Nothing,' Logan said through gritted teeth, mentally counting down the minutes until his head carpenter would arrive so he could get the hell out of here.

If arriving early to see Hope had been a bad idea, sticking around afterwards had been worse.

When he'd heard her play that song…man, he'd been blown away. He'd never heard anything so beautiful and he felt as if she'd reached a hand into his chest, wrapped her fingers around his heart and squeezed. He'd been out of sorts ever since.

He didn't do deep and meaningful conversations, especially not with women who knew the score. But she'd been so damn vulnerable he hadn't been able to help himself. He'd wanted to reassure her that he wasn't the kind of guy to break her heart, yet that was exactly what he'd do.

He could see it playing out all so clearly. Despite telling her he would move on shortly, he had seen the gleam in her eyes: she wanted more. More than a guy like him could ever give any woman.

So he'd taken his foul mood out on his workmen, something he never did. For all he knew, Mike had probably called Rick and ordered him here to calm him down. He'd fire Mike's sneaky ass if the guy weren't a shit-hot electrician.

'Is Hope the woman I spied through the front glass of the place?' Rick smirked, annoyingly smug. Yeah, he knew exactly why Logan was edgy and out of sorts.

'Yep.'

'Try using bigger words next time.'

Logan flipped Rick the bird.

'She's pretty, in that English rose kind of way,' Rick said, oblivious to the minefield on which he trod. Logan was all talked out for today.

'Leave it alone—'

'You like her.' Rick studied him, uncomfortably appraising and nothing like his usual jocular self. 'I've never seen you like this on a job, so it has to be about her.'

Logan knew he'd have to give his friend something or he wouldn't let up. Rick didn't tolerate bullshit, yet another thing they had in common. 'We're hanging out. No biggie.'

Rick guffawed and slugged him on the shoulder. 'Never thought I'd see the day, the great wanderer falling for a woman.'

'We're fucking, that's it,' Logan said, instantly regretting the declaration, feeling disloyal to Hope for belittling the sensational physical connection they shared.

'Yeah, right.' Rick shook his head. 'You're such a schmuck. What's wrong with admitting you like her?'

'Because we're not in grade school, dickhead.'

Besides, if he admitted it out loud to his mate, it made this strange, out-of-control desire to spend time with her beyond the sex all the more real. And he was in enough of a funk since hearing her sing and would prefer not to exacerbate it.

She'd said all the right things about continuing

their sex-capades yet keeping it casual and he should be rapt. Instead, he couldn't shake the feeling he'd taken on too much with this one.

'Heard from your dad lately?'

And, just like that, Rick transformed a bad situation into a shitty one. He knew why his friend had changed the subject and what he was alluding to: that Logan had never had a serious relationship with a woman because of his past, tangled up in a big ball of resentment towards his dad.

So he never wanted to foster ties that always ended in disappointment. To have a woman wait around for him while he travelled, her discontent and frustration growing until their relationship inevitably imploded. Or, worse, bring a kid into the situation, the kind of kid he'd once been, hero-worshipping his dad only to be kicked in the fucking heart by the constant let-downs.

No, he didn't want any of that. Besides, he was happy. He had a kick-ass company, enough work to keep him busy for decades and a bank account that ensured he didn't have to work if he didn't want to. Long-term relationships bred nothing but unhappiness and heartbreak. Not for him.

'No, haven't see him,' Logan said, his voice clipped and brooking no argument. 'I really need to get back to supervising the guys...'

'They've done a thousand of these jobs without you standing over them, I'm pretty sure they'll cope for another few minutes.' Rick folded his arms, disapproval radiating off him. 'Doesn't he live in Melbourne? Why don't you—?'

'Rick, you're my best mate, but if you keep spouting this drivel I'm going to have to deck you.'

Not that he would; Logan had never hit anyone in his life. But, if talking about Hope wasn't high on his list of discussion topics, talking about his dear old dad fell into a definite no-go zone.

'You need to see him some time,' Rick said with a shrug. 'Might put the rest of your life and this warped view you have about relationships into perspective—'

'That's it, I'm done.' His hands curled into fists as he pushed open the back door to Hope's property so he could escape into a world of hammering, sawdust and drilling. Familiarity with his work would ease the confusion, courtesy of his friend's too accurate assessment of why he didn't do relationships. 'Go rest up and I'll see you soon.'

Logan didn't wait for his mate's response. He'd had enough.

If thinking about his earlier reaction to Hope had him reeling, mulling over Rick's unwarranted advice regarding his dad had the potential to send him into a tailspin.

Time to focus on work like he always did. And a few stolen hours here and there with Hope when he could. Keep things simple. Uncomplicated.

Just the way he liked it.

CHAPTER TWELVE

WHEN HOPE WANTED clarity she visited her favourite place, the Victorian State Library. Entering through the giant marble arches on Swanston Street flooded her with peace.

It had been the first Melbourne landmark she'd explored when she'd arrived five years before, her love of books undeniable. When she walked through these arches, her muscles slackened and her limbs loosened as any residual tension drained away. She loved strolling through the Red Rotunda and seeing the nineteenth-century paintings and sculptures, followed by a tour of the Blue Rotunda with its twentieth-century portraits of artists, authors and other notables who were part of Victorian history.

If she yearned for a history fix, she'd spend a few hours in the Redmond Barry Reading Room, poring over non-fiction journals featuring musical legends she had listened to on occasion. The library soothed her soul and calmed her mind.

Except today.

Today, Logan had accompanied her and she had no freaking idea why.

It had been bad enough yesterday, coming to terms with the fact she'd agreed to a short-term fling while he was in town. This, hot on the heels of scorching sex in the confines of her mini-studio, followed by her revealing far too much of herself by playing that song she'd written about him. Not that he knew it. The lyrics could've applied to anyone yearning for a real connection. But then she'd come clean about feeling out of her depth around him and he'd been way too understanding and sweet.

Rugged, tough guys like him shouldn't have a soft core. It made him all the more appealing. She could cope with viewing him as a sex object, a gorgeous guy to shift her out of her comfort zone, to shake up her rather mundane existence. But since the moment he'd shown a genuine sincerity yesterday she'd been mulling 'what if?'

What if she'd made a big mistake in letting this guy in a little?

She'd done a fine job of protecting her heart since Willem. But in the short time she'd known Logan she'd already spent too much time thinking about him and that didn't bode well for when he left in a month. Guys she'd dated before had never had this impact on her. She'd deliberately kept them at bay and ended things quickly if they wanted more.

Thinking about Logan so much made her re-evaluate the wisdom of her choice. Maybe the smart decision would be to end this fling now.

'Why did you come here with me today?'

He didn't flinch at her blurted question, which

bordered on rude. 'Already told you. This library has the most famous dome in Melbourne and I want to get a few ideas to see if we can soundproof yours while restoring it to its former glory.'

Why did he have to sound so damn logical? His reasoning sounded plausible but deep down she would've preferred him to say he wanted to spend time with her.

It was crazy having those kinds of delusions, because they weren't dating and she had no expectations. But when he'd heard she was coming here and he'd asked to accompany her, she hadn't been able to help but hope he liked her for more than her body.

'The dome is rather spectacular,' she said, relieved she managed to sound offhand despite her whirling thoughts. 'Have you been here before?'

His lips compressed and a shadow scudded across his hooded gaze. 'Once. A lifetime ago.'

'School excursion?'

'Something like that,' he said, half-turning away so she couldn't read his expression. But she heard the tightness in his voice, as though she'd hit a sore spot.

She should drop it. That would be the smart thing to do. But she'd stopped being smart around the time she'd demanded he screw her up against an alley wall at the back of a pub.

'You mentioned growing up in a small outback town far from Melbourne. Did you go to school there too?'

He took so long to respond she wondered if she'd really stuffed up. After what seemed like an eternity, he said, 'Rally-Doo is too small so I went to school in nearby Swan Hill. A small, unknown public school. You wouldn't have heard of it. Hills High.'

She hadn't. 'I'm ashamed to say that, though I've lived in Melbourne for five years, my Australian geography is lacking.'

'You haven't done the touristy thing and travelled around?'

She grimaced and shook her head. 'I've been to Sydney and the Gold Coast, both times for an indie music concert; that's it.'

He'd lost the haunted look and the corners of his mouth quirked into a teasing smile. 'And you call yourself an honorary Aussie.'

Glad he'd lightened up enough to tease her, she tapped her chest. 'I love living here but I'm still an English girl at heart.'

'Let me guess. You prefer toasted muffins over donuts, you drink tea over coffee, use a fine porcelain cup and do it like this.' He held up his pinkie and wiggled it.

She laughed. 'I'm far from clichéd.'

'Don't I know it,' he murmured, so softly she barely caught it, the sudden heat in his gaze making her aware of her quickening heartbeat. 'Seriously, though, you need to sightsee. Travel. See more of this wonderful country.'

The fluttering in her chest elicited by the intent behind him alluding to her being anything but clichéd, combined with his sizzling look, had her inadvertently leaning into him, craving his touch.

But they were in a public place and there was a huge difference between a back alley and one of Melbourne's most prestigious landmarks.

'I will travel, once I get my recording studio up and running.'

A blatant lie, because she knew once she started recording she intended to be busy into the next decade, fostering the talent of unknown musicians while producing her own music and sharing it with the world. It was what she'd always wanted to do. It had been her secret dream and she'd only ever shared it with one other person—who'd proceeded to take her prized songs and record them as his own.

The kicker was that she would've gladly shared her songs with Harry if he'd asked. Instead, the one person she'd thought she could trust in the world had callously shattered her illusions, like everyone else before him.

Logan eyed her with scepticism, as if he knew her profession of plans to travel in the future was a load of bollocks, before snapping his fingers in an apparent epiphany. 'We should go camping.'

'I'd rather stick a fork in my eye.'

Her loathing of sleeping under the stars in a tent had nothing to do with her privileged upbringing, during which she had only holidayed in the best five-star resorts, and everything to do with her fear of Australian snakes and spiders. She'd watched enough documentaries to know that she preferred solid walls between her and the creepy crawlies, not thin canvas.

She shuddered at the thought and he chuckled. 'Have you ever done it?'

'No and I'm not about to start now.'

An eyebrow rose in blatant challenge. 'Bet I can change your mind.'

'Bet you can't.'

He leaned in, close enough she could smell his addictively clean crispness mingled with something decidedly earthy—a heady, tantalising scent that had imprinted on her receptors and made her hormones go a little crazy.

'One of the benefits of camping is the closeness of snuggling in a sleeping bag.'

Her nipples tightened at the thought of being up close and personal with him that way but she still wasn't convinced. Tiger snakes, funnel-web spiders and any number of nasty critters with eight legs could slither and crawl into a sleeping bag.

'A bed can be just as snuggly.'

'Granted, it can.' The pale blue flecks in his eyes glowed as a wicked grin curved his lips. 'But you should know, guys love nothing better than a challenge, and I'm going to make sure you live a little over the next few weeks.'

'Hey, I'm not some hermit. I get out.'

To the supermarket, the occasional yoga class and the arts centre for an infrequent recital. Though all that was on a need-to-know basis. She already sounded like an unadventurous recluse.

'To places like this?' He threw his arm wide, his teasing smile making him even more irresistible.

'Yeah. And I wander through the laneways, dine at the trendiest restaurants and attend dingy clubs to listen to music.' She sounded too defensive, well aware he'd hit a sore spot. Being a loner had its down sides: namely daydreaming about what it would be like to open herself up to a real relationship rather than shunning any connection beyond superficial. 'What of it?'

'Whoa.' He held up his hands, his smug grin infuriatingly gorgeous. 'I just meant that you need to step out of your comfort zone. And if camping is too much too soon maybe you can start with a footy game?'

He smacked his lips together in an exaggerated parody of hunger. 'Nothing like a hot meat pie drenched in tomato sauce while cheering on the Echidnas.'

Another thing Hope hadn't paid much attention to since she'd moved here: Aussie Rules football. She knew a few of the teams, including the Eastern Echidnas, but that was about it. She'd never been a soccer fan back in the UK so watching Aussie Rules wasn't high on her agenda.

And what did he mean by suggesting she needed to live a little…? Damn, she almost slapped herself upside the head.

He wanted to spend time with her.

Outside of the bedroom.

She should protest, insist that she wanted nothing beyond his dick. Or was she reading too much into this? Was he just a guy who liked to tease her, to have some fun when they weren't screwing?

Or did he like her enough to want to get to know her beyond the sex?

The latter terrified her. She didn't want to let him get close. But there was something utterly appealing about this man that had her wanting to throw caution aside and have fun.

Whatever his rationale, in that moment she came to a decision.

She would make the most of their time together.

She wouldn't second-guess her impulsiveness, mull over his motivations or sabotage this as she had every fleeting connection that had come before him. She'd enjoy Logan, for more than his body, and wave goodbye at the end.

Simple.

'Okay. Take me to the footy.'

His eyes glittered with approval. 'Great. They're playing the Sylphs in Melbourne this weekend. It's a date.'

'You know, if you're taking me out of my comfort zone, maybe I should return the favour.'

'What do you mean?'

'I'm taking you on a laneways tour of the city.'

He rolled his eyes. 'Why would I want to stroll through a bunch of graffiti-covered alleys?'

'You're not averse to all alleys,' she said, with a wink, and he laughed.

'Okay, drag me through the city. But I get to pick the place we eat.'

'Deal.' She stuck out her hand, unprepared for him to tug her towards him when he took it.

'You're incredible,' he said, slanting a soft kiss across her lips that made her melt against him. 'I love sparring with you.'

'I can feel how much.' She pressed against him, glad they were sheltered in an alcove off the library's main entrance. 'We better go check out that dome.'

'The dome's not really that important,' he said, holding her upper arms and easing her away. 'I only tagged along to spend some time with you.'

Stunned by his admission, and quelling the instinctive urge to flee because of it, she stared at him.

'Because we've basically fucked twice and that's it,' he continued, sounding endearingly bashful. 'I wanted to show you I really do want to hang out while I'm around.'

She searched for the right response to convey how much she appreciated his effort without alerting him to how the thought of getting closer by 'hanging out' struck terror into her heart.

When she came up lacking, she settled for 'Thanks, I like spending time with you too.'

'So shall we check out the dome or leave?'

Her body clamoured to leave but she had this gorgeous guy alongside her in one of her favourite places; she'd be a fool to pass up this opportunity to enjoy his company.

'Dome, but we'll make it quick.'

He nodded his approval and took her hand. It felt surreal as they took the elevator to the sixth floor, walked out onto the highest level of the La Trobe Reading Room and surveyed the stunning room below, eight long tables fanning out like the tentacles of an octopus.

She loved the reverent hush, the whisper-quiet of students lining those tables, heads bent over books, backlit by green lawyer lamps.

'Impressive,' he said, barely glancing at the tables below before the dome above drew his attention. He gaped a little and she knew the feeling; the massive soaring architectural feat never failed to make her feel insignificant in the grand scheme of things.

'This is one of my favourite places,' she said, pointing to the ancient books in shelves that lined the alcoves of the room. 'There's over thirty-two-thousand books in here alone and I wish I could curl up and read every one of them.'

'I can barely bring myself to read the newspaper,' he said, an odd wistfulness lacing his tone. 'My mum was the bookworm.'

She noted his use of the past tense and dithered over whether to ask him about her or not. She knew nothing about him beyond his job and the small town he'd come from. If they were going to spend time together, maybe it wouldn't hurt to know more.

'She died when I was eighteen,' he added, before she could question him further.

'And your dad?'

'He's around but we don't get on.'

From his clipped tone and deep frown, she could tell there was a world of untold angst there, but his clenched jaw and the visible cording of the muscles in his neck alerted her that now probably wasn't the best time to delve.

Time to change the subject. 'Now that you've seen the dome, can we do a quick tour through the red and blue rotundas before we leave? They house some fabulous paintings from the nineteenth and twentieth centuries.'

He visibly relaxed, his shoulders lowering and his expression easing into curiosity. 'You really are an artsy-fartsy cliché,' he said, sounding amused rather than judgemental. 'Okay, let's go look at these paintings.'

However, his mobile buzzed at that moment. 'Excuse me,' he said, fishing it out of his pocket and moving slightly away to answer. He spoke in low tones so she couldn't really hear the conversation but one look at his lips compressed into a slash and his narrowed eyes told her she'd lost her library partner. He grimaced when he hung up and thrust the phone back into his pocket, cursing under his breath.

'Sorry, I have to go. There's some glitch at the council with a permit that needs sorting. Rain check?'

She hid her disappointment and nodded, tilting her face up for his incoming kiss. It was all too brief, a bare glance of his mouth across hers, before he eyed the door.

'I'll call you,' he said, touching her lightly on the arm.

'Okay.'

Then he was gone, leaving her feeling giddy, hope-

ful and looking forward to the next few weeks with
him way too much, while pondering what lay beneath
the surface of this enigmatic man.

CHAPTER THIRTEEN

IT HAD BEEN way too long since Logan had seen Hope at the State Library: four long days.

He'd intentionally stayed away because he felt like a bastard for lying to her.

There hadn't been a glitch with a permit.

There'd been a glitch in the form of his father calling.

The second he'd heard Stephen Holmes's gravelly voice in his ear, he'd known he couldn't hang around Hope for the rest of the day. Dear old Dad always put him in a foul mood so he'd begged off and left. She hadn't seemed fazed, but he'd maintained his distance for the rest of the week, not because he wasn't clamouring to see her but because he knew he wasn't fit company for anybody for days following his dad's calls.

He'd had to give in today because he'd invited her to this football game so he'd swallowed his resentment at his father and manned up.

'The team's about to run out,' he said, nudging her carefully so she wouldn't drop her meat pie.

'We're barracking for the Sylphs, right?'

Her eyes twinkled with mischief and he clamped down on the urge to cover her mouth with his. She had this way of lightening everything around her and he needed that today. His dad's pleas still rang in his head days later and this time it was taking him longer than usual to get over his funk.

'You know very well we're supporting the Echidnas.'

Her eyes widened in mock surprise. 'Oh yeah, we've already been over all this. Eighteen men on the field per side who can kick, hand-ball and mark the ball, along with tackling each other, with the ultimate aim being to kick goals.' She pointed at one end of the stadium. 'Through the big sticks is a goal, through the big and small goalpost is a behind.'

She grinned and tapped her temple. 'See? All that useless information you spouted earlier is stored up here.'

He laughed, her teasing just what he needed today. 'You can't live in Melbourne and not support a footy team. It's un-Aussie.'

'Lucky I'm a Brit,' she said, blowing on her pie to cool it. 'Though I am partial to these pies. They're delish.'

Her contrasts never seemed to surprise him. Considering her privileged background—he'd looked her up online—he'd expected her to be a Michelin-star kind of girl who'd think the humble Aussie meat pie was gross. But she'd demolished one and was onto her second before the game had even started. Intriguing indeed.

'Did you get your permit issue sorted?'

Great. Now he'd be forced to lie again. 'Yeah.'

Unable to meet her curious gaze, he focussed on the players warming up on the stadium's pristine grassy surface. Who knew watching a bunch of athletes running through warm-up stretches could be so fascinating?

'There was no hitch, was there?'

Damn, how did she do that? He hated lying; he had no tolerance for it after his childhood. But telling her the truth could result in more questions and he had no intention of discussing his warped family life. Even now, days later, he still couldn't forget his father's pleading tone asking to meet. Asking for a second chance.

His gut churned with repressed anger. He owed his father nothing, even after he'd digested the startling news of how close he'd come to losing him.

When she continued to stare at him in open curiosity, he knew he had to come clean.

'My dad called. He never fails to rile me and I often end up yelling at him. I didn't want you privy to that so I begged off to talk to him in private.'

He prayed silently she wouldn't delve further as thinking about their last call made him want to thump something.

Stephen Holmes had survived a cancer scare.

And the fact Logan had learned about it after the fact rammed home how shitty their relationship was.

His choice, of course. Once his mum had died—and Logan had found out the real cause—he hadn't wanted anything to do with his father. He'd been blaming his dad for years for abandoning them so it hadn't been difficult. What had been hard was his father's constant overtures to mend their relationship. No matter how many times Logan hung up on him, or yelled or called him names, Stephen persisted. His father never gave up despite not being able to get through to him. Until last Wednesday, when Logan had learned about his father's battle with testicular cancer, and how he wouldn't have known until he got a call from the hospital if things had gone south with his dad's op.

It made him feel like shit.

Maybe Rick was right. Maybe it was time to confront his dad and lay the past to rest. But every time he contemplated it he developed an eye tic and he sweated bullets. He'd already lost enough sleep over the years, mulling over his father's callous abandonment and subsequent overtures to make up for it. He'd be damned if he developed an ulcer over his dad's latest attempt to reunite.

But he couldn't get the C-word out of his mind. Cancer. What if it returned? What if his father died before Logan said all that needed to be said?

He'd dealt with his anger and bitterness over the years, usually by wielding a hammer at work. But he'd been off the tools for a long time now and his dad's latest call kept playing over and over in his head like a damned earworm.

'You mentioned you didn't get on with your dad before.' She laid a hand on his forearm, the tiniest speck of ketchup dotting her thumb. 'Want to talk about it?'

'No,' he spat, tempering it with a sigh when she withdrew her hand. 'Sorry, force of habit. I have this theory that if I don't mention him he doesn't exist.'

He risked a glance at her, not surprised to see a raised eyebrow. 'Childish, I know, but it's complicated.'

'We all have complicated family tales but if yours is affecting you this much maybe you should do something about it.'

He wanted to chastise her for the psychobabble but didn't want to spoil their day out. This was supposed to be fun, exposing her to a taste of Melbourne culture, to something new she'd never done before. He should never have mentioned his father.

'The game's about to start,' he said, raising his beer to his lips and wishing he could down the whole thing in one go to ease the tightness in his throat. 'Go Echidnas.'

She stared at him through slightly narrowed eyes for what seemed like an eternity before averting her gaze and focussing on the field.

Relieved, he slumped into the hard, uncomfortable plastic seat and took another slug of beer. He should be enjoying himself. He had a beautiful woman by his side, he was watching his favourite football team and he intended to celebrate with her later back at his place. Instead, the beer burned a trail down his throat and settled in his gut like acid.

'You need to face me some time, Son.'

That fucking phrase reverberated around his head, impossible to dislodge no matter how hard he tried. Football, beer and sex: it should be a no-brainer for clearing his head. But if the football and the beer weren't doing the trick maybe he needed to fast-forward to the sex.

He rested a hand on Hope's thigh and leaned across to murmur in her ear. 'Want to get out of here?'

'But the game's only just started.' She stared at him like he'd lost his mind.

'Yeah, but maybe I want to get started in a different way.'

She liked his bluntness. She'd told him so. But this time he knew what she'd say before her mouth opened because it pursed in disapproval and a tiny frown slashed her brows.

'As much as I want you, I won't be any guy's temporary diversion.' She tilted her nose in the air in the characteristically snooty move he usually found endearing. Not today. 'I want to watch the game.'

Okay, so she was paying him back for freezing her out about his dad. But how could he articulate all the shit he'd endured because of that man to a virtual stranger when he could hardly face up to it himself?

He itched to get the hell out of there, to leave and go drown his sorrows somewhere else. But he wouldn't run at the first sign of the tough stuff.

He wasn't his old man.

When she continued staring at him with that all too probing stare, he nodded. 'Fine. We'll stay.'

But he'd ruined the day and not even an Echidnas victory by forty-five points or her apparent enthusiasm for his team could salvage what he'd screwed up.

When they left the stadium and headed for his ute, he felt compelled to ask, 'Do you fancy having dinner somewhere?' even though the thought of spending an evening across a table from her seemed unpalatable, considering his mood. She didn't deserve this.

'No thanks. Take me home please.' Her clipped tone alerted him to exactly how unimpressed she was by his behaviour and he didn't blame her.

It took less than twenty minutes to get from the Docklands Stadium to her place and when he pulled up outside the front of *Hope and Harmony* she already had the ute's door half-open.

'Hey.' His hand shot out to still her. 'I'm sorry.'

'For what? For acting like a jerk all day? For not speaking to me? For treating me like a hanger-on you couldn't wait to ditch?'

He winced and scrubbed a hand over his face. 'I deserved that.'

'Yeah, you did.' Her tone softened and he felt the rigid muscles of her shoulder relax under his touch. 'Look, neither of us signed up for a relationship. We're having fun for a short time not a long time or whatever other kind of fling cliché you'd like to use. But today wasn't fun for me and by that residual scowl on your face I'm guessing it was shitty for you too.'

She gently removed his hand from her shoulder. 'So why don't you sleep on it? Deal with whatever's bugging you? And we'll catch up some other time.'

Logan managed a terse nod, appalled he'd treated her so badly but unable to salvage something from it, not in his current mood.

'I'll call you,' she said, broaching the gap between them to place an all-too-brief kiss on his lips.

Then he watched the woman who invaded his every waking thought get out of his car and head inside her place without looking back.

CHAPTER FOURTEEN

HOPE DIDN'T HAVE much time for social media, other than using it to post video clips of her music online. But she hoped it would prove fruitful when she researched Logan Holmes. Something major had gone down with his dad for him to act so out of character yesterday. The fun, flirtatious charmer had been nowhere in sight; instead, he'd turned into a brooding, glowering shadow of his former self.

It had unnerved her, the need to comfort him when they weren't emotionally invested, so she'd responded in kind, feigning interest in the game while casting surreptitious glances at him every few minutes. It had been one hundred and twenty minutes of sheer torture. To make matters worse, he'd asked her out to dinner from obligation rather than any real desire to spend more time with her and it had been the last straw.

So she'd called him on it. Told him to get his shit together. But would he?

Guys weren't so great at facing feelings and it looked as if he had a whole carousel of baggage regarding his father.

She knew all about the burdens of family. Even now, five years after she'd left England, her parents alternated between patronising and interfering, condescending and threatening. They would say anything to get their own way and she'd learned that way too young. Her parents lied without compunction and ultimately that was what had driven a wedge between them a long time ago.

If she'd known the truth about her grandmother's trust fund she would've cut ties earlier and followed her heart into a music career. Instead, they'd lied and said she'd be penniless when they cut her off if she persisted in her 'frivolous nonsense'.

So she'd done what had been expected of her, a stupidly naïve, frightened eighteen-year-old following the path set by her parents.

Ironically, it was after another person she'd trusted had betrayed her that she'd learned the truth. Willem had done his research well in order to ingratiate himself and had alerted her to the fact she had a small fortune waiting for her courtesy of a long-dead grandmother.

She knew her parents loved her in their own way but their lack of compassion for what *she* wanted out of life and the lengths they'd gone to in order to control her never failed to grate.

It had taken her a long while to be able to have some kind of relationship with them no matter how fraught, and her music had helped.

She hoped Logan would find peace with his father too. And while it had nothing to do with her—

getting emotionally involved with the rugged CEO wasn't on her agenda—she had to know what was bugging him so she wouldn't inadvertently tread on any virtual landmines again.

She'd resisted the urge to pry into his life last night but after minimal sleep she had no such compunction this morning. Firing up her laptop, she sipped at her favourite breakfast tea. A few seconds later, she put her cup down and typed 'Logan Holmes' into the search engine. Stacks of hits popped up but most were in association with his business. He had no social media accounts. Bummer.

Feeling like a snoop, she typed in another name, 'Stephen Holmes', and bingo. Stephen had a bio on a major entertainment website, describing him as a stand-up comedian. She clicked on the link and perused the scoop on Stephen, gleaning more from a few paragraphs than Logan had divulged in several conversations.

Stephen toured the country, performing in small venues for the comedy club scene. Considering his extensive CV, he must've started before Logan had been born. He'd won a few awards in the early days for his routines and had performed in Vegas twice. There was mention of a son, but no name, and a snippet on a recent health scare. It also mentioned that Stephen currently resided in Melbourne.

She checked out a few more links but didn't learn anything new. If Stephen lived in Melbourne and had had a recent health scare maybe that call had been him reaching out to Logan. But what was so dire in their past that Logan couldn't forgive his father and had made a mere phone call rattle him to the point of withdrawing like he had yesterday?

She shouldn't interfere. She wouldn't. But she knew what it was like to resent a parent and sometimes it helped to share. Harry had been her sounding board; who did Logan have? For whatever time they would be shagging, maybe she could be his.

Picking up her mobile before she could second-guess her decision, she fired off a text.

U free?

The answering ping surprised her with its speed, as she'd expected him to leave her hanging.

Depends.

On...?

What U R wearing.

She smiled and responded.

Come over & find out.

His response came swiftly.

B there in 30.

Okay, so the text flirting was good. He'd moved on from yesterday. But as she quickly showered and dressed, she couldn't help feeling guilty for luring him under false pretences. He would be thinking this was a booty call.

She had something else in mind first.

'Tell me again why you're dragging me through the back streets of Melbourne.'

Logan sounded like a whiny kid, deliberately baiting Hope because he knew she loved this. This was the fifth alley she'd shown him and, despite his fake indifference, she saw the gleam of interest in his eyes.

'Because this is culture,' she said, pointing at a giant ebony mouth in a scary crimson face plastered across a laneway entrance. 'You showed me yours yesterday; today I'm showing you mine.'

She waggled her eyebrows and he chuckled. 'I'm talking about the essence of Melbourne, in case you were wondering.'

He ducked down, his lips grazing her ear and sending a shiver of longing through her. 'I'd much rather see something else of yours,' he murmured, nipping her ear lobe before soothing it with a flick of his tongue that sent a jolt straight to her nether regions.

'Later.' Her grip on his hand tightened as a silent promise of things to come. But for now she had to come up with a smart way of broaching the sensitive topic of his dad without alienating him. 'Did you do anything last night after you dropped me off?'

He stiffened but didn't pull away. 'Went back to my place and emptied the mini-bar, which I keep stocked for my occasional trips to Melbourne. Easier than having a regular fridge.'

She didn't know if that jibe about him being transient was directed at her, a pointed declaration that he wouldn't be around for long so she should shut the hell up. It didn't stop her but she didn't want to sound judgemental. 'It's always more fun drinking from those teeny, tiny bottles.'

'It's what's inside that counts.' He sounded resigned rather than bitter and she hesitated, searching for the right words to ask what was bugging him. 'It's not like a hotel mini-bar. I stock regular sized cans in there. Much more effective for kicking back and forgetting everything.'

Before she could say anything, he continued. 'I'm not an alcoholic. I've had a rough few days and I apologise for my shitty behaviour yesterday.' He huffed out a deep breath. 'I'm not some dickhead trying to jerk you around, so maybe if I give you a little insight you might actually forgive me.'

'Hey, there's nothing to forgive.' She lifted his hand to her mouth and pressed a kiss on the back of it, trying to clamp down on her curiosity and failing. Thankfully, she hadn't had to pry much at all and he seemed ready to divulge snippets of his past.

The tension bracketing his mouth lessened but the haunted shadows flitting across his eyes didn't. 'My dad wasn't around much when I was growing up. He tried to make it as a comedian so was on the road a lot. Mum and I missed him a lot, particularly Mum.'

His eyes turned flinty as he hesitated, as if struggling to find the right words. 'She was a different person when Dad was around. She'd light up, and then when he left again she'd clam up. I thought that maybe she had depression but she wasn't on any meds and didn't display many of the symptoms when I looked it up.'

Hope clung to his hand, wishing she could infuse him with strength. She understood more than he knew. Having a physically present but emotionally absent parent could be just as hard as not having a parent at all. She'd often felt invisible around her parents, or worse, regretted, as if they'd never wanted a child and didn't really want her around. They tolerated her, doing their utmost to bend her to their will, to make her their clone.

When she hadn't acquiesced, they'd lied to force her into it and, while she might have forgiven them, she'd never forget.

'So what happened?'

His brows pulled in as he cleared his throat. 'Dad started to make some serious money when I was in my teens so he barely made it home. Mum got worse to the point she pretty much ignored me most days.'

He stiffened, his expression contorting with pain. 'Then she died.'

Sadness tightened Hope's throat as she leaned in and rested her head against his shoulder. 'That must've been heart-breaking.'

'It was.'

Two short, sharp words that hinted at sorrow, pain and devastation. Her parents might be narcissistic liars, and she would mourn them out of obligation when they eventually passed, but the audible anguish in Logan's gruff voice told her exactly how much he'd loved his mum.

He remained silent for a long while and she waited out his pause, surprised by his candour, relieved she didn't have to pry it from him but regretting causing him pain by his recounting of the tale.

'I blamed Dad for her death. At the funeral, he stood up in front of everyone in the town and waxed lyrical about how much he loved his family, how everything he did was for me.'

His upper lip curled in a sneer and his eyes hardened to a steely blue. 'Bullshit. He happily abandoned us because it suited him. It was always about him. His career, his opportunities,' he spat out, bitterness lacing every word as his face reddened. 'He tried to reach out to me after the funeral, saying we should catch up more often now that I was moving to Melbourne for my apprenticeship; saying how the men of the Holmes family had to stick together, how we had to look forward to the future together. I told him to shove it up his ass.'

He stood rigid, his nostrils flared, a vein pulsing at his temple, and Hope slipped her arms around his waist and buried her face in his chest, trying to convey silent comfort. He held her but his arms were unyielding, his back stiff beneath her hands.

'The other day when he called and I was with you he told me he'd had cancer.' His voice cracked a little and he cleared his throat before continuing.

'He's okay but he laid a heavy guilt trip on me and I've been mulling it over ever since.'

Helplessness filled Hope as she released him. She'd wanted to know what was behind Logan's funk; it looked as though she'd got more than she'd bargained for. She had no idea whether Logan wanted comforting or to be left alone. His body language screamed 'hands off' but the torment in his eyes gutted her.

'What are you going to do?'

'Fucked if I know.' His mouth twisted with resentment and she had her answer right there. He didn't want her comfort. Which was probably a good thing because anything she could offer would be lame and ineffectual in the face of his dilemma. 'The thing is, I can't see how meeting up is going to change anything. He'll always be a selfish asshole to me. But then I think about how shitty I'd feel if he died before I got to say a bunch of stuff...'

'Then I think you've figured out what you need to do.' She rested her palm against his cheek. It was a simple gesture she hoped would convey that she understood and wished she could do more. 'See him. You might purge the past and move forward. At the very least you'll get to voice your opinion. And who knows? You might even find yourself reconnecting—'

'Not going to happen,' he said through gritted teeth, his lips flattening. 'But, yeah, I think it's time.'

'Do you want to do it now?'

'Hell no.' He pulled her into his arms again and squished her so hard she could barely breathe.

'Thanks for listening. I'm not a sharer but it kinda felt good to get all that off my chest.'

Hope hugged him right back and they stood that way for a long time. She'd never been into overt displays of affection as a kid—no great surprise given that her folks considered an air-kiss on birthdays more than enough—but being able to convey so much by wrapping Logan in her arms felt good. They might not be indulging in anything more than a fling but she hoped he derived some comfort from confiding in her and knowing she'd happily be his sounding board if needed.

When he released her, he stared at her with a tenderness that made her ache.

'You sure you don't want to call your dad now?'

'No. I want to do something else.'

She couldn't fathom the determined spark in his eyes but it was better than the pain of the last few minutes. 'What?'

He lowered his head to whisper in her ear. 'I want to do what I should've done last night with you.' His tongue traced the whorl of her ear in a slow, deliberate swipe. 'And it doesn't involve watching a footy replay.'

Hope almost felt guilty as relief seeped through her. This, she could do. She understood their intense physical connection. The riotous confusion of emotions him having confided in her elicited, not so much.

'Oh?' She arched an eyebrow and struck a provocative pose with her hand on her hip, responding in kind to his switch to a playful mood.

His wicked laugh rippled over her, loaded with intent. 'Ever checked into a hotel for a quickie?'

A wave of heat swamped her at the thought, most of it pooling in her cheeks that had to be a beacon for the surge of excitement making her skin pebble. 'No.'

His fingertip grazed her blazing cheek before trailing along her jaw, her chin, eventually tracing her bottom lip with deliberate lightness. 'Well, we're in the heart of the city, surrounded by a billion hotels, so why don't we save the laneways tour for another time?'

The old Hope would've been appalled by such a suggestion. But the new Hope she'd become through letting go of her old insecurities one layer at a time leapt at the raunchy thought of ducking into a hotel with the sole intention of having sex.

'These laneways aren't going anywhere,' she said, glancing up at him coyly from beneath lowered lashes. 'We should definitely do our bit for inner-city tourism and check into a hotel.'

'I love how spontaneous you are,' he said, grabbing her hand and tugging her close for a quick kiss that did little to assuage the sudden burning of her body. 'Let's go find the nearest one.'

She didn't have to be asked twice and they almost stumbled from the dark laneway in their quest to find the nearest hotel. Thankfully, it wasn't far; they both spotted the sign on the corner of the next block at the same time.

'Fortuitous,' she said.

At the same time he said, 'Fate.'

They laughed and picked up the pace, almost bounding up the three concrete steps and pushing through a heavy glass door into a cool interior. The lobby had a shabby, understated elegance to it, like an old lady who'd seen better days. Faded chintz sofas were strategically placed around mahogany coffee tables, with fringed lamps casting a warm glow over the place. The polished parquetry floor and the brass-lined check-in desk appeared faded, but Hope didn't care. All she cared about was getting naked with Logan as fast as humanly possible.

'Be right back,' he said, squeezing her hand before releasing it.

As Hope watched him check in, her impatience growing as the receptionist dropped his credit card twice, she wondered what had got into her—but she didn't care because soon it would be him.

CHAPTER FIFTEEN

THE HOTEL WAS A DIVE.

Logan had stayed in fancier places in smaller towns around the country. But he needed to obliterate the ache clawing at his chest like a trapped animal desperate to escape. The ache that talking about his father had elicited. Sex with Hope was guaranteed to do that.

He'd never talked to anyone about his dad. Rick knew a fair bit of what had gone down because they'd been friends when he'd first moved to Melbourne and had been privy to the conversations—more like yelling matches—when his father had reached out several times after his mum's funeral. But he'd never divulged the truth to a woman before and the fact he'd done it with Hope spoke volumes.

He was in too deep.

Since when did a fling signify a real connection for him?

He'd dated extensively around the country over the years. Tradesmen held a certain appeal for some women and as CEO of a booming company with a healthy cash flow, he'd become popular with women in general. It didn't make him a bighead to admit it; it made him a realist. Women were attracted to money and ruggedness, and he had both.

Except Hope didn't give a fuck about his fortune; she had more than enough dosh of her own. As for his looks, she trumped him in that department too. Even now, as he palmed the key card from the hotel receptionist and strode towards Hope, she stared at him with those big grey eyes, all-seeing, all-knowing. She wore funky faux leather pants today, with a green flowing top that set off her eyes. He'd been hot to trot from the moment he'd seen her. Then he'd blurted all that stuff about Stephen to explain his shoddy behaviour towards her and had felt like shit ever since.

Logan didn't depend on anyone. He'd been his own man for a long time and confiding in Hope had been an anomaly. It mystified him in a way he didn't like. The last time he'd felt this befuddled had been at his mum's funeral and he hated feeling out of his depth.

He liked being in control. He didn't like vulnerability. Revealing too much about his family, having Hope listen, discuss with and support him, had shown that he had a weak spot and that didn't sit well with him.

He didn't want her getting too close: it would only end badly for her. Bonding while they fucked was one thing; feeling comfortable enough around her to reveal too much was another.

He had to get this semi-date back on track and

that meant focussing on the sex. But she was right. He had to see Stephen. Settle this once and for all.

But what if seeing his dad after all these years made everything worse?

Spending all his time on the road wasn't just about enjoying the spoils of being CEO of his own company. It wasn't about keeping his hand in with the building industry. It wasn't about being a demanding boss who had to oversee the commencement of projects personally.

It was about not growing close to anybody.

More importantly, not having anyone depend on him.

Because that was his ultimate fear: that he was more like his dad than he cared to admit and disappointing anyone who got too close because of his fear of commitment would be inevitable.

He'd seen what his mother's dependence on his father for her happiness had eventually done to her and it hadn't been pretty. The emotional rollercoaster Stephen had inflicted on her had taken its toll and he'd been privy to the fallout. It made him resent his dad all the more because somewhere deep inside, in a place he hated to acknowledge, he'd begrudged his father his ability to escape.

Stephen hadn't born the brunt of his mum's mood swings, Logan had, and it made him determined never to become so emotionally invested in a relationship that it produced an unhealthy dependence that always left one partner worse off. No fucking way.

Logan never wanted to be responsible for any

woman's happiness, ever. Flings that lasted no longer than a month before he moved on suited him fine.

Gritting his teeth against the urge to call this off because of his mood, he forced a smile. It must've come
out a grimace because that fucking pity was back in
Hope's eyes and it slayed him all over again.

'Do you really want to do this—?'

'Come on,' he growled, grabbing her hand and
holding on tight.

He strode towards the lift, determined to douse
his moroseness with a warm armful of woman. They
rode to the fourth floor in silence but he was acutely
aware of her: the heat radiating off her skin; her light
floral fragrance faintly reminiscent of roses and vanilla; the brush of her hair against his arm.

When the elevator doors slid open, he spied their
room number two doors to the right. She squeezed
his hand when he fumbled the first card swipe and
he cursed. He got it on the second try and pushed the
door open, immediately regretting this decision as
a faint, musty odour tickled his nose and he caught
sight of the room.

Hope deserved better than this.

She'd be a five-star kind of girl and he'd brought
her to this dive because…what? Because he wanted
to use her to eradicate his over-sharing regarding his
father, when he should've had the balls to confront
him a long time ago?

'Stop over-thinking this,' she said, slipping in behind him and closing the door. 'It's okay.'

'This place is a shithole,' he muttered, leading her

further into the room, which only cemented his first impressions. Worn carpet the colour of English mustard, pale blue bedspread torn in one corner, a small scratched desk, a single chair with scuff marks on the legs and heavily kinked olive drapes that sat askew, partially hiding the view of the brick wall of the apartment building next door. 'It was a mistake bringing you here—'

'Shh...' She pressed her fingertips to his mouth, silencing him. 'I'm not a princess.'

She lowered her hand and gently nudged him backwards towards the bed. 'And I want to be with you.'

She palmed his cock with one hand as his knees hit the back of the bed and shoved him down onto it with the other. Determination glittered in her eyes as she stared at him, daring him to put a stop to this.

He should. His mood, this place, it was all wrong. But when he opened his mouth to say so she increased the pressure on his cock, tracing the rigid outline with her fingers, massaging him. Fuck, he was a goner.

'This is going to be good,' she said, not breaking eye contact as she knelt at his feet and nudged his thighs apart, her hand continually stroking his cock through his jeans, making rational thought impossible.

All the angst of the last twenty minutes faded as Logan watched her unzip him. Anticipation made him light-headed as he propped himself up on his elbows as this amazing woman slid her hand into his jocks and took out his hard cock as if it was the most precious gift she'd ever unwrapped.

Yeah, this was exactly what he needed. Sex with a hot woman. No time to think or feel. Just live it.

When she swiped her tongue across the head in a slow, languorous sweep, he couldn't think about anything beyond this moment. Fucking perfect.

Her tongue circled him again as her hand gripped his shaft, strong and confident, and he gave himself over to enjoying this. Having her stare at his cock like she couldn't get enough was a huge turn-on and he thrust his hips up a little.

She didn't need the encouragement and when her lips enclosed the tip the feeling of her hot mouth encasing him ripped a groan from the back of his throat. She slid her lips over him, her hand rising up to meet her mouth. Sucking and squeezing. Up and down, over and over again, blanking everything but the hot moistness of her mouth and the strength of her grip.

His hips bucked as she sped up, sucking and squeezing, until the delirium of release overtook him. It felt as if his balls lifted up clean into his body as he thrust into her mouth and came, the milking of his release so strong his ass arched off the bed.

She didn't speak as she slowly slid him out of her mouth. But she kissed the tip of his cock and he trembled again, his super-sensitive skin tuned to her every touch. She stood and sat next to him on the edge of the bed, tucking him back into his jocks when all he needed was some time to get back in the game.

When she rested her head on his shoulder and didn't speak, he had no idea what the hell was going on. He reached for her and she held a hand to his chest to stop him.

'This was about you,' she murmured, snuggling into him when he wrapped his arm around her. 'I can wait.'

He didn't want her to. He wanted to bury himself in her. He wanted to annihilate the uncharacteristic ache in his chest that her unselfishness elicited.

He wanted to fuck and forget.

His cock had better get with the programme because the faster he recovered from her sensational blowjob, the faster he could focus on what he did best. Fun for a short time, not a long time, then leave.

Anything else, anything remotely resembling an emotional connection, wasn't an option.

CHAPTER SIXTEEN

HOPE HAD NEVER brought a man to her apartment so the fact Logan currently lay sprawled in her bed, fast asleep, spoke volumes.

As if she hadn't already known he was different from all the other guys she'd dated.

She'd learned to guard her heart in England when her relationship with Willem had imploded and she'd discovered the truth: that trust is easily broken and lies are cheap.

Having her heart broken had been bad enough but it had been a hard lesson learning of her parents' lies close on the heels of Willem's deception. And Harry's betrayal soon after had cemented what she'd already learned: never trust anyone.

Ironic, considering her parents had tried to instil that very value into her from a young age, but for a different reason. The McWilliamses' fortune ensured they had dealt with usurpers sucking up their entire lives. They'd wanted her to spot the have-nots wanting to take advantage of the haves, to question everyone's motives. It meant she'd rarely dated as a teen and at twenty had fallen hard for Willem, naïvely optimistic. She'd been a prime target for a jerk like him.

In a warped way she'd been grateful to him. Her momentary lapse in trusting him and having him crap all over her meant she'd never make the same mistake again. People were fickle, whether they were related to you or not. Lesson learned.

So she'd hardened up when she'd landed in Melbourne five years ago. She didn't emotionally invest and she never fully trusted. Expiration dating suited her just fine and resulted in less angst.

This thing she had with Logan was casual. And she had to keep it that way, which was why inviting him here, into her home, could signal a change of heart she might not be ready for.

Discouraging trust-building meant not letting anyone get too close. It was why she'd never brought any of the other guys she'd slept with to her place. But inviting Logan here had seemed like a good idea at the time. They hadn't stayed in the grungy hotel long. Not because she had an aversion to dirt—okay, maybe she did—but he'd revealed so much of himself to her when talking about his family that she'd wanted to put him at ease.

She'd seen how fraught he'd been after divulging the truth about his past and had wanted to distract him. Giving him a blowjob had been a start but she'd wanted to do more, which was why they'd ended up at her place. She'd hoped that by showing him her personal space it would return the favour of revealing a small part of herself and make him less angsty about disclosing so much of himself.

However, him falling asleep while she showered hadn't been part of the plan because having him here, touching her things, seeing more than she'd revealed to any other guy, made her too vulnerable and she seriously wanted to jump his bones to get this fling back on track. But when she'd seen him spread-eagled on her lemon bedspread, his expression more serene than she'd ever seen it, she'd let him sleep.

It would give her time to compose a few songs. She'd been lagging lately, consumed by travelling all over Melbourne to her students, rather than them coming to her for lessons, because of the renovations. The moment her new recording studio was up and running she wanted to lay down enough tracks for an album. The sooner other local indie musicians heard her work, the more interest she could drum up and hopefully launch their careers too.

She paused in the bedroom doorway and glanced at Logan one last time: the tough guy with a marshmallow core. He snored softly, his lips emitting small puffs of air as he slumbered, oblivious to how much she liked seeing him in her bed. He dwarfed the small space, which had barely enough room for her queen-sized bed, matching side-tables and a dresser. Yet he fit somehow, as though he'd spent many nights here instead of this being his first.

The first of many.

The moment the thought popped into her head she

spun on her heel and padded into the lounge, where she'd set up one corner as a mini-music-room.

Logan wouldn't be around for long. He'd made that perfectly clear. So that stupid stab of pain in the vicinity of her heart at the thought of him leaving couldn't be more unwelcome. She knew the score. It was why she'd started up with him in the first place. He was exactly like the rest of her short-term fixes for the loneliness that plagued her at times. But the more time they spent together the more he sucked her in with a hint of susceptibility beneath an iron facade. The bad boy with a soft centre. Irresistible.

With a sigh she sat at her desk, picked up a pencil and took out a clean sheaf of paper. She already had the lyrics to this new song hovering at the edge of her consciousness.

Pierce my heart...
Make me ache...
It's just the start...
Please don't take...

They made no sense in their current format but as the first strains of a haunting melody filled her head she started writing. Slowly at first, mixing quavers and semi-quavers, alternating tempo. C-C-D-E-B-B-C. As she jotted the notes, the words started to coalesce and she wrote the first few stanzas in total free-flow. She loved this part of the creative process, letting everything pour out of her, words and music, in a frenzied burst that she could refine later.

She had no idea how long it took but it seemed like the blink of an eye when she'd completed the first song and moved onto the second. And the third. And the fourth. By the time her fingers cramped from clutching the pencil so tightly, she'd written four songs that leapt off the page. Her fingers itched to play and she swivelled on her seat towards the keyboard next to her desk.

Not wanting to wake Logan, she plugged in her headphones and let her fingers take over, gliding across the keys, getting a feel for the new songs. As each song flowed into the next, effortless and real, Hope knew she'd stumbled onto something special, something almost magical. She'd never been this inspired, had never experienced the sheer joy of getting her songs right the first time.

She usually scribbled down a few notes and words and took a break, before returning to her writing when the inspiration struck. She'd never written four songs in a row and certainly hadn't played them like this: as if her fingers were one step ahead of her brain.

She could attribute her new-found creativity to any number of things: the stars aligning, her musical talent finally coming to the fore, the balmy spring weather. But she knew the real reason behind this flawless creative streak—and he currently resided in the middle of her bed.

Swiping her hand across eyes gritty from studying sheet music too long, she headed for the sofa and curled into a corner. A sudden chill overcame her at the realisation her creative happiness might depend on a guy who'd leave sooner rather than later, and she reached for the cashmere throw on the back of the sofa and drew it around her.

This couldn't be good.

Flowers inspired her. Melbourne's artistic laneways inspired her. Watching loved-up couples inspired her. Long walks through the Royal Botanic Gardens, strolling through the museum and listening to jazz on the banks of the Yarra River inspired her.

A rugged, sexy construction king destined to break her heart shouldn't.

The moment the thought that he had the power to break her heart popped into her mind, Hope stifled a groan and hung her head. Resting her forehead on her knees, she tried a meditation technique she'd learned at yoga to wipe her mind and blank it of all thoughts of Logan.

It didn't work.

The thought had lodged front and centre in her impressionable brain and she couldn't dislodge it no matter how many low-level chants she internalised.

She'd never depended on anyone for her happiness. Her parents were typical upper-class refined English gentry. Children were raised by a well-paid, well-educated nanny and only seen at mealtimes, where they'd mind their manners and respond when spoken to. She'd never known any different until she'd hit her teens and had started escaping to the local village to hang out at the pubs with Harry. Back then, books had made her happy. Music made her happier. People, not so much. Then she'd met Willem and had never known joy like it. Which had made it all the harder when he'd hurt her.

She'd been a loner ever since and it had served her well.

Until now.

What was it about Logan Holmes that had her in a tizz?

She should go to him. Should wipe away this uncharacteristic dwelling on emotions with a rousing bout of sex.

Instead, she tugged the cashmere throw tighter around her, slid down the sofa and rested her head on a cushion. She needed some time to mull over this latest realisation because if she woke him now on the pretext of having sex he'd probably take one look at her face and know there was something going on.

She'd wake him in the morning and by then she would've eradicated the odd ache in her chest, ready to get physical with the guy who'd rocked her world without even trying.

CHAPTER SEVENTEEN

Logan had no idea how long he'd been asleep but his eyelids felt gritty and his mouth dry when he woke. Worse, when he glanced to his side, Hope wasn't tucked next to him and he lay on top of her fancy coverlet, not under it.

'What the fuck?' He pushed into a sitting position and swung his legs over the side of the bed, swiping a hand over his face to wake up. He blinked several times in the semi-darkness, trying to remember how he had ended up in Hope's bedroom—not having sex.

He remembered strolling the laneways, blabbing about his dad, a mind-numbing blowjob then coming back here and…crashing. She'd taken a shower. He'd rested his eyes. And she hadn't woken him.

Way to go pleasing a woman, dickhead.

He padded to the bedroom door and opened it. Moonlight cast a glow over the lounge, along with the reflected city lights scattered outside her window. Her apartment, situated on the tenth storey of an upscale building in Parkville, looked like something out of a magazine, all sharp angles and shiny chrome and designer furnishings. He'd felt uncomfortable the moment he'd set foot inside. Not because he couldn't afford a place like this—he could buy this entire apartment building if so inclined—but for the fact it looked exactly like something he didn't want: a real home.

Hope had put her personal touches everywhere, from the red tulips in elongated vases strategically placed throughout the room to the geometric black-and-white shaggy rug beneath the glass-topped dining table for four. Music magazines were stacked neatly on the coffee table, jostling for space alongside biographies of long-dead musicians and the occasional thriller, with an open notebook covered in scrawl taking pride of place on top of the lot. Plump cushions of various size and colour lay scattered across the furniture, managing to appear artistic rather than messy.

It brought a lump to this throat, looking around this room, because his mum had had the same talent for taking a hotchpotch of things and making them appear elegant. He remembered trawling the local secondhand shops with her, being dragged from one to another, acting as a packhorse for her purchases. He hadn't minded, despite his token protests, because decorating their house had made his mum happy and that had happened less frequently as he'd grown up. Later, she'd let slip that she'd been doing it for his father, thinking that if she made their home pretty maybe he'd return more often. When Logan had heard that he'd wanted to take a knife to all her cushions and slash them to pieces. Stephen hadn't deserved a home, let alone a good woman to keep it nice for him.

Rubbing his chest at the inevitable burn that thoughts of his dad elicited, Logan moved into the lounge in search of Hope. A small lamp caught his eye to the left and he walked over to a desk covered in paper. By the looks of it, she'd been working while he'd been sleeping. He didn't mean to pry but his glance landed on the top page, a song called 'Yearning'. He skim-read the lyrics and was damned if that lump in his throat didn't swell. He had no idea who the guy was in the song but he hoped to God it wasn't him.

He could never be any woman's 'everything'.

Swivelling away from the desk, he spied Hope curled up on the sofa. Her eyes were closed, her breathing even and, with a pink rug draped over her, she looked like a sleeping fairy. Feeling like a voyeur, he drew closer, watching her. She wasn't classically beautiful—her nose was too large and her eyes too far apart—but that mouth... Discounting the wicked things she could do with it, she had a smile that transformed her face to pretty in an instant. Her lips were parted slightly and he'd never wanted to kiss a woman so badly.

But she'd let him sleep so the least he could do was return the favour.

For now, he had something important to do, something to get him out of this funk once and for all. Blurting out truths about his past to a woman, falling asleep rather than fucking... He really needed to get his head back in the game.

He padded back into the bedroom, closed the door and slipped his phone out of his jacket pocket, where it hung on the back of a chair.

He didn't care about the early hour. It would be the best time to call his father as he remembered Stephen always liked to sleep late so leaving a message rather than talking to the old man suited him just fine.

He didn't have Stephen's number in his contacts list but he'd saved every one of his father's messages over the years: forty-five in total. Initially, Logan did it as a reminder of the pain Stephen had caused, a self-flagellation tool in case he ever weakened and let his father back into his life. But more recently, after he'd heard the news of his dad's cancer battle, those messages had become a symbol of something more.

A reminder of his foolishness if his dad pegged out and he maintained his distance until it was too late.

Calling his dad to arrange a meeting could only be a good thing. Purge the past. Confront the lies. And maybe, just maybe, move on without the guilt of his hate eating away at him.

He scrolled through his recent call history and saw the familiar number. His thumb hovered over it for what seemed like an eternity before he tapped it.

His chest tightened and his breathing grew choppy as he held the phone up to his ear, clenching it so tightly his fingers spasmed. After two rings, the voice mail kicked in and Logan exhaled in relief.

'This is Stephen. I can't take your call right now because I'm busy making people laugh. So, if you want to make me chuckle, leave a message.'

Something twanged in Logan's chest. His father hadn't changed his message in years. He'd heard the same cheery recording many times as a kid, when his mum had encouraged him to call Stephen so they could maintain a strong bond.

What a fucking joke.

If Stephen had wanted to maintain a bond with his son he would've come home more often rather than staying away for fifty-one weeks of the year. Asshole.

Logan dragged in a breath and blew it out before speaking. 'Hey, Dad, it's me. Been thinking about a lot of stuff lately and maybe we should meet up to discuss it. I'm busy this week but one day next week should suit. I'll text you the details.'

Logan hit the 'call end' button before his father heard the tremor in his voice. He hated himself for allowing long-suppressed emotions of the past to bubble up now and threaten to consume him. He needed to get a grip. Confronting his dad might be long overdue but it was a start.

The bedroom door creaked open and he quickly shoved the phone into his pocket. The last thing he needed was Hope asking who he was ringing and why.

Not that she'd given any indication of being the clingy type but since he'd revealed too much of himself to her he'd been on edge.

'You're awake,' she said, swiping a hand across her sleep-filled eyes. 'Okay, so that was an obviously stupid thing to say.'

She looked so goddamned cute standing in the doorway, wrapped in that fuzzy pink rug, wearing a long black T-shirt that hung halfway down her thighs, one barefoot balanced on top of the other. Her hair frizzed around the crown like a halo and a deep sleep-wrinkle slashed her cheek where she'd been pressed against the armrest, but even sleep-tousled she was the most captivating woman he'd ever seen.

His chest twanged and there was only one thing he could do to get rid of the uncharacteristic sappiness.

'I'm glad we're both awake so we get to finish what we started earlier.' He crossed the short space between them and swung her up into his arms.

'Hey, I'm heavy, put me down—'

'You're a lightweight and when I put you down I'm going down,' he said, laying her on the bed gently, rucking up her T-shirt and settling between her legs.

'Oh…' That one muttered syllable gave way to a drawn-out moan as he swiped her pussy with his tongue, the first taste going straight to his head. Sweet. Addictive. Yeah, this was exactly what he needed to obliterate feeling and focus on doing.

He slid one hand under her ass and lifted her to his mouth, using the other to spread her slick folds wide. Her pussy glistened, inviting him to explore. So he did, thrusting his tongue into her over and over, alternating with grazing her clit with his teeth until he had her writhing.

'So good,' she muttered, her hand resting on his head and when he raised her a little higher her fingers convulsed, tugging at his hair. He didn't mind a little pain mingled with pleasure but he must've made some kind of sound because she lifted her head to look at him.

With her eyes wide and her lips parted, she looked wanton, ready for anything.

'You like me fucking your pussy with my tongue?'

He deliberately baited her with his crudeness to see what she'd do. She didn't disappoint.

'Lie on your back and put your hands behind your head,' she commanded, surging into a sitting position and scooting back on the bed.

'Why?'

He threw the question out there, not caring for her rationale, because he liked this take-charge woman and the way she owned her sexuality.

'Because I'm going to sit on your face.'

No murmur, no whisper, just a blatant statement that had him obeying her command in record time.

'You're so fucking hot when you're bossy,' he said with a smug grin. 'You know that, right?'

'I know you're about to stop talking.'

She spread her legs either side of his head, giving him another up close and personal look at that pretty pussy as she lowered herself until she had her clit positioned just right over his mouth.

He inhaled her muskiness as the tip of his tongue grazed her clit in a feather-light tickle designed to tease. He did it again, and again, until he heard her whimper.

'Logan…please…'

Only then did he increase the pressure, lapping at her with quick little licks, faster and faster until she was practically grinding her pussy into his face.

That was when he sucked the sensitive nub of nerve endings into his mouth and bit gently. She came apart on a raw, primitive yell that raised the hairs on his arms. So fucking hot.

When his tongue darted out to lave her clit again she trembled and scooted down his body.

'You are a master at that,' she said, her expression of bliss making him grin. 'Condom?'

'In my wallet. Left pocket of my jacket.' He made to get up and she pushed him back down.

'Let me.'

Thankfully, she made quick work of finding it while he unzipped and pushed his jeans and jocks down. It would've taken too long to get undressed completely and with the taste of her still on his tongue he needed to be inside her now.

Sensing his urgency, she rolled the condom on with skilful precision, her firm grip reminding him of the way she'd handled him in the hotel, the way her mouth had felt on him…

'I need to fuck you,' he said, reaching for her, but she slapped his hands away.

'Put them back behind your head,' she said, swinging a leg over him. 'I'm calling the shots.'

'Yes, ma'am,' he drawled, doing as he was told

and settling back into this real-life fantasy of having this sexy, uninhibited woman taking what she wanted.

'That's better,' she said, positioning her pussy over his cock before slowly lowering herself.

She'd only taken him in an inch and he gritted his teeth against the urge to drive upward. With deliberate slowness she peeled her T-shirt up, revealing those beautiful breasts and rigid nipples that begged to be sucked.

'I want to taste you, to touch you—'

He bit off the rest of what he was going to say when she impaled herself on him, taking him in to the hilt. Enclosed in velvet heat, he found he had nothing else to say as she started to move up and down, riding him with a resoluteness that soon had his hips bucking of their own accord.

'If I can't touch you, you do it,' he growled, thrusting up as she drove down, the delicious friction sending him nuts.

'I'm the one in charge but I'll give you this one.' She slid her hands up her torso until they cupped her tits, before proceeding to tweak her nipples, rolling them between her thumbs and forefingers.

'Fuck yeah, just like that.'

His throat tightened with lust and he bordered on panting as she licked one thumb, then the other, before resuming plucking at her nipples.

'Fuck me,' he muttered, his balls tightening in pre-release.

'Only because you asked so nicely,' she purred,

jamming down onto him with renewed vigour until he was blinded to everything but her.

When she reached down to touch herself she grazed his cock with a fingertip and he fell into the abyss, coming with a ferocity that tore a shout from deep within.

She followed him a second later, their cries mingling and echoing as the spasms subsided. She collapsed forward onto him, her hair tickling his nose, but he didn't push it aside. He liked having his face covered so she couldn't read his expression.

He didn't want her seeing the longing.

Longing that he could prolong this mind-blowing physical connection they shared beyond a few weeks.

Ironic that he'd blasted away the maudlin thoughts about his dad with a rousing bout of scintillating sex, but in doing so he'd come to a startling realisation.

He could never have a long-term relationship with Hope, with any woman, but for the first time ever he would miss this when it ended.

CHAPTER EIGHTEEN

HOPE STOOD IN the middle of her new recording studio and spun a slow three-sixty.

Magnificent.

It was everything she'd imagined and more, and she couldn't wait to thank Logan in person. He'd worked a small miracle in getting his crew to finish the renovations in just over a week, giving her the opportunity to kick-start her dream sooner rather than later.

It went some way to earning her forgiveness, considering he'd snuck out of her apartment in the early hours of the morning three nights ago, leaving nothing but a barely legible scrawled note.

Crazy, considering she was the one who usually absconded from a guy's bed to avoid any mushy stuff the morning after. But the sex with Logan had been incredible and she'd wanted more, so finding he had gone had left her oddly deflated. He'd loved it when she'd taken charge and it had got her off in a way she'd never imagined. As she'd tumbled into sleep she'd expected to wake next to the sexiest man alive and do it all over again. Instead, she'd found he was gone in the morning.

They'd spoken twice on the phone since: the first time when she'd rung him to ask why he'd snuck out early and he'd cited work as a lame excuse she had no option but to accept in order not to appear like a clingy girlfriend; the second when she'd called to invite him out to dinner tonight, when she intended to present him with her surprise.

It had been ingrained in her from childhood that doing something special as a thank you would ensure you were remembered.

With what she'd bought Logan, she hoped he'd never forget her. They might have put an expiration date on this fling from the start, and she might have gone into this with her eyes wide open, but now that his impending departure grew closer she couldn't help but feel a tad lost.

Because another thought struck her as she checked out her new studio. Had he instructed his crew to finish this job sooner rather than later because he couldn't wait to get away?

His motivation for finishing ahead of schedule shouldn't bother her, but it did. It made her second-guess her decision-making. She'd wanted a hot fling, and she'd got one, but had lines blurred somewhere along the way? Had she invested more than her body?

She didn't like the implications of that, not one bit. She'd never trust a guy with her heart again. But what if it was too late?

Her mood soured so she did what she always did

when confronted with something unpleasant: drew her shoulders back, lifted her head and focussed on the positive.

Starting with dinner tonight.

Logan had said he'd meet her at the Melba Room, the Langham's signature restaurant that boasted fabulous views of the city and equally fabulous food. She'd quelled her initial disappointment at not travelling to dinner together, ignoring the niggle at the back of her mind that insisted he had already started distancing himself. Though it was more than a niggle, considering the way he'd snuck out of her place the other morning. Maybe he'd already started laying the groundwork then and that was the real reason he'd absconded before dawn.

Or maybe he knew she was a phoney.

She hated herself for not owning up that she'd been awake when he'd called his dad. She'd felt him watching her so had pretended to sleep, waiting for him to come to her, willing him to kiss her awake, sweep her into his arms and carry her to the bedroom. But when she'd overheard his phone call, she'd realised he'd been checking up on her to ensure he wouldn't be disturbed.

Considering what he'd told her it had been a momentous step to contact his dad, and she hadn't wanted to get in the middle of all that, so she'd feigned sleep after he'd hung up, waiting a few moments before entering the bedroom. He'd appeared startled to see her and in that split second between her opening the bedroom door and seeing his stricken expression she'd known what he needed.

Someone to distract him, to take away the pain and focus on the good stuff, so she'd released her inner vamp and gone for it. The sex had been phenomenal as a result but when she'd woken to his terse note she'd cried a little.

The tears had been for him and the upcoming confrontation with his father and nothing at all to do with acknowledging she already cared too much for this man and wished she could be there for him while he went through the impending emotional upheaval. *Yeah, right.*

As she entered the restaurant, she spied him at the cosy corner table for two that she'd requested when she'd made the booking. She wanted privacy tonight for what had to be said.

The hostess led her to the table and it gave her a few brief moments to study him. His handsome profile: strong jaw; long eyelashes; slight bump on the bridge of his nose that prevented him from being too perfect. An accident with a hammer in his apprentice days, he'd explained when she'd asked about it. She'd traced that bump with her fingertip before kissing it. And she yearned to explore every inch of him with her mouth again.

The first song she'd written the other night had been about him. 'Yearning'. Because that was what he made her feel. He'd never know it, but she'd never felt like this about any guy, and by pouring her soul into her music she had some chance of getting him out of her system when he left.

She might not be willing to trust him fully with her heart but she hoped that after tonight she would've taken the first monumental step to admitting that maybe, just maybe, she might be willing to try.

He chose that moment to glance up and their gazes locked, the instant sizzle of heat arcing between them tugging them together like an invisible string.

Right then, she knew she had no chance in hell of a song helping her forget him.

Resisting the urge to smooth down her chartreuse silk halter dress, she fixed an upbeat smile on her face and strode towards him. His gaze started at her coral-painted toenails and travelled upward in a slow, languorous sweep that made her skin prickle with heat.

He stood when she reached the table and kissed her cheek. 'You look amazing.'

'Thanks,' she said, fighting a rising blush and losing as he pulled out her chair, waiting until she sat before sliding it in.

'Do you always dine in fancy places like this?' He gestured at the elaborate buffet featuring mouth-watering cuisines from around the world.

'Frequently. I like feeling special.'

It sounded lame but she couldn't tell him the real reason: that cooking for one lost its appeal fast and coming here reminded her of visiting the Langham in London with her parents every birthday. They might've ignored her for most of the year but they'd always made a big fuss on her birthday and being here helped her focus on good memories rather than bad.

'A classy woman like you deserves that.'

The compliment sounded offhand but it wasn't the first time he'd alluded to the supposed class divide between them. Considering the gift she intended to give him, it needed to be addressed.

'Do you think there's some kind of socio-economic gap between us?'

His eyebrows shot up and he held up his hands. 'Whoa. That's heavy talk on an empty stomach.'

'You didn't answer my question.'

'That's because it's irrelevant.' He shrugged, his nonchalance forced, considering the way his fingers gripped the water glass in his right hand. 'We're having fun. So what if you're the English princess slumming it with the Aussie builder?'

She was right and it annoyed her that he thought he was her plaything when he was so much more. She hoped her gift would prove that. 'Technically you're a CEO and I'm certainly not "slumming it".'

He laughed at her overt snootiness, which completely undermined her refuting the 'princess' tag. 'Hey, it's okay. We've got a good thing going on. Don't let the motivation get in the way of a good…fuck.'

He'd been about to say something else and the fact he'd ended with deliberate crudeness while unable to meet her gaze told her so.

'Pity there hasn't been much of that going on this week.' She met his gaze boldly, challenging him to tell her the truth about why he'd left in the wee small hours several days ago. 'I didn't like waking to find you gone.'

He grimaced and swiped a hand over his face. It didn't eradicate the tension bracketing his mouth nor the creases around his eyes. 'Sorry. I needed to be on the job site early to personally oversee a delivery.'

His guileless smile didn't fool her for a second. 'But you're pleased with the results and the fact we finished ahead of schedule, yeah?'

'I'm thrilled.'

He'd given her the perfect segue so she slid her hand into her bag to grab the box. 'And, to show you how much I appreciate the amazing job you've done, here's a little something to say thanks.'

She handed him the gift-wrapped box, hoping he liked it. She'd never bought a gift for a…lover before. Heck, it felt weird labelling him that, even in her head. But what was he? More than a friend, less than a boyfriend—lover seemed to fit even if they hadn't done much of the physical loving this week, worse luck.

'You didn't have to do this,' he said, taking the gift tentatively, as if handling a ticking bomb. 'I provided a service for you, nothing more.'

Even though he was referring to renovating her studio, that stung. Was that how he viewed their relationship too?

Swallowing her disappointment, she pointed at the box. 'Go ahead, open it.'

He took a painstakingly long time tugging on the

crimson bow, sliding his thumb beneath the tape on either side before lifting the wrapping and finally undoing it completely. He slid the box out and smoothed the embossed ebony gift-wrap, as if he didn't want to open the box.

Hope bit down on her bottom lip to stop from blurting, 'hurry up.' She held her breath when he finally lifted the hinged lid on the box.

When he caught a glimpse of the gift inside, his jaw dropped.

'This is too much.' He shook his head, a disapproving frown slashing his brows as he placed the box on the table and nudged it towards her with his forefinger. 'I can't accept this.'

The breath she'd been holding whooshed out in disappointment as he averted his gaze from her and the box, his mouth compressed into an unimpressed line, his eyes narrowed.

He didn't like it.

'I bought it for you. I can't return it—'

'Yes, you can.' He snapped the box shut so loud she jumped. 'You've spent twenty grand on a watch for me and you don't think that's over the top?'

'I can afford it...' She trailed off, realising her mistake when he pushed his chair back from the table and stood, his expression resigned.

'I can't do this, Hope.' He held up his hands as he backed away. 'The fancy restaurant, the expensive watch...this isn't me.'

To her mortification tears sprung to her eyes and he muttered, 'Fuck,' when he saw them.

'I have to go. I'm sorry,' he said, spinning on his heel and striding towards the steps leading to the marble exit.

She wanted to go after him, to explain how they were more alike than he thought, two loners with major trust issues searching for a way to fulfil an emptiness in their lives for however long it lasted.

She wanted to tell him that the watch was nothing more than a thank-you gift and it was more than she'd given any guy since Willem.

She wanted to assure him that she had the end date in sight too, that no man could convince her to put her heart on the line ever again, that she didn't want anything from him bar his body.

But she didn't.

She reached for the watch, placed the box in her bag and gestured a waiter over.

She would order the most expensive wine on the menu, choose her favourite dishes and finish with a melt-in-the-mouth crème brûlée.

She might have the safety net of her grandmother's trust fund, but she made her own money and spent it the way she wanted to, and she'd be damned if some guy with a hang-up would make her feel guilty for enjoying the spoils of her success.

And she sure as hell wouldn't have her memories of this wonderful place ruined by an insensitive clod.

Time enough to kick his ass later.

CHAPTER NINETEEN

LOGAN HAD ACTED like an asshole yet again. But that fucking watch had been a trigger for a deeply repressed anger, even if Hope didn't know it.

The moment he'd lifted the lid on that box and seen the glittering silver and gold wristband, the mother-of-pearl face with exquisitely detailed numbers, he'd been catapulted back in time to his fourteenth birthday.

Stephen had actually come home for once, making a special trip for his birthday. Logan had been annoyed and ecstatic simultaneously: annoyed that his mum would spiral yet again when Stephen left and ecstatic because his dad might love him after all. Because his present proved it, right?

They'd never had a lot of money so when his dad had gifted him a shiny new watch that had cost more than the family's second-hand car Logan had been blown away. He'd considered that watch a symbol of hope, that if his dad could afford something so expensive he must finally be succeeding with his career and would be home more often.

His euphoria had lasted a week.

Not only had Stephen left in the middle of the night, he'd taken Logan's prized watch with him.

His note had been brief: he had a golden opportunity to travel to New Zealand to do a stand-up show in Wellington that could propel his career internationally, but he couldn't afford the airfare so needed to pawn the watch, promising to get it back as soon as he had the money.

Logan never saw the watch again.

And he hadn't wanted to. He hadn't wanted tangible proof that his father was a shallow, narcissistic bastard who only cared about his own needs and didn't give a flying fuck about his son or wife.

That had been the beginning of the end for Logan. On his father's next visit home, Logan had made himself scarce. He hadn't been able to stomach seeing the man who had killed his dreams of actually having a father who cared; and who'd eventually killed his mum too with his callous disregard.

Seeing Hope's gift brought all the old resentment flooding back.

Was her gift a way to buy his affection too?

It stuck in his craw, the way she tried to suck him into her world. The elegant apartment, the posh restaurant, the exorbitant gift. Not that it was her wealth that bothered him—he had more than enough zeroes in his bank account to match hers—but that whole moneyed scene left him cold.

He didn't need tangible proof to know he'd made it. Give him a night in his humble two-bedroom house in front of the TV watching the football and nursing an ice-cold beer rather than any of the fancy palaver in Hope's world.

But he'd reacted badly to the watch and even now, two hours later, shame made his gut gripe. Or maybe that had more to do with the four lagers he'd downed on an empty stomach. He'd tried watching a football talk show, a replay of last week's game, even the last quarter of the Echidnas' last grand final win. Nothing soothed him.

He should apologise to Hope, but what was the point? They were over. He'd be moving on to Sydney next week to quote a new job. Better they end it now.

Before...what? Before he felt something more than lust for her? Before he divulged the whole truth behind his moods lately? Before he blurted out that she was the only woman he'd ever met who made him contemplate doing the unthinkable: staying put for once?

He couldn't say any of that let alone admit it to himself so he lashed out at the nearest inanimate object, an old armchair, giving the rickety leg a re-sounding kick. The resulting throb in his big toe wasn't worth it. Cursing his stupidity, he crushed the empty beer can in his fist and lobbed it into the rubbish bin in the corner as a loud pounding started on his door.

Nobody visited him, ever. In fact, not many knew his address, apart from Rick and the post office, which redirected his mail more often than not. And he certainly didn't receive visitors at ten p.m.

Disgruntled, he trudged to the door and yanked it open, shocked to see Hope glaring at him with open hostility.

'You'd better let me in.' She jabbed a finger in his direction. 'Otherwise I'll throw stones at every one of your windows, not caring if they break or not.'

Logan bit back a smirk. While he wasn't pleased to see her, was there anything more magnificent than a riled woman in full confrontation mode?

Her eyes flashed fire, her cheeks were flushed and her chest heaved, her breasts straining the silk of her dress. Her rigid nipples stuck out like emblems of her passion—even if it was anger in this case—and his dick reacted even while his head yelled, *Down, boy.*

'Come in.' He opened the door and stepped back, waving her in with an exaggerated flourish. 'I don't intend to call out a glazier in the middle of the night.'

'Wise choice.'

She sailed past him, leaving a cloud of her expensive floral fragrance in her wake. He loved that smell, a heady mix of jasmine, rose and something deeper, maybe vanilla mixed with musk… Whatever it was, whenever he smelled those flowers in the future he'd think of her.

He closed the door and followed her into his humble lounge, barely big enough for the both of them. Before she could speak he held up his hand. 'Don't waste your breath talking about the watch. It was a nice thought but I can't accept it, end of story.'

A frown slashed her elegant brows. 'It was nothing more than an expression of gratitude, that's it.'

'You're talking about it when I asked you not to.' He shook his head, hating that he felt compelled to justify himself and knowing he couldn't, not without telling her too much. 'How the hell did you find me?'

She flashed a sickly sweet smile. 'Your foreman is a lovely man.'

'I'll kill the prick,' he muttered, knowing this would be Rick's idea of matchmaking. Dickhead. 'Now that you're here, do you want a drink?'

'No thanks.' She clasped her hands together and stood in the middle of his lounge, a bright splash of colour against the drabness. It made the contrast between his life and hers all the more vivid. 'When are you leaving?'

Her bluntness startled him. Most women played games and skirted around the tough stuff. Not Hope. She was assertive both in and out of the bedroom.

'Early next week. There's a job in Sydney I need to quote. A music recital hall.'

'Your reputation for producing fine acoustics is preceding you.'

'The indirect promotional grapevine is the most effective,' he said, sounding like a stilted marketing advertisement as he gestured for her to take a seat. 'So please feel free to tout me to any colleagues.'

'But that might mean you'll return to Melbourne.' Her hand flew to her mouth in mock horror. 'And, oh my, we might even get to hook up again.'

He had no idea if she meant it as a flippant remark

or was testing the waters to see if he'd be amenable to the idea. Either way, he had to shut this down.

No way in hell would he ever have a woman waiting for him to return, her happiness dependent on him.

He wasn't his fucking father.

So he dredged up the worst insult he could, ensuring that by belittling what they'd had she'd never want to see him again.

'Being a refined Englishwoman, you've probably never heard the term "hit it and quit it"?'

She might not have heard the term but she understood the meaning, if her thinned lips and blazing eyes were any indication. 'I said that in jest. I'm not an idiot, Logan. I know this thing between us was nothing more than a fling and that you wouldn't look back once you "quit it".'

She'd got the message. Good.

Why did it make him feel like the lowest slime?

'What are you really doing here, Hope?'

If he deflected this onto her, it might stop him from hauling her into his arms and giving her the explanation she deserved.

'I don't like being walked out on. First at my apartment, then tonight at the restaurant.' She took a step towards him, chin high, glaring and defiant. 'Unlike you, I finish what I start.'

Another step brought her within touching distance. 'And, seeing as we're almost at the quit part, don't you think it's only fair we have one last "hit"?'

Logan stood his ground, gritting his teeth, his fingers curling into fists by his side.

He didn't want to be responsible for hurting this woman more than he already had. He wasn't a fool. He'd seen the pain in her eyes several times now, pain he'd caused in his lousy attempts to push her away. So no matter how badly he yearned to have her now, he wouldn't initiate it.

'Hope, this isn't a good idea—'

'Shh.' She placed a fingertip against his mouth. 'I'm calling the shots.'

'You always have,' he murmured, experiencing a jolt as her fingertip traced the shape of his mouth.

'What can I say? I like being in charge.'

And she set about proving it by pushing him down onto the sofa and straddling him. Her dress was rucked up, revealing smooth thighs he had previously explored in great detail. Her skin glowed in the light cast from the sole lamp he'd switched on, pale and luminous. She rested her hands on his shoulders, pinning him to the back of the sofa.

Blood pounded in his head, drowning out any last resistance. He averted his gaze and swallowed, trying to regain control of his rampant libido when it came to this woman, and losing as she writhed against him a little and his cock throbbed.

'You want this as much as I do,' she said, grinding against him again, determined to make him lose it.

He sucked in a breath as their eyes met, her raging desire no match for his splintering resistance.

He shifted his pelvis so he was pressed against the spot he wanted to be and surrendered. 'Fuck yeah.'

'Good.' She flicked her hair so it draped over one shoulder in a flowing golden cascade. 'If this is our last time, let's make it count...'

He surged forward to claim her mouth, anchoring her with his hands on her waist, desperate for skin-on-skin contact. His fingers plucked uselessly at the silk and sensing his need she eased her mouth away and untied the knot behind her neck. The top of her dress slithered forward to reveal the tight buds of her nipples and he groaned, lowering his head to swirl his tongue over one, then the other.

They puckered to rigid nubs as he sucked and licked, flicking each nipple with his tongue before blowing on them. Her chest arched forward, thrusting her tits into his face, leaving him in no doubt that she loved what he was doing.

'More—' He cut off her demand in a searing kiss that made him lightheaded. She might enjoy being in charge but he got off on making her crazy just as much. He plundered her mouth as he tweaked her nipples, plucking at them with the barest pressure, her soft cries of encouragement spurring him on.

His right hand trailed down her taut abdomen, teasing her with a feather-light touch that raised goose bumps on her skin. She wriggled in an attempt to get closer to him and he smiled against her mouth. 'Easy, babe, there's no rush.'

'Yeah, there is,' she said, her voice husky. 'We had phenomenal sex the other night then you left before we could have round two and I've been fantasising about doing it again ever since.'

He didn't want to think about that night he had snuck out of her apartment after calling his dad, or the fact that Stephen hadn't called him back, so he nuzzled the column of her neck, nipping gently with his teeth. She shivered and reached between them, covering his rigid cock with her hand, rubbing him.

'You want that?' He thrust up into her hand, rewarded by a smug smile curving her lips.

'Oh, yeah.' She scooted back, giving her access to his fly.

He held his breath as she unzipped him, slid her hand inside his jocks and wrapped around him, her grip firm. So fucking good. Then she took him out and her hand started to move up and down his length, sure and skilled. She watched from beneath lowered lids, the tip of her tongue poking out between her lips.

He pushed her dress up so the entire thing bunched around her waist, leaving her gloriously bare. With her legs spread wide her pussy glistened, so fucking beautiful, and he pressed his thumb to her clit, making her jolt.

He stilled her hand on his cock. 'Sit back and enjoy,' he murmured, wanting her to watch him get her off.

She complied, straightening and leaning back a fraction. He kept her anchored with one hand on her waist, the other between her legs slick with her juices. His thumb circled her clit slowly as he slid one finger into her, another, mimicking a lazy pumping action that quickly had her writhing and panting.

Beads of perspiration dotted her skin as he increased the tempo until she was riding his hand with abandon. Her head flung back, elongating her neck, her tits thrust towards him; she was seeking pleasure and proud of it. She gave one final gyration before coming on a cry that sent a jolt of longing to his cock. He loved this about her, her sheer wanton enjoyment, in stark contrast to the prim exterior she presented to the world.

He made fast work of digging a condom out of his wallet and rolling it on so that when her eyes finally fluttered open he was ready for her.

'You are…' She shook her head, like waking from a daze. 'There are no words.'

'Good, because I'm not one for talking.' He guided his cock to her pussy, nudging in exquisitely slowly.

'Watch,' he said, and when she looked down he surged all the way in, letting rip with a low growled 'Fuck!' as she tightened around him.

He flexed his hips upward, grasping her ass with his hands to guide her. She didn't need it. She matched him perfectly. As he thrust up, she bore down, riding him with an expertise that made the tension pool in the base of his cock all too fast.

It had been like this that night at her apartment, wild and hedonistic, her enjoying the control that being on top gave her, him loving every fucking minute.

Everything began to blur into one erotic kaleidoscope as she rode him frantically: her sexy, throaty moans; the slide of her against his cock; the musky scent of their bodies joining.

His fingers dug into her ass as he gripped her tight, moving her faster, his hips pistoning as the fucker of all orgasms clawed at him. She arched back and the change in friction drove him over the edge with a brutal ecstasy that robbed him of everything.

'That was so hot,' she murmured, bringing him back to the present, and he blinked rapidly to dispel the fog clouding his brain.

All he could manage was a trite 'Yeah,' because he knew, deep down in a place he rarely acknowledged, that no matter what they said it would be hard to walk away from a connection this strong.

They'd meant it as a goodbye fuck.

But what if he wasn't done with her yet?

CHAPTER TWENTY

HOPE WASN'T ASHAMED to admit she liked the finer things in life. Aged Shiraz, vintage champagne, handmade chocolates. She worked hard to be able to afford her luxuries, keeping her granny's trust fund money for major purchases like the studio and her apartment and their maintenance. She'd never been ashamed of her wealth but she hadn't flaunted it either, considering it had attracted the wrong sort of male attention in the past.

Because she didn't trust easily she never knew if guys liked her for her or if they were more interested in her money. She'd been on great dates that ended in one of two ways: the guy feeling intimidated and emasculated because of her wealth and begging off, or the guy not offering to pay because he felt entitled. Both scenarios were incredibly unattractive.

She'd felt safe in the knowledge that Logan wasn't like those other men. A self-made millionaire, he wasn't interested in her for her money. In fact, he'd gone to great lengths to explain their relationship was nothing more than transient.

So why did the obvious poverty of his home leave her questioning if he'd been entirely truthful with her?

She could tolerate many things, but lies weren't one of them, and the thought he might've withheld the truth from her set off a deep-seated panic.

She hated the anxiety clawing at her common sense, a small insistent nagging that Logan could be yet another person she'd let into her heart who would ultimately lie and betray her.

Could she ever really trust anybody again?

As he showered, belting out some ancient rock classic, she strolled through his home. All six rooms of it: a lounge, a kitchen, two tiny bedrooms, a dingy bathroom and a makeshift sunroom tagged onto the back. The size surprised her but not as much as the shabby air that clung to the faded surfaces.

The kitchen decor hadn't been changed since the seventies, with every cupboard and tile a burnished orange. The stove top resembled an antique, the mini-fridge the same. The sunroom was empty bar an old rocking chair with a frayed purple cushion.

She hadn't taken much notice of the lounge when he'd been pleasuring her but now she took her time studying it: an old brick fireplace with a bluestone mantel, a dull grey carpet worn threadbare in patches, an ancient box TV and a sofa with two matching chairs covered in a chintz print. She'd stuck her head in the master bedroom door for a quick glance, having time to take in a modest double bed and a side table. That was it.

The sparse furnishing could be a guy thing, considering he spent a lot of time on the road for work. But the overall air of abandonment, of an empty shell of a house filled with old, ugly furniture, didn't gel with her image of Logan.

Why would a successful CEO of his own company reside in a place like this?

Unless he had money problems. A secret gambling addiction? Debts? Alimony?

The doubts started building, swamping her. She'd been in this position before—discovering a man she loved had duped her, had gained her trust by careful manipulation, only to rip the blinders from her eyes in the cruellest of ways.

Loved?

Crap. She couldn't love Logan. A self-confessed wanderer would not a good boyfriend make. Besides, love meant opening her heart completely when she entered into a relationship, trusting him one hundred percent, and Hope seriously doubted she had the ability to trust anyone that explicitly.

She'd tried before. Even after Willem had broken her heart she'd put herself out there, hoping to find someone who would change her mind and make her a believer again.

But when it looked like a hook-up with the right guy had the potential to develop into something deeper, she'd sabotaged it every single time, too terrified to trust.

So she couldn't love Logan. She wouldn't. But what if she already did?

Anger at her stupidity made her want to lash out and unfortunately he chose that moment to stroll back into the lounge, wearing soft cotton boxer shorts and a smug grin.

'Why is your place a hovel?' she snapped, falling into that age-old pattern of sabotage, desperate for him to push her away before she fell any deeper.

His grin faded and sudden fury sparked his eyes, as intended. 'I prefer "understated" but, hey, nice to know what you really think.'

She tried not to wince and squared her shoulders, preparing for a battle she'd lose. She didn't want to do this but she had to. It was the only way to salvage anything when she walked away as she always did.

'I'm curious as to why…all this?' She swept her arm wide, gesturing at the furniture. 'You're a CEO, living in a very humble dwelling. It doesn't make sense.'

She hated herself for prodding at an obvious sore spot with him and he reared back as if she'd poked him in the eye. 'What's it got to do with you how I live?'

What could she say? That she wanted to know more about what made him tick because she'd fallen for him? That she wanted more than a fling? That he'd wheedled his way into her heart without trying and she knew it would take a long time to get over him?

She had no answers so she reached for a little white lie. 'I've had a guy lie to me before about his monetary status. I didn't care for it.'

'Listen to yourself.' He sneered, his upper lip curled in derision as he folded his arms in a classic defensive posture. *'I didn't care for it,'* he mimicked, shaking his head. 'Who the fuck do you think you are?'

Hope knew exactly who she was: a foolish woman who'd fallen for the wrong guy. A woman so damn terrified of telling him the truth because he could turn out to be as untrustworthy as every single person in her past. A woman hurting so badly her throat seized with the effort of withholding her feelings for him.

He started pacing and she couldn't help but ogle the flexing of his back muscles rippling beneath that splendid expanse of tanned skin. 'You contact my foreman to get my address. You turn up here like a stalker when I obviously didn't want to see you. Then you act like you've stepped in dog shit because my house isn't good enough for you?'

He marched into the bedroom with a resounding 'Fuck,' followed by a wardrobe door slamming.

She should be happy: objective achieved. She'd pushed him away before he could wangle his way any closer, tempting her to blurt out the truth. But happiness was a far cry from the pain making her chest ache.

When he stomped back into the lounge she lamented the loss of all that beautiful skin. He'd tugged on jeans in a hurry, leaving the top button undone, and shrugged into a white T-shirt that highlighted the muscular chest beneath. 'I want you to leave.'

Yeah, she'd got what she wanted all right. She disgusted him so much he couldn't wait to see the back of her. But her feet couldn't move. She willed them to but they remained rooted to the spot as she struggled not to blab the truth.

'I said leave. We're over.'

He almost yelled the last part and she flinched. Not from the cadence of his voice but from hearing the finality of those two words. Words she'd provoked him into saying but words that tore her apart regardless.

'Goodbye, Logan.'

He couldn't meet her eyes and stared at the TV relic in the corner. Stupidly, she wished he'd look her in the eyes so she might glimpse something, anything that proved he felt half of what she was feeling for him.

She wished he'd question her on her irrational behaviour, that he'd push for answers. Because she loved him she might've told him the truth about everything.

Instead, he backed up a few steps and opened the front door. Only then did he meet her gaze, defiant and challenging. But behind the defiance she glimpsed hurt. A world of pain she knew too well.

She understood pain. She'd channelled hers into being a productive, proud human being who'd broken free of the disappointments of her past. Yet a flawed one, because by falling for Logan she'd screwed up in a big way.

She couldn't trust him with the truth; she couldn't trust him, period. And while that choice was all on

her it left her alone, devastated and yearning for
something she could never have: a man to love.

So she did what had to be done.

She walked out the door without looking back.

CHAPTER TWENTY-ONE

LOGAN SLUNK INTO the comedy club and found a seat in the darkest corner. The buzz of happy voices filled the air, mingling with the soft pop playing in the background. There were plenty of empty seats scattered around the periphery of the small room. He'd guess his dad wasn't as popular after all these years as he used to think he was.

Stephen had never known that Logan had scoured the newspapers and online sites for any snippet in relation to his dad. There hadn't been a lot in the early days but as Stephen Holmes had become better known on the comedy circuit the mentions had increased. Logan had systematically printed out those articles, no matter how innocuous, and pasted them into a scrapbook.

Which he'd burned after his mum's funeral.

Stephen had been dead to him; why keep a physical reminder of the man who had consistently let him down his entire childhood?

He shouldn't be here. Not when disappointment still clogged his chest an hour after he'd ended things with Hope.

She didn't get it. Didn't get *him*. She'd taken one look at his house and virtually accused him of lying about his wealth. Fuck. Just because he didn't flaunt his money she'd labelled him a douche, or something akin to it.

If she'd given him a chance to explain, he might've taken it. He might've opened up about how the humble weatherboard in Footscray was the only place he felt truly at home. That he'd purchased it after saving for two years on his meagre apprentice's wage. That he purposefully kept it simple because it reminded him of where he'd come from.

He might not have been back to Rally-Doo since he'd packed his bags after his mum's funeral and headed down to Melbourne, but every time he set foot in his place he felt like he'd come home again.

He hadn't picked Hope for a snob. So the fact she'd misjudged him so badly rankled and he'd over-reacted.

The sex had been phenomenal as usual but there'd been something more this time…a deeper connection that had terrified yet exhilarated. He couldn't stick around in Melbourne for her, and he certainly wouldn't have her waiting around for whenever he lobbed into town, but while he'd showered he'd actually contemplated various scenarios as to how they could make this work.

Then she'd looked down her snooty nose at his place, he'd exploded and that had been the end of that.

He should be glad. They'd had a clean break. No

emotional declarations, no drawn-out goodbyes. He hated fuss.

But he wasn't glad. The hollow ache in his chest testified to that. He felt empty, like the day he'd discovered his mum dead on the kitchen floor, as if the only good thing in his life had been wrenched away.

A waitress approached and he shook his head. He didn't want a drink. He wanted to confront the demons of his past and finally get some closure. Having this unresolved tension with his dad, combined with the guilt that he wouldn't have known about Stephen's cancer until after he'd died, didn't sit well. He would meet with his father and have the conversation they should've had over a decade ago.

Stephen had returned his call, leaving a message about potentially meeting up next week.

Logan hadn't been able to wait that long.

He preferred the element of surprise and turning up to one of his dad's shows for the first time, with the intention of confronting him afterwards, would have to do.

A few more patrons filtered in as show time grew closer. The eclectic crowd, ranging from old hippies to young yuppies, made him feel out of place. He preferred a simple pub to this faux trendy club with its black tables, black carpet and silver-draped walls, the small stage taking pride of place front and centre featuring the clichéd crimson velvet curtain drawn shut.

It was stupid to feel this nervous as the lights dimmed. Logan would soon see his father for the first time in twelve years and his throat tightened. His heart pounded in time with the introductory music blaring through speakers around the room and his mouth grew dry.

The curtains drew back ridiculously slowly as Logan wiped his sweaty palms down the front of his jeans. Now that the moment had arrived, he wanted to make a run for it.

Then his father stepped forward to the microphone stand and Logan held his breath. His chest caved in on itself, as if all the air had been sucked out of the room. Tears stung his eyes and he blinked rapidly, willing the urge to hyperventilate away.

This was crazy, his over-the-top reaction. Grown men didn't feel so weak.

Then his father grinned, catapulting Logan straight back to his fifth birthday, when his dad had presented him with a massive hardback dinosaur book and smiled at him just like that.

Rage made his hand shake as he dashed it across his eyes. This man had stolen so much from him. What could they possibly say to each other now that would erase the pain of the past?

But Logan had never been a quitter so he sat through his dad's show.

With every joke, every anecdote, his anger faded until he found his mouth reluctantly quirking into a semi-smile. Stephen was good. He commanded the room and held the audience captive. He delivered punch lines with impeccable timing. He related everyday incidents and made them funny. But what

captured Logan's attention the most was his dad's
self-deprecation—because he had the same sense
of humour.

When the show wound down and Stephen gave
a mock bow to signal the end, Logan couldn't believe an hour had passed. Raucous applause filled
the room and he found himself clapping too. As wait-
resses moved through the room, taking drink orders
before the next act, Logan knew the time had come.

Time to confront his father.

CHAPTER TWENTY-TWO

THE FIRST THING that caught Hope's eye as she entered her apartment was the letter propped against the fruit bowl. Stupid, how her parents still favoured snail mail in this age of cyber speed. She'd tried guiding them towards video-conferencing, even simple calling, but they stuck to their fancy embossed stationery to connect with their only child thousands of miles away.

Now probably wasn't the right time to read the letter, considering she'd cried all the way home from Logan's after her sabotage and his curt dismissal of their short-lived relationship, but she needed comforting and a tenuous connection to her old home might provide that.

She slipped off her shoes, picked up the letter she'd left there since yesterday and curled up on the sofa. Sticking her finger beneath the flap, she wiggled it a little, then yanked, tearing open the envelope. As she slid the thick sheets of paper out, the faintest waft of lavender tickled her nose. Her mother's signature perfume. And just like that tears stung her eyes again.

Blinking, she unfolded the sheets, three in total,

and started reading. Her parents' letters were always the same. Her mum wrote the first page, her dad the second and her mum finished off the third. They gave her mundane updates of their life in an English country manor: the housekeeper's grandson had started walking early at ten months of age; the gardener's wife had been caught flirting with the mayor at the pub; winter promised to come early this year.

These trivialities usually annoyed her but Hope found herself re-reading the letter, deriving some comfort from the familiarity of it all. Some things never changed and her parents' reliance on the traditional made her feel warm and fuzzy this time rather than intolerant and bored.

Interesting that she'd urged Logan to confront his dad when she hadn't visited her parents in five years. At her parents' continual insistence she visit, she'd given the excuse that she was establishing a business and her students relied on her, and asked them why they couldn't visit her. They begged off flying the twenty-four hours from London to Melbourne, yet would happily fly first class around the world on a whim.

She'd taken it as yet another sign they didn't give a fig about her, that they never had. But their letters arrived monthly like clockwork and they obviously read her emails, by their written responses. They weren't demonstrative and a touch of approval on her head as a child had been the most she'd been able to hope for, maybe a hug to accompany the usual air-kiss on her birthday. It made her wonder, was she emotionally repressed too?

She didn't think so. She wouldn't have responded to Logan so openly and wholeheartedly if she were. But there was a world of difference between physical openness and acknowledging emotions.

She'd been more than happy to have sex with Logan but when she'd had the opportunity to explain herself an hour ago she'd clammed up and walked away without a backward glance. She could blame her parents' lies, Willem's too, and Harry's ultimate betrayal, but emotional obtuseness was in her DNA.

They'd all changed her in a way, but she'd been more optimistic than her parents...until Willem. He'd been the one really to change her. To shatter her faith in love and following her heart, then to devastate her completely by revealing the truth of her parents' duplicity when she hadn't given him what he wanted. She hated him for it.

With her resolve to stay away from Logan wavering, this would be a good time to remind herself of exactly why she couldn't trust those she let into her life.

Sighing, she stood and stretched out the kinks in her back, before padding into the bedroom to get her memory box, her one concession to sentimentality. She hadn't looked at it in years but kept it as a reminder of who she'd been and how far she'd come. The trusting, naïve young woman had morphed into an independent cynic. She should be proud of how well she'd protected her heart.

So what had gone wrong with Logan?

Standing on tiptoe, she tapped the top shelf of her wardrobe, encountering the long, flat box tucked away beneath a stack of jumpers. She gripped it and slid it forward carefully until she could grab it with both hands. A little larger and longer than a shoebox, it hardly weighed a thing. Her keepsakes were scarce but meaningful.

Plopping down in the middle of her bed, she jiggled the lid of the box until it gave, revealing reminders of a time gone by. A programme from a play in Hyde Park; a menu from high tea at a posh London hotel; a matchbook from an overnight stay at a luxurious B&B in Bath.

Willem had been extravagant, wooing her with high-end dates and expensive gifts, inveigling himself into her life as if he'd been born to it. But he hadn't been. He'd used her. He'd duped her into believing their three-month relationship had been real, only for her to discover his potent feelings and unwavering attention had been a sham. An elaborate lie perpetuated by an unscrupulous freelance journalist who'd gone to any lengths in order to get the story he wanted: in her case, an exclusive interview with her parents, the reclusive and wealthiest family in Yorkshire.

He'd wanted a story and hadn't cared how low he had to stoop to get it, unrepentant that he'd hurt her in the process. He hadn't cared about her and he certainly hadn't loved her as he'd professed two weeks into their whirlwind romance. Despite watching people suck up to her parents because of their money her entire childhood, she'd fallen for a swindler. A stupid, gullible fool, taken in by smooth words, a charming smile and a man who'd appeared to be her equal in every way.

When she'd lashed out, he'd served up the truth about her trust fund as a parting gift. She hadn't wanted to believe him and had confronted her parents, demanding answers. To her horror, they hadn't baulked or shirked from the truth. Hell, they hadn't even apologised. In their eyes, they'd been entirely justified in lying to her in order to bend her to their will.

'It's for your own good, dear,' her dad had had the audacity to say, while her mum had looked on, dry-eyed, as Hope had crumpled in the face of their deception.

A month later Harry had recorded her songs and passed them off as his own to the world, cementing what she already knew.

Never trust anybody, ever.

She knew the screw-ups in her past were the reason she had pushed Logan away earlier. Seeing the overt poverty of his house had set off something inside her; the thought he might have fooled her too, that everything they'd shared to date might be based on a lie, had seemed too unbearable to contemplate.

But what would Logan hope to gain by pretending to be a rich guy? He'd made no moves to gain access to her fortune. He didn't crave a cushy lifestyle. He was a man's man who enjoyed the simple pleasures. He'd appeared uncomfortable when she'd taken him to the State Library and the Langham. He'd been more at home at the football and in his favourite pub.

It didn't seem like a ruse but then, she'd been duped before.

'Screw this,' she muttered, slamming the lid back on the box. Reminiscing about the past wasn't helping her gain clarity about her future.

As she shoved the box back in its spot, she realised something. She had no keepsakes from her time with Logan. Nothing but memories.

It saddened her. She'd have to make do with the studio, and remembering him every time she recorded a song.

She'd never forget him.

That would have to do.

CHAPTER TWENTY-THREE

As Logan wound his way through the club's patrons, he had plenty of time to second-guess his decision.

But he'd come this far; he had to go through with it.

A burly bouncer stopped him from slipping backstage so he gave his name and asked to see Stephen Holmes. The bouncer eyed him with suspicion before heading off, reappearing a few moments later and beckoning him to follow.

The air backstage smelled musty, making his lungs seize. Though that probably had more to do with stopping short when the bouncer pointed to a red door at the end of the corridor.

'Thanks,' he said, earning a grunt from the bouncer as he headed back to the stage door.

Logan glared at the damn crimson door, all too aware that what lay behind it was worse than anything he'd ever confronted before. He had no idea how long he stood in that dimly lit corridor but eventually he willed his feet to move and he trudged the remaining steps towards the door. Sweat beaded on his forehead and trickled down his cheeks as his fingers curled into a fist, ready to knock. But his arm rose halfway before the door opened and his father smiled *that* smile. The one he'd seen on stage. The one that made him feel five fucking years old, filled with hope and joy to have this man in his life.

His dad.

What a crock of shit.

Stephen Holmes didn't deserve the title and never would.

'Good to see you, Son.' Stephen held the door wider, nothing but guileless expectation on his face. He'd aged gracefully, with creases fanning from the corners of his eyes, grooves bracketing his mouth and greying at the temples the only signs of him being fifty-something.

He wore a stylish black open-necked shirt and black denim with cowboy boots, adding to his age-lessness. But when Logan met his gaze, he glimpsed the same mix of emotions rioting through him— fear, regret, sorrow—and saw that what his father must've recently gone through with the cancer scare had aged him.

'Wish I could say the same,' Logan growled, steeling his resolve as he pushed past his dad without a handshake.

He couldn't do this.

What had he been thinking?

The rage had returned, swamping him in a suffocating wave that had him clawing to the surface, desperate to eradicate the past and forget he even had a father.

He dragged air into his lungs, willing the breath-lessness compressing his chest to ease. For a horri-fying second he felt faint and clamped down on his anger by focussing on something good... An image of Hope, sexy and sated at his place, sprang to mind. Fuck. The last thing he needed now was to think about her.

'I'm glad you've dropped in unexpectedly,' Ste-phen said, and gestured to a seat. 'We've got a lot to talk about—'

'Do we really? Because from where I'm stand-ing there's nothing you can say that will change a goddamn thing.'

Logan shook his head, desperate to clear it. A roar-ing filled his ears, as if he'd held shells up to them and could hear the ocean. 'I came here for one rea-son only. To say what I should've said years ago but didn't, out of some warped respect for the man who gave me DNA and little else.'

Stephen's expression crumpled a little but his eyes were defiant. Logan knew that look. He'd seen it in the mirror too many times to count, when one of his dad's promised visits had never eventuated.

'Son, I know I screwed up with you—'

'*Screwed up?* Is that what you call it?' Logan barked out a laugh devoid of amusement. 'You ripped our family apart. You abandoned us for your own selfish reasons and didn't give a shit.'

His voice had risen but he didn't care. He had to get this out. All of it. 'You swanned in whenever you felt like it, lifting our hopes, before tearing us apart all over again. Mum...' Logan's throat clogged with emotion but he continued. 'She lit up when you were around, then spiralled into moroseness when you weren't. She shut down with me too so I actually lost a mother as well as a father.' He thumped his chest. 'I became the primary carer in our house. *Me.* I had to do everything and it pissed me off that you didn't bloody care!'

Tears filled Stephen's eyes but Logan wasn't done yet. Not by a long shot.

'You killed her, you know. That heart attack was precipitated by ongoing stress, considering she had no other risk factors. So how does it feel to know you're responsible for that?'

Logan didn't care that he was yelling now. He wanted—needed—to get a reaction out of this man, whose stoic acceptance of the accusations flung his way riled Logan even more.

'I'm sorry for a lot of things I've done, Son, but I can't change the past.'

Of all the things his father could've said, Stephen's half-assed apology achieved nothing.

Logan slow-clapped. 'Wow, great insight. Any other pearls of wisdom you care to share before I leave?'

'I love you, Son.' A lone tear trickled down Stephen's cheek as he took a step forward. 'I always have. That's why I kept returning to Rally-Doo to visit even though it would've been better for your mother if I had made a clean break.'

The roaring in Logan's ears intensified to the

point he couldn't hear a thing. Spots danced before his eyes and he found himself being guided into a chair by his father. When his vision cleared, he flung up his arms to dislodge his father's grip. 'Get your fucking hands off me.'

Sorrow darkened Stephen's eyes as he released him and backed away, taking a seat opposite. The dressing room was so cramped their knees almost touched. To his father's credit he remained silent, giving Logan time to process what he'd revealed.

Stephen's infrequent visits home had been because of him?

He had to ask, even if he didn't want to know the answer.

'What do you mean?'

'I didn't want to have to tell you any of this.' Stephen scrubbed a hand over his face. When it lowered, it appeared as though his dad had aged years.

'Your mum knew I had dreams to become a comedian when we met. It's all I ever talked about. But she was a born and bred country girl who hated leaving Rally-Doo even for a day trip. So, after a month, I tried to break it off. She didn't take it well.'

Stephen bit down on his bottom lip. 'She rang constantly, left messages, turned up at my parents' house. I thought by confronting her one last time she'd get the message, and she seemed more reasonable and very sweet so we ended up...' His father blushed. 'Anyway, two months later she was on my doorstep, announcing she's pregnant. In a town the size of Rally-Doo unwed mothers are destined for a hard life, so I married her.'

He halted, as if struggling to find the right words, before continuing. 'I didn't love her, and I doubt she loved me, but I had hopes we could make a go of it. Then you arrived...'

His dad's voice broke and Logan waited, unsure whether to be appalled by this confession or thankful he was finally learning the truth behind his dad's flakiness.

'You were the best thing to ever happen to me,' Stephen said, his tone fierce as he pinned him with a glare. 'I would've done anything for you, so I did.'

Confused, Logan shook his head. 'By leaving me?'

'I wanted to take you with me so badly.' Stephen's fingers dug into his thighs where his hands rested in his lap. 'But it would've killed your mother. She had obsessive tendencies that started with me and morphed into things like magazines and soaps and... well, anything.'

Stunned by the revelation, Logan racked his memory. He'd once tried to move his mum's staggering stacks of magazines tucked into every corner of the lounge and she'd gone berserk. He hadn't thought much of it at the time because those magazines brought her comfort when his dad wasn't around. She'd sit for hours with them spread across her lap, flicking through pages at random. He'd found it quirky but not testament to a deeper-seated problem.

As for the countless cakes of soaps in the bathroom cabinet, the many tubes of untouched lipsticks and the teetering pile of cookbooks in the kitchen, he'd put it down to his mum being a hoarder clinging to memories of the past.

'She wouldn't acknowledge her problem let alone see a doc, so to stop from fighting a losing battle I distanced myself. Physically. I thought by removing myself from our sham marriage she'd be happier and in turn your life would be easier.' Sombreness downturned Stephen's mouth. 'No kid should grow up in a tension-filled household. I thought I'd done the right thing when I visited and saw how happy she was and how rapt you were to see me.' He tapped his temple. 'I had it all figured out up here. Visit when I could, keep everyone happy.'

Stunned, Logan stared at his father in disbelief. 'Is that what you really believed?'

'It's what I saw. Even though I didn't love your mum, I saw she loved you as much as I did, so when we played happy families for however long my visits lasted I thought it was the right thing to do.' He clasped his hands together so tightly his knuckles stood out. 'If I'd had my way, you would've lived with me. But a nomadic life is no good for a kid and I'd seen evidence of how obsessive your mum could be when I wanted to break up with her; I didn't want to risk setting her off again. If I'd taken you, she would've become obsessed with getting you back, and who knows what that kind of instability would have resulted in or what she would've done to have you? I didn't want you seeing that side of your mum so I stepped back.'

Logan needed time to process the revelations that

kept on coming, overwhelming and stifling. 'So why did you stop visiting as I grew older? Why did you stay away if you *loved* me so much?'

Stephen sighed and pinched the bridge of his nose. His spine bowed, a man defeated, before he slowly straightened his shoulders. 'Because you were a smart kid and you started eyeing me with suspicion and anger rather than excitement and anticipation.'

'You mean you couldn't buy me off any more with toys and books?'

'What I mean is, you were starting to ask me the hard questions and I couldn't disparage your mother, not when she was doing a good job of raising you.' His jaw clenched and he looked away. 'So I made you hate me by staying away deliberately.'

'What the…?'

'It almost killed me. In here.' Stephen thumped his chest over his heart. 'I loved you, but I made a choice. I wanted you to have a stable home life, not be dragged from one town to the next, living in seedy motels and eating greasy fast food. I wanted you to be happy, your mum too. But there wasn't a single day I didn't wish I had you with me.'

Sadness filled Logan, expanding until he felt as though he'd explode with it. His eyes burned and his throat tightened, but he managed to ask the one question that had plagued him his entire life.

'Then why didn't you stay?'

'Because I didn't want you growing up resenting me, hating me, and that's what would've happened if I'd stuck around—trapped in a marriage I never wanted, dying on the inside while trying to fake happiness on the outside. You would've seen straight through me and I wanted you to be happy with your mum, even if it meant you and I could never have a real relationship…' Stephen ended on a sob and to Logan's horror he felt like bawling too.

He didn't have it in his heart to tell his father that he had ended up hating him regardless. Because he didn't. Not really. He understood his father's warped motivations, even if he didn't like it.

'Why didn't you tell me this years ago?'

Stephen dashed a hand across his damp eyes. 'I tried to reach out many times, Son, but you didn't want a bar of me. I hoped that would change in time. Then the cancer hit and I knew I had to do something to repair the breach between us.'

A jumble of emotions whirled through Logan and he couldn't process it all. He needed time. So he settled for 'I'm not sure if I can forgive you. But I'm glad you told me everything.'

Stephen nodded, stood and held out his hand. 'All I'm asking for is a chance.'

Logan stared at his father's outstretched hand for a long time, before finally standing and taking it.

His father's grip was strong, firm, his hand as icy-cold as his. Logan was glad Stephen didn't try to embrace him.

For now, the handshake was a start.

CHAPTER TWENTY-FOUR

IT HAD BEEN a whirlwind week for Hope. She'd recorded her first five songs, ones she'd written months ago in preparation for this opportunity when she had her studio up and running. And another song she'd intended to keep private but couldn't resist recording: 'Yearning'. When three of her students had given feedback, insisting it was her best work, she'd released it online last night to a surprisingly high number of downloads. She knew, because she'd been checking compulsively ever since.

A crazy, bad-for-her compulsion, similar to cherry-choc-fudge sundaes, but she couldn't resist. Because every time she heard herself singing the lyrics she pictured Logan: strutting into the inner-city café the first time they met; wiping tomato ketchup off her chin at the football; screwing her up against the alley wall behind the pub; donning a tool belt for an all too short time when one of his workers had called in sick with gastro.

So many moments with a man she needed to forget but couldn't.

It was slowly but surely driving her crazy.

She wanted to call him. Swallow her pride and make the first move. Apologise, tell him the truth and set the record straight.

And, okay, maybe slake her insatiable lust for him.

That was the worst of all, the constant dreams and fantasies. Despite her mind trying to forget him, her body wouldn't get with the program. She craved his touch, his tongue, his dick, like she'd never craved anything in her life. It was nonsensical, irrational and totally mind-messing.

She should know. She'd spent the entire morning trying to draft new songs and only had twelve sheets of screwed up paper to show for it.

Her muse had left the building along with the sexy tradesman-CEO.

Then a few hours ago she'd had a phone call from a radio station asking to interview her. Not one of the majors, but a small station focussing on indie artists. She'd been rapt. So she'd waxed lyrical about her new recording studio in Melbourne, putting a call out for indie artists.

And had been inundated. She'd booked her first two to start recording next week with another three for the weeks after. It had taken time, listening to the artists' songs, wading through all those who had contacted her, but she had high hopes that the ones she'd chosen would help launch her humble studio on the indie scene.

But first she needed more songs of her own.

However, after another hour of random doodling and staring at blank sheet music with a pencil poised in her hand, she admitted defeat.

Something wasn't right. She'd never had trouble composing before. Even when Willem had broken her heart she'd sought solace in her music. The familiarity of her favourite songs had soothed her back then and, when the initial shock of Willem's deception had worn off, her creativity had taken flight. The music and words had flowed out of her and she'd barely been able to keep up with getting them down on paper.

So what was wrong now? Her love for Willem had been intense, passionate and heady, and she hadn't allowed herself to feel anything remotely like it for Logan. He'd been her fling: her short-term sexy time. It didn't make sense that walking away from him would affect her creativity if Willem breaking her heart hadn't stopped her producing songs.

Maybe the excitement of the last twenty-four hours had sapped her energy.

Or maybe your creativity is tied in to your happiness and you haven't been happy since you ended things with Logan.

Damn her voice of reason. She was a real bitch.

Hope didn't need a man to feel happy. Not any more. Willem had put paid to that particular fantasy.

But that was the kicker in all this, that by falling in love with Willem she'd learned how incredible it could be: the giddiness, the excitement, the sheer optimism that everything in the world seemed brighter because of that person.

And, despite all her proclamations that she'd never let any man get that close again, she knew deep down she might have opened her heart to the possibility of something *more* with Logan and that was why she felt so damned off-kilter now it had ended.

This was why she didn't depend on anyone to be happy. It was much easier being bold, confident and independent.

So why the glumness that wouldn't quit despite her apparent overnight success?

She needed to shake things up. Get out of here. Try writing somewhere else.

However, as she gathered her writing tools and slid them into a leather satchel, her mobile rang and one glance at the screen had her heart stalling.

Logan.

CHAPTER TWENTY-FIVE

THE MOMENT LOGAN heard Hope's voice singing those haunting lyrics, every hair on his body snapped to attention.

His hand clenched his almost empty beer schooner as he glanced over his shoulder, half-expecting to see her on the makeshift stage in this working man's pub in the back streets of Sydney's Darlinghurst. Wishful thinking; his gaze landed on the empty stage and his disappointment was almost palpable.

Her voice, husky and sexy as all fuck, drifted from speakers set up strategically around the room. Most of the patrons, the yuppie office crowd who'd just finished work, were oblivious to her soulful voice. Only he seemed to be listening and he wanted to clamber on the nearest stool so he could plaster his ear against a speaker.

'She's great, huh?' The barman, polishing a clean glass, gestured at the speaker he'd been staring at. 'Some new indie artist. I'm a big fan of the scene and this song got posted online last night and has gone viral.'

'Really?'

Wow, good for her.

Pride made him sit straighter, until he realised he had no claim on her. He'd made damn sure of that after the way he'd spoken to her at his place, effectively ending any chance of civility.

'Yeah. Everyone's been asking me to replay it.' The barman wrinkled his nose. 'Though the lyrics are a bit too sappy for my liking.'

Logan remembered the lyrics. He'd read them, first-hand, that night he'd stayed at Hope's apartment. They'd made him feel an uncharacteristic surge of emotion then and had the same effect now.

When he'd first read them, for a stupid, delusional moment he'd thought she'd been referring to him. Back then, it had scared the shit out of him and he'd continued putting up barriers because of it.

But now, as she sang of fresh starts, aching hearts and yearning, he wished he hadn't been such a dickhead.

When the barman glanced at him quizzically, expecting him to say something, Logan responded with 'She's very talented.'

And not just in the singing department. His cock thickened to half-mast thinking about the many ways she'd got him off and her sheer enjoyment of sex. Not many women were that uninhibited. Hope had matched him in every way, always turned on, always up for it. Man, just thinking about that alley sex...

Relieved the barman had moved on to serve other customers, Logan fished his phone out of his pocket.

He'd ended things badly with Hope, deliberately pushing her away so they wouldn't have the awkward break-up when he moved on. But he'd been in Sydney an entire day and he couldn't shake the feeling he'd done the wrong thing. He'd confronted the past and his dad last night, and the immense relief afterwards ensured he'd had the best night's sleep of his life once his plane had landed here.

He had no idea if the relationship with his father was salvageable but Logan found he was willing to give him a chance. It also made him ponder: his parents had never been in love. His mum had virtually trapped Stephen into marrying her and he'd stood by her when he hadn't had to. His mum being dependent on Stephen for her happiness had been all on her. She'd created the family she craved, but at what cost? She'd had a kid who had become a burden once his dad had left. She'd spiralled into further obsessiveness when Stephen hadn't given her the love she'd wanted. It wasn't his dad's fault that his mum hadn't been able to live a joyful, independent life without him.

Which made him wonder: had he made a big mistake in blaming his parents' dysfunctional marriage for his resultant fear of commitment?

Stephen's infrequent visits and consequential abandonments had ensured that Logan never wanted to disappoint anybody in the same way. He sure as hell didn't want a woman's happiness dependent on him, and moving around, being a nomad by choice, ensured he'd never have to fully commit to anyone.

But what if Hope's happiness wasn't dependent on him?

She'd never given him any indication she hung on his every word. She hadn't called or texted him daily, even when they had been fucking. She hadn't made demands on his time or slyly probed for information about the future, all things he'd tolerated with other women he'd casually dated.

Instead, she'd let him…*be*.

And he'd fucked it up royally by being an emotionally unavailable prick who was petrified of commitment and all it entailed.

He'd blamed his dad for his hang-ups for so many years—knowing deep down that he might be more like his father with his quest to avoid ties than he cared to admit—that it took him a few moments to realise he didn't have that piss-poor excuse any more. He knew the truth about Stephen and why he'd done what he'd done.

His dad had had a valid reason for doing what he'd done.

Did Logan?

He feared commitment because it fostered dependence, disappointment and ultimately resentment. He moved around because of it and he never let any woman get too close.

While Stephen had done it out of some warped sense of duty, Logan avoided entanglements because of…fear.

And he was through letting it rule his life.

Which left Logan with two options: carry on with

his plan not to be tied down, to keep moving, to not have anyone depend on him ever; or to take a chance.

Entering a committed relationship would be the hardest thing he'd ever done. More terrifying than taking out a loan to launch his business all those years ago. More gut-wrenching than losing his family, if it went pear-shaped.

But he'd always been a risk-taker. And, now that he had more insight into his dysfunctional past, he wouldn't allow it to taint his future.

He wouldn't make the same mistake his father had, leaving behind a person he cared about.

He'd give Hope the opportunity he never had.

Before he could second-guess his decision, he tapped on Hope's number and held the phone up to his ear. His gut churned as he waited for her to pick up, the ringing tone harsh and taunting. After five rings, his call went through to voice mail.

'Hi, can't take your call right now. Leave your details and I'll get back to you.'

Hearing her posh English accent made his insides clench with longing and he cleared his throat.

'Hey, Hope, it's me, the rude prick that blew you off. Anyway, I thought you might like to hear this.' He held the phone away from his ear and directed it towards the nearest speaker for a few moments, before pressing it to his ear again. 'You're amazing, you know that, right? Congrats on releasing your first song. I'm in Sydney quoting a job and this pub can't get enough of you. Anyway, I'll be back in

Melbourne later tonight and was hoping you'd see me tomorrow. Call me, okay?'

He hung up before he could sound any more desperate and cursed under his breath. He'd rambled, almost gushed. Dickhead. He should've hung up and called back later, waiting until she picked up. Then again, considering how he'd ended things between them, she might never pick up. He didn't blame her for screening his calls.

Now all he could do was wait.

Though, if she didn't return his call by tomorrow, he had a sneaking suspicion he'd be paying a visit to *Hope and Harmony*.

He wouldn't quit.

What he had to ask her was too important.

CHAPTER TWENTY-SIX

AFTER PLAYING BACK Logan's message for the eighth time, Hope admitted it.

She'd let him back in a little.

Hearing the deep timbre of his voice made her tingle and she replayed it several times just to get that buzz before actually listening to his words.

He thought her song was great.

He wanted to see her.

She should be ecstatic. And a small part of her was. So ecstatic, in fact, that after hearing the message for the tenth time she sat down and a song poured out of her. Which pretty much confirmed what she already knew: he made her happy and when she was happy she composed much better.

Her muse was such a fickle bitch.

She wrote three more songs before she called him back. He answered on the second ring. Eager. She liked that.

'Hey, thanks for calling me back.'

'No problem,' she said, managing to sound cool and aloof while she clenched her thighs together at the sound of his voice. 'So you're in Sydney?'

'Yeah, finished up a quote today. I'm at the airport now.'

Hope bit back her first impulse to blurt an invitation to come see her when he landed. She couldn't sound desperate, not when she wanted to do this right.

But what was right? If she invited him to her place, they'd end up in bed before they had a chance to talk. And she couldn't go to him, not after the last time at his house. He wouldn't appreciate it if she booked them into a fancy hotel. Unless...

'How about we catch up when you get back?'

'Tonight?'

He sounded surprised. Not as surprised as he'd be when he saw what she had in mind. She intended to keep their reunion simple, no frills, appealing to the heart of the man who'd captured hers without trying.

'Yeah. I'll text you the details of where to meet me. It's not far from the airport.'

He hesitated before responding. 'Okay, sounds good.'

She exhaled in relief. She intended to do this right and not screw up like last time.

'And, Hope?'

'Yes?'

'I'm looking forward to seeing you.'

He hung up before she could respond, leaving her breathless with anticipation.

She'd been mulling over her plan since the previous evening and his call today had confirmed she was right in following through. Logan mistakenly thought she was shallow and hung up on wealth because she'd let him believe it at his place. So she intended to prove the opposite before divulging the truth, all of it.

She knew a simple roadside motel in Mickleham, which would be perfect for what she had in mind. A date. No frills. Just the two of them, confronting this thing between them and articulating all that they'd left unsaid.

She fired off the details to him, surprised when he didn't respond with more than a thumbs-up emoji. He had to be curious. Or maybe he'd taken one look at the motel's name and address and thought all she wanted was a quick fuck. When actually she wanted so much more this time.

She wanted time.

Time for her to learn to trust.

Time to explore this connection between them.

Time to develop resilience against her fear of betrayal.

The next three hours dragged. Anticipation fizzed in her blood, making her light-headed as she cleaned her apartment, showered, chose a simple outfit and headed for the motel. She made a quick stop on the way to pick up their supper. She fully intended to make Logan see that she wasn't so different from him despite what he thought.

She'd booked a suite at the motel because the pictures on the website showed it had a dining table and sofa, items conducive to talking. Booking a room with just a bed would give him the wrong idea. Not that she didn't want him but that could come later. Talk first.

As she checked in, she heard the roar of a descending plane at nearby Tullamarine. It drowned out her doubts momentarily, until she realised Logan's plane would've already landed and he would be on his way here.

She hoped to God she was doing the right thing.

The suite didn't disappoint. Clean, plain, with a simplicity that she craved. The faintest aroma of vanilla hung in the air, courtesy of a dispenser plugged into an outlet. Her gaze fell on the bed, covered in a daffodil-yellow spread, the one bright spot in the room. She had high hopes for that bed.

Slipping off her flip-flops, she closed the door and laid the food parcel in her arms on the dining table. The smell of fish and chips soon overpowered the cloying vanilla and her mouth watered. She hoped Logan was hungry. For more than food.

A knock sounded at the door and she jumped, the butterfly farm in her stomach taking flight. Shaking out her arms did little for the sudden buzz zapping through her body so she dragged in a deep breath, let it out and opened the door. And promptly sagged against it, that damn buzz making her knees weak.

An unshaven Logan wearing a plain white T-shirt and denim, with a wild look in his eyes, overloaded every damn thing she'd planned to say when she first saw him.

Instead, she grabbed at his T-shirt, hauled him inside and slammed the door. Then he was on her, his mouth seeking hers, his hands grabbing her butt, hoisting her up so he could carry her to the bed. She clawed at him, desperate for skin, losing her mind a little when he nibbled his way down her neck to the hollow between her collarbones. Her pelvis arched of its own volition as his mouth trailed lower and, when he captured a taut nipple between his teeth, she almost came.

'So responsive,' he murmured, untying the knots of her cotton dress at her shoulders and sitting up long enough to tug the whole thing off her body. 'So beautiful.'

He lowered his head again and this time he zeroed in on where she wanted him most. Her thighs fell open as he settled between them, the intensity in his gaze making her heart jackhammer.

'I've missed you,' he said, a second before his tongue swiped her. She whimpered and he did it again and again and again, long, slow sweeps that had her writhing, panting and clutching at his head. He lapped at her clit like he couldn't get enough and, when he changed the pressure from soft to hard, she came apart, bucking her hips like a wild thing. It was her fastest orgasm on record and she didn't care. This reunion wasn't about slow and steady. She craved him with every cell in her body and she wanted him now.

Thankfully, he didn't give her time to recover. She didn't want it. She wanted more; everything he had to give. He stood, whipped off his T-shirt, unzipped his jeans and pushed them down to the floor along with his jocks. His cock sprang out, thick and long, and she licked her lips in anticipation.

She throbbed with wanting him and as he rolled on a condom she couldn't wait any longer. She surged up to meet him but to her surprise he steadied her and slowly lowered her to the bed.

'I want to take my time savouring this,' he said as they lay face to face. She couldn't read the expression in his eyes, or maybe she didn't want to. She'd never seen him like this, laid bare, his emotions simmering beneath the surface.

'I want this to be special.' He hooked her knee over his thigh and slid into her, inch by exquisite inch. 'I want you.'

He wasn't just talking about the sex and they both knew it. But with him filling her, and her body clamouring after another release, she didn't want to analyse or speculate. He'd said, 'I've missed you,' which in the throes she'd assumed meant he'd missed the sex.

But his gaze told her differently and as he started to move, slowly at first, sliding in and out with the single-mindedness of a man hell-bent on pleasure, Hope knew something had shifted between them. Something momentous. Something that could give her the future she wanted no matter how much it terrified her.

His eyes never left hers as he started to thrust harder, the delicious friction making her heart pound. He grasped her hip with one hand, the other cupping her cheek, the heat generating from their sweat-slicked bodies making her face burn.

His mouth tightened as his eyes widened and she knew he was close. With a saucy move, she slid her upper leg tighter over him, changing the angle of their pelvises, and he groaned, driving into her like a man possessed.

When she strained forward to kiss him he slid his thumb over her lips and held her face in place so he could see her when he came. With two more thrusts he stiffened, his face contorting with pleasure, his groan so deep it reached down into her soul and tugged something free.

He knew it too, because he'd seen it in her eyes, seen every damned thing she was feeling.

But instead of running like he had every other time, instead of closing off like she still half-expected him to, he brushed a tender kiss across her lips before wrapping his arms around her and holding her tight.

In that moment, Hope knew she'd made the right decision in taking another chance on this guy.

He could be her future.

Time to let it happen.

CHAPTER TWENTY-SEVEN

'YOU SURE KNOW the way to a guy's heart.' Logan swiped a chip through a puddle of ketchup in the middle of their newspaper feast. 'Who knew fish and chips could be just as delicious lukewarm?'

'I prefer them hot.' Hope wrinkled her nose as she popped a piece of fish into her mouth. 'You haven't had real fish and chips until you've tried the ones from our local village where I grew up.'

She rubbed her stomach and made appreciative moaning noises that had him hard in an instant. 'Just the right amount of salt and vinegar, and piping hot. So good.'

'I'd rather have lukewarm if it means I can have you first.'

A blush stained her cheeks as she flashed him a coy smile. 'I think I could get used to that too.'

A shadow passed over her face and her smile faded. 'I'm glad you contacted me.' She dabbed at her mouth with a napkin. 'I think it's a good idea we talk.'

Just like that, his appetite vanished. Crazy, considering that was exactly why he'd called, but now that the time had come he found the words lodged in his throat like a fishbone.

'Yeah, we need to talk.' He gestured at the newspaper between them. 'Finished?'

She nodded so he balled up the remains of their supper and stuffed it into the bin. Pulling back the tabs on their sodas, he passed her one and downed half of his. It did little to ease the tightness in his throat.

'I saw my dad,' he blurted, not surprised when her eyebrows shot up. 'I went to one of his shows, then caught up afterwards.'

'How did it go?'

'Awkward. Tense.' He shrugged, the memory of his father's eagerness and his own recalcitrance making him want to wince. It had been painful but cathartic and, if it enabled him to move forward with Hope, it had been a good thing. 'But it was something I needed to do in order to confront my past and move on.'

'Good for you.' She nodded, tenderness softening her features. 'It can't have been easy.' She gave a short, sharp laugh. 'I moved halfway around the world to get away from my parents.'

He wanted to ask about her background, about her desire to leave her family behind, but if he lost momentum now he'd never say what had to be said.

'Facing up to my dad made me realise a few things.'
'Like?'

Curious, her head tilted to one side as she studied him, causing a lock of hair to tumble over her face. His fingers itched to reach out and tuck it behind her ear, but if he touched her now his brain would fry as it usually did whenever he touched her, and he had to focus.

'That he wasn't the selfish asshole I pegged him for. That he had reasons for leaving.' He huffed out a breath. 'That while we're probably more alike than I care to admit I'm not going to make the same mistakes he did.'

She didn't speak, giving him time to continue, and he started to sweat. It broke out along his forehead and his palms grew damp. Fuck. Why was this so hard?

'I want you to come with me.' The words tumbled out on a growl and he cleared his throat. 'I latched onto the way you reacted to my simple place as an excuse to drive you away. But in reality I ended things between us because I didn't want you waiting around for me, your happiness dependent on me, like I thought my mum's was dependent on Dad. But I see things differently now.'

He scooted his chair closer to hers and reached for her hand as she stared at him in open-mouthed shock. 'I want you, Hope. You're incredible and I'd be a fool to walk away from you for fear I'll end up in a messy relationship like my folks. But my job's on the road and I want you with me.'

He lifted her hand to his mouth and pressed a kiss on the back of it. 'What do you say? Care to take a risk on a wanderer?'

She stared at him in wide-eyed wonder so he saw the exact moment his dream died, the expectation and excitement in her eyes replaced by sadness and regret.

He released her hand and when she lifted it to touch his cheek he reared back.

'I'm sorry, Logan, I can't—'

He didn't wait around to hear the rest.

CHAPTER TWENTY-EIGHT

HOPE WOULDN'T LET him walk away. Not this time.

She flung open the door and almost ran into his back. 'Please come back inside so we can talk.'

'Nothing to say.' His gravelly voice hinted at a world of pain. Pain she'd caused. 'I'm calling a cab.'

'You're more like your dad than you know,' she said, reaching for the lowest blow in her arsenal to get him to stay. 'You're a quitter. How many times does this make that you've walked away from me when things get tough?'

He spun around so fast she stumbled back and would've fallen if he hadn't steadied her. 'I'm no fucking quitter.'

'Prove it.'

She tilted her head up, daring him to follow her back inside.

'Fuck,' he muttered, releasing her so she could open the door wider.

'After you,' she said, with exaggerated sweetness as he barged past her.

As she closed the door and studied his rigid shoulders from behind, she realised she'd never met a more infuriating man—and that was one of the things she loved about him. He challenged her. He infuriated her. He confounded her. But she couldn't let that derail her from what needed to be said.

He'd asked her to go away with him, to hit the road like some gypsy. And, while her heart longed to take the plunge and see what kind of an adventure that could bring, she couldn't do it.

If it was in his DNA to run, it was in hers to prove her independence no matter what the cost.

'Logan, look at me.' She approached him carefully and held out her hand, as if confronting a wary dog.

This time, when he turned to face her, she saw his anger had given way to hurt. Bewilderment. As if he couldn't fathom how she'd turn him down.

Damn it, she had to make him understand this had nothing to do with him and everything to do with her own insecurities.

'I want you too.' Her hand dropped to her side. 'I've been miserable without you.' She gave a self-deprecating snort. 'Heck, I couldn't even write a song without you around, that's how crazy I am about you. But I can't put all my faith in you and walk away from my dream, and that's what you're asking me to do.'

A spark of hope flared in his eyes. 'But you can write songs anywhere. Play in pubs and clubs. Get your work out there first-hand—'

'Stop.' She shook her head, hating that he had this all figured out in his head and that she'd have to stomp on his dream in order to get hers. 'This isn't just about me. I want to foster talent, get unknown artists the recognition they deserve, and to do that I have to be here, in Melbourne, in my new studio. Surely you can understand that?'

He seemed to deflate before her eyes, his shoulders slumping as he thrust his hands into his pockets. 'I understand that your work is as important to you as mine is to me. But I have to be on the road. Quoting jobs takes me all over the country and my company would lose momentum if I was stuck in one place.'

She understood what he was implying: that her business was a start-up and wouldn't suffer if she postponed. Or maybe she was being overly sensitive. But Hope had been betrayed by too many people close to her before and what he was asking was too great. Logan might be nothing like Willem, Harry or her parents but she couldn't ignore her own desires and sacrifice her dream for his.

Sensing she may be prevaricating, he took a step forward, broaching the distance between them. 'This is a big deal for me, sweetheart. I've never lived with a woman let alone wanted to be with one for more than a short time. But I hate the thought of leaving you and we're so great together—'

'Shh.' She pressed her fingertips to his mouth. 'You have no idea how tempted I am. But I can't throw away everything I've worked so hard for.'

What she really meant was *even now, when I know I love you, I can't fully trust my own judgment and, in turn, you.*

But she didn't say it. Instead, she lowered her

hand. 'Why don't we trial long-distance for a while? See how that goes?'

His lips compressed in a mutinous line and he shook his head. 'Never works.'

His gaze darted away, evasive, and she knew right then her dream of him giving her time to trust, time to develop their connection, was just that—a fanciful dream.

'I get why my dad left us, and my mum had demons that had nothing to do with him, but I won't put myself in a similar situation of you sitting around, waiting for me to show up in Melbourne whenever it's convenient.'

His tortured gaze finally met hers. 'You deserve so much more than that.'

She wanted to rant at the injustice of this. She'd finally been willing to open herself up to trust a guy and he couldn't compromise. She loved him. He loved her enough to want her with him all the time. Yet they couldn't make it work.

Fuck trust and relationships and this incredible man who'd made her fall in love with him without trying.

'I understand,' she said, sadness making her voice quiver at their stupid impasse.

He wanted her with him.

She had to stay.

And she hoped to God she wouldn't regret this decision for the rest of her life.

'So that's it, then?' He removed his hands from his pockets and reached for her.

She let him haul her into his arms where she rested her cheek against his chest. His heart thudded beneath her ear, strong and steady, like the man himself, a reminder of what she was giving up in sticking to her principles, in holding on to a deep-seated fear that could ruin any chance she ever had at lasting happiness.

'You're so special to me,' she murmured, wrapping her arms around his waist and hanging on tight. 'I wish I could be with you.'

'I wish for that too, babe,' he said, burying his face in her hair.

Hope had no idea how long they clung to each other, silently wishing for things that could never be.

But this time, when he released her and headed for the door, she didn't stop him.

CHAPTER TWENTY-NINE

'IT's GOOD TO have you back on deck.' Logan shook Rick's hand. 'You must've done a number on that physio to get early clearance to return to work.'

'My back's fine.' Rick did a twist and side-bend to demonstrate. 'Good as new.'

'Yeah, well, take it easy for the first week back on the tools. I can't afford to lose you again.'

Ironic, that those latter words were what he'd envisaged saying to Hope yesterday. Instead, he'd ended up blurting his proposal for her to accompany him on the road, she'd turned him down and he'd been reeling ever since.

How had his plan to confess his feelings been so monumentally fucked up?

He could blame his upbringing, how he'd learned to suppress his feelings young, but that was bullshit and he knew it. He wasn't his mum, he wasn't his dad; he had to take full responsibility for this cock-up. It was all on him.

'So what's this meeting about?' Rick wedged into the booth opposite Logan. 'I've read all your emails and seen the plans for upcoming jobs. No need to roll out the welcome wagon personally.'

Logan took a deep breath. Here went nothing.

'I want to talk to you about shaking things up a little.'

When Rick's brow furrowed in confusion, he clarified. 'With the company structuring.'

Rick shook his head. 'You've lost me, mate.'

Logan hoped this hare-brained idea wouldn't sound as stupid articulated out loud as it did in his own head. 'I want to delegate more jobs and install you in a higher management role.'

'You're giving me a promotion?' Rick's eyebrows shot up, before his mouth eased into a lop-sided grin. 'Maybe I should take time off work with a crook back more often.'

Logan clasped his hands together and rested them on the table between them. 'I'm making a few changes for the benefit of the company, that's all.'

'Bullshit.' Rick thumped the table. 'You're a control freak. That's why you insist on quoting every new job personally, no matter where it is.' He guffawed. 'So the fact you're even talking about delegating means something major has happened.'

Logan should've known his oldest friend wouldn't buy the professional spiel. The last thing he wanted to do was discuss his relationship with Hope but after he'd got home late last night he'd spent a sleepless night re-evaluating his priorities.

He wanted her, but on his terms.

She'd refused.

So what did he have to do to convince her that his feelings were beyond the physical?

He'd mulled over various scenarios, discounting them all, until he came up with one he hoped she'd find doable. If not, he was plain out of options.

'Fuck me.' Rick snapped his fingers. 'This is about that woman, Hope, isn't it?'

'Maybe.'

Rick didn't buy his offhand shrug for a second.

'Never thought I'd see the day, my friend.' Rick leaned back and folded his arms, his wide grin annoying as fuck. 'You've gone and fallen for a woman for longer than a nanosecond.'

'Fuck you,' Logan said, his grouchiness more to do with the fact he was so easy to read these days than his friend's intuition.

Rick laughed and fake knuckled his eyes. 'Quit bellyaching and tell me what your grand plan is.'

'No grand plan,' Logan said, managing to sound offhand. 'I wanted her to travel with me, but she's starting up a new business so that's not possible. So if I delegate more jobs, that means I can stay in Melbourne more often.'

Rick mouthed, *Wow*, and Logan balled up a napkin and flung it at him.

'You're actually thinking the C-word?' Rick continued mocking him. 'You're actually *committing*?'

Logan flipped him the bird and he laughed again.

'Seriously, mate, this is a good thing you're doing. Why the change of heart? For as long as I've known you, you've determinedly avoided staying put in any one place and hooking up with a woman…oh.' Rick lost the goofy expression. 'You saw your dad?'

Logan nodded. 'It helped clarify a few things.'

'Good for you.' Rick studied him. 'Can I ask you something?'

'No.'

'You know I'm going to ask regardless,' Rick said. 'You're not planning on sticking around Melbourne permanently?'

'That's right.'

'So what happens if things get serious between you and Hope? What then?'

'Fucked if I know,' Logan muttered, well aware that was a major flaw in his plan.

But at least he had a plan, when after leaving Hope last night he'd had nothing. This new plan involved making her see that he wasn't some spoiled brat who expected her to give up everything to be with him, that he didn't only want their relationship dependent on his way or the highway.

This way, he was making sacrifices too. He'd stay in Melbourne some of the time, she could accompany him on the road some of the time. Win-win.

Now all he had to do was convince her.

'Just so you know, women rarely change their minds, mate.' Rick held up his hand, the gold wedding band on his ring finger shining in the morning sunshine. 'And you don't need one of these to know it.'

Logan hoped to God he could convince Hope to change hers. 'Hope and I are on the same page. She wants to be with me; she said as much last night. But she doesn't want to give up her business, and neither do I, so this should work for both of us.'

Rick held up his hands in mock surrender. 'Hey, I'm not the one that needs convincing. But if your relationship does take the next logical step towards long-term commitment, be prepared that one of you may have to give up everything.'

Logan didn't want to contemplate that yet. He knew he was in for a fight trying to sway her to accompany him on the road even some of the time. And he had to do it. He wouldn't be the only one compromising but spending longer periods of time in Melbourne would be a good start. He wouldn't do long distance. It hadn't worked for his folks and it sure as hell wouldn't work for him. He wanted all of Hope all the time and if that made him a selfish prick so be it.

This plan was doable. Time in Melbourne for her life, time on the road for his. Simple.

So why did his gut gripe at the thought it was anything but?

'Good luck, mate.' Rick slapped him on the back. 'Hope it works out for you. And in the meantime, I'm ready to step up in the company in any role you need me.'

'Thanks, I couldn't do this without you.' Logan pulled Rick in for a man hug that lasted the requisite less than five seconds. 'I'll email you the revised job description and the upcoming quotes I'll need you to do.'

An uncharacteristic sombreness made Rick hesitate. 'Do you want to wait and see what your girl says before you go ahead with the company restructuring?'

It had crossed Logan's mind that Hope might still say no to his new proposal. But he hadn't got this far in life by second-guessing decisions. He'd left home at eighteen to live in a big city, supporting himself. He'd embarked on his career with gusto. He'd launched his company with loans and a will to succeed. If he'd dithered over any of those life choices he'd still be stuck in Rally-Doo mourning his mum and hating his dad.

So he wouldn't hold back on this plan with Hope. He was all in. And if he failed he'd deal with the fall-out then.

'Regardless of what happens with Hope, I think it's time I cut back on the constant travel and put down some roots for a while.' He pointed at the rolled up newspaper on the table they'd just vacated. 'Dad's done an interview featured today. He's got some gigs in Melbourne for the foreseeable future so I thought it wouldn't hurt to spend more time here, getting to know him.'

'That's great.' Rick's goofy grin returned. 'You're a changed man and I like it.'

When Rick held out his arms again, Logan waved him away. 'Cut the sentimental bullshit and get back to work.'

'Sure thing, boss.' He snapped a quick salute. 'Let me know how it all goes.'

Logan nodded, determined that nothing would stop him from presenting his plan to Hope and convincing her to agree.

CHAPTER THIRTY

IT HAD TAKEN Hope five long, lonely days to figure out what she really wanted out of life.

Her song 'Yearning' had gone viral, with downloads increasing exponentially each day, and the resultant airplay and feedback equally astounding. She'd launched a new song for an unknown artist that was already climbing the indie charts. And she had enough bookings for her recording studio to keep her busy for the next year. She should be floating.

Instead, when she walked into her apartment at the end of a long day and toed off her shoes, the emptiness crashed over her. She loved her place, a sanctuary from the increasing demands of her job. Ironic, that in launching her dream she'd achieved what she'd always wanted—an endless stream of music and almost every hour of the day filled with creative energy—yet it wasn't enough.

She craved...*more*.

And that more was in the shape of one very tall, very hot, very rugged, Aussie builder-cum-CEO.

So, after her sixth sleepless night in a row, she'd instigated steps to satisfy her craving.

She knew several musician junkies in the indie scene in Melbourne and she'd just interviewed her third for the day. She needed a part-time manager, someone to shoulder the load alongside her, freeing up more of her time to chase another dream.

Happiness.

She gave the interviewee the usual wind-up spiel and walked him to the door, leaping back in surprise when it flung open to reveal a mussed, unshaven, crazy man on the other side.

Logan.

'I'll be in touch,' she said to the interviewee, managing to keep her voice from quivering when every nerve ending in her body had gone on hyper alert at the sight of Logan.

The guy nodded and skirted around Logan, who stood on her doorstep like an avenging angel, shoulders squared, heat blazing from his eyes, his hair bristling from some unseen energy force.

'What are you doing—?'

She didn't get to finish her sentence as his mouth claimed hers in a toe-curling kiss that left her clinging to him and making embarrassing pleading noises in the back of her throat. He tasted of coffee and mint, the challenge of his tongue entwining with hers so familiar she wanted to cry.

But Hope couldn't do this any more, this weird push-pull where they ended things then started up because of a sizzling sexual chemistry. She wanted more and, despite the way she'd refused his last offer, she hoped he still did too.

Placing her hands on his chest, she pushed gently and eased her mouth from his. 'Stop.'

He stared at her in wild-eyed confusion, as if he hadn't meant to kiss her but had got carried away. 'I came here to talk but seeing you does crazy things to me.'

He made loopy circles at his temple. 'Completely bat-shit crazy.'

She laughed and led him in, closing the door behind him. 'Actually, I'm glad you're here.'

'You may not be when you hear what I have to say.'

That sounded ominous but Hope didn't let it discourage her. She knew what she wanted. Him.

She'd spent the last five years pushing men away, trying to prove that she didn't need anybody; that trust was overrated and she could do just fine on her own; trying to prove that she earned her breaks and didn't get them handed to her on a silver platter despite her entitled upbringing. In a way, that was what the recording studio was all about, her final fait accompli to show how far she'd come from a privileged life in a gentrified English manor. The pinnacle of her independent achievements, a real 'up yours' to the people who'd ruined her faith in practically everybody.

She'd achieved her dream, but at what cost if she couldn't have the man she loved too?

And she did love him. Wholeheartedly, unreservedly, the kind of love to make her take a risk on fully trusting again, the kind of love to inspire grand acts of passion. Like this.

'That guy you saw on the way out? He's my new manager for the recording studio. So I can come with you sometimes when you hit the road. If you still want me too...' She trailed off, her babbling cut off by the shock bracketing his open mouth. 'All that stuff I said when you asked me to go with you still stands. This studio is my dream, and I want it to flourish, but this week has been hell without you regardless of my musical success so I want to be with the man I...love.'

She almost whispered the last word but he heard. To her relief his face relaxed and his lips eased into a goofy grin.

'You love me.' A statement, not a question, reverent and not smug in the slightest. 'That's great, because I love you too, and I came around to tell you I've promoted Rick so I can stay around in Melbourne for longer periods.'

Hope flung herself at him and smothered his face with smoochy kisses, laughing and almost crying at the same time. Her heart ached with joy as he wrapped his arms around her waist, picked her up and swung her around until they were both breathless.

'Are you for real?' He lowered her carefully until her feet touched the floor but didn't release his clamp-hold on her waist.

'Yeah, I wanted to be with you, and sticking to my principles born of fear would've left me heartbroken,' she said, basking in the wondrous affection from his steady gaze. 'And before you ask, yeah, I'm

a big old scaredy-cat when it comes to trusting people. My parents lied about my trust fund for years.
My first serious boyfriend was faking his feelings
to get an interview with my parents and broke my
heart in the process to the point where I deliberately
sabotaged any possible relationship since. And my
oldest musician friend, Harry, who I've mentioned
before, plagiarised my songs after I'd confided in
him for years.'

Concern quickly gave way to outrage in his expressive eyes. 'Is that the real reason you didn't agree
to hit the road with me, because you don't trust me?'

She bit her bottom lip and nodded. 'The thing is,
I've learned to trust myself. At some point, I need to
take a chance on my feelings again and I want to do
that with you.' She paused, hoping he understood the
enormity of what she was telling him. 'I may need
you to be patient with me, because it's hard for me
to trust anyone implicitly. But I know you love me,
and I feel the same way about you, so let's do this.'

He placed a hand over her heart. 'You can trust me.
I won't let you down.'

'You'd better not,' she said, giving him a playful
shove. 'Thanks to my past I've been so fixated on
my trust issues and fears that I didn't realise I don't
have to give up my independence to be with you, I
just need to tweak it a little.'

He nodded. 'And I figured that relinquishing
control of my company doesn't mean my world
will become dependent on you. And that I'm more

fearful of failing at a relationship than making an actual commitment.'

'We're a couple of goofballs,' she said, unable to keep a grin off her face. 'You know that, right?'

'I also know I love you and I'm sticking around to prove it.'

He cupped her face and lowered his lips to hers in a tender sweep that left her blinking furiously to stem the flow of tears.

'We're going to be together,' she murmured, awe-struck that this incredible man was all hers. 'All the time. On the road and here. Think you can handle that?'

'Yeah, babe, I can handle anything with you by my side.' He slid his hands lower to caress her butt. 'And I'm thinking of getting a grip on this handling thing starting now.'

EPILOGUE

One year later

FROM THE SOCIAL PAGES, *Yorkshire Gazette.*

The esteemed Mr And Mrs McWilliams of Hedge Manor, along with renowned Australian comedian Stephen Holmes, were proud parents at the nuptials of their children yesterday.

Hope McWilliams, raised in Yorkshire but residing in Melbourne for the last six years, wore a strapless ivory chiffon dress embossed with tiny silver treble clefs as she wed Australian construction tycoon Logan Holmes.

Logan, a native of Rally-Doo, a small rural town in outback Victoria, surprised his wife with a serenade of her hit song 'Yearning' at a small reception at the McWilliams estate.

Five-hundred-pounds-a-bottle champagne flowed freely alongside boutique Australian beers, while guests dined on beef Wellington, fish and chips, fruit pavlova and Tim Tam cheesecake. A true melding of cultures indeed.

White lilies, pink roses and Australian natives blended seamlessly as table centrepieces, while potted eucalypts decorated the entrances. A local band, started by the late Harry Remme over a decade ago, played a foot-tapping mix of original jazz and pop tunes, some of which were written by the bride, who has gifted copyright to the band.

'Harry fostered my love of music for many years and I'm proud that his band continues his legacy in singing some of my songs,' the bride said.

Guests danced the night away before retreating to their rooms in the manor.

The newly wed Mrs Hope Holmes also had this to say: 'This has been the happiest day of my life. I'm so glad I followed my heart to Australia and found this amazing man. He's my home, my love, my everything.'

At that point the groom, Logan Holmes, burst into a rousing rendition of his wife's newest hit 'Love of my Life' that didn't leave a dry eye in the house.

Melbourne Morning Chronicle:

Fresh from a tour of London following a family wedding, popular comedian Stephen Holmes

*has announced an upcoming project with his
son, construction king Logan Holmes.*

*After acquiring prime land on the outskirts
of Melbourne's CBD, Logan's company will
construct a state-of-the-art, purpose-built comedy club to showcase up-and-coming young
talent.*

*Stephen, a veteran of the stand-up scene in
Australia, will personally mentor the comedi-
ans lucky enough to be a part of this venture.*

*A proud Logan had this to say about his fa-
ther: 'Dad pursued his dream when it was the
hardest thing he'd ever had to do, and I'm so
proud of him now for fostering the dreams of
others. I'll be in the front row on opening night
for all his shows and those of his protégés.'*

*When asked for a comment, Stephen said
this: 'While I love my job, and am looking
forward to this new challenge, Logan is my
greatest achievement. He makes me smile better than any joke I could ever tell, and I'm
looking forward to coming up with some new,
innovative knock-knock jokes to tell my first
grandchild.'*

Hope chuckled and stabbed at the article in the
paper. 'Is your dad trying to tell us something?'

'He's turned into a sentimental old fool,' Logan
said, snatching the paper from her and rolling it up
before gently tapping her naked butt with it. She
loved their Sunday morning lie-ins, when the glori-

ous Melbourne sun poured through the blinds and bathed them in warmth. 'Besides, it's not his fault he doesn't know that we intend on doing a lot of practice first before we get to the baby-making stage.'

'Practice is fun.' Hope wiggled her eyebrows and winked at her husband. 'How about another session?'

He picked up the sheet and glanced under it. 'It's only been five minutes but give me another two to recover and you've got a deal, Mrs Holmes.'

'Lucky me.' She batted her eyelashes and snuggled into him, revelling in their total skin-to-skin contact.

'I'm the lucky one,' he said, brushing soft kisses across her eyelids, the tip of her nose and finally her lips.

'You are my world,' he whispered against her mouth, his breath tickling her lips.

With her heart full to bursting, she started humming her song with the same title. His eyes lit up because he knew. Every song she wrote, every word she sang, was about him and for him.

The love of her life.

Her muse, her partner, her husband, her world.

Lucky, indeed.

* * * * *

WICKED HEAT

KELLI IRELAND

To all the readers around the world who have found
joy in the pages I've written.
This one's for you.

CHAPTER ONE

ELLA MONTGOMERY PRESSED her forehead against the plane's small window, her stomach wedged near the top of her throat. She watched as the ground rapidly approached, the pilot executing what felt like a slimly controlled descent through the trade winds. Flying always reminded her just how fragile mortality was. A small mechanical failure. A miscalculated approach. Hell, an unpredicted shift in the wind. Any of it could change her round-trip ticket to a one-way. No refunds. No guarantees.

She held her breath as the tires skipped across the crumbling asphalt runway, the wings flexing far more than anything metal ever should. A flock of feral chickens scattered into the thick brush, necks extended in alarm, the rooster frantic to keep up with his ladies.

The pilot hit the brakes on the twin engines, and the momentum thrust Ella forward in a seat designed to be comfortable for individuals still mastering the fundamentals of addition and subtraction. With her hands gripping the armrests, she gritted her teeth and rode out an arrival more in line with a dirt runway in remote Wyoming rather than her actual destination: Bora Bora, French Polynesia.

The Cessna puttered down the short airstrip before turning sharply and taxiing to the private airport. Two visibly harried baggage handlers tended the luggage. One crouched in the belly of the plane at the next gate over and tossed luggage out the plane's belly button while the other caught said luggage and created a small pile on the tarmac. To the side of it all stood a lone airport representative in a starched white uniform sporting several leis draped over his arm.

The plane was small enough that the pilot didn't use the intercom but instead emerged from the cabin. He opened the front exit at the same time a rolling ladder hit the side of the plane, a metallic clank resonating through the cabin.

Then the pilot stood—as much as he could in the compact space—and addressed the passengers in the eight-seat cabin. "Ladies and gentlemen, welcome to Parkaire Field in beautiful Bora Bora. If you'll gather your personal belongings, your baggage will be available at the foot of the stairs, where you or your driver may retrieve it."

Seated in the second row from the front, Ella decided to wait out the minirush of fellow travelers anxious to be off the puddle jumper. She watched people contort their bodies into amusing shapes in an effort to retrieve their luggage and make their way to the front. A man who'd sat in the row opposite her tugged with ferocious intent on the handle of the large briefcase he'd shoved under the seat in front of him. The handle gave way and the man lunged ass first into the aisle, plowing into another traveler who stood beside Ella's seat.

The assaulted passenger lurched sideways, flailing as he tried to regain his balance...but failed. Not just failed, but *failed*. He tumbled into her lap, all long arms and longer legs. A button from his suit jacket popped free and skipped across Ella's forehead. Paperwork scattered as the stranger's messenger bag was upended and a laptop landed on top of her foot.

"Sorry, sorry, sorry," the assailant repeated as he retrieved his briefcase and clutched it to his chest with one hand, mopping his forehead with the other.

"No worries. It's bound to happen in such cramped quarters."

Without offering to help Ella up, the pardoned man shuffled the few steps to the front of the plane and down the stairs.

"Right," the stranger on her lap mused in a proper British accent, amusement saturating each word. "Because it's certainly de rigueur to hip-check fellow passengers." He twisted around to look down at her, mischief darkening his gaze. "Is it not?"

She shouldn't engage with him—she *knew* she shouldn't—but he was so damned attractive, sitting there in her lap flirting, with the challenge in his eyes so open, that she couldn't stop herself. Tilting her head in a coquettish manner, she met his gaze head-on. "I suppose it depends, really."

"Oh?"

She nodded somberly.

One corner of his mouth twitched. "Pray tell, what does it depend on?"

She sat up a little straighter just as he leaned in. Her lips brushed the shell of his ear as she spoke. "I suppose it all comes down to one thing. Is your ass in the habit of assaulting laps?"

"I'll be honest. I've been considering it as a side job."

"Obviously."

"Obviously?" he said on a choked laugh.

The stranger twisted and turned as he tried to free himself from the narrow alleyway created by the seat in front of her and her upper body. He managed, but not without accidentally brushing the outer edge of her breast.

His touch made her draw in a sharp breath.

The man cleared his throat and eyed his laptop bag, which rested between her legs.

She wasn't going to help him retrieve it. Nope. Not any more than she'd stop him *from* retrieving it.

He considered her for a second before reaching for the bag, twisting a bit more than necessary. The result allowed the back of his free hand to skate down her bared calf.

He might have shivered, but she couldn't be sure given her own reaction.

She looked him over then let her eyes linger on

his face as she answered. "You're clearly in need of additional funds. The charity shops in your neighborhood must have stopped carrying the best quality Hermès socks or Rolex watches like they used to." Her gaze landed on his, and eyes the color of dark chocolate stared back with unerring intensity.

If I were a strawberry, I'd totally dip that.

The thought made her grin.

The stranger grinned back. "Penny for your—"

"Not even for a hundred thousand pennies, but thanks." She barely managed to stifle a sigh. Of course, he had a British accent. Her personal kryptonite.

Ella smoothed her hair, fighting the urge to fan her face. "You know, if you told me this was your first lap dance, I'd have said you were doing pretty well…right up until you broke that no-touch rule."

"My first? Ha." He pushed a lock of errant hair back into place. "You're perfectly aware that this is precisely how these things go. I impress you with my moves on the first dance. The first is always gratis, by the way. Then you're enticed to pay for the second dance, wherein I employ my signature moves and render you speechless. And trust me, my lady," he all but purred, "I'm highly skilled at keeping things professional. Everything is part of a job, even pleasure."

She chuffed out a laugh, gathering her own things. "Signature moves. You think pretty highly of yourself, Oxford." Man, he smelled good—cologne that smelled like windblown shores laid over the warm wool of his suit and heat from his skin that carried the essence of *him*. Drawing a deep breath, she briefly closed her eyes before glancing up to meet his gaze. "I would imagine you've had ample opportunities to perfect those moves. Particularly the keep-it-professional routine."

He tilted his chin down and leaned forward, closing the distance between them. "Pay up and find out," he said in a soft but unquestionably suggestive tone. "For your convenience, I take all major credit cards—even Diner's Club. Cash as well. Lady's preference."

Her mouth twitched, and she blinked with slow suggestiveness. "I save my bills for tipping."

"Lucky me," he murmured.

From the front of the plane, the pilot cleared his throat, clearly fighting laughter.

Ella shot the stranger a sly look. "It seems we're causing a scene."

"This is hardly a scene."

"No? You're an expert, then?"

He leaned close enough that, this time, it was his lips a whisper from her ear. "A bona fide professional."

A moment of sheer hysteria ensued. What if this guy actually *was* a gigolo? Wouldn't that be the icing on the wedding cake she had yet to design.

Patting the man's outer thigh in dismissal, she shook her head. "Unfortunately, I'm scene averse. Time to go."

"Pity, that." He gave a short nod toward the small messenger bag in the overhead bin. "Yours?"

"Yep." She straightened her skirt and moved to

stand only to find he'd retrieved the bag and held it for her.

He looked at her then, no pretense. No artifice. No sexy banter. It was *that* look, hunter to hunted. "I'll see you to the bottom of the stairs. It is, after all, the least I can do."

"Thanks," she managed, the sheer sexual pull of his person making her fight the urge to rub her thighs together. Nothing like starting the most critical job she'd ever had by engaging in seriously unprofessional behavior with a gorgeous man.

And she *was* here for a job. No, not *a* job. *The* job—the one that would revive a career that had been on life support ever since her business partner, Rob Darlain, had bailed on her.

Rob had taken *their* pitch for a TV show to a local cable network. They'd offered him the gig, which catapulted him to regional fame. Then the national network had come calling. Ella had been left to plan children's birthday parties and bar mitzvahs instead of the exclusive, high-end events for which she and Rob had become recognized. And it didn't help that he'd claimed to be the exclusive coordinator/designer while labeling Ella the help. The contract she had in her bag was her shot to not only prove her ex-partner wrong but to really, truly make a comeback. This event would park her business, her *name*, at the top of the list of event planners favored by society's upper echelon.

Ella preceded the stranger to the exit, hunched over due to the low ceiling made lower by her heels' height. Every woman had a list of things she refused to cut corners on, from the brand of her coffee to the skin care line she used to the gym membership she ate noodles to afford. For Ella, her shoes were near the very top of that list. The heels she'd worn today had been a careful choice. They were her only pair of Louboutins, and she'd saved for months to buy them when times had been good. They were her power shoes, her I-can-do-anything-I-set-my-mind-to shoes. They were ass-kicking, name-taking shoes. She saw them as her personal totem, her symbol of power and control. Some might find her foolish. But those people didn't fuel the voice in her head, the voice that demanded she be the best at what she did.

Ella sighed.

If she could pull this job off... No. *When* she pulled this job off, it would mean no more choosing between groceries or gas, electricity or water.

With the Los Angeles elite being what they were, the culture being what it was, she'd been required to sign a confidentiality clause. She wouldn't even know who the bride and groom were until the day before the rehearsal. So instead of dealing with the bride, Ella had agreed to work with the bride's personally appointed representative. She, or he, would have the final say in approving the plans and could, per contractual agreement, make suggestions and changes as she saw fit. If Ella hadn't been desperate to relaunch her career, and if she wasn't sick and tired of eating noodle packs to survive, she'd have balked at that stipulation. But she needed this. More than the bride needed an "unrecognized" event planner no one would suspect had been hired to coordinate the wedding of the year.

Whatever. It would work.

It had to.

Ella was prepared to realign the heavens if it meant making this wedding go off without a hitch. She'd worked too hard and for too long to settle for anything less. If she failed?

"Not going to happen," she said to herself.

The resort's shuttle pulled up near the plane. Stepping around several chickens that had wandered back onto the tarmac, she hoisted her messenger bag onto her shoulder, extended her suitcase handle and headed toward the vehicle.

She had seven days to pull off the social event of the year—the event that would put money in her account, restore her professional reputation and maybe, just maybe, give her back the most valuable thing she'd lost over the last couple of years.

Self-respect.

Liam Baggett made his way from the plane much slower than the woman he'd crashed into. Pity he'd failed to charm her. Had he possessed an ounce of the infamous Baggett charisma, he'd at least have procured her number. No reason this whole trip had to test his moxie. Especially not when there was a gorgeous distraction within easy reach.

He glanced her way again and watched as she dodged a rather large rooster. The woman was stunning in a nontraditional way. Mouth a tad too wide but lips decidedly lush, eyes a devastating green, her hair varying shades of brown that said someone with talent had taken what nature gave her and enhanced it to suit that pale complexion. She possessed a lovely figure he'd briefly—*far* too briefly—had his hands on. He hadn't noticed her legs until she'd made for the plane's front exit. In truth, he'd been so distracted as he admired their toned length that he'd nearly knocked his skull on the door.

Blinking rapidly, he chastised himself for allowing the distraction, no matter how fine. He had one life to save and another to destroy before he returned to London and resumed the helm of his late father's empire.

Trade winds blew with predictable unpredictability, tousling his hair.

Should have cut the damn mop before flying out. "If there'd been time, I *would* have," he groused to no one save the hen who'd taken a liking to the shine of his shoes. "Bloody bird. You're a barnyard animal, not a magpie." He scooted her away with his foot, but she returned post haste to continue the burgeoning love affair.

The one benefit to the breeze was that it kept the temperatures tolerable. For an Englishman who saw the sun roughly every third day, and only if he was able to leave the office before dark, it was bloody warm.

Searching the tarmac, he found the shuttle to the resort waiting, both side and rear doors open and the driver posted at the back to load passengers' bags. Liam gathered his bags and briefcase, strode to the van and delivered all but his briefcase into the driver's care. He rounded the passenger doors, set one foot on the running board and stopped. The woman who'd fascinated him only minutes before was in the far seat and rapidly entering notes on her iPad.

He wordlessly moved into his seat, all the while keeping watch on his travel companion.

The driver shut the doors with authority before clambering into his seat. Putting the van in gear, he took off down the road. Less than one hundred yards later, he was looking in the rearview mirror instead of out the windshield and talking to the woman with an easy demeanor. "The roads between here and the resort can be a bit trying, miss, so you may want to forgo typing until arrival." Then he hit the gas and they shot away at breakneck speed…right through a massive pothole.

The woman fumbled her iPad, recovered it before it hit the floor and caught the driver's stare. "A bit trying, huh?"

He laughed. "Wait until we hit traffic. Here in Bora Bora, traffic includes cars, motorcycles, scooters, and even the occasional cart and donkey."

She stuffed her iPad into her bag without further comment, yet Liam couldn't help but notice the way her shoulders didn't move with the bus's motion. The muscles in her neck were visible and appeared rigid. And despite her sunglasses, there were faint lines that radiated from the corner of each eye. Lines that clearly represented both stress and worry.

He was about to speak, to restart the banter they'd shared on the plane, but she turned away, reaching in to her bag and retrieving a travel pack of ibuprofen. She ripped the package open, retrieved two pills and tossed them into her mouth. Without water available, she struggled to get them down but managed.

What could be so bad a woman lands in paradise and has to take something for a headache? And why am I obsessing? I have my own issues with this god-forsaken trip.

Still…

The gentleman's code Liam lived by demanded he do something to distract her. Leaning toward her, he said, "My travel agent assured me the resort was a guaranteed headache-free zone."

The woman whipped her entire upper body toward him, eyes wide as she pushed at a strand of hair that had worked its way out of her chignon. Recognition dawned, and her eyes warmed. "You," she said, smiling.

"And you as well."

"What are you doing…" She shook her head. "Never mind."

"You have impeccable taste in locale as well as accommodation." He nodded at the driver as the man wove between slower moving traffic as if the ten-seat bus were an IndyCar, their route Le Mans. "The Royal Crescent is a lush resort. If you didn't reserve a cabana over the water, you should consider upgrading."

"I actually have a room in the resort proper." When he said nothing, only watched her, she shrugged. "It suits my needs."

"Sometimes simply meeting one's needs should be abandoned in favor of obtaining one's desires, don't you think?"

She stared at an indeterminate point over his shoulder, tapping her forefinger against her lower lip as she considered his question. It was only seconds before she shifted her gaze to meet his. The wicked gleam in those impossibly green eyes told him she'd give as well as she got. "Actually, no. I'm of the opinion that a woman shouldn't leave desire on her wish list. A smart woman places her desires, whatever...*whomever*...they might be, near the very top of her list of necessities. Wouldn't *you* agree?" She arched a dark brow, the wordless gesture a direct challenge.

He had intended to bait her. Clearly, she knew it. What Liam had never expected, though, was that she'd take the bait. The image of reeling her in had his heart beating a bit faster, breath coming a bit shorter. He liked it, liked *her*, and found himself hungering for the thrill of the chase.

He traced his fingers over the tanned skin on her shoulder.

She drew in a deep breath.

He smiled, knowing full well that the look he gave her was leonine. How often had he been accused of letting that particular look loose in both boardroom and bedroom when he discovered exactly what he wanted? Today, this second, what he wanted was this woman.

"Touché," he murmured, shifting slightly to accommodate his rising desire.

She laughed then, the sound as sultry and evocative in its richness and depth as the first sip of the finest scotch rolling across the palate. Her laughter whipped through him, muddying his thoughts and fogging his awareness of everything but her.

"You're staring," she murmured.

"So I am."

The woman's brows rose slightly. "So…stop?"

"I will."

"When?"

Liam lifted one shoulder in a partial shrug. "When I'm done looking."

Turning in her seat, she glanced out the window. "The scenery is beautiful."

"It certainly is," Liam murmured. She twisted back around and drew a breath, certainly to deliver a sharp rebuttal, but Liam wasn't looking at her—he was staring at the lush jungle landscape outside.

The faint flush that spread across her exposed décolletage and crept up her neck was quite adorable, though he doubted she'd agree with his assessment. In his experience, few women were keen on being considered cute, and those that favored the more juvenile assessment weren't the type he desired. But this woman—with her singular focus, quick wit and physical appeal—was exactly the type to pique his interests.

With her staying at the same resort, their paths were certain to cross.

Liam smiled.

Perhaps this trip wouldn't be such a chore after all.

CHAPTER TWO

THE DRIVER SPED up to the resort's elegant porte cochere and stopped with enough force that the van bounced back and forth on its shocks like a child's rocking horse. When Ella could convince herself they had truly stopped, she mentally logged the travel time in case the wedding guests wanted to know...or take a cab. She peeled her fingers from her armrests. Her muscles suffered mild rigor as she attempted to move toward the open door. That meant she had to accept the hand offered to help her down. Only it wasn't the driver. Her fellow passenger, the stranger she found all too alluring, had quickly and quietly exited and then, quite unexpectedly, rounded the shuttle and waited by her door. She paused.

He waited.

Chastising herself for hesitating, she took his hand and stepped out of the vehicle. After all, the gesture was nothing but a courtesy. Yes, he'd clearly been flirting earlier, but it had been innocent. Or innocent enough. The problem was that she'd wanted to flirt back. And flirty banter led to things she'd forbidden herself this trip, things like a tryst that could call her professionalism into question. It was just...

She glanced at him and found him staring at her unabashedly.

Damn it.

She turned her back on him, reaffirming her decision to avoid personal entertainment. Men like him were few and far between, and thank God for it. He was the exact type of distraction she couldn't afford. Not on this trip. Not when her future hinged on the success of this job.

Stepping forward, she returned the doorman's smile as he ushered her into the air-conditioned lobby. "Welcome to the Royal Crescent. Your luggage has been tagged. Once you've checked in, a valet will deliver your bags to your room."

"Thank you," she said.

Ella sighed as cool air swept over her bare arms and legs. Thank God for air-conditioning.

The resort seemed classy and sophisticated, giving an impression of subtle but irrefutable wealth and luxuries both small and large. A gentleman wearing all white and bearing a tray of champagne approached, offering her a glass. A single strawberry churned up bubbles as it gently bounced about the glass bottom.

She sipped and sighed again. Chilled to perfection, the dry bite was ideal with the fruit's sweet tartness.

This place was going to be the perfect backdrop for the wedding Ella had planned.

Scanning the lobby, her gaze landed on the concierge desk and the three people staffing it. The obvious leader of the group, a uniformed man who appeared to be in his fifties, rose and headed her way with a grin. He stopped and said something in the ear of the waiter bearing the champagne. The younger man nodded and stepped to Ella's left, proffering a glass to the person behind her, a person she didn't need to see in order to identify.

Heat—*his* heat—spread across her back and chased away the air's artificial chill. Her muscles, finally relaxing after the harried trip, became fluid, languid even. The urge to close the distance between them, to move back into what she knew was a solid torso, to feel the strength in the hands and arms that had effectively pinned her to her seat, had her instinctively shifting her weight onto her heels.

What the hell?

Sure, she believed in instant and undeniable attraction. Some called it chemistry. But her reaction to this total stranger was far beyond anything she'd ever experienced, and she didn't like it. At all. It pushed against her self-control with the wildly rapid, incessantly repetitive tap-tap-tap of a crack-addled woodpecker.

Lust, untamed and unchecked. There was no other name for it.

The word wound through her senses and made her more aware of the earthy undertones of his cologne, the smell of hot leather from his briefcase and the susurrus of silk against wool as he moved.

"Madam?"

Ella blinked rapidly and brought the man she had assumed was the concierge into focus. "I'm sorry. Would you repeat that? I was lost in thought for a moment, I'm afraid."

"I said my name is Arvin. I'm the resort's head event coordinator. And a woman soon to be wed certainly cannot be blamed if her mind wanders a bit." He grinned wider. "Particularly in an environment so conducive to romance, yes?"

Ella's brow wrinkled as her brows squinched together. It was her typical reaction to stress, one her mother swore had begun at age three and would have Ella bearing deep, undesirable ridges in her forehead before she was forty. She absently pressed her fingertips against the ridges in an attempt to smooth her skin. "I'm sorry, but…who's going to be newly wed?"

The coordinator's smile faltered as he glanced between her and the stranger she knew still stood within earshot. "I…well…*you* are, madam." He raised a clipboard that held several sheets of paper with printed information and handwritten notes in the margins. "My staff and I have worked diligently on the preparations for the ceremony, just as you requested." He looked at the list and began ticking off items. "We've made arrangements for cake tasting, set up appointments with three florists, have a string quartet that will play in the lobby this evening so you might hear the quality of their performance. Then there's the—"

"I'm not getting married," she said. "I'm *coordinating* the wedding."

"No." The denial, issued in that decidedly uppercrust British accent, was ripe with disbelief. "Not you."

Ella slowly turned to face the handsome stranger, working to keep her composure. "I'm not sure what you mean by that."

"You're the one my sister hired to pull together this…this…" He dropped his briefcase and waved both hands wildly, the gesture encompassing the entire lobby. *"This."*

"Do *not* tell me that you're the family member my unnamed bride has chosen as her surrogate decision maker."

"Oh, bloody hell. You *are* her. The event coordinator." The last few words were enunciated with whip-like consonants and gunshot vowels.

"Yes, I am."

The stranger downed his champagne in two long swallows then held the empty glass out with one hand while the waiter retrieved it. "You're Ella Montgomery."

"Again, yes, I am. You are?"

He watched her through narrowed eyes. "Liam Baggett. The bride's brother."

"Baggett." Her mind raced through the list of starlets she'd compiled as possible brides, but none was named Baggett. In fact, the name didn't ring any bells at all.

Confusion must have decorated her face, because

Liam finally offered, "Half brother. Same father, different mothers. My mother died when I was very young, and my father remarried roughly five years later. My sister was born from that union."

"Still, Baggett isn't ringing any bells." Closing her eyes, she drew in a deep breath, held it for a count of ten and then let it go to a second count of ten. What had she done? How had she let herself invest everything she had, from money to the last of her reputation, in an event she was expected to plan without contact with the bride? Had she been set up to fail? The thought made her stomach lurch, the motion as nauseating as it was violent. "Tell me I'm not being punked. Tell me I haven't flown more than halfway around the world to be made a fool of. Tell me—"

"What I'll tell you is that my sister used a different name for the screen to keep some type of separation between her private life and her public persona. It's a closely guarded secret, hence the reason you'll be dealing with me, not her."

The event coordinator had watched the verbal volley with interest. "So you're arranging your wedding while here, yes?"

"We're not getting married," they both said at the same time.

"I'm sorry. I don't understand," he said, small beads of sweat dotting his hairline as he glanced from his clipboard to Ella and finally to Liam.

"I'm not the bride," Ella said through gritted teeth. "I'm the wedding planner for Mr. Baggett's half sister and her fiancé."

Arvin's hands shook as he flipped through the paperwork on his clipboard, crossing out certain things and adding notes to others. "I see." He looked up, pupils dark in wide eyes. "As I said before, my name is Arvin, and I am—"

"The resort's event coordinator." Ella shook Arvin's hand by rote. "It's nice to meet you, Arvin. I need to make sure that you understand that I am absolutely *not* the bride."

"I'm clear, Ms. Montgomery, and I sincerely apologize for the misunderstanding. My staff took to heart your admonition that all must be perfect. We have two team members plus myself at your disposal around the clock." He glanced at the last page and paled radically. "Oh, sweet and merciful..."

"Arvin?"

"As a show of our appreciation for choosing the Royal Crescent, your room was upgraded to the honeymoon suite bungalow."

"I appreciate the gesture, but it certainly wasn't necessary." Ella felt her brow furrow and let it do as it would, wrinkles be damned. "But the change doesn't seem like something that would warrant panic."

"Normally, it wouldn't." Arvin dragged his arm across his forehead to wipe away sweat that only popped right back up. "But there was, as I also previously indicated, the belief that you were the bride." He began to fan himself with the clipboard. "And that...that...Mr. Baggett was your..."

"Groom," Ella whispered, throat so tight the word emerged as a strangled wheeze.

Behind her, Liam made a choking sound.

Ella didn't bother turning around. Surely he couldn't be any more dumbfounded than she was. "I can't, Arvin." And she couldn't. Proximity to that man would destroy every good intention she had. If she didn't succumb to his flirtation, he'd likely succumb to hers. What happened after that was precisely what the honeymoon suite had been created for.

This was bad.

The event coordinator touched his earpiece and gave a fractional nod. "Your bags have been tagged and will be delivered within the half hour."

"I can't do this," she whispered. "Rooming with Mr. Baggett is *not* an option."

"I… I…" Arvin stood very straight.

Ella closed her eyes. This couldn't be a portent of what lay ahead. It just…it couldn't be. "If you'll simply assign us separate rooms, I'll retrieve my luggage and get to work on the wedding."

Arvin tugged at his shirt collar, his face flushing a horrid fuchsia. "I'm so sorry, Ms. Montgomery, but the resort is booked solid. When we upgraded you and Mr. Baggett to the suite, the rooms that you each originally booked were assigned to guests on our waiting list."

Ella took a second glass of champagne and threw it back, eyes watering with the bubbles' bite. "Waiting list? How can there be a waiting list when this is supposed to be the beginning of the off-season?"

Arvin shrugged. "It's our annual carnival."

"That wasn't advertised on the resort's website."

Panic clawed its way up the back of her throat and threatened to choke off her air supply.

"I am sorry, Ms. Montgomery. Our website has been undergoing a complete redesign, and—"

"Surely there's a neighboring resort. I could get a room there and commute back and forth to the Royal Crescent. A rental house. A house with a room for rent. A yurt. Something," she muttered, looking around the crowded lobby. "Anything."

The Brit behind her leaned in close, and the crisp smell of champagne that lay over a hint of tart strawberry wrapped around her as he spoke quietly into her ear. "This is the equivalent of the French Polynesian Mardi Gras, Ms. Montgomery. There won't be rooms available anywhere on the island for a solid ten days. I'd have thought you, as a professional wedding planner, would have known as much."

He was right. She should have known. But even her embarrassment wasn't enough to stop his whispered breath from skating along her jaw and caressing the shape of her ear. Shivers threatened to shatter her composure. Things low in her belly tightened, and she stepped closer to the other man. "I can't stay with him," she said, the words tumbling over one another. "I can't."

"As I said, miss, the resort is booked to capacity. I'm certain we can find a…rollaway bed…perhaps?" There was a sense of undisguised pleading in his entire persona, from his nearly vibrating frame to the pitch of every word. "I cannot afford this type of mistake on my employment record, Ms. Montgomery. At the very least, I could be demoted. At worst?" He shook his head as he swallowed, the gulp loud enough to be heard over the hum of the crowded lobby. "And my wife—it would reflect poorly on her as well. Please, allow me to do whatever I may to make this right."

Ella took a deep breath, held it for a count of ten and then let it out slowly. Squaring her shoulders, she faced Liam and offered a small approximation of a smile. "Surely we're adult enough to make this work? I'll take the rollaway; you take the bed. We're going to be working together so much, this might even work to our benefit."

Liam's eyes narrowed farther. "What do you hope to gain?"

"Nothing." She looked back at Arvin. "It's what I don't want him to lose."

Liam was quiet long enough Ella was certain she'd have to plead with him to go along with it. Then he spoke, his voice rich with implied debauchery. "Surely, as two grown adults in command of their faculties and capable of informed decision making, we can share a room for a few days."

Ella swallowed hard and nodded. "It's just for a few days."

CHAPTER THREE

DESPITE HIS IRRITATION with the situation, Liam had to admit he admired the woman in front of him. She obviously didn't want to room with him, and, while that stung his damnable pride as much as it piqued his equally damnable interest, he found a solid sense of respect blooming alongside his lust. No matter who'd made the mistake, she wouldn't let this hotel employee suffer for the error.

The singular good thing that came from this debacle? Proximity to Ella would make manipulating the situation much, much easier. A few well-placed comments, a nudge here, a suggestion there and voilà. The unrealistically short engagement following an even shorter committed relationship would *not* result in the worst possible outcome: a wedding. No, the event would be canceled, and Liam could go back to his day-to-day operations in London while his sister, Jenna, came to her senses about the type of man her fiancé truly was: gold digger, fame seeker, all-around narcissistic bastard and someone whose short-fused temper didn't suit Jenna's go-with-the-flow demeanor. Sure, she'd be livid at first. And likely a bit heartbroken. But when she realized the future Liam had saved her from? She'd be grateful. He could weather the emotional storm until that understanding dawned. She was an exceptionally bright woman. It wouldn't take long.

He nodded to the other gentleman. "I've been a guest here before, so I'll show Ms. Montgomery to the appropriate over-the-water bungalow if you'll provide general directions." Arvin began to speak, offering to take them himself, but Liam gently interrupted. "Ms. Montgomery would likely benefit from a chance to quietly settle into her living quarters before she begins her work. My sister, the bride, is a bit, hmm. Let's call her exacting."

Ella stood tall, strong, as she drew in a sharp breath and her spine went a fraction more rigid. A fraction was all she had to spare, though, without outright shattering from the afternoon's stress. He felt a bit bad for her, but his primary objective was postponing the wedding if not outright stopping it. For good.

Directions were provided without hesitation, and Liam offered Ella his arm. "I suppose calling you 'darling' at this point wouldn't go over so well. Shall we?"

Ignoring the gentlemanly gesture, Ella rolled her eyes and bit her lip. He watched as she licked her lower lip with slow, smooth sensuality. "Well, this is about as bad as it can get." She looked up through thick lashes. "Right? Tell me this is as bad as it can get."

Liam blinked a couple of times and rolled his shoulders in an attempt to dislodge the guilt draped around his neck like a heavy stole. "It can always get worse."

She shook her head. "Just once, I wish someone would lie to me when I ask them to instead of lying to me when I don't expect it."

The guilt wound around his neck like a garrote, strangling his response. "Bungalows are this way." He gestured to the nearest door and, taking her messenger bag for her before cupping her elbow, gently steered her toward the exit. The nagging voice in his head, the part that made him good at reading people in the boardroom, wouldn't hush. He had to know what she'd meant. "People lie to you often?"

"I'm a wedding planner." She shot him a short look and snorted with incredible derision. "I see people lie to me, their parents, their significant others all the time. People tend to lie the most when it matters the most."

"Are you always so cynical?"

"Practical." Gently pulling her elbow from his grip, she held out her hand and waggled her fingers. When he didn't respond, she plucked her bag from his shoulder. "And I can manage."

"No doubt." Still, he opened the door for her. He'd do what he had to do to spare his sister, but he'd still treat Ella Montgomery like the lady she was. Until he couldn't, for Jenna's sake. If Ella had siblings, she'd understand. Surely. "How, exactly, do people manage to lie the most when it matters the most?"

"Honestly? Lies always matter." She navigated the narrow bridge that led away from the sand and out to the bungalows.

"To the right, here," Liam said, pointing toward a bungalow set away from the others. "I suppose they wanted to provide us some privacy, being newly-weds and all."

She laughed softly. "Sound carries more efficiently over water than it does land."

An image of her, hair out of its neat twist and spread around her, linen sheets rumpled and draped across her naked body, one breast bared, a long leg exposed to the hip... Sweet Mary, save him from his suddenly overactive imagination. Heat burned through him like fuel exposed to a lightning strike. He had to focus, to remember what they'd been talking about and remind himself she'd failed to answer his question. "For clarity's sake..." Irritated at the tightness in his throat, he reached up and, with rough execution, undid his tie and the top button of his dress shirt. Then he tried again. "For clarity's sake, does a white lie qualify? Particularly if it's meant to spare one's feelings?"

She paused at the door and waited while he retrieved one of the two keys in the little envelope and swiped it across the electronic door lock. He handed her the spare key and then pushed the door open to a spacious, elegant bungalow complete with a small infinity-edge pool, glass-paneled floor in the living room, small kitchen and, through the open French doors, a mosquito-netted king bed with an abundance of pillows.

"Go on then," he said as he moved into the bedroom and dropped his briefcase on the desk. An enormous fresh flower arrangement was situated on one nightstand and scented the ocean breeze with the smell of freesia, roses and something utterly wild. He paused to trace a finger along a single rose petal before calling out, "I'm all ears."

"Just forget it." Her voice was muffled, as if she were in the bathroom.

"Can't. Sorry. Nature of the beast."

"Look, bottom line is that I've come to believe there's not a time when being lied to *doesn't* matter. If it's important enough to lie about, it's important." She leaned around the corner, inhaling as if to say something else, but her eyes widened and she gasped. "This is the honeymoon suite?" She walked through the room and headed straight out the second set of French doors that led to the expansive deck and the view of the crystalline waters and colorful reefs teeming with sea life. "This is incredible!"

"Almost makes it worth being married."

She shot him a sharp look. "Consider our marriage annulled."

"Such short wedded bliss," he said on a sigh. "I didn't even get to kiss the bride."

She laughed, the sound soft but reserved. "You wish."

"I do."

This time, she truly laughed. Liam found himself caught between wanting to watch versus taking her mouth with his and swallowing the sexy, sultry sound. He hadn't realized he'd been waiting to hear her laughter, but he had. She had the kind of laugh that would turn men's heads, would compel them to seek out the siren responsible. And though he wasn't one to wager, Liam was absolutely willing to bet Ella was a fun lover, one who laughed when she loved— right up to the point that teasing and laughter were consumed by passion that would be as avaricious as it was unreserved.

Her laughter trailed off, but Liam continued to stare. He couldn't look away. Never had a woman enchanted him like this, and she'd done it unintentionally and without an ounce of pretension. And suddenly, he had to know—had to fill in a blank his imagination had created.

"What would our kiss have been like?"

Her gaze darted to his, her lips parted and the tip of her tongue swept out and touched the edge of her cupid's bow. Different emotions ranging from surprise to curiosity flashed across her face, but Liam was most interested in the emotional revelation that struck.

Desire.

He stepped closer and paused, giving her every chance to tell him to bugger off. Instead, she shifted so their hips lined up, her body acknowledging what she verbally denied. "There wouldn't have been a kiss."

"You won't kiss your groom? Rather odd, don't you think?"

"You're not my groom." Her voice was raspy, husky and told him everything he needed to know.

"And you're not my bride, yet I still can't stop myself from wondering."

"Stop putting ideas in my head."

"Where would you rather I put them?" he teased.

"Oh, God," she whispered, moving fractionally toward him. "You're temptation incarnate."

He leaned forward, bracing a hand on the railing on either side of her. "And what's your position on temptation?"

"Never turn it down."

"Why?"

She moved into him, closing that final distance so their bodies touched. One slender hand rested on his chest; the other wound through his hair, gripping just tight enough to exert control. Eyes locked with his, she pulled him toward her at the same time she rose on her toes. "You never know when it might come around again."

Liam groaned as their mouths came together in a rush of heat and hurry and hunger. There was nothing tentative about the kiss. It would burn hot and then hotter until it became a supernova that consumed them both.

Her body was pliant, yielding to his, pushing back against him in every critical place. Liam wondered that their clothes didn't turn to ash at every point of contact.

And he wanted more of her, then and there, than he'd ever wanted of another woman.

He hesitated a split second, but it was enough.

Ella broke the kiss, slipped under his arm and took several long strides toward the bedroom. Pausing, she reached down and slipped her heels off. Liam watched as she curled her bare feet into the fluffy rug and then uncurled them.

He couldn't believe that this woman, this siren, would have toenails painted the faintest seashell pink. It seemed like a secret that he alone knew, and he had the strangest urge to keep anyone else from knowing this tiny private thing about her.

This had to stop.

He hadn't come here to engage in a tryst. The only reason compelling enough to take him away from the office mid–corporate takeover was his little sister's well-being. When she'd told him she needed help planning the perfect wedding, he'd met her and her fiancé in London for dinner. The man, semi-professional baseball player Mike Feigenbaum, had been attentive at first. That had quickly devolved following a phone call the man had taken midmeal—answering without apology and leaving the table without excusing himself. He'd missed most of the main course and had snapped at Jenna when she went to check on him. She'd been upset, and her proposed groom had done nothing to console her. Instead, he'd shown signs of a temper Liam wouldn't allow Jenna to become tied to.

So he'd flown halfway round the world to stop his sister from marrying a domineering asshole following a whirlwind romance that had been documented by all the gossip rags.

Rolling up his sleeves and strolling with feigned casualness to the hammock, Liam lay down and locked his hands behind his head. He watched Ella from under half-lowered eyelids. She was temptation incarnate. Her body was in lush profile to him, her unapologetic stare locked on his.

"So that's what our kiss would have been like?" He rubbed his chin between thumb and forefinger. "Sufficient."

She chuffed out a sound of indignation laced with disbelief. "If that driving wood behind your zipper is *any* indication, that kiss was far more than sufficient." Bending, she scooped up her shoes. "And seeing as I've been more than clear on my lack of appreciation for liars, I'd suggest you cut the crap."

"Testy." Liam gently set the hammock to rocking and continued to watch Ella. "Tell me, have you always had this aversion to fibbers, or is this something new?"

"I've never been a fan of lying. What's the point?"

"To get what one wants, I assume."

Her face closed up, any and all emotion under lock and key. "No matter whom you hurt?"

"Who hurt you?" The question wasn't meant to

be as weighty as it sounded, but Liam found himself desperately wanting to resolve the problem for this fiery woman. It would cost him little and potentially relieve her of some personal baggage.

She looked at him askance, worrying her bottom lip.

"Tell me."

"Ask nicely," she retorted.

He waited.

So did she.

Liam rolled his eyes. "Please."

"You've heard of *Two Turtle Doves*?"

He shook his head.

"It's a prime-time TV show. I was supposed to be half of it. My business partner sold me out, took our idea to the network and they bought it...without me as a cohost."

Liam set his foot on the deck and stopped the hammock's rocking. "Threw you under the bus, did she?"

"He, and yes. Clients followed the fame, and that left me coordinating children's birthday parties and bar mitzvahs to make ends meet. No one wanted the event planner who hadn't been good enough for the network to pick up."

"But you were excluded. It wasn't a matter of being good enough," he countered.

"That part didn't make the network news. All people knew was that I was cut out of the deal. They assumed."

"So your partner lied..."

"And everyone believed him. He ruined my life with a single lie." She shrugged. "That pretty much made me a stickler for the truth. And now your sister's wedding is going to put me back on the map and reestablish my reputation as the premier event coordinator for the upper echelon of Los Angeles."

The truth pricked the little guilt he allowed himself, but he couldn't let that sway him from his course of action, no matter how deliciously tempting he found Ella, nor how heartbreaking her story was. Jenna's happiness and well-being *had* to come before all else, including Ella's business. After all, she would have a multitude of opportunities to reclaim her place in the who's who of society planners. But Jenna? She had one real shot at a happily-ever-after, and it was *not* going to happen with some semiprofessional baseball player from Wisconsin.

Settling deeper into the hammock, Liam set the swing into motion once more. He closed his eyes and forced his breathing into a rhythmic pattern—in, two, three, four, five…hold…out, two, three, four, five, six, seven, eight. His heart rate slowed. The churning in his stomach eased. And he was able to address Ella, who'd moved to stand at the foot of the hammock.

"I can't speak to the reputation you once had, but I've no doubt you're perfectly capable. My sister wouldn't have hired you if you weren't." He opened his eyes. "Seeing as we're going to be spending the next seven days together, how do you propose we best handle our close proximity?"

She tilted her head toward the bedroom before flicking open the top button of her blouse. She grinned, backing away from him. "I can handle the… proximity issue…if you can. First thing I'm going to do is put my dive suit on and check out the resort's dive excursion. Your sister and her fiancé wanted some fun prewedding activities for their guests, so I'm planning a group dive. But I want to check out the instructors myself and make sure the experience not only meets but exceeds the hype. Sunken ship, hammerhead sharks, colorful reefs with abundant life—all that jazz."

Liam stood and moved toward her, closing the distance with measured steps until he stood mere inches from her. He looked down and stared into light green eyes rimmed with ebony lashes. Reaching out, he tucked a stray hair behind her ear.

"I, uh…"

He leaned toward her, quietly amused at the way she responded, instinctively moving closer to him before she caught herself. Undoubtedly, it was her need for control that forced her to pause midmotion. But she didn't retreat, didn't recover the steps she'd taken toward him.

Good to know.

"I thought we'd cleared this up," she said. "Business before pleasure."

"Oh, we did." He deftly removed the earring that had been about to fall free of her ear, handing it over. "I didn't want you to lose this. It looks like the real deal."

She took it from him, closing her fingers around the earring and stepping back. "Thank you."

He began to unbutton his shirt, thrilling as her eyes followed each button until he hit his waist and pulled his shirttails free. Then she looked up, eyes wide.

Someone knocked at the door.

His mouth kicked up in a small smile, though his eyes never left hers. "I'll get that, as it's likely our luggage."

"Sure."

He started for the door. Several steps away, he glanced back and found her rooted in the same spot, her eyes locked on his backside.

"I'll have our bags put in here. If you'll give me five minutes, I've a mind to grab my suit and head out with you."

"You dive?" she blurted out.

"I do."

"Is your future brother-in-law certified, do you know?"

He tried not to scowl and, by the worried look on Ella's face, achieved far less than even 50 percent success. "I'm not certain. But I suppose he's like anyone else—he'll either dive or drown."

Her brow furrowed at the comment, but she didn't reply.

He shrugged out of his shirt and tossed it on the bed. "Be right back."

He rounded the corner but still managed to hear her reply.

"Please, God, let them be trunks. But if You're listening, it would be fine if they're small."

Long before they reached the dive center, Ella was certain she'd been cosmically destined to face death by drowning. Why? If Liam Baggett was a menace in a power suit, then he was lethal in swim trunks. Yes, *small* swim trunks, at that. God's existence had been verified the moment Liam walked out of their bungalow, towel slung over one broad...broad...shoulder, his lips still slightly swollen from their kiss.

Their kiss. What had she been *thinking*? The answer was simple: nothing. She'd been living on the sheer influx of desire that had clouded her brain and determined conservative thinking—and living—to be a crime given proximity to *him*.

She sneaked another look, this one longer. And she wasn't any sorrier this time than she had been when she'd stolen the first, second or third looks.

His upper body had the professionally chiseled look that came from long hours in the gym and, for good measure, a little physical work on the side. His thighs were lean but corded with muscle. If she touched his calves, they'd be solid. But his arms were the most arresting part of him. They were nothing less than sculpted perfection, a wordless covenant that protection could be found within their embrace.

Ella shook her head. *Covenant? Protection? You're thinking Henry Cavill as Superman, not British surrogate wedding decision maker.*

They passed the bar, and she eyed it longingly. If she stopped for a drink, just one, they'd miss this excursion but could still catch the last outing today. Watching the bartender muddle the mint as he put together a mojito almost made the decision for her...

"Ella?"

Instinct had her rubbing her furrowed brow and forcing herself to take a deep breath. "Yes?"

Liam waited several feet ahead of her, a knowing look in his eyes. "If you want another..."

Kiss. Say kiss.

"...drink that badly, I'm sure we can make the next excursion. We've plenty of time before the wedding party's arrival."

Wedding party. Job. Stay focused.

"No." The word registered clear and sharper than she'd intended. "No," she said again, this time more pleasantly. "I need to... *We* need to use every minute to our advantage to ensure your sister's wedding comes together without a hitch. No cutting corners, and certainly no making do."

That same shadow she'd seen earlier passed over his face. "Of course."

"Wait. What's that look? Is there something I should know?"

He glanced away, his gaze fixed on some unseen spot in the water. "What, specifically, are you referring to?"

"I'm referring to the wedding. I mentioned it being perfect and your face went totally blank. Is there something you aren't telling me? Something

I should know?" She hesitated. "Is it something between the bride and groom?"

"I assure you, Ella, that my interests lie solely
in securing my sister's well-being. Nothing more,
and certainly nothing less. Understand that I will do
whatever I must to ensure her happiness is secured.
She's the priority here, not me."

"Of course." Ella gripped her shoulder and pulled,
stretching, before repeating the same with the other
side. She was wound so tight she couldn't tell up
from down, left from right, or brotherly concern from
familial dissatisfaction. His answer struck her as a
bit odd, though. Aggression created a solid founda-
tion for every word he spoke. What was he willfully
omitting?

The answer wasn't right there for the plucking, but
she'd figure it out. One thing was certain, however.
He loved his sister and, like he said, she was the priority. At least they agreed on that much.

"About that drink?"

A shake of her head before she resumed the trek
to the beachfront dive hut. "It's best I don't give in
to temptation before hitting the water."

The wind carried his response to her, soft and so
sexually charged it seemed lightning should have
struck. "On that, Ella, we very much disagree."

Fighting to keep from visibly clenching her thighs
at the impact of his words, she focused on retying the
sarong around her waist. Her dive suit wasn't skimpy,
but it fit tight, and the thin neoprene did nothing but

enhance every movement. So she'd suffer a little discomfort. It wouldn't kill her.

Liam remained silent the rest of the walk, lagging behind just far enough that she felt his eyes caressing every line of her body, every inch of her bare skin.

CHAPTER FOUR

WAVES ROCKED THE 109-foot catamaran, the slap of water against the fiberglass hull soft. Rhythmic. Every now and then, the breeze would gather enough momentum that the sails swelled and billowed. The fabric would snap taut only to fall back to its lethargic default when the winds quieted. Clouds were sparse—brilliant white against the endless azure sky. If the Garden of Eden had been anything like this particular slice of paradise, Adam had been a fool to risk it all over a mediocre piece of fruit. For Eve, though? Particularly if she'd looked anything like Ella...

"I'd have eaten brussels sprouts if she'd offered," he murmured.

Ella had started the trip by grilling the dive instructors, asking for everything from credentials to referrals. The poor men had been overwhelmed, though she hadn't understood why. And wasn't that just like her. She was everything brilliant and strong and professional...yet kind...and wearing a bikini. The poor dive instructors had been tripping over themselves to satisfy her every request. If they knew how the woman kissed? They'd be lost—land or sea, it wouldn't matter.

As for himself? Well, he'd simply watched with avaricious appreciation as she took off the short dive suit and revealed the little number beneath. Thankfully, she hadn't required anything of him. Even so, they hadn't cleared the outermost harbor buoys before he'd lost the little bit of temper he'd packed for the afternoon.

"For God's sake, Ella," he bit out. "Leave the men to their jobs. I'm certain your questions will be answered in due course, either by the instructors or through the experience."

Ella's chin had set, and she'd shot him a sharp look. "I get your point, Liam. I'm annoying him by *doing* my *job*. Let me make something perfectly clear now, before we go any farther. You seem like you'd be the type who's more comfortable dealing with women as accessories. That's fine if it's okay with the women in question. But I'm absolutely *not* that woman. I don't require a man to intervene, to handle the difficult tasks—the proverbial heavy lifting. Thanks for feeling the need here, but I'm good. If you think I should retire to the deck and lie back, get a little sun and let the men do their jobs, think again." She smiled sweetly at Liam. "Unless you're willing to join me."

"Well, shit," he muttered. "Insult my manhood when I'm just trying to help you relax. What's the old saying? 'Out of the frying pan—'"

"Oh, you have no idea the fire you've just waltzed

into," she murmured, retrieving a glass of punch offered by the boat's deckhand. "See, if you had grown up in the United States, Smokey the Bear would have taught you not to play with fire unless you were prepared to get burned. But after that interruption? You better hope there's a first aid kit onboard, because I'm about to blister your ass."

"Foreplay in such a public manner?" Liam teased. "I'll take my chances."

She grinned into her cup. "You're just that type, aren't you?"

"What type is that?"

Shaking her head, she wandered over to an unclaimed space on the deck and lay down before shooting him a quick, devilish look. "You know— the type to make things a little public."

He sank down beside her, propped himself up on one arm and leaned over her, seeing his reflection in her sunglasses a split second before his subconscious made the decision his conscious mind would've eventually landed on. He kissed her. Quick. All heat and passion, without apology and certainly without regret. He'd only had the one taste of her, but he craved more. She was an instant addiction.

Breaking away, he smiled down at her. The stunned look on her face sent a thrill through him. Seducing her, or being seduced by her, would be worth every effort. Or almost any compromise. So she was clear, however, he leaned closer and said, "I don't mind public displays of affection."

"Apparently not." She cleared her throat and

shifted so his lips could easily find her neck. "Liam..." Her gaze slid to his and then away. "While I don't know who your sister is and, yes, that irritates me like you wouldn't believe, I do know she's high profile. Seriously high profile. And people—everyone from guests to trade magazines to gossip rags—will name me as the event coordinator. You're obviously the bride's family. Do you really think it's wise to be seen cavorting with the hired help?"

He buried his nose in the crook of her neck and nibbled his way across the expanse of skin to her collarbone. A quick nip elicited a gasp and he pushed up to lean on one elbow again, thrilling at the sight of her nipples pearled beneath her bikini top. "Don't be confused here, Ella. *I* didn't hire you."

"True, but—"

He cupped her jaw and rested his thumb over her lips. "Don't borrow trouble. Wherever this goes, we're two consenting adults. No one need worry about anything else."

A small grin tugged at one corner of her mouth. "Do you really believe you know what's best for everyone—what they should think or how they should behave..."

He arched a brow. "Darling, when people want to be right the first time around, they seek out my opinion. So, in a nutshell, yes." Something whispered through his consciousness, something as uncomfortable as it was unintelligible. Ella, in taking his advice, was going to be dead wrong. He smothered the feeling as he waited out her response.

She laughed and shook her head. Instead of replying, she shifted her gaze and stared out at the seemingly endless expanse of water behind him. The rapid tap-tap-tap of one bare foot against the deck created an anxious rhythm in the conversational void.

Liam grew twitchy as the silence continued. He wanted Ella to say something that would stop him from examining his response too closely, something that might soothe the discomfort left by the vague thought he'd taken a misstep. He'd always been at the conversational helm, directing people wherever he wanted them to go. Now, to have Ella stop like this left Liam out of sorts. Suddenly *he* was the one tapping his foot, and *he* struggled against the urge to say something, *do* something.

He moved to take her hand, wanting the physical contact, hoping it would assuage the unpleasant pressure on his conscience.

She picked up her punch, shutting down his attempt.

"Like that, is it?"

"For now."

"And why, exactly, should that be the case 'for now'?"

She sat up, crossing her legs and spinning to face him. The move put her at arm's length. "You're clearly suffering delusions of grandeur, believing you know what's best for everyone." She took a demure sip of the punch. "What's best for *me* is to finish this, suit up and get in the water as soon as possible."

"And why, pray tell, do you believe that?"

She tipped her glasses down her nose and looked up at him, sun already bronzing her skin to reveal a smattering of faint freckles over her nose. "You'll follow, and that means you'll either have to shut up and breathe or chastise me...and drown."

Laughter erupted from him in a rush. No one—*no one*—talked to him like this. Ella Montgomery must have a set of stainless steel balls *and* a spine to match. He liked that about her. Far more than he should, in truth. She was compassionate, professional, quick thinking... And she was starting to become more than a short-term distraction.

She'd never be a potential bride, despite his earlier joke, because Liam didn't do forever. He leased his car. He leased his plane. He leased his flat. Hell, he had term versus whole life insurance. Everything in his life had an end date, even his career. Thanks to sound financial planning, he would retire in sixteen years at age fifty.

So that mythical woman, the one capable of enticing Liam to rethink a forever type of commitment? She didn't exist. Not for him and, given what he'd witnessed within his peer group, within the business world and, God knew, within his family, not for anyone.

It struck him that if Ella had him shoring up his emotional boundaries and personal beliefs, he should be careful.

Standing, he moved to the front of the catamaran, leaned against one of the masts and quickly outlined his plan.

Seduction would necessarily come first. His. Hers. Theirs. It mattered little so long as it occurred.

Second, mutual physical pleasure—always a fine goal.

Third, he'd get her out of his system, thus removing any craving he might have for her.

Fourth, and finally, he'd ensure there were no strings.

That gave him roughly forty-eight hours to complete his plan before he got back to business as usual.

He'd worked with less.

The dive had been a complete success, and Ella signed the paperwork that made the excursion an official group activity for the wedding guests.

Headed back to the bungalow with Liam, she laid a hand on his arm, hoping the physical contact would smooth the way to her next task. "I know you don't want to give me guests' names in order to protect your sister's identity. I get that. I do," she emphasized when he looked down at her, face entirely deadpan. "I'm not asking for names. I don't need them. I just need the guest preferences from your spreadsheet. I can't do my job, can't represent your sister's best interests, without them."

His arm stiffened beneath her hand before he broke contact, stepping away. "Ella, I understand you need the spreadsheet, and I'll get it to you as soon as I have a chance to amend it and remove names. You'll have it in plenty of time to do what my sister hired you to do."

Irritation brought a hot flush to her cheeks. A fallen coconut lay in the middle of the path, and for a brief moment she envisioned braining him with the shell before stealing his computer and running off to print the mysterious list. Sighing, she toed the coconut off the path and continued walking beside him. "This isn't a want, Liam. It's a need. No matter what you may think of my profession, that's precisely what it is. A profession. I'm a professional. It's a business, not some fun little hostess-styled sideline thing I do to break the daily ennui of living as a high-society wife."

"My mother might take offense to that assessment of her monthly luncheons."

"Then I'll issue an apology. *To your mother.*" She shoved her hands through the mass of hair she'd unbraided and let dry in the sea breeze. "If you'll just give me—"

He wrapped an arm around her waist and led her into the dense tropical foliage that lined the path. It was cultivated but had grown up, taken on a wild feel.

She let out a small squeak of surprise when he took her hips and backed her into a palm tree. Looking over his shoulder, he found the greenery had closed behind them. For all intents and purposes, they were well off the beaten path, not steps off a cultivated one. *Perfect.*

"Let's talk about want versus need." Shifting, he pressed against her. The fabric of their swimwear did nothing to hide his full, throbbing erection.

"Let's," she murmured. Her hands went to his

hips. He arched a brow, and she knew she'd surprised him. "Seize every moment or there might not be another, remember?"

"I guarantee there will be another."

"Then perhaps..." She made as if to step away, and he took one hand gently, firmly.

"I wanted you earlier, Ella. Now?" He swallowed and looked askance, and she wasn't sure if it was his confession or the sun that deepened the color of his cheeks. "Now, this is sheer, unadulterated need."

"I understand."

He cupped her chin and lifted her face to his. "Do you? I'm not playing around, Ella. I hunger for you in a way that defies logic and explanation."

"Feeling's mutual," she murmured.

A group of young adults passed by only feet from where they stood. The teens never paused, never glanced their way.

Ella adjusted her stance so that the length of his cock pressed along the soft, bare skin of her belly. The fabric of his swim trunks was stretched beyond manufacturer recommendations, no doubt.

His hips thrust forward as he sucked in a breath. His heat branded her skin. "Please, Ella. I'll get down on one knee and— Holy *shit*."

She dropped to *her* knees and freed him from the constrictive fabric. He was much larger than she'd thought, and she'd guessed he was big. She had a moment of doubt. Could she manage him?

One way to find out.

She slid the tip of her tongue up his pulsing length

and then slipped her lips over his broad crown. The palm tree trunk at her back scraped across her skin. That strange dichotomy of sensations—smooth, silky skin on her tongue and rasping bark against her back—heightened Ella's every sensation. She lowered herself down his length, the tang of salt water and man saturating her awareness. He ran his hands through her hair, his fingers spasming as she lifted herself off his length and found a sensitive spot just beneath the corona. She paused, thrilling at the command she wielded over the powerful man who stood before her. He shook so that his legs seemed to almost fail him. His breaths were so harsh he sounded like a racehorse nearing the finish line. And the way he had to remove one hand from her head to prop himself up on the palm tree at her back? She ruled his body just then, and she relished every second.

Reaching up, Ella cupped Liam's sac, gently rolling it in her palm at the same time she sank down his length. The tip of his cock brushed the back of her throat, and she hummed her approval.

He groaned, knees bending so she had to adjust her position.

"Ella," he ground out. "I can't…"

She worked him harder, feeling the subtle change as his testicles drew tight just seconds before he lost control. It was all Ella could do to keep from touching herself, bringing herself over that beautiful edge and joining him in the fall, but this was about him, about her command of him, her control, his pleasure.

Next time, and there would be a next time, she'd see to it that he gave as well as he received.

Releasing him, she found him staring down at her, his forearm propped on the tree, his forehead resting on his arm. The sated look in his eyes was sexy as hell, but it couldn't compare to the slightly swollen bottom lip—he must have bitten down on it to keep quiet. She'd done that to him, driven him to the point he'd nearly cried out.

And she suddenly wanted nothing more than to drive him so far beyond rational thought that he lost all reason and simply let go.

Next time.

Liam offered her a hand, and she rose with his help. He nuzzled her neck, her sensitive skin erupting in goose bumps. She wanted him, more than she'd ever wanted anyone. Even a short affair would be enough. Enjoy him while she was here, removed as they were from everyday life stress, and take the memory with her when she left. That would do.

It would have to.

She sagged against him, something akin to disappointment sneaking in and leaving a dark smudge on what had been a bright moment. Reality was always such a quick way to go from thrilled to simply breathing in and out. The only option was to live in the moment and enjoy what little free time she had between work and related obligations.

"Ella?"

Her name, a soft question on his lips, had her lifting her face to his. "Hmm?"

"Thank you."

She grinned. "Not what I expected, but I suppose you're welcome."

He smiled and then surprised her by bursting out laughing. "Well, 'you're welcome' wasn't what I expected, either. No matter. What I meant was, that was absolutely incredible. And generous." He kissed her, soft and swift. "And you'll get your own back soon enough."

One eyebrow shot up. "Is that so?"

"It is." He ran a thumb over her eyebrow. "Have dinner with me."

"Agreed. But you have to do one thing for me."

"And that is?"

Irritation prickled along her spine. "You won't agree out of gratitude?"

Liam blinked slowly. "Darling, I learned early on to never make blind promises to old friends or new lovers. It tends to sully the relationship."

Relationship. Not the word she would use for a tryst, but he could call it whatever he wanted.

He hooked a finger under her chin and drew her attention back to him. "What is it you want from me?"

"The revised list." The request was flat, even to her ears.

"Have dinner with me, Ella, and I'll bring the list. The event coordinator texted me on our way back from the dive. He's coordinated a banquet on the beach with local performers, and you'll make your final menu choices then as well. The goal, I believe, is to have you consider the same or similar event for the post-ceremonial reception. He and his staff have contracted quite a few entertainers, and they want you to pick your favorites."

"Why did he text you?"

"I'm not sure. He did ask me to pass the information along to you. I would speculate he simply assumed we'd attend together."

"Why don't you let me have the list. I'll attend the dinner and then bring back suggestions based on what they've put together. There's no need for you to come with me. It's really a simple event. No need to..." She took his hand and squeezed it before letting go. "I can do this more quickly and efficiently if you're not there to distract me."

"First, I'm here on behalf of my sister and her groom. It only makes sense that I see what's being proposed. Second, dining alone is never as entertaining as dining with a partner." He traced the line of her jaw, a smile playing at each corner of his mouth. "Distractions aren't necessarily a bad thing, Ella."

"Clearly you've never tried dating in Los Angeles."

He arched a brow, inquiry unspoken.

"My dates usually wrap up with me trying to avoid the awkward good-night kiss while wishing I'd told the guy no when he asked, picked up Chinese takeout and brought it home to watch *The Big Bang Theory* reruns...*alone*."

Liam shook his head, the look on his face one of disappointment. "You are, without a doubt, choosing the wrong men."

She tapped a finger against her pursed lips and

pretended to consider his words. "You know, you might be on to something."

He studied her with an intensity that left her shifting her weight from foot to foot, and then he spoke, each word registering low but clear. "Have dinner with me, and I'll show you how the men who've taken you out should have done it."

She considered him, truly curious as to what he'd do differently. Before she could respond, he pulled her close, pressed a kiss to her temple and said softly, "Those are my terms, Ella. Accept them and I'll provide the list of amended guest preferences as well as a night you won't forget."

"Deal."

He tucked a wayward strand of hair behind her ear. "I'd say I'll pick you up at seven, but to make things easier, why don't we meet in the living room?"

"Again, deal."

He kissed her then, kissed her like he meant it. Stepping back, he set himself to rights before offering a hand and leading them back onto the path. An approaching couple smiled and looked away.

Ella blushed.

"That color looks good on your cheeks," Liam murmured. "I've a favor, if you don't mind."

"What's that?"

"Would you allow me to shower first? It will give me a few extra minutes to revise the list and print it for you."

Visions of him in the shower, wet and soaped up,

rendered her mute. An answer was necessary, but words eluded her. All she could do was nod.

Her mind flashed over dinner and went straight to the point when they would head back to the bungalow, where Liam Baggett had promised to show her how a date *should* end.

Even her imagination knew there were things he'd be able to show her, things she'd never considered. But come morning, she'd know.

Firsthand.

CHAPTER FIVE

LIAM DID AS PROMISED, showering first and then retrieving and printing the list. What he hadn't told Ella was that the list had already been modified. Well before his arrival at this tropical paradise, Liam had created several versions of the list, unsure which would be necessary. So while Ella had showered, he'd found the list with no names but guest characteristics, some accurate and others, well... He'd switched guest preferences, omitting some items and outright changing others.

He hadn't once hesitated, had never questioned the outcome because he'd been so clear in his focus, had known what he needed to do to unravel the wedding at its very seams. He'd done all this well before he'd met Ella. Long before he'd even considered he might suffer some form of remorse for setting the wedding planner's career back. Not destroying it, certainly. That hadn't been the plan. But even now, as drawn to Ella as he was, he would do whatever he deemed necessary for his sister, Jenna, to emerge happy and whole. He'd just be sure to help Ella recover from whatever societal storm resulted from his sister's dissolved nuptials.

Printout in hand, he wandered through the bungalow's living room and stood on the deck. The sun had settled low on the horizon. Everything was cast in broad, rich strokes of pinks and purples and oranges. Night would follow quickly, and the stars would dominate the night sky.

Soft footfalls drew his attention, and he turned. The barefoot woman in the doorway dulled the sunset's brilliance. His thoughts swung from planning a seduction to being seduced.

"Ella," he said, his voice saturated with something akin to reverence.

She wore a dress that, at first glance, appeared to be a full-length, sleeveless number in predictable black. But the simple sheath enhanced her silhouette. Every curve seemed like a fantasy yet unfulfilled, hidden by a touch of shadow here and a hint of promise there.

His mind was so jumbled that his entire vocabulary disappeared in a blink. He couldn't do more than stare like an obsessed idiot who wouldn't have been able to reply had he been at gunpoint.

She was flitting about and, thank God, didn't seem to notice the effect she had on him.

"I'm not wearing shoes since dinner's on the beach. Voluntary sand between the toes is one thing. Sand in the shoes? Entirely different sitch." She cleared her throat and, on a small smile, turned back into the room. "Two seconds. I forgot my earrings."

The move revealed the other side of the dress. Liam's ability to form coherent thoughts went the way of his vocabulary, leaving him staring wide-eyed and slack jawed. How many years would he spend dreaming about the soft, exposed skin of her back or the faint suntan lines earned this afternoon? He saw it all, more even, because the dress's back wasn't just open, it was *open*. Nothing but a maze of thin crisscrossing straps that dipped so low it was millimeters from that scandalous point where her back and her back*side* met.

Adjusting the front of his trousers, he spun away and walked to the balcony railing, gripping it with strength fueled half by fury, half by desire. Fury at his inability to control his reaction to the woman he'd planned to seduce. As for the desire? That was self-explanatory. He glanced over his shoulder and watched her approach him with such grace and composure he had to remind himself to breathe. Yes, this was desire of the most destructive kind. A single glance and she rendered him mute. Senseless. *Common.*

"Ready?"

There were a thousand things he wanted to say, and not a single damn word came out. Instead of stumbling through some inane compliment and embarrassing himself, he wordlessly proffered his arm, squashing the small thrill that coursed through him when she laid her hand across the exposed skin of his forearm. Never before had he thanked God he'd rolled his sleeves up.

First time for everything, I suppose.

A shake of his head to clear it, and then he was guiding Ella down the steps to the walkway and toward the beachfront. He watched her from the corner of his eye, this woman who threatened to undermine his plans. And she seemed completely unaware she had derailed him, turned him inside out, tied him in knots.

"You're quiet."

Her softly spoken comment drew him out of his musings. Looking down at her, his breath caught all over again, and he had to smile. He'd always prided himself on laying out intelligent plans and executing them with logic paired with practicality. It was, for all intents and purposes, his modus operandi.

But with her backless black dress and bare feet and shell-pink toes, Ella Montgomery had shattered that MO as if it were an illusion. Part of him wondered if he shouldn't be irritated. The larger part of him couldn't bring himself to care. Falling slave to her siren's call sounded like an ideal plan. He would come to her call, allow her to draw him down to the depths of dark passion, where he would willingly drown.

"Liam?"

His gaze met hers, inwardly thrilling at the sharp catch of her breath, the involuntary widening of her pupils, the slight tightening of her fingers on his forearm.

"Apologies. Woolgathering at an inopportune moment. What did you say?"

"I said I'm sure you have a lot on your mind with your sister's impending marriage, and I hope you'll tell me about her so that I get this right."

"Of course." She would instinctually assume he was at a loss over the wedding details. He wouldn't correct her. Not yet.

Guilt's sharp fingers clawed their way up his back, caressing his nape before scraping along his scalp. His skin crawled in response. He was going to ruin this woman's career—at least superficially...temporarily—and he knew it. Of course, he fully planned to use his connections to help her rebuild. Hell, he'd buy Ella's way into society's good graces if he had to. But Ella would have to trust him to help reestablish her reputation when all seemed lost. For that to happen, he had to first earn that trust. *While lying to her about the wedding plans. And seducing her.*

Guilt's weighted talons sank so deep they scraped bone.

It was a new feeling, this particular level of guilt. He'd dismantled businesses, sold pieces and dissolved personnel departments with less apprehension than he experienced just then. Frankly? He didn't understand this sensation any more than he liked it.

So master the moment and deal with tomorrow, tomorrow.

Right. Time to take control, to set aside the unfamiliar apprehension where Ella was concerned, to focus on her as a woman—one he found disconcertingly appealing. Show her that the men she'd dated in Los Angeles were just overgrown boys who hadn't been equipped to satisfy a woman of her caliber.

He'd deal with the fallout when it came.

Ella was hyperaware of the man at her side. The slight abrasion of his skin against her palm. His spicy cologne, faint but distinct enough to tease her senses. The way the breeze mussed his otherwise perfect hair. He'd been suspiciously quiet despite her attempts to draw him into conversation, his responses short and without elucidation.

Irritating man.

He hadn't been so quiet this afternoon.

It seemed that she'd needlessly worked herself into a minor frenzy over this evening. He was absolutely calm. Of course, he had the list she needed. He didn't have a client showing up in a few days who expected a perfect wedding, much of it based on revisions she wasn't yet privy to.

God, that *list*. It was her invisible nemesis. She needed it now. Particularly if it was an updated version of what she'd been provided by the bride's personal assistant. Without up-to-date information, Ella was effectively working blind. So she'd have dinner, tease Liam about the way dating *should* go, flirt and play a little, and then she would get down to business. First thing she'd do was coordinate the hell out of this wedding and, immediately after that, she'd ensure that her reputation was back in working order.

Arm in arm, they stepped off the cultivated path, feet sinking into the white-sand beach.

Ella gasped.

Arvin and his staff had taken the plan she'd given them and outdone themselves. It was as if they'd crawled into her mind and plucked images, bringing thoughts and feelings together to create the perfect montage, from the big picture to the finest details. They'd hit every mark.

Pale blue porcelain fire pots lit the path to the lone dining table, small clusters of seashells encircling the base of each pot. All around the entertaining area, tiki torches had been placed in seemingly random places in the sand, their flames swaying in the breeze.

The table had been set up with low ottoman-style pouf chairs done in clean, unembellished linen. It was adorned with a white linen tablecloth, and a burlap runner ran the length, anchoring a fresh flower arrangement done in a long, low style that would allow guests to easily converse over it. From the place settings to the crystal to the candlelight, the presentation was immaculate. Every color was precisely what Ella had ordered, right down to the shade of navy blue in the accents, the bright white hydrangea, the pale ivory of the calla lilies and the rich colors of local flora.

"This is amazing," she breathed, her fingers tightening on Liam's arm as she sought to slow her breathing. It was going to be okay. Everything was going to be beyond okay if the resort's planning crew could pull off something like this. "Absolutely amazing."

The bride's taste was disturbingly similar to Ella's, and, seeing it all come together, she had the briefest flash of what her own wedding would be like. Someday. Far, far away. Probably around the same time she became eligible to collect retirement.

Forcing herself to let go of Liam's arm, Ella strode forward to check the silver pattern. She was almost to the table when Arvin, the event coordinator, intercepted her.

He gave a small bow and, just beyond the firelight's glow, musicians began to play softly. The classical piece drifted across the air. Arvin rose and met her gaze head-on. "It is my sincerest hope you will find everything to your approval. My staff and I worked straight from the specifications and sketches you provided prior to your arrival."

He wrung his hands as he spoke, his wide, bright eyes searching her face. She took his hands in hers and squeezed gently. "It's positively the most beautiful setup I've ever seen, Arvin. I mean it. The entire presentation is stunning. It's like you crawled inside my head and looked at my imagination's snapshots. I'm certain the bride and her future husband will be thrilled. You and your staff should be commended on doing such a spectacular job. In fact, I'd like the name of your supervisor. She, or he, needs to know what incredible talent this resort possesses in you, your leadership and your people."

He closed his eyes for a brief second before replying. "Thank you, Ms. Montgomery. I want to apologize once more for the misunderstanding regarding whose wedding had brought you to the resort. I spent the afternoon calling all over the island trying to secure another room, but there isn't a single vacancy. I even tried a couple of homes with rooms for rent, but everything is booked. I would willingly offer you the bedroom in my home if you find yourself strongly opposed to the current arrangement."

Disappointment spiked through her—a way out of her current situation when, in truth, she no longer wanted one. She hesitated, not sure what to say, when a deep voice drifted through the dark and saved her.

"That's very generous of you, Arvin, but we'll manage the current arrangements without any trouble. And in regards to the current setup, Ms. Montgomery is right in saying that you and your staff have done a beautiful job. We'll only make a few minor changes."

Ella spun, the sand churning under her feet and tipping her off balance. She grabbed Liam's arms to keep from falling. Looking up, she searched his face. "Changes? What changes? This is precisely what your sister asked for. It's her dream setup."

"You're right. It's *her* dream, Ella. But it's certainly not her groom's vision of the perfect wedding. My sister discussed her wishes with her fiancé, and there were a few things in particular he wanted to see changed or added."

"I need that list," she all but growled. "Now."

"As agreed, I'll provide it after dinner." Adjusting her hold on his arm, he gently turned her toward the table. "Where would you have us sit, Arvin?"

"You may choose whichever seat you prefer, but I had planned for you and Ms. Montgomery to sit in the seats reserved for the bride and groom. The northern seat places the bride closest to the water with a slightly better view of the performers." He pulled out one of the two ottoman-style seats and gestured in a genteel way. "Once you've been seated, madam, sir, I'll have the meal served. We've adhered to your request for local custom and cuisine. The chef will serve pork, chicken and an optional fresh-caught parrot fish, all locally sourced and cooked in a traditional *himaa*, a pit dug in the ground and heated with volcanic rock. There are marinated plantains for those who prefer a vegetarian or vegan diet. The central proteins will be accompanied by dishes of *po'e*, *fei*, *uru* and *fafa*. The drink served with the meal will be *miti haari*, which is coconut milk diluted with spring water and lime. We will, of course, also provide a variety of beer in the bottle and a selection of white wines. Champagne will be chilled and provided later in the meal for the traditional toasts to the bride and groom."

Ella relaxed fractionally at the realization that the meal was exactly what she'd asked for—local tradition combined with a handful of dishes that would cater to Hollywood's particular, more diet-restrictive tastes. "It sounds divine."

"We'll want to ensure that a bottle of that new sports drink—what's it called? Power something—

is at each place setting." Liam dug out his phone and thumbed through a couple of screens before nodding. "Here it is. Yes, it's PowerBoost. The company is the groom's newest sponsor, and he wants them represented. He's asked that place settings alternate flavors between Manic Melon and Electrified Kiwi."

A faint film that tasted suspiciously like shock seasoned with a hefty dose of denial coated Ella's tongue. "No. That shit is either fluorescent pink or neon green."

Arvin paled.

Liam shrugged. "And?"

"It's *not* going on these tables."

"Groom's wishes. Bride concurs." Liam tapped his phone screen, and it went dark. "Shall we eat?"

Liam wrestled dueling urges: he wanted to cringe at his undiluted lies. He wanted to laugh at the look on Ella's face. Neither won. Instead, he smothered both urges with brutal efficiency.

Murdering emotions and flights of fancy. A new tagline for my personality type.

His mouth tightened until he felt the corners curl down.

Sitting next to him, Ella made small talk, guiding the conversation with an easy grace through each course, from appetizers through salad and well into the main course. She was a great conversationalist, seeming to truly listen to what Liam had to say and asking intelligent questions in turn. She was an anomaly, a complete about-face compared to the women he typically entertained, who were interested in his money and his social status and focused almost exclusively on what he could do for them. They were piranhas in Prada, jackals in Jimmy Choo. They looked at him and saw unlimited dollar signs and a season's pass into society's elite, whereas Ella—without knowledge of who he really was—saw a relatable man.

It dawned on Liam that, for the first time in his life, he had the chance to get to know a woman without presumptions laid out by society matrons and their husband-hunting daughters. Those women had proven time and again that they'd do anything to become Mrs. Liam Baggett, and he'd shut them down, each and every one. Yet now, having met a woman who genuinely piqued his interest, he was unable to capitalize on the opportunity.

My, how the tables have turned.

"Liam?"

He glanced up. "Beg your pardon?"

Ella paused, fork held out with a seared scallop on the end. "I asked if you were aware scallops had been added to the main course. I thought the groom hated seafood, particularly shellfish." She set her fork down and picked up her wineglass, sipping slowly as she watched Liam with undisguised assessment.

"I know he doesn't care for seafood in general, but I was under the impression scallops were the lone exception to that rule. It's shrimp that will send him into a righteous fit of temper."

"Shrimp? Why?"

"The first time I met the man was at a private dinner with my sister. She was in London for…" He waved off the explanation, not ready to disclose his sister's identity. "Regardless, that's where she chose to introduce me to him."

"I take it things didn't go well."

"He ordered steak. There was a shrimp skewer on his plate as garnish, and the guy absolutely lost it. Berated the server, demanded to speak to the manager, told my sister to mind herself when she attempted to intervene and defuse the situation. Her fiancé humiliated her. Over shrimp." Liam picked up his wineglass and swirled the contents but set the glass down without drinking. "It's safe to say I'm not his biggest fan."

"I'm sorry."

Liam looked up, focusing on the woman across from him as the last wisps of the memory fanned the flames of temper. That had been a disastrous night. "Why are you sorry? You had nothing to do with it."

"It's clear it still bothers you."

Liam shrugged then forked up a scallop and popped it into his mouth, enjoying the buttery flavor. He picked his glass up again but, this time, followed through and drank. The tannins in the wine cut the richness of the butter, the pairing perfect. If only he could say the same of his sister and her choice of groom. Setting his glass down once more, he met

Ella's direct gaze. "It's over and done. She's marrying him despite my suggestion she do otherwise."

Arvin approached the table, stopping at Liam's seat. "How is everything?"

Liam rose from his low seat and offered the other man a brief handshake. "Your staff has outdone themselves. The meal was incredible and the musicians positively brilliant."

Arvin stammered as he tried to articulate his thanks.

Liam interrupted, waving him off. "I understand how much effort went into the planning and execution. You have my thanks and the same from my sister, I'm sure. If you'd have dessert served while the event's primary entertainment performs, that would be lovely."

"Of course, sir." Arvin bowed deeply and then gestured to the musicians, saying something in Polynesian. The music grew softer and softer until it completely faded away. The ocean's susurrus rush and retreat filled the void. Liam found himself able to breathe and, for the first time, truly appreciate the perfection of the locale Ella had selected for Jenna's wedding. His sister was going to be thrilled with every aspect Ella had selected and designed.

And he was going to ruin it all.

He had no choice, though. Jenna's fiancé was a fame-seeking, moneygrubbing, coattail-riding leech. Mike had moved in to her home, assumed use of her staff and drove her cars at his leisure. To the best of

Liam's knowledge, Jenna was footing the entire bill until the baseball player "made it big."

Perhaps Liam would be able to convince her to spend a few days here with him after the wedding plans dissolved. She'd need the downtime. This would be the perfect place for her to recenter herself before she headed back to Hollywood. And, with Jenna here for a while, her publicist would be able to spin the breakup and place his sister in the best possible light. As for the groom? Mike could rot in hell as far as Liam was concerned. Let his dime-store publicist work out his personal spin.

A low, slow drumbeat began, and Liam swiveled to find a group of six women making their way onto the stretch of sand between the table's edge and the surf. Each carried a large, lit tiki torch. They took their places and began to move as the drumbeat increased in tempo. Hips undulating, the women— clad in sarongs and bikini bottoms—swung the tiki torches like they were batons, splitting into two groups of three and holding the lights high before stabbing them into the sand as the drum thundered a final beat. Two performers moved to stand in front of the table. They swayed as the drums began to beat out a hypnotic rhythm, their hips seeming to move independent of the limitations set by the human body. They swiveled and shook while the women's shoulders stayed straight and almost still, their arms so fluid as to seem boneless. Two more women joined, and then two more, and all six moved in a way that embodied the allure of the tropics, the appeal of intimate meals shared on fire-lit beaches and the promise of seduction that lay in the music's every note.

One stepped forward and held out a hand to Ella. "Come."

"Oh, no," she replied, laughing, her eyes bright. "I don't dance."

The moon cast its light on Ella's lush mane, highlighting it with luminous silver streaks. Her face was flushed from wine. The self-deprecating smile that decorated her face was so open, so unapologetic, so real. The last thread of his control began unraveling. When the dancer reached for her and Ella shook her head, Liam found himself moving forward without any awareness he'd set himself in motion. All he knew was he had to touch Ella. Right then. To see if the silver streaks in her hair were as cool as they appeared or, just maybe, as warm as the woman who bore them.

The distance between them disappeared, and Ella turned just as Liam reached out.

Warm. She was so warm.

"Liam?"

He didn't say anything, simply took her glass and blindly held it out with the unspoken command that the dancer take it.

She did.

"Dance, Ella." The murmured command rumbled up from within him, so deep that his chest vibrated with the sound. With the need that fueled it.

"I don't dance," she whispered.

"Tonight you do."

"Liam—"

"If you won't dance there, with them, then dance now." He took her hand and pulled her into his embrace. "Here." He began to sway in time to the lilting notes of the traditional bamboo flute, its sound as light as the drums were heavy. "With me."

She began to move in time to the music. They swayed back and forth, letting their bodies go where the music led them.

His hands slid across the smooth, silky skin of Ella's back. He loved her dress, the way it hugged her body, hinted at its lean form but enhanced her lush curves. He would have a dozen made so she had one to wear for every occasion. Hell, he'd plead with her to never wear anything else.

When he pulled her closer, Ella glanced up through thick lashes, her eyes burning with untempered heat. "Is this how you'd treat a date in Los Angeles?"

"This is how I'd treat you, Ella. Only you." He spun her around, guiding her to the water's edge and into the very edge of the surf, the waves rushing in to slip over their bare feet and wick up the fabric of his trousers and her dress. "Just dance."

She closed her eyes then, and gave herself to the music. Her chin tilted toward the sky. Starlight shone brighter than he ever remembered it, bathing her in a surreal glow. The hand that held his tightened, and the hand on his chest fisted the linen of his shirt. "You're a dangerous man, Liam Baggett."

Something in him snapped. No one could have heard, but it was as clear to him as the starting bell at a horse track. He moved with as much grace as he could muster, leading Ella from the water's edge and back onto the sand.

The surf rushed after them, licking at their heels.

Ella's lips parted on a sigh. Lifting her face to his, her gaze came to rest on Liam's mouth.

His cock swelled in response to the undisguised hunger that swam in those green depths.

Ella didn't look away, didn't try to hide the emotional riot she experienced. Instead, she whispered his name, just his name, in that sultry voice of hers. In it lay a plea he heard and responded to in kind.

"Ella."

She rose on her tiptoes, clutching his shoulders for balance in the shifting sand, and closed the distance between them...then stopped less than an inch from his mouth, waiting.

She would pursue so much as she was pursued. She would give what she was given and take what was offered. Nothing more. Nothing less.

Liam could live with that.

He dipped his head low and brushed his lips over hers. She tasted of crisp white wine and the sun's warmth and just a hint of mint in the dessert she'd sampled. He could get drunk on her. His senses heightened even as his mind grew sluggish, intoxicated by the woman in his arms. Never had it been like this with anyone.

Breaking the kiss, he took her hand and started toward the bungalow.

CHAPTER SIX

Tension raced through Ella's body like her nervous system was a never-ending zip line. Fine tremors in her hands made her clumsy as she gathered the hem of her dress before climbing the stairs that led into the thatch-roofed hut. Liam stood across the room, his shirt unbuttoned and one thumb hooked behind the button of his pants. He drew in a deep breath and let it out slowly. "I haven't been able to think clearly since I saw your toes."

She glanced down. "My...toes?"

"They're pink, Ella." He chuffed out a short, harsh laugh. "You've reduced me—the head of Europe's premier financial firm—to obsessing over the color of your nail polish."

She smiled at him, a wicked gleam in her eyes. "So, you get off on feet, then. Or is it the color pink? Because if it's pink, you're in for it. I'm wearing one other item that's pink."

"If you're telling me your lingerie is pink, don't expect to find them in the morning."

"You'd steal my underwear?"

He met her curious stare, his eyes filled with a predatory hunger that made her want to run *only* to ensure he chased her. Took her down. Commanded her body as the spoils of some as-yet unfought war. Then he sealed her fate as well as his.

"Of course, I'd steal other things from you first."

"Such as?"

"I intend to steal your breath followed by your sense of reason followed by your self-control."

Her heart tumbled through her chest like she had just come off a carnival tilt-a-whirl. "You're telling me you're capable of taking all of those things. And with such confidence."

He leaned against the bathroom door frame and, with one flick of his wrist, undid the top button of his trousers. "Yes, Ella. I am."

"How can you be so sure?" she asked, voice strangled.

He pinched the zipper tab between thumb and forefinger. "I haven't been able to stop staring at you all night. That dress... God, Ella. That dress. I want to peel it off you slowly, but I'm afraid I won't have the patience. I want to see you bare, wearing nothing but candlelight, far too badly. I want to touch you, to find out if your nipples are a similar pink to your toes or if they are, in fact, paler."

Ella traced a hand along the outside of her breast, his eyes following her every move. It was thrilling, knowing she had seduced this man simply by being herself. Erotic in a whole new way.

Liam's gaze slid back to hers. "I'm done chatting, Ella. Lose the dress."

She smiled, the coquettish move morphing to something more carnal as her gaze dropped to the smattering of dark hair revealed just above Liam's zipper. He had an impressive erection going on. Mouth dry, she forced herself to swallow. "We need to set the ground rules."

"Fine, but be quick about it." He pulled his zipper down an inch.

"What happens inside this bungalow has no bearing on what happens outside."

"Spell it out clearly, Ella."

"What we do here, privately, has nothing to do with who we are professionally. The two—personal and professional—are essentially two different people."

"I'm fine with that, but I'm more interested in the rules that apply right here. Right now. Tomorrow will be whatever it is."

Ella licked her lips. Liam's gaze zeroed in on the movement, and her nipples pearled.

"Lose the dress."

"Bossy bastard."

He shrugged, eyes blazing with unchecked desire.

Clutching the bodice of her dress with one hand, she reached up and untied the slender bow at her nape. Strings fell away and the dress sagged around her, held in place but not covering much. "Bedroom rules are simple. If either of us doesn't like something, we say so, and whatever it is stops."

"And if you don't tell me to stop, Ella? What then?"

"Then take it as an official endorsement—hell, take it as a challenge—to pull every other damn word in the English language out of my mouth using only your body. Make me scream, Liam. Make me forget my name. Make me forget every man who has been here before and be the man I'll compare every future lover to."

Liam's lip curled. Before Ella could ask what his issue was, he'd dropped his pants, stepped out of the puddled linen and started toward her, his long strides eating up the distance between them with alarming quickness.

He stopped so close to her she could smell the fragrant musk of his cologne. "Here's hoping you have a huge vocabulary, Ella. Challenge accepted."

Then he kissed her.

Ella's self-control dissolved under Liam's undivided attention. She let her dress fall to the floor, the silky fabric puddling around her feet like spilled ink. Kicking free, she moved closer to the scalding heat of Liam's bare skin. She gave herself free rein to explore his chest's contours with hands and lips, discovering the sculpted hills and salty valleys of muscle defined in stark relief in the moonlight. She shoved his shirt off his shoulders and let it go. It landed somewhere. They'd find it later. For now? There was only her.

Him.

Them.

And the moment demanded her full attention if she was going to keep up with his agenda.

As if he read her mind, he broke away from the kiss and leaned in to nip her earlobe. "Stop trying to make sense of this, Ella. Let it be what it is."

"And what is this?" she whispered, letting her head tip back, exposing her neck.

His answer, whispered in kind, raked over her skin. "Madness."

Madness.

She intended to respond, but Liam chose that moment to dip lower and, lifting the globe of her breast, take the nipple into his mouth, where he attended it with lips and tongue and teeth. An invisible line ran through her breast, down her abdomen and settled in her sex. It was hot, tantamount to a lit fuse, and it promised an explosion when it reached her core. Already the embers were burning.

Ella rubbed her thighs together and moaned, raking her fingers through Liam's thick hair and fisting it. She pulled him closer.

He hummed his approval against her skin.

The fine vibrations did impossible things to her already distended nipple.

"Please," she gasped. Desperation made her awkward, but her hands sought out his erection and she gripped it, sliding the broad girth through her fist. So smooth. Hot. Hard. She followed the length back up with slow calculation and discovered a fine sheen of arousal coating the head. Shifting her grip, she smoothed her thumb through it and across the sensitive tip.

Liam huffed out a wordless sound and then lifted

his head to reclaim her mouth. Their tongues dueled, desperation flavoring every touch, fueling every nip, shaping every sound. Alternately pushing and pulling, he directed her toward the bed as if he were a choreographer. Mosquito netting slithered across her bare shoulder and arm, and Ella shivered. Then the edge of the mattress was there, and she found herself being laid down with extreme care, his kiss never ending, his touch never ceasing.

She wallowed in myriad sensations, her body fluid, molten, under his heat.

Liam broke the kiss, and she mewled in protest. There were no words to ask him to return to her mouth, particularly when he began trailing kisses down her body, tracing his tongue around each nipple, circling her belly button and then—

Ella arched off the bed when Liam's mouth closed over her sex, where she most craved touch, stimulation, manipulation. Anything.

Everything.

She cried out in protest when he let go, falling back on the bed as he tugged her hips to the very edge.

"Patience," he said, mouth barely touching her overheated skin.

"Screw patience," she ground out, lifting her hips to him in a wordless demand.

She felt him smile. "That's the plan."

Liam's control had begun to unravel on the beach when he'd taken Ella's mouth in that first kiss, but this—the taste and sound and feel of her—dismantled him in a rush. His mouth worked her hard, driving her to the brink of orgasm before backing off, until Ella shook with the need.

Her frustrated cry had him sliding a single finger into her tight sheath and using his thumb to caress that sensitive nerve bundle as he used his free hand and teeth to rip open the condom he'd tossed on the bed. Unchecked need had him shaking so badly it took both of his hands to roll the condom down his length, but he managed. Barely.

Looking up, he found Ella's glazed eyes locked on the jutting length of his cock. She whimpered, hips undulating with primal need.

Liam was undone.

He gripped her hips and pulled her toward him. Then, eyes on hers, he surged forward and sheathed himself in her tight, hot sex with a single thrust.

Ella arched her back so hard only her shoulders and feet were on the bed. She took him to the root even as her hands scrabbled and fisted the duvet, seeking purchase.

There was little finesse and even less control as instinct took over, driving his hips in a base thrust-retreat-thrust motion echoed by the sound of skin striking skin with a rhythm that spoke of bodies in motion.

Ella gripped his arms for leverage and gave as well as she received, lifting her hips to meet his every drive. She was wild and uninhibited and everything he'd ever dreamed of in a lover. He wanted more of her, all of her, and would settle for no less as he fucked her with a brutally raw passion he'd thought himself incapable of.

Reaching between them, he found her swollen clitoris and pinched it.

"Liam!" she cried out, eyes going wide.

The first flutters of her orgasm clutched his cock, and his balls drew impossibly tighter. The base of his spine burned with warning a mere second before heat scorched his length and his own orgasm overtook him. No more warning than that.

He was reduced to a frantic pumping of hips and ragged breaths and shattered thoughts as he rode out the sensations that threatened to dismantle him, body and soul. Grinding his hips into hers, he gave a final thrust as she went limp. Straining, a final pulse rocked him and he collapsed forward onto her.

Their hearts thundered one against the other, the frenzied beats adopting a kindred rhythm.

She shifted beneath him, and he managed to move his body onto the bed beside her, rolling to take her into his arms in a move as foreign to him as democracy was to dictatorship. He'd never been one for postcoital cuddling, but just then, the idea of letting Ella go wasn't acceptable.

His chest tightened with an unnamed emotion when she snuggled back into him so that he spooned her. They fit together as if they were a two-piece puzzle. He felt like he should say something, offer some sort of commentary on their situation, but Ella beat him to it.

"You're way behind, Webster."

"Webster?"

"The dictionary. I suggested you pull every word in the English language from my mouth. All you managed was your name."

He smiled into her hair. "That was enough, darling." The pet name fell from his lips with ease and, for once, it wasn't just an empty platitude meant to pave the way for a smooth departure from his lover's bed. The truth rattled him, and he lost his train of thought.

She was quiet, presumably waiting on him to finish his thought.

He rolled onto his back and took her with him, situating her so she straddled his hips before offering her the truth. "Dawn is hours away. We've plenty of time to work on your vocabulary."

CHAPTER SEVEN

ELLA SAT NEXT to the pool, laptop open, and flipped through the list Liam had given her before he slipped out this morning. The warmth of the early-afternoon sun soothed muscles that ached from overuse through the night.

She grinned.

Maybe she'd arrange for a massage later this afternoon. Or she'd talk Liam into doing it. Yeah, that had some real potential.

Her grin widened.

"Work first, play second." She murmured the reminder under her breath.

Getting back on task, she continued to read through Liam's paperwork. There, at the bottom of the first page in bold male handwriting, was a note with the groom's request for a shellfish pairing with the main course. She typed the request into the file she'd started to track Liam's changes. It wasn't that she didn't trust him. She didn't know him enough to either trust or distrust him when it came to her career. But she felt better keeping their individual choices clearly defined in the event the bride or groom wanted to know why a specific change had been made.

She continued through the notes. There were quite a few handwritten amendments on the second and third pages—things like the flowers to be used in the bride's bouquet, the number of guests attending, requested activities, food choices, the orientation of the chairs relative to the sea and more. Each change left Ella a little more concerned than the last. Sure, the revisions were minor, but they altered the feel of the preceremony celebration and the nuptials…enough to make Ella question whether she'd had it right from the beginning. Was she losing her touch? Liam had been so confident in giving her the changes, so sure about what the couple desired for their big day. And he would know, wouldn't he? Had she misread the bride's wishes so significantly?

At the thought, her belly rolled over, the sensation as lazy as it was insolent.

A shadow cut across her computer screen. "Finding everything in order?"

Ella glanced up and discovered the very man she'd just been thinking about standing beside her lounge chair. Liam's broad shoulders blocked the sun. He wore nothing but a pair of pale blue board shorts. Water dripped from the hems and puddled around his bare feet. His dark hair was slicked back, making his deep brown eyes all the more prominent in that sculpted face. He shifted his weight from one foot to the other, and the waist of his trunks slipped a fraction of an inch down his hips. Tanned warmth gave way to a thin white strip of skin.

He moved to tug the shorts up, and she reached out to rest a hand on his knee. "Don't."

A smile teased one side of his mouth. "Don't what?"

"Don't pull your shorts up."

"The lady allows me to command her body in the dark but thinks to command mine in the light of day?"

She tugged on the end of the wet suit, exposing a bit more skin, and took him in, one visual gulp at a time.

"If memory serves, you were quite vocal in your approval."

"I'm all about positive reinforcement."

He chuffed out a small laugh.

"Besides," she continued, "how else was I supposed to let you know you were doing what—*exactly* what—I wanted?" Batting her eyes, she lowered her voice. "And if *my* memory serves, you were all too anxious to have me command your body under yesterday's sun."

He touched two fingers to his forehead in mock salute. "Touché."

A short laugh, breathy and shallow, escaped her, and she fought the urge to cringe. She'd never been *that woman*, the one who flirted with inane comments and superficial behavior. This man wouldn't turn her into that woman, no matter how spectacular a lover he'd been.

Ella cleared her throat, gathered her paperwork and then stood, forcing Liam to take a step back and give her some space. She needed to do something proactive on this account, something to prepare for the arrival of the bride and groom in just four short days.

Four days.

The timeline was so tight. If she screwed this up, there would be no time to fix it. This was a one-shot opportunity to reclaim her career and her self-esteem. She wouldn't, *couldn't*, screw it up.

"I have some questions about the changes you requested."

Liam crossed his arms over his chest, took a deep breath and widened his stance as if preparing for battle. "Do you, now." His tone was measured. "I was under the impression my notes were self-explanatory."

She tilted her head to one side, looking him over. "Does this happen often?"

"Does what happen often?"

"This." She gestured toward him. "Do you have frequent episodes where your superiority complex interferes with common courtesy? If so, you might consider seeing someone about it."

His eyes flared for a moment before his lids slid down and gave him the appearance of bored but focused irritation. "A little respect, Ella."

"Absolutely, Liam," she said, emphasizing the two syllables of his name and meeting his stare head-on. "When it's earned." She squared her shoulders and tipped her head toward a table situated in deep shade. "Let's move over there. We'll be able to spread the paperwork out, and I can share sketches and initial plans on the guest seating, ceremony timing and reception setup. I believe that when you view the ideas your sister first approved, you'll be able to help me incorporate the modified requests."

"Certainly, though I'm deferring to you and your expertise."

"Yes, but you know the couple. I don't." She moved past him, still talking as she went. "Consider it a different type of boardroom negotiation and you'll be fine. But treat me like the expendable lackey, and we're going to butt heads all the way to our departing flights."

"And that wouldn't do, would it."

Ella rounded on Liam and forced herself to hold her ground when she found him much closer than she'd anticipated. Tilting her head back and shielding her eyes from the sun, she fought to keep her tone level. "You're trying to provoke me. I'm not sure why, but stop it. Neither of us gains anything if this wedding is a wreck just because you couldn't separate the personal and professional aspects of our acquaintanceship."

"Acquaintanceship." Liam's brow furrowed and his eyes darkened. "Is that what you're calling this thing between us?"

Ella shrugged. "I don't need to label it to enjoy it, so feel free to call it what you want. But whatever you do? Don't, and I mean *do not*, allow it to interfere with my job. Understand?"

He inclined his head but didn't meet her challenging stare as he waved her toward the table she'd indicated moments before. "After you, then."

And that…that easy capitulation left the skin across her shoulders tight even as he placed a hand so low on her back that a small shift let him slip lower, one finger caressing the skin below her sarong and bikini-clad bottom, sending warmth coursing through her. Both sensations were strong, both messages loud and clear.

The question was, which one should she listen to first?

Five hours later, with the sun beginning to set, Liam had demanded Ella take a break. The woman had grown frazzled, frustrated and kept retracing steps she'd already taken. She'd argued with him, as predicted, so he'd signaled the waiter, signed off on the check and asked her to meet him at the bungalow. Then he left, Ella still stewing in her seat. There was time yet to get her to come around, even if the timeline was tight and growing tighter. The approach had to be gentle, even subtle. If he pushed her too hard, too fast, she'd become suspicious. He didn't want to lose the best chance he had in getting his sister to see the truth about her fiancé. Though he was feeling inexplicably guilty about the consequence to Ella should he successfully dismantle the wedding.

Settling deeper into the porch hammock, he used one foot to push off and start the swing rocking. He could fix whatever went wrong, set Ella's business to rights with just a few well-placed calls, a timely recommendation or two and a couple of high-profile jobs he'd create on his own if he had to. And surely Jenna would use her star power and social influence to help as well. His sister was softhearted. Too much so. That had gotten her into this mess of an engagement in the first place. If she'd been more practical instead of so emotional, she'd have seen what her fiancé was after from the beginning. Thankfully, Liam had no qualms about protecting his sister. He would do what needed to be done to ensure Jenna wasn't taken in by a con man. If love existed, his sister deserved nothing less.

One of the bungalow's French doors opened with a soft *snick* before closing with a sharp *kabam*.

No apology followed.

Yep. Ella was still irritated. Maybe "pissed off" was more accurate. His insistence that Jenna wanted freshly imported tulips from Holland had seemed to send Ella over the edge. She'd typed the amendment into her computer, fingers slamming against the keys in rapid-fire fashion, and then eyed him through narrowed lids. "Anything *else*?"

That's when he'd made his stage-left exit.

He knew he needed to smooth the proverbial waters between them to keep her focused on his revisions. The trick was to do so in a way that wouldn't make his concerns seem overdone or his directives too controlling. He couldn't allow her to get to the point she considered reaching out to Jenna's assistant for confirmation. There had been a moment, maybe two, this afternoon where it had been a near thing.

The woman was sharp as hell. But he'd been able to redirect her by suggesting outrageous alternatives to his "amended" requests in the hopes of making his changes seem less, well, outrageous. Which they were. He was well aware some of what he'd written in was over-the-top. He'd drafted a mental checklist of things he would need to handle himself. Then he had offered to take those tasks off her plate to help her. The blatant lying didn't sit well with him. At all. But he'd do that and more, even worse, to spare Jenna the heartache Mike would, without a doubt, foist on her.

Liam had watched over Jenna since she'd taken her first steps, always there to ensure she wasn't hurt if she fell, helping her get back up and take her next steps with confidence. And she had because she knew he was right there to catch her should she fall again. Liam had tended her wounds, from skinned knees after falling off her bicycle to a broken arm following a horseback-riding incident. He'd talked her through her first broken heart. He'd celebrated her first major nomination for lead actress. He'd always been there for her. Always. She'd even once admitted to him that part of her fearlessness was the knowledge he'd always be there to support her.

And then there was the oath Liam's father had demanded from his deathbed.

First, Liam had to give his word that he would watch over Jenna. Second, his father had demanded that Liam keep Baggett Financial Services in the family and ensure that voting rights and ultimate ownership would remain at 51 percent or greater in the Baggetts' favor. Should Liam fail, the board was ordered to replace him with a second cousin. The boy was only fourteen but had already proven a head for numbers in his boarding school. Liam had been insulted. He'd also been emotionally wrung out. The former his father dismissed; the latter was never acknowledged. Not by either Baggett.

And while he'd resented the hell out of his old man, he fully intended to keep true to his word. He didn't take vows lightly.

Ella stepped closer, scattering his darkening thoughts like light permeating shadow. The wind toyed with loose curls that had slipped free of her sloppy topknot. Her semisheer sarong fluttered around her long, toned legs.

Liam let his eyes drift closed even as his sex awoke with a hard pulse.

He knew exactly how those legs felt when they were wrapped around him.

The wind shifted and carried with it the floral bouquet of her perfume. She was a siren. How could she be anything else? She was smart as hell, beautiful, charming, witty—all traits Liam valued in friends as well as in lovers. He'd never been lucky enough to find all of those things in one person, though. Until now. The realization was a stinging buzz in his chest, a feeling not unlike the vibration of a large gong struck in close proximity. It vibrated through him until he was forced to rub the valley between his pecs in an attempt to assuage the feeling.

"The tulips will be here on Tuesday, in tight bud condition, with a guaranteed arrival of no later than 3:00 p.m. That gives me time to put together the bouquets and boutonnieres without the heat forcing the flowers open prematurely." She sighed. "I have Arvin speaking to the resort's contracted fishermen about harvesting the scallops, but he's not sure what they'll be able to gather this time of year. We may have to add them to the seafood croquettes, but there will be shellfish in some form or another."

Liam hooked his arms behind his head and watched Ella pace the length of the deck. "You need to relax, Ella."

She sucked in a short breath, tension carving deep grooves in the soft skin beside her lush mouth. "I'll relax when this wedding is a success. There'll be time and opportunity then. But right now? I can't. Too much is riding on luck showing up to play for my team, and in my experience she tends to avoid critical situations where I'm involved. She'll show up afterward and be all, 'What? You needed me? My cell never rang.'"

Liam smiled. "You're sexy when you're strung out."

"You think so?"

"I do."

She shook her head and laughed softly. "Then you ought to find me completely irresistible by Monday night."

"It will work out the way it's supposed to, Ella.

Trust me on this. And I find you irresistible right now."

"Sweet talker." Her smile faded. "If all that mattered was an exchange of vows, I'd agree. But there's so much more to making a bride's dream manifest as reality. I was under the impression she wanted butterflies, not birds, released at the close of the ceremony. Now I find out she wants four dozen birds released with the kiss. So while I figure out the best place to release the butterflies that will arrive Monday, I have Arvin trying to source the birds. It's all last-minute, of course, and all he can come up with are pigeons. Not quite the same effect as white doves soaring free."

Sitting up, Liam straddled the hammock and motioned her forward.

She moved toward him like a cautious cat, lithe and smooth but ready to bolt if threatened. "What?"

He wiggled his fingers in an impatient gesture. "You need to take a few minutes and relax."

"I don't *have* a few minutes to relax. I 'relaxed' last night and slept through my alarm this morning."

He stood and moved toward her, silently celebrating when she held her ground and squared her shoulders. This woman was no shrinking violet. It made the battle of wills sharper and conquest that much sweeter...no matter who won. And Liam wasn't averse to being conquered now and again.

Pulling her into his embrace, his hands skated down her back, over the expanse of bare skin and, cupping her butt, pulled her into his semierect cock.

"If you won't take a break for your own well-being, take one for mine."

Ella slid her arms around his waist at the same time she twined her right leg around his left. "You're bribing me to slack off on your sister's wedding."

"No." He lowered his head and nibbled his way along her jaw to her neck, down and then down some more until he reached her collarbone. A quick nip drew a sharp intake of breath from her, and his cock swelled hard and fast. "I've no doubt you'll handle what needs handling." Taking her hand, he rested it on his erection, his nostrils flaring when she closed her hand over his length and stroked him through his shorts.

Ella's breath came faster, scalding the skin of his neck. Backing toward the bedroom, she tightened her hold on him and whispered, "And what about you, Liam? Do you need to be handled?"

"By you?" he asked. "Always."

CHAPTER EIGHT

ELLA'S PHONE BUZZED. Face buried under her pillow, she blindly searched the tabletop until she found it, but the call went to voice mail before she managed to answer.

"Don't you dare leave this bed." The commanding male voice was still laced with sleep. "Whoever it was will call back, and whatever they want will keep until then."

Sunlight slipped through the window, softened by the gauzy mosquito netting that surrounded the bed and created a haven within the tropical paradise. "Says the man who left me without even a note yesterday morning." She stretched until her muscles shook and then went limp, letting her arms flop onto the expansive mattress. One hand made contact with her lover's arm.

He grunted his objection.

The temptation to lie there until noon was too real. "I need sustenance." She weakly clapped her hands. "Breakfast in bed, man. Make it happen."

The bed shifted. Small electronic notes indicated

Liam was placing a call. Still, it surprised her when his sleep-roughened voice greeted the person on the other end with "And good morning to you, Marise. This is Liam Baggett. I'd like to place a room service order, please." A pause. "Crepes with fresh cream and strawberries, fruit, granola, Belgian waffles, sourdough toast, bacon, orange juice and a carafe of regular black coffee." Another pause. "That's it. Just charge it to my room. Oh, and if you would have the meal set up on our patio, that would be lovely."

Ella's stomach rumbled in appreciation. The man certainly had good taste. She rolled onto her back and draped one arm over her eyes as the beep of the phone said Liam had disconnected the call. "How long before I can put caffeine in my system?"

He chuckled. "Twenty minutes."

A warm hand slid across her abdomen, and she sucked in a sharp, short breath. "Too long."

"Just long enough for me to distract you," he countered, reaching for her.

She rolled away before he could get a good grasp on her. "No. Nope. Not happening." Standing, she swayed with a bit of dizzy exhaustion. They'd stayed up too late last night, making love in far too many locations in and around the bungalow—the porch, the hammock, the bed, the tub, the floor. She was satisfied—so satisfied her muscles felt like overcooked noodles. It was a wonder she was able to stand without support. Not that she was complaining. At all. But the time she'd spent in personal indulgence was time that hadn't been spent working on the wedding.

Snatching up her cell, she thumbed to the messages and read the transcription of Arvin's voice mail.

> Birds located. Aviary only had one dozen available. Breeder recommended another aviary on neighboring island. If the expense is acceptable, let me know and I'll have the doves delivered. I need to order them today in order to receive them in time for the ceremony. Arvin.

Ella pinched the bridge of her nose and focused on taking slow, deep breaths. This was another expense she hadn't planned on. Every change Liam made came with a new cost. Like using flowers flown direct from Holland. She had expressed her concerns, but Liam dismissed them with a wave of his hand. He'd insisted that his sister had given him free rein to go over the budget. Ella had asked him to send her an email confirming that the additional costs were acceptable. He'd pulled out his phone and written the email on the spot, going one step further by promising he'd cover any cost to which his sister objected.

But Ella was still anxious. The energy drinks, the doves, the excursions…additions and subtractions to the welcome baskets. If Liam failed to honor his word to cover costs, the bride and groom could come after her and demand she pay out of pocket.

Driven by caution, she figured she'd improvise. Somehow. Maybe hold a less expensive group activity than the private sail and scuba dive currently scheduled for the bride, groom and their guests the day prior to the ceremony. That would be one place Ella could cut a few corners.

Leaving Liam lounging in bed, she went into the living room and opened her computer, pulling up the resort's activities website. She traced a finger along the keypad, scrolling—scuba diving, deep-sea fishing, snorkeling, hiking. She paused. *Parasailing and horseback riding.* Each activity was easily one hundred and fifty dollars less per person, and she'd bet she could negotiate a better rate.

"Liam?"

An inarticulate sound was her only response.

"What do you think about parasailing and horseback riding?"

"I'd never recommend trying the two at the same time."

"I'm sure that's sound advice, smart-ass. I'm asking if you think either of those activities might be a better choice for the guests instead of the sail and dive."

Covers rustled followed by the sound of bare feet padding across the hardwood floor. Liam appeared in the doorway, a sheet wrapped about his waist. Sunlight came down from the skylight, showcasing the hard planes and muscles of his torso, making him look like a chiseled work of art. Natural highlights in his hair softened his features. But his eyes—they were infinitely deep and far more sensual than she'd ever seen them.

Ella wanted to abandon all attempts at work and take this man back to bed. He might frustrate the hell out of her, but he had learned his way around her body in no time at all. He could dissolve stress better than a stiff drink, relieve anxiety better than any prescription. Yeah, she'd take one of him to go, thanks.

Blinking rapidly, she shook her head. "Stop distracting me."

He smiled then, slow and suggestive, and tilted his head toward the bedroom. "We still have ten minutes before breakfast gets here. Enough time for a quickie."

The problem was, she didn't want a quickie. She wanted more time with him, wanted more time than this event would afford them. Already she'd begun dreading the day they'd part ways. This wasn't like her. At all.

But the truth was what it was.

The only practical solution was to keep things between them light. Fun. Relaxed. She needed to keep her head in the game and her heart off the table. Period. And there was no better time to enforce her "no emotional connections" pledge than the present.

Closing her computer, she set it aside and stood, stretching her arms above her naked body.

Liam's eyes grew hooded as he pushed off the door frame he'd been leaning against.

She started toward him. "What can you do with six minutes?"

He reached out and pulled her close, his erection prodding her belly. "More than enough, Ella." His lips brushed hers and he smiled, the look utterly wicked. "More than enough."

Liam spread out the newspaper and read through the financials before opening his computer to do a little catching up with the London office. He answered a handful of critical emails and delegated the rest to his personal assistant. He was in the process of reviewing a high-profile client's returns, making notes on changes and calculating potential returns on amended investments when his cell rang. The ringtone was a snappy show tune, one he'd set for his sister after taking her to see a live performance on the West End for her sixteenth birthday.

He reached for the phone and swiped to answer the call, silently thanking the powers that be for getting Ella out of hearing distance so he could speak freely. "What's going on, squid?"

Jenna laughed. "How long are you going to call me that awful nickname?"

"Until I can forget you clinging to me, afraid to jump off the diving board unless I went with you."

"I was being cautious!" she retorted.

"You nearly drowned the both of us," Liam groused, though even he could hear the undiluted affection in his voice.

"Whatever. How's the wedding stuff going?"

Liam leaned back in his chair and closed his eyes, focused on keeping his breathing even, his tone level. "Right on schedule. You hired a stellar event coordinator."

"My assistant said she was pretty awesome. I hate doing this so cloak-and-dagger, but it's the only way to keep the paparazzi off my ass."

"What are you telling your guests?"

She laughed. "Nothing. We've handwritten notes to invite them to join us on a brief getaway. Doesn't look like a wedding invitation at all. That was the event coordinator's idea. What's her name again?"

"Ella."

"Right. Anyway, we're inviting everyone like it's an individual thing and asking them to keep it tucked under their hats so we have a chance of a paparazzi-free vacay. Most are Hollywood names and faces, so they'll appreciate the opportunity for a private vacation. It wouldn't surprise me if most of them suspect a wedding, but the guest list is small enough I'm not too worried about gossip."

"I'll bet you a hundred pounds one of them sells you out."

"You're such a cynic."

"Yet you didn't take the bet."

"Oh, I'll take it. But when I win, make sure you pay up in British pounds. Don't try to cheat me by giving me American dollars. Not with the exchange rate what it is."

Liam chuckled. "As if you'd best me. I'll take *my*

winnings by way of a single Benjamin, you trusting soul."

"We'll see who's handing out money when this is all over." She sighed, a small hitch sounding across the connection. "Is the wedding really coming together well, Liam? I've been worried. It's not that I don't trust you. You know that. It's just..." Jenna hesitated, seeming to hunt for the right words.

It's not that I don't trust you. Liam felt as if his heart had been steamrolled, backed over and steamrolled again. She had entrusted this—what was supposed to be the happiest day of her life—to him. And for the first time ever, he was going to absolutely disappoint her.

His chest tightened at the realization. Every breath grew shorter and shorter until he struggled to breathe at all.

"Leem?"

She hadn't been able to pronounce his name as a toddler. Instead, she'd called him "Leem," and it had evolved into her nickname for him. Now she only called him that when she was out of sorts and unsure of herself. It didn't happen often anymore.

"Ella is top-notch, Jenna, truly in a class of her own. She has ensured that every idea presented, whether from you or I, becomes a reality." Total truth so far as that went. Perhaps the most truth he'd spoken regarding the wedding since he'd set foot on the island.

"There haven't been any issues with the stuff I asked for? I know some of it will be hard to manage in such a remote location, but she was positive she could make it happen."

"Jenna, there's nothing to fret over." *Except the groom.* "What was it your mother always told you about getting married to our father?"

"That she could've been married in a cornfield under the blazing noon sun wearing nothing but a gunny sack while holding a bouquet of thistle. She married the man she wanted to spend the rest of her life with, and *that* was what mattered."

"So hold on to that."

"I am."

"Are you quite certain about this, squid? You don't have to marry him simply because he asked, you know."

"I know you and Mike haven't exactly hit it off, and it's clear you don't like him much, but he's the one. *My* one, Liam. I love him."

"Then that's the answer, I suppose." But it didn't have to be. She didn't have to marry this guy just because he'd convinced Liam's softhearted sister he was a prince among paupers.

"It is," Jenna answered in kind, her voice soft. "And you'll be there to stand in for Dad, to walk me down the aisle and give me away. I wouldn't have it any other way."

Emotion welled, stealing Liam's ability to speak. He made a noncommittal noise and then choked on the sound, coughing harshly.

"Leem?"

"I'm fine."

"I've got another call. Hold on." She was gone and back in a flash. "That was Mike. The car service is here to pick us up. We're headed to the airport!" she nearly squealed. "This is really happening, Liam!"

She sounded so damnably happy...

Leaning forward, he propped his elbows on his knees and raked his free hand through his hair. "Travel safe, squid. You're all that matters, you know."

"Don't worry so much," she chastised. "I'll be there soon enough and you'll see."

"Jenna," Liam wheezed. "I gave our father my word that I'd look out for you, ensure your happiness before all else..." He couldn't finish that particular train of thought because a new realization was barreling down on him at breakneck speed.

What if I'm wrong—wrong about the groom? Wrong about stopping the wedding? And, God save me, wrong about what would truly ensure Jenna's happiness?

If he was wrong, his sister was about to pay the price for his mistake.

But he'd seen Mike treat Jenna poorly, and more than once. His boorish behavior, lack of manners and general indifference had soured Liam on the man. There was no undoing the damage. He had to protect Jenna.

"Leem?" she prompted.

"I only want you to know you have options. Even if you're pregnant, we can—"

"I'm not pregnant, Liam," Jenna said in as sharp a tone as she ever took with him. "Would you please relax? It's going to be fine. After all, you said so, and who would dare defy you?" She sighed. "We'll be there soon, Liam. Please stop worrying. Mike is my one. I know what I'm doing."

Liam remained silent, unsure what to say in the face of her frustrated plea.

Jenna took the decision out of his hands, disconnecting the call without a goodbye.

Liam was left holding the phone, still wondering what he should've—could've—said that stood even a remote chance of making things better between him and Jenna. Things couldn't be broken now, before the rug was pulled out from under her.

With their father gone and her groom likely to bail when things got tough, Liam would be the only one there to help her pick up the pieces of her dream.

Even though he was the one who would shatter it.

CHAPTER NINE

ELLA SAT AT the beachside bar, the seating chart for the wedding dinner spread out in front of her. Her initial notes had stipulated no bride and groom table— Jenna and Mike had wanted to sit *with* their guests. The revised arrangement had guests clearly segregated, each one labeled "B" for bride or "G" for groom. The two groups had been seated in different locations, each one opposite the new table where the bride and groom sat. Alone. The arrangement made little sense. It felt wrong, far too unlike the original plans.

Shoving her hands through her hair, a low growl escaped her. Should she follow Liam's revised plans and ignore the inner voice that was screaming at her to disregard his changes? Surely Liam wouldn't screw her over. What could he possibly gain from ruining his sister's wedding? More than once he'd said that he wanted his sister's happiness above all else.

But things weren't adding up, and Ella couldn't swing many more changes. Not with the wedding so

close. The resort—thanks to her relationship with
Arvin—had been willing to extend a significant rate
reduction for horseback riding on the beach. Liam
had never answered her about substituting horseback
riding or parasailing for the dive trip, so she'd chosen
horseback riding based on his notes. No one indicated a fear of animals. No one claimed any allergies.
So she'd offer two excursions, each with the bride
and groom present, and guests could choose which
one they wanted to participate in. That would work.

Letting her gaze drift over the seating arrangement, Ella traced her fingers along the far table, the
one labeled with the groom's guests, then finger-
walked across to the bride's guest table. The groups
were small, but... "This can't be right."

"What's wrong with it?"

She looked up sharply into eyes the color of luxurious dark chocolate—sweet but with a bite.

Liam's brows drew together. "Ella?"

Shaking off the ridiculous wanderings of her mind,
she focused on the moment at hand. Now was the time
to get this mess straightened out. Ella had a short
window of time left to make sure everything was in
order for the Wednesday morning walk-through and
Wednesday afternoon excursions. Then? The wedding.

Two. Days.

The butterflies in her stomach took up dogfight
maneuvers, zipping left and then right, flying up
only to plummet to the depths of her belly. Rather
sickening, all in all.

"Ella?" Liam repeated.

"I have two days to piece together what you say your sister wants versus what her personal assistant said she wants. I have to make sense of this and make it work, Liam, because anything less could potentially doom me to planning children's parties for the rest of my life." Running her hands over her face, she traced the lines marring her forehead and the grooves etched alongside her mouth. She had to look as haggard as she felt. "This is wrecking me. I'm going to need a week at a spa just to undo the damage the stress is doing to my skin. I swear I've aged five years in four days. This is ridiculous, Liam."

He sank into a canvas sling chair and scooted forward, pulling together the plans she'd scattered around her. It took him seconds to organize them, but then he seemed to hesitate. With careful consideration, he folded up the sheet he'd given her and moved the original plan to the top of the pile. "Trash the seating plan I gave you and go with the one my sister's assistant originally laid out."

Ella started and then sank back into her chair. "What? Why?"

"Because this is more in line with what she truly wants." Liam looked at her, smile sardonic and eyes sad. "It's something I shouldn't have messed with."

The knot that had formed in Ella's stomach unraveled, and she drew her first full breath since hearing Liam had a modified wish list. Until now, she hadn't realized exactly how messed up she'd been. Not really. But this...this sudden about-face Liam was pulling? It eased her fears. Surely there was a reason behind it, but she wasn't going to look for it. All that mattered was she'd suddenly found the confidence to move forward. "So what would you say to horseback riding on the beach or parasailing instead of snorkeling and diving?"

He was shaking his head before she had finished asking the question. "Groom has allergies. I'm not sure if horses fall under that umbrella, but I'd avoid it just to be safe."

"Good to know." Reaching across the table, she laid her hand over his, which was resting on the original seating chart. "Thank you, Liam." There was more to those words than courtesy. There were layers of gratitude and an acknowledgment that she knew this was hard for him. She wanted him to know, to realize she understood he was struggling.

He squeezed her hand in return before pulling away. Looking out over the quiet beach, his mind seemed even farther away than his gaze. "Ella, do you know who my sister is?"

No reason to play games or be coy. "I have an idea."

"Who do you think she is?"

"I'm guessing she's Paige Jennings."

He smiled. "Nope. Guess again."

Ella sat farther forward and rested her crossed arms on the table's edge. "I almost asked if you were sure," she said with a small smile. "I was pretty sure myself."

Liam's gaze came back to her. "No idea, then?"

"I suppose she could be any number of starlets in Hollywood."

He grinned. "Don't let her hear you say that."

"Now you're scaring me."

"My sister is Jenna Williams. Her fiancé—"

"Is Mike Feigenbaum." Ella swallowed hard. "Award-winning actress meets the rookie MVP for minor league baseball and starting pitcher for Utah's triple-A team, the Hellcats. An insanely fast, well-publicized romance follows, culminating in a proposal right before Mike opts out of his contract negotiations and very publicly becomes a free agent. He then moves to Hollywood to be with Jenna." Flopping back into her chair, she shook her head. Or maybe it was her whole body shaking. Yeah, that was more likely. "Jenna Williams is your sister?"

"My father married Jenna's mother when I was seven. They had Jenna when I was nine." One corner of his mouth curled up in a tender smile. "I couldn't stand her when she was born. But then, when she was about nine months old, she took her first steps…and they were toward me. She followed me everywhere after that. And when she began to talk? Good God, she chattered at me nonstop. It didn't matter if I understood a single word she said. Like everyone she meets, she won me over by simply being herself."

"Jenna Williams," Ella repeated through numb lips.

"You'll love her." It was half statement, half command.

"I'm sure I will—if she's even half as lovely in person as she has been in every interview I've ever seen. But why tell me now?"

She watched as something haunted passed through his eyes. "You need to know who she is."

Ella heard the two words he'd left unspoken. To me. *You need to know who she is* to me. She scooted her chair closer to the edge of the pavilion and wiggled her toes until they were buried in the sand. There were a hundred things she could say, at least two dozen she probably *should* say, and not a single one seemed absolutely right.

As if he read her mind, Liam said, "I expected something…more."

"More?"

"In your reaction to my sister's fame."

Ella shrugged. "I've dealt with celebrities before. And everything I know about her indicates she's a delightful woman. I don't know much about her fiancé, but I'll meet him soon enough."

At the mention of the groom, Liam's face clouded over.

"So it was an understatement when you said you're not his biggest fan." Ella leaned over and picked up her mimosa, sipping the drink slowly as she considered what to say next. She needn't have bothered, as Liam plowed through the opening she'd provided.

"There aren't civil words strong enough to accurately convey my feelings toward the groom," he snapped.

"Good thing you're not the one marrying him, then." The words hung between them before falling with an inaudible *splat*.

"No, I'm not." He stood, brushing invisible lint

off his shorts before tugging at his linen shirt. "But the most important person to me in the whole world is, and she deserves better."

"Is she happy?" Ella asked quietly, the knots that had unraveled beginning to bind themselves all over again just behind her belly button.

Liam slipped his sunglasses on and looked at her, eyes blocked by the dark lenses. "If he's not good enough for her, if all he's doing is riding her coattails to fame and fortune, does it matter?"

She opened her mouth to answer, but he waved her off, spun and, with a spine that appeared totally unbending, stalked away.

Despite the fact that he couldn't hear her answer, she offered it anyway. "I'd be willing to bet it matters the world to her."

Liam stomped into the bungalow, his insides a bloody riot of opposition. He wanted to throttle himself for thinking he could disrupt a wedding by giving poorly placed and outright gaudy suggestions.

He wanted to strangle Mike Feigenbaum when he got off the plane. Liam would send the body to some remote region to be dumped. He had the funds to pay people who knew people.

He stumbled to a halt. Sweet mother of God, what was he thinking? He'd never order a murder even under the worst of conditions.

Doesn't this qualify—breaking a deathbed vow?

He shook the thought off and then stilled as he realized what he really wanted to do: grab Ella

Montgomery and run. He wanted to stay in bed with her for a week, to talk and make love and order room service and, shockingly, talk some more. Everything about her calmed him. She was the counterbalance to his personal crazy, and he craved her nearness, hungered for her touch, longed for the scent of her perfume on his pillow. All that and more. So much more. Emotions he refused to look at head-on and was unwilling to name thundered around him in a war chant, demanding he take up the fight to win her, claim her and, above all, keep her.

But it would never happen. Liam wasn't programmed for happily-ever-afters. Hell, he was trying to stop that very thing from happening because if life had taught him anything, it was that fairy tales were best suited to paperbacks and afternoon matinees. They didn't hold a place in the real world because *they weren't real*.

He'd seen friends marry and divorce and become bitter shells of their former selves.

He'd seen heartbreak and hurt in abundance, but never had he seen that thing called love, *romantic* love, rise above any given situation and conquer all.

It simply didn't happen.

Loyalty was a far more desirable trait. Tangible. Reliable. Measurable.

Liam rolled shoulders gone tight with that bevy of emotions. What lay ahead of him was a combination of obligation and love of family. That kind of love could be compared to loyalty, and Liam was comfortable with that. It was, after all, the characteristic he valued most.

The latch on the door snicked open, and Liam turned, expecting housekeeping. What he found was a wedding planner, arms overflowing with fresh flowers and a flush of sun on her skin.

"Hey. I wanted to tell you I didn't mean for us to part like that earlier. I really—oomph!"

He crossed the room and pulled her into his arms, crushing delicate blooms between them so that the spicy fragrances swirled around them like nature's perfume. His mouth found hers and swallowed her gasp of surprise even as one hand grabbed her ass to pull her closer and the other hand relieved her of the floral bounty. One word repeated through his mind.

Mine.

There were whispers of other words, words he'd spent the last hour denying.

Liam didn't care.

The only thing that mattered was finding the solace he'd been so sure he could do without. Solace only this woman offered him. He needed it like a diver needed air.

Their tongues dueled in the most intimate dance— thrust, parry, retreat. She met him move for move, never backing down, never giving him permission to take the lead. No, not this woman. She was fierce. A woman who held her own, and he found her strength, her determination, her give-as-good-as-she-got absolutely sexy as hell.

Her hands went to his chest and yanked at his

shirt. Buttons flew, plinking across the hardwood floor. She shoved the destroyed garment off his shoulders, her hands roving over his upper body with a possessiveness he'd never cared for...until now. She nipped his bottom lip before breaking the kiss, her mouth tracing his jaw, down his neck, between his pecs—all with stinging nips followed by soothing kisses.

A wildcat. That's what she was.

And he loved it.

Reaching his pants, she made an inarticulate sound of frustration when the tie at his board shorts knotted. He tried to help, but she pushed his hands away. Warm feminine hands and nimble fingers slipped underneath the waistband of his shorts and the fabric slithered down his legs, setting his cock free.

Ella dropped to her knees and, before Liam could say a word, she took the length of him in her mouth. Deep, so deep. The head of his cock bumped the back of her throat and she hummed around him with pleasure as he shouted out the same. She swallowed his length even deeper, cupping the ridged underside of his cock with her tongue as she worked him slowly, so slowly. Then she eased off and started all over again.

Clever fingers slipped up his legs, higher and higher until she parked one on his thigh for support and the other—

Liam shouted again, louder this time.

Ella gently cupped his balls, rolling them deftly

between her fingers as she squeezed tenderly and pulled on his sac. Never did she cease laving him from root to tip, cheeks hollowing as she sucked him deep, tongue working magic he had never fathomed she possessed.

Winding his hands through her hair, he found himself mesmerized by the sight of her kneeling before him, surrounded by the flotsam of scattered flowers. She'd spread her knees, bracketing his feet. Her hair mounded around his hands. Her breasts were lush. Sun kissed. He knew what they tasted like, knew the way her nipples felt as they pearled on his tongue. Knew the way her breath hitched if he drew a bit stronger, if he let his lips pluck at the hypersensitive skin before letting go to breathe cool air across their tips.

He was torn between wanting to experience Ella's gifted mouth and wanting to lose himself in the pleasures of her body. Watching her for another moment made up his mind.

He reached down and lifted her chin.

She let his cock go with a soft sound of disapproval.

"Up," he ordered.

"Bossy bastard. I'm not done."

"While I appreciate your damn fine skills, we'll get there together or not at all." He let go of her hair to grasp her arms and pull her to her feet. Their mouths fused once more, her lips swollen, and he pulled her close, groaning when she shimmied out of her bikini bottoms without breaking the kiss.

Wrapping a long leg around his waist, she ground

her sex against his. His grip on her tightened as her desire slickened his shaft. Passion fogged his mind.

"Take me to bed, Liam."

"As my lady commands."

Without warning, he swept her up in his arms, grinning at her alarmed squeak. He delivered her to the bed, setting her down with tender care, and left a trail of kisses in his wake as he moved up her body. They fit together like two pieces of a puzzle, his cock nestled against the apex of her thighs, his forearms resting comfortably on either side of her shoulders.

She wrapped one leg around him and, with a swift push-pull, reversed their position so she straddled him.

Resting his hands on her hips, he stared up at her. "My body is yours, Ella."

A shadow crossed her face, so fleeting he half wondered if he'd imagined it, particularly when she took his hands and moved them to cup her breasts. But he knew what he'd seen. "What's wrong, love?"

She shook her head, her hair tumbling around her shoulders. "Not a thing."

Rising, she let him slip the condom on before she took over again, gripping his cock at the base and positioning him between her slick folds. With careful control, she slid down his length, her heavy-lidded gaze locked on his.

Liam took hold of her hips and thrust up, the move driven by sheer instinct.

She squeezed her thighs around his hips. Hard. "Uh-uh. I'm in control here. Patience."

He growled, the sound reverberating deep in his chest. Patience wasn't what he was after. He wanted fast, hard, blank-the-mind sex. He wanted to make love to her with mind-numbing results. Instead, she was the one working him over, demanding his body acquiesce to her demands, attentions, skills. Then she wrecked him.

"Let me take care of you."

She rose on her knees so high that the very tip of him nearly slipped free, then she sank back down. Every inch she took was pleasure paired with pain. The tight grip of her sheath stole his control and he bucked.

Again, she squeezed her thighs around his hips.

The urge to protest tripped over his tongue, but she placed a finger on his lips at the same moment he started to speak. "Hush, Liam. Let me."

So he did. Relaxing the hold he had on her hips, he lay back and gave her something he'd given no woman before: absolute control.

Ella rode him, slow and sure, until a fine sheen of sweat broke out over her skin. It shone in the afternoon sun, casting an ethereal look over every inch of her body. Running her hands up her torso as she rose and fell, she cupped her breasts and then tweaked her nipples.

Liam shuddered beneath her, twisting his hips in an effort to be still as she took him all the way inside her.

"Do that again," she said, voice husky with passion.

He hadn't meant to move that way, but if she

wanted more of that? Yeah, he could give her what
she wanted.

Hands on her hips, he let her set the pace, occa-
sionally twisting his hips as directed. Every time he
did, her core tightened around him to the point her
sex gripped his cock like a damn vise. The urge to
give her what she wanted warred with his need to
drive into her, to force the orgasm she was dragging
out for both of them, to make her scream his name
to the heavens.

She must have been on the same page because,
without warning, she leaned forward, parked her
hands on his shoulders and began to ride him in ear-
nest. Sounds of hard, fast sex—skin on skin, harsh
breaths, little moans—saturated the air, filled his
head and dominated his awareness. There was only
this moment, only this woman, only one possible
outcome.

Liam's balls drew up tight. Release roared toward him, and he was a slave to its timing. But he
could—*would*—bring her with him. Reaching between them, he found her clitoris and stroked in time
with the pace Ella set. She faltered before increasing
her speed, pumping harder, digging her fingers into
his shoulders until her nails scored his skin. Her eyes
widened a fraction, and Liam struck.

Knees bent, he pitched her forward at the same
time he pinched that bundle of nerves between two
fingers and strummed it with his thumb. He rolled
his hips and drove into her, meeting her thrust for
thrust.

Ella's head fell back and she called out his name.

Liam increased the tempo even more, thrilling as she lost control and called out his name.

Hair loose and wild, she let go of his shoulders and reached back, gripping Liam's knees as she ground her sex against him, taking him as deep as she could. Her cry was magnificent, seeming to originate from the very heart of her before flinging itself free without a care as to who heard her or what they might think.

Liam's own release ripped through him, boiling out of the tip of his cock as if she'd summoned it.

Nothing had been this good. This right. This whole. Not ever.

Ella was brilliant, wild, so fucking alive he couldn't look away. She was everything.

And he was lost.

CHAPTER TEN

STORM CLOUDS DOMINATED the horizon, obscuring the setting sun as Ella stepped out of the shower. Body lax, muscles loose, she toweled off and wrapped up her hair atop her head. There were a dozen different things she needed to focus on, but her first priority was sorting herself out.

She and Liam had been right on the cusp of falling into each other earlier when Liam had said four words—just four words—that had shredded Ella's heart. *My body is yours.* His body. And only his body. She'd realized then that she wanted more. Not that she had any right to any of him, particularly after they'd agreed this was a fun-while-it-lasted affair. No strings. No regrets. Hell, she'd even given herself a stern talking-to a couple days ago about keeping things light and enjoyable until they left the island.

But somewhere in there, she'd begun to feel... something. What that something was, she couldn't be sure. Not yet. And with the way Liam viewed relationships, not ever. That meant Ella needed to stick to her initial ground rules or remove herself from the equation altogether.

Touching her fingertips to the tops of her breasts, she watched the peaks swell and rise, and she wondered if she could actually give him up. He loved her body like no one ever had. He made her tremble with a single word, yearn for his touch, forget how to breathe, come apart on command. She was the instrument to his virtuoso. Her sex throbbed, a sweet ache of memory.

His form filled the doorway, mouth fluttering at the corners in a half smile. "And I was under the impression I'd done a thorough job so you wouldn't need to supplement my efforts."

She dropped her hands and shrugged, looking away as she unwound the towel from her head. "Condition check. Nothing more."

"Everything okay?"

She smiled at him in the mirror. "You'll be pleased to know you left everything in working order." Grabbing her brush, she began working the tangles from her wet mass of hair. Sometimes she loved having naturally wavy hair; others, not so much. Like now. She pulled a little too hard and winced.

"Here," he said, closing in behind her and taking the brush. "Sit. Let me."

She sat on the vanity stool, body vibrating, heart numb. How could she possibly keep her emotional distance if he was going to do things like brush her hair? That certainly wasn't some random act of kindness. It was blatant intimacy, the one thing he had kept out of their interactions.

Except the dance on the beach.

Except for ordering breakfast served on the porch.

Except carrying you to the bedroom.

Her heart ached like a bad tooth, and she fought the need to rub her chest and soothe the discomfort that bordered on pain. It wasn't like this could be serious anyway. People didn't fall for each other this fast. Not if it was real. Infatuation? Sure. She had that in spades. And, if she were honest, she'd had *that* particular affliction since he'd landed on her lap on the plane.

If her feelings for him were serious, she'd be... what? What would she be feeling that would be any different than what she felt now?

Ella's breath caught.

She was so not falling for Liam Baggett, brother of Hollywood's darling, famous in the world of finance, infamous among socialites as the unattainable, unchainable bachelor. Yeah, she'd looked him up this afternoon. Article after article labeled him a jet-setting playboy, a millionaire so many times over even *Time*'s Top 100 had lost count, a shark in the boardroom and a lover of women worldwide.

I'm one of those women.

It shocked her that it stung to be one of ten, twenty, fifty, one hundred women he'd called "lover." She'd had affairs before, but she'd never become so emotionally involved that she struggled with the inevitable end.

Liam paused behind her. "What's with the long face?"

She forced herself to smile. "My face is oval, thank you. Not long."

"Talk to me, Ella." The quiet command hung there, his eyes on hers in the mirror.

"If you don't get the tangles out before it dries, my hair turns into a giant nest that will haunt me until I shower again."

He began brushing. "Don't hide from me."

"I'm sitting right here. Naked, in fact." She smiled brighter but couldn't maintain eye contact, instead leaning forward to reach her moisturizer. Removing the lid, she scooped out a dollop and slapped it on her face, rubbing in the expensive cream with brisk, sweeping strokes.

"Ella," he said in that warning tone of his.

As if she were a child to be admonished.

She huffed out a sharp sigh. "Leave it alone, Liam. I'm fine."

He paused. "There's this look on your face—"

"That's probably because I keep thinking about the metric shit ton I have yet to accomplish before this wedding." He opened his mouth to say something else, likely to press if she knew him at all. Reaching back, she held his wrist. "Let it go, Liam. I'm stressed. That's all."

"Don't regret the time we've spent together." A command couched as a request.

"I don't," she said, fighting for a normal tone and nearly succeeding. She tried not to focus on the words he hadn't spoken—that their time was limited, that they had best make the most of what was left—over what he'd said.

"Neither do I." He stared at her for what felt like an eon before handing her the brush. "I need to answer a few emails from the London office. Shouldn't take more than an hour. Join me for dinner when I've finished?"

She considered, thinking how nice it would be to have a quiet dinner with him, to get to know him better, to discover who he was beneath the polish and responsibilities. And she realized she'd only be setting herself up to fall harder.

"I shouldn't," she said around the bitter regret lodged in her throat. "I have so much to do before Jenna and Mike get here."

"You…we…have another full day. Dinner, Ella." He rested his hands along her jaw, gently turned her face toward the mirror and waited until she had no choice but to look at him. "Please."

She might not know Liam well, but she knew enough to be sure he didn't use that word often.

"Say yes." Again with that half smile.

She debated with herself, going back and forth as she rapidly created a mental list of pros and cons. But then Liam leaned in and sealed his mouth over hers in a persuasive kiss.

He broke the kiss but his lips still caressed hers when he spoke. "Dinner, Ella. One meal where we're just a couple of people on holiday. No talk of the wedding or my work or anything remotely related."

She looked into eyes fringed with dark lashes—

eyes she'd seen amused, angry, aroused—and she answered the way she'd known she would from the beginning.

"Okay."

A quick buss of the lips and he was walking out of the bathroom, calling over his shoulder, "I'll meet you back here in an hour."

"Make it two," she called after him.

If she was going to do this—go on a date with this man—she was going to make sure he remembered everything about her. From what she wore to what she didn't, she would etch herself into his memory.

It was only fair seeing as he'd already done the same to her.

Liam had sent word via a runner asking Ella to meet him at the head of the beach path nearest the main pavilion. The runner had returned with the message she'd be there. But she was late. Fifteen minutes, to be exact. Every second felt like ten. Every soft footfall against the boardwalk had him searching the evening shadows for her. And then she was there, rounding the bend with the resort lights behind her creating a nimbus around her lithe form.

She wore a short, sleeveless dress in a green silk that was so dark it appeared black in the shadows. Around her throat was a black choker with a single diamond-encrusted emerald in the center. Matching earrings hung from her ears. The sides of her hair had been pulled up to a loose knot at the crown of her head, leaving waves hanging down her back. The style emphasized her natural beauty. Whatever makeup she wore was understated and enhanced her elegant features. Her tan legs were bare. Dark stilettos with heels so high she moved in a hip-swinging strut made him want to forgo dinner and have her for dessert. His cock was ready to place that order.

She stopped a couple feet short of him. The air carried the hint of her perfume, a scent he would always associate with her—earthy with a floral undertone, so bold yet feminine.

He wanted to tell her she looked amazing, but the words were lost, carried away by the flood of testosterone raging through his veins. Every thought in his head involved her, him and a Do Not Disturb sign on a door that would remain locked for the next three days.

She arched a brow. "Either I'm overdressed or I look like hell and you're trying to find a nice way to say it."

"I've been trying... That is, there aren't words..." Liam cleared his throat. Twice. When he finally spoke, the words were gruff, one hand reaching for her. "Come here."

She laughed then and stepped forward, allowing him to pull her into a warm embrace.

On the patio nearby, a quartet struck up soft dinner music. Liam spun Ella away from him and brought her back, turning her in slow circles, watching her carefully.

She looked up at him, then tilted her chin even farther and stared at the night sky. "What?"

"I'm trying to figure out what's different about you tonight."

"Nothing."

"Not true. There's an air about you, something less…intense, maybe? Different, definitely."

"My give-a-damn broke."

"Pardon?"

She laughed, softer this time.

He couldn't help but think that, if he had to name the color of her eyes tonight, it would be Somber Green in Starlight.

When did I become such a bloody maudlin poet? Next thing, I'll need a cigarette and bottle of cheap wine as I tap out bad rhymes on a run-down laptop.

"So what broke your give-a-damn? I didn't even know that was a real thing," he teased.

"Oh, it absolutely is. And you, Mr. Baggett, will be receiving a bill for breaking it. Shattering it, really."

His brows shot up. "Me?"

"You."

"How?"

"You invited me to dinner without work as a buffer."

"I fail to follow your logic."

She stopped following his lead, forcing him to cease the intimate dance he'd begun. Moving out of his arms, she took a few steps down the cultivated path, stopping where the sand began. Ella, one hand on a palm tree, balanced on one foot and then the other as she removed her shoes. Then she headed toward the beach.

"Ella, stop."

A short glance back and she did as he bade.

It took him a second to catch up to her. Toeing his dress shoes off, he retrieved them in one hand and took hers with the other. "I had dinner set up on..." He paused, surprised to find he didn't want to ruin the romance of the moment he'd spent the last hour creating. "Would you do me the honor of allowing me to escort you to our table?" She started to put her shoes back on, but he stopped her. "You won't need those."

One of the event staff approached with a small basket extended. "For your shoes. They'll be returned to your bungalow, Ms. Montgomery, Mr. Baggett."

Curiosity made her tuck her chin in, but she handed her shoes over without comment.

Liam did the same and then reclaimed her hand. "This way."

He led her down the beach and around a bend to a private cove. There, a teak daybed had been set up complete with a champagne bucket staked in the sand, bottle open and chilling. Flowers were scattered across the daybed, and a plate of hors d'oeuvres sat near the foot. A blanket lay artfully over a top corner. At least four dozen large pillar candles were scattered about, their flames whipping in the slight breeze. The flickering candlelight made the night feel more alive and yet more secluded, like they were miles from civilization. On a portable table, four silver domes—two large, two small—covered the meals the chef had prepared.

Ella paused, seeming to take it all in. She didn't say anything, but her hold on Liam's hand tightened.

He would have given anything to know exactly what that squeeze was meant to convey. Irritation? Surprise? Joy? Anxiety? Too many options ran through his head. She'd reduced him to this person he'd never been, someone who sought the approval of another, someone who wanted nothing more than to make his lover understand what she meant to him.

He'd been unable to articulate that and so much more, so he'd tried to show her.

He squeezed her hand back after several more seconds.

Still, she was silent.

And he broke. "For the love of God, woman, would you say something?"

Her eyes sparkled as a wicked grin spread across her face. "Something."

The single whispered word took a moment to register. When it did, Liam let go of her hand and doubled over with laughter. He couldn't catch his breath. No one was that ballsy with him, pushing him when he was so clearly on edge. He loved that about her, that she refused to let him intimidate her. She was perfect the way she was.

The sobering thought stole the last peal of laughter, cutting it short.

...*loved that about her*, he'd thought. *Perfect the way she was.*

Too much was happening at once.

"Liam, I can't believe you did this."

"Neither can I," he said. Liam had discovered the one woman who possessed the ability to convince him love might exist after all.

And after the last-minute wedding changes he'd made late this afternoon, love might not be enough to save them.

CHAPTER ELEVEN

ELLA HADN'T REALIZED that Liam could be quite so charming. While they ate, he was as entertaining as he was attentive, asking about her childhood and telling her stories of his boarding school days and, later, tales that involved a younger American half sister who wanted nothing more than to be one of the boys—right down to her poorly imitated British accent.

"My mates would chuckle at her behind her back, but Jenna knew. She'd get so cross she would stomp her feet and threaten to divest them of their bollocks long before she knew what bollocks were."

He'd been so descriptive that Ella could imagine the pigtailed girl's tantrums. "Where did she get the idea bollocks were important?"

"I'm quite sure, us being strapping young lads with quite exaggerated prowess where young ladies were concerned, that she heard us bragging."

"As boys…and men…are wont to do," she added.

He tipped his wineglass toward her in unspoken agreement. "She's a smart girl—always has been.

She'd have figured out that, whatever bollocks were, we valued ours greatly, so why not threaten to take what we clearly held in highest esteem?" He laughed then, eyes warm with love for the girl his sister had been. "And what of you, Ms. Montgomery? Any siblings?"

"I was an only child."

"Ever wish for siblings?"

"All the time." She sipped her wine, opening her mouth to accept a piece of fruit Liam offered. Exotic flavor burst across her tongue, something similar to cantaloupe but with a slightly softer aftertaste.

Head canted to the side, he considered her. "Would you have had a brother or a sister?"

"One of each, if I'd been able to choose, and I'd have been the baby."

"And if you could only have one?"

"A sister, hands down."

Liam clutched his heart with his free hand and furrowed his brow. "A shot to the heart of all mankind. A brother would have looked out for you. What would a sister have done but steal your dolls and borrow your clothes?"

"Since it's my perfect world, my sister would have been my best friend. Older than me, she would have had all kinds of worldly advice about men, clothes and—" she cringed "—makeup that would have spared me the humiliation of my seventh-grade yearbook photo."

"That bad?"

"Baby blue eye shadow and white lipstick immortalized together, forever." She raised her glass in a mock toast. "Top that."

"I share this with no one, so repeat it and I'll disavow any knowledge of this conversation before I hunt you down and—"

"Not a word." With two fingers, she made a zipping motion across her lips.

"I had my hair permed so I could style it like Donnie Wahlberg from New Kids on the Block."

Her laughter bubbled up and escaped, peal after peal. Nothing tempered her reaction as she considered this man first in perm rods, then with perm solution dripping around his hairline and, finally, using a plastic hair pick to gently tease out the curls of his new hairdo. "A...perm..."

"Oh, it gets worse."

"Worse?"

He grimaced. "The band was an American sensation, not so well known in the UK, and my stepmother's stylist didn't know who he was. First time around, I ended up looking quite like Weird Al. I believe it's called a bouffant?"

That did it. Ella handed him her wineglass before rolling onto her side and, clutching her aching stomach, laughing until she cried.

Liam set the glasses down on the side table, retrieved a cloth napkin and handed it over. "You mock me?"

"I don't need to," she gasped. "I'm sure your friends did quite well on their own."

He grinned and chuckled. "They took the mick out of me, that's for sure."

"Why in the world did you use your mother's hairdresser?"

"I could hardly go to a salon, now could I? All of thirteen and wanting to be cool. What if a girl from the area had seen me or, God forbid, been in having her hair done as well? Mum's hairdresser came to the house, so I had the privilege of being attended privately."

"And after? When she'd finished with your hair?"

"I may have been single-handedly responsible for the introduction of the ball cap into British society."

Ella flopped onto her back and dropped one arm over her face. She'd laughed so hard her belly hurt, grinned so wide her cheeks ached. "I can't imagine you like that. You're so polished now. So *GQ* in all the right ways."

"I'll take that as a compliment and respond simply by saying a good stylist goes a long way in making the man fit the mold."

Dropping her arm, she rolled her head to the side. "What mold?"

This time he didn't look at her when he answered. "The one my father expected I shoehorn myself into."

She rolled onto her side again, curling her knees so her feet tucked up behind her, her head resting on one arm. "He had expectations, I guess. Given that you came from society."

"Not just society, but high society. My lineage has been charted since the 1400s. My family tree has been propagated by arranged marriages and pruned by a pragmatic hand when things weren't just so. I was the only son, so my father was determined from my first breath that I'd carry on the Baggett legacy, and he raised me, groomed me, with that singular goal in mind."

"And if you didn't want to be a financial investment guru?" She waggled her hand at his quizzical look. "Or whatever it is you do."

The bed shifted slightly as Liam rolled onto his back and stared at the star-saturated night sky. "I was never given the option, Ella. Had I gone to him and said I wanted to be a teacher, he would have simply told me, 'Baggetts do not engage in common occupations.'"

"Teaching is far from common," she said a bit tartly. "My mom's a teacher."

"I'm not demeaning the occupation by any means." The short laugh that followed was decidedly bitter. "I had him to do that."

"So what did, or does, being a Baggett mean?"

"I was raised to understand that it meant loyalty at all costs. Behaving honorably, but 'honor' was measured by the outcome of one's choices, not by any bourgeois definition. Carrying on tradition no matter the cost. Carving out the most direct path to your success no matter whom you had to cross, run over or destroy to get to that end goal." He sighed.

"It meant doing your duty even at the cost of extinguishing your desire."

To hear him speak so calmly of a household with such dogmatic, patriarchal values simply crushed her. She wanted to comfort the child he'd been before the worst of the rules were instilled in—or inflicted on—him. He never had a chance to just be a boy, to get his Sunday clothes dirty, put frogs in his pockets or build forts out of cardboard boxes. Ella might not have had siblings, but she'd had friends. She had been encouraged to run and play and discover and dream, to figure out who she was and where she fit in the world. Happiness had been her parents' end goal for her. Nothing else had mattered. Certainly not to the extent that they would've robbed her of free will, enforced antiquated expectations on her contemporary lifestyle or forced her to follow in the footsteps of ancestors who were long since dead.

But nothing she said would change his past, and she had the distinct feeling that showing pity would force him, by conditioning, to defend his heritage. More specifically, his father.

Instead, she asked the only question she could think of. "Are you happy?"

He looked at her, really looked at her, and a slow smile carved its way across a face that had been bordering on solemn. "Right now? Very."

Her heart tumbled, and not because she rolled onto him and straddled his lap.

Not because his hands slipped up her bare thighs,

his thumbs discovering that she, too, could pull off the commando routine with aplomb.

Not because he said, "Gladly," when she whispered, "Take me to bed, Liam."

No, her heart tumbled because he'd given her more than a glimpse of who he was, where he came from and what had shaped him into the man he had become. Her heart longed for him in a way that was personal.

Intimate.

Profound.

And what she wanted from him was more than a love affair. She craved the thing she'd never wanted from another man. Not an affair of bodies but of hearts. The free-fall sensation she'd heard about, read about and listened to in songs her whole life. She wanted to feel her stomach wobble, her heart quake and her sense of reason dissolve. She wanted to fall in love.

As she took her own measure, checking off symptom after symptom, feeling after feeling, she realized she was already out of control—well and truly falling.

She could only hope Liam would catch her.

Linen sheets slid over Liam's body as he stretched, slowly coming awake. A glance at the clock surprised him with the late hour. Breakfast would be over. He'd have to make arrangements to have lunch brought in for Ella.

Ella.

He glanced over at the woman sprawled out beside him, the sun pulling rich highlights from her hair where it fanned out over her pillow. Last night seemed like a dream now, and if it weren't for the fact she was here he might wonder if he'd imagined the whole thing.

Conversation had flowed so easily. Hell, he'd even talked about his childhood—something he didn't do with anyone, even Jenna.

After hearing about how Ella had been raised—in a loving, happy home—Liam couldn't help but think she'd make an excellent mother. The kind who made a house into a home. Someone who'd bake cookies and have pillow fights but wasn't a pushover. A woman who would be able to act as parent and friend to her children.

He respected her even more than he had before, and that respect drove him out of bed, albeit silently, and had him pulling on his shorts before, shirt and shoes in hand, he tiptoed to the front door.

The pile of paperwork she'd left next to her computer caught his eye. Given what he was about to do, he thought it wise to lift the list he'd given her. Maybe he could amend a couple of items before giving it back to her. Nothing major, just…

Without trying to rationalize his actions, he slipped the stapled list free and stepped out the front door, closing it as quietly as possible. He shoved the papers in his back pocket and then finished dressing on the porch before heading toward the resort's main building. The one benefit to having slept in was that Arvin and his staff should be at work. Arvin would be Liam's best—only—chance of undoing what he'd done yesterday. And the lead guilt weighing on his shoulders meant he had to try.

Scanning the massive lobby, he didn't see Arvin anywhere. The event planner's area, right beside the concierge, was vacant. So he opted for the concierge instead.

"Good morning." The chipper young woman behind the desk smiled at him. "How has your stay been so far?"

"Excellent, thank you," Liam answered absently, scrubbing his hands through his hair. "Do you know where I might find Arvin?"

The woman affected a concerned look. "I'm sorry. Arvin is off island this morning retrieving some materials for a private event. He should be back by midafternoon, late afternoon at worst. May I leave a message for him?"

"Right. The event he's out for is actually mine."

"Congratulations," she said, beaming up at him.

"It's not…" He shook his head. "Never mind. Does he have any other staff on hand, anyone who might help me resolve an issue with a change I made to the event?"

"His staff is out this morning, running errands related to your event. However, I'll certainly have someone call you as soon as they're back."

"I really do need to—"

"Liam!"

He whipped around in time to catch the petite blonde who threw herself at him. His mouth opened and closed several times before he set the woman back. "What are you doing here?"

"Um… I'm the bride?" Jenna answered, laughter making her eyes sparkle.

"You're earlier than I expected."

"Liam."

The deep voice drew his attention to the man standing several paces away, arms crossed over his chest.

"Mike," he returned.

"Nice place," the groom said, looking around.

"It's perfect!" Jenna chirped. "I love it. It's exactly what I wanted. And everyone is so friendly." She stepped out of Liam's embrace only to slide an arm around his waist and snuggle into his side.

He instinctively settled an arm around her shoulders as he looked down. "I'm confused, Jenna. Your flight left New York yesterday with a long layover in Paris. I wasn't expecting you until tomorrow."

"Nope. We got to Paris so early that we were able to get seats on an earlier flight."

"The guy at the airline desk was a huge fan," Mike said, smiling down at his bride-to-be.

Liam tried to think, tried to put things in order, but his mind had blitzed out. Jenna was early, and Ella was going to flip out.

Ella.

Again, her name whispered through his mind like an invocation, his heart beating faster and breath coming a bit short.

"Liam?" Jenna asked as she wiggled in his embrace. "I mean, I know you're glad to see me and all, but you're going to bruise me if you clutch me any tighter."

"Apologies." He forced himself to relax and take a deep breath. Ella was going to flip her shit when she found out Jenna and Mike had arrived a day early.

"Mr. Baggett?"

The young lady from the concierge's desk held out a cordless phone. "I have Arvin on the line for you, sir."

"Thank you—" he glanced at her name tag "—Becky." Taking the phone, he stepped away from Jenna and Mike. "Arvin."

"What may I do for you, Mr. Baggett?"

Liam lowered his voice. "Arvin, my sister and her groom have arrived a day early. I need to know where you're at on the task I gave you yesterday."

Arvin swallowed so loud Liam heard it. "It's done, sir. It wasn't easy, but I do think you'll be pleased with the…results."

Stomach clenching hard, Liam lowered his voice further still. "I'm not certain it will be in the bride's best interest to have it done as I requested."

"I—I'm sorry, sir? Are you asking me to undo it?"

"Yes. That's exactly what I'm asking."

"It's temporary color, sir, but it won't wear off for several days."

Damn it.

"I'll figure something out, Arvin. Thank you."

"Yes, sir. I'll be back this afternoon and—"

"I'll see you then." Liam hastily disconnected as Jenna bounced over to him.

She poked him in the ribs. "I hope you weren't working."

"Uh, no. It was nothing." Handing the phone back to Becky, he smiled. "Thank you. It's all in order."

He turned back to Jenna. "So what would you like to do since you're here early?"

"I want to walk through everything for the wedding, see what it's going to look like." She grinned back at her fiancé beatifically. "It's going to be incredible, getting married in paradise. Perfect way to start our lives together."

"If it makes you happy." Mike moved closer and held his arms open.

Jenna slipped out from under Liam's arm and into Mike's embrace. She whispered something in his ear, and the man leaned down and kissed the top of her head. "You're footing the bill, so I'll shut up. Most important thing is that we end up husband and wife."

Liam bit back the caustic words that burned his throat. Mike had just confirmed what Liam most feared—that the minor league baseball player was, indeed, riding along on his sister's dime. And now the guy was officially a free agent, which was sports-speak for "unemployed."

Jenna deserved better than a tag-along kind of guy. She deserved someone who was her equal. Sure, Mike might be considered a handsome man, but there were issues beyond looks. Serious issues. Things like the guy's temper and his tendency to take his frustrations—*any* frustrations—out on Jenna. Add his just-confirmed financial leeching and it came together to equal one fundamental truth: the man wasn't remotely fit to be Jenna's husband.

If Liam were to compare Mike to, say, Ella, she would take the win in every category. She was far more loyal, driven and accomplished than the baseball player ever would be.

As if she'd heard his innermost thoughts, Jenna glanced up at Mike and said in a rebellious stage whisper, "I'm telling him."

Her groom rolled his shoulders, looking back and forth between his soon-to-be wife and future brother-in-law. "It hasn't hit the news, sweetheart."

"So? It's happening, Mike." She twisted inside his embrace and faced Liam. "Mike's been called up."

Liam's brows rose. "To what?"

"You're so British," she said, laughing. "The major leagues, Liam. He's been called up as their relief pitcher. He'll be going to spring training with the team."

"I assume that comes with a paycheck." He stared at the other man, who simply stared back.

"A good one."

"And what, exactly, is 'good' in your ledger? Does 'good' provide for my sister under any and every circumstance?"

"Liam!"

Mike moved in front of Jenna, all but physically shoving her aside. "What the hell is your problem, Baggett?"

"Problem?" Liam laughed out loud. "It begins, and ends, with you."

"Stop it." Jenna's hissed command was ignored until she wedged herself between the two men. "Just stop it. This is my wedding."

"Our wedding," Mike corrected, his sharp tone cutting through the air.

She shot him a look. "Our wedding." Rounding on Liam, she drove a finger into his chest. "You need to stop provoking Mike. Now. And I don't want either of you ruining the wedding with this bullshit posturing and chest thumping. Do you hear me?"

"I wouldn't dream of it," Mike said softly before kissing the top of her head.

Liam said nothing.

Jenna glared at him.

Silence.

Mike broke into what was fast becoming a battle of wills. "The concierge was able to get us into rooms early. Some family ended up having to go home early, so we're taking their rooms until the ceremony, when we'll be moved to the honeymoon suite."

Liam almost choked.

Mike continued, unaware. "Let's go check out our rooms, unpack and get settled in. Then you can call Liam, maybe have him introduce us to the event coordinator you hired. She can show us around."

"Sounds good." Jenna's words were tight. She grabbed the handle of her carry-on bag and walked away. She stopped after several feet, seemed to think something over, then turned back to Liam. "Don't be a dick, brother mine." Then she gave him her back and stalked across the expanse of tile floor to the elevator bank, where she jabbed the Up button several times.

"Wouldn't dream of it," Liam muttered.

"Good," Mike said. "Do *not* ruin this for her…or you'll answer to me."

The warning couldn't have been any clearer.

Liam wanted to respond with his own warning, to tell this clown that he knew why the guy was marrying Jenna, but all Liam could do was stare and say nothing at all.

They wanted to see what was in store for their wedding. But what they were going to encounter over the next twenty-four hours would show Jenna exactly what type of man Mike was. Because watching Mike physically move Jenna aside, speak over her, tell her how they'd handle check-in followed by the suggestion that Ella could show them around, thus bypassing Liam?

No. To all of it, no.

Liam could only hope for two things. First? He hoped Jenna would understand what he'd done to make her see the truth about Mike's character…or lack of.

And second, he had to hope Ella would forgive him and accept his efforts to make amends when the wedding went straight to hell in handbaskets she'd decorated.

CHAPTER TWELVE

ELLA WAS UP to her elbows in fresh flowers. She loved floral arranging and had taken on some of those duties as a sort of indulgence. Designing was cathartic, forcing her to focus on the flowers and their shape and size and smell, the orientation of each bloom and the way they were placed for maximum impact.

Working beside her was a master baker who was applying fondant to the cake for tomorrow night's rehearsal dinner. Both this cake and the wedding cake would be adorned with floral toppers made by Ella herself.

She'd just placed a water pick on a bird of paradise stem when her cell buzzed. Gently setting the flower down, she dug her phone out of her back pocket. The display showed a number she didn't recognize. "Ella Montgomery."

"Don't panic."

"Any time you tell someone not to panic, Liam, it's the first thing they do. Hold on a second. I need to step outside." She waved at the baker and mouthed, "Be right back." Maneuvering around the work space, she made it to the side door and stepped into the sunshine. The air felt warm, especially after working in what was essentially a cooler. A bloom of sweat decorated her hairline, and she rubbed it off with the back of her forearm. "Go ahead. Tell me what I'm not supposed to panic over."

When Liam spoke, the urge to scream welled up in her throat, choking off her air and, with it, any ability to respond.

"Did you hear me, Ella? Jenna and Mike are here."

She nodded as she tried to force her lungs to work, her mouth to open, her lips to form words. "When you say 'here,' what exactly do you mean?"

"I'm not sure there's another way to interpret 'here.' They've checked in to their rooms, are currently getting settled in and would like to do a walk-through of the event this afternoon," Liam bit out.

"You know, if I'm not allowed to panic, you don't get to be an ass," she retorted.

"I'm not being... Never mind. The point is, they want you to take them through the rehearsal plans and ceremony setup. They're calling me after they've unpacked their bags and want me to perform introductions."

"I'm not ready! I was supposed to have another day! There are some key things I need to finish before I can do a proper walk-through with them!" She fought the suffocating panic that ballooned in her chest.

"What would you have me do, Ella?"

There was no good answer. "Buy me some time and I'll find a stopping place here. Can you do that— entertain them, walk the resort, something? Just let me finish this bouquet and I'll meet you in the lobby in—" she looked at her watch "—an hour. What have they asked to see today?"

"They want to see what you've put together. All of it. Jenna's excited."

The tone of his voice told her he was anything but.

Yanking at the tie that held her hair up in a loose topknot, Ella dropped her phone. A wide crack split the screen corner to corner. "Shit," she snapped. Retrieving her phone, she looked it over. Hopefully, it would keep working until she could get home and replace it.

"What's wrong?"

Hysterical laughter rose up the back of her throat and emerged as a croak. "Everything is wrong, Liam. If you're asking what just happened? I broke my phone. It's one more expense I don't need, one more thing I'll have to pay for because I can't do without it. And you're calling, asking me to do the walk-through when only half of what needs to be done is actually *done*."

"Ella, I can't do this for you."

"I'm not asking you to. I'm asking you to stall them, Liam. Make small talk over drinks until I can pull together a walk-through that won't leave them regretting the choice to hire me."

Swallowing past the almost debilitating fear, she closed her eyes and focused on her breathing.

"Ella?"

"Just…give me a second."

She ran through the list of things that had been fully prepped, things she could share with the bride and groom. There were excursions to walk through, the menu, entertainment, the ceremony site. She could call Arvin and get him to set up a taste test of the wedding dinner. All that would take up the rest of the day. There would be plenty of time to finish the flowers tonight. Then tomorrow she could actively manage the guest excursions and the rehearsal, see the couple and their guests through the rehearsal dinner, and, finally, put the finishing touches on the wedding ceremony and the reception. The end was in sight. She just had to push through and get there in one piece.

The initial shock having passed, she took a deep breath and relayed her plan to Liam.

"That's fine. Jen and Mike will meet you in the lobby. What time?"

"I said an hour. I'll stick to that. After I've finished here, I'll grab my portfolio so I'll be able to show them the sketches. That'll help them visualize what the actual ceremony will look like. Otherwise? They'll be wholly dependent on my descriptions to fill in the blanks."

"I'll be there."

"You're coming, too?"

"I want to support my sister no matter the outcome."

"'No matter the outcome?'" she parroted. "What does that mean?"

"Poor choice of words. I'll see you shortly."

An odd feeling settled low in her gut. "Don't screw this up, Liam."

"Pardon?"

"Just…forget it. I'll see you in a little while."

A single tap on her cracked screen and the call disconnected. She finished the bouquet and headed back to the bungalow, thankful that her phone at least worked. She'd struggled with this event so much she'd begun to think the universe hated her, but maybe—just maybe—she was wrong. Maybe the universe didn't hate every cell in her being.

Just most of them.

Liam stood on the balcony just off the lobby. Jenna and Mike were several steps away, their heads together as they whispered, laughed and sneaked kisses. They were trying to stay away from the main foot traffic at the resort, but they'd insisted they wanted to get a feel for the ambience and see some of the decor.

Mike said something to Jenna and she laughed, a low, throaty sound that moviegoers worldwide would recognize. Liam looked over to find them slow dancing on the balcony.

"Get a room."

"We got two," Mike said, sotto voce.

"I'm sure Jenna did."

Mike stilled.

Jenna turned and looked from one man to the other. "What? What did I miss?"

Tension built until it crackled on the air like a summer storm. Mike didn't look away from Liam when he answered. "Your brother's suggesting I'm a gold digger."

Jenna's eyes flashed with anger. "Liam? What is wrong with you?"

"Just protecting your assets, sister."

"My assets are mine, Liam. I'll do as I please with them. That means if I want to invest in an alpaca farm in Nepal, you'll smile and wish me good returns. Likewise, if I want to pay for my own wedding, you don't have a say in that choice."

Liam clenched his jaw tight, but it wasn't enough to stop his damning judgment from spilling out. "No? Fine. But your choice doesn't change my opinion. I'd rather you had someone willing to carry his own weight in the relationship."

Mike took a step forward. "And how do you know I don't?"

Liam's laugh was so bitter it left an aftertaste. "How do I know? You certainly didn't buy that designer three-carat bauble on her finger on a farm league salary. You moved in to her place instead of her moving in to yours. You're driving her cars everywhere you two go. You were unemployed and now claim to be moving up to the big leagues, but it hasn't hit the trade papers. Need more examples?"

"You have no idea what I make or what I'm worth."

Liam arched a brow, his sole intent to piss the other man off. "It so happens that I do. Your farm salary was reported in the trade papers. The right word in the right ear and I found out what your endorsements paid. Added together? Your value isn't even half of what Jenna makes for a single film. I can't imagine it has improved since you quit."

"You son of a bitch," Mike spat, starting for him.

Ella cleared the large French doors just then, taking in the situation. In one fluid move, she stepped between Liam and Mike, extending her hand to the groom. "Hello. You must be Mike Feigenbaum, the lucky groom. I'm Ella Montgomery, your event coordinator."

Mike drew up, social custom and common courtesy partnering to halt what would likely have been a bloody good fight. Liam watched as the other man shook Ella's hand and forced a tight smile. "Nice to meet you, Ms. Montgomery."

"Please call me Ella." Then she turned to Jenna. "And you, Ms. Williams, are even more beautiful in person than on screen, which I wouldn't have believed possible. It's lovely to finally meet you. Your brother has spoken so highly of you."

"It's lovely to meet you as well, Ms. Montgomery... Ella." Jenna smiled the smile she used for publicity shots, paparazzi and interviews. "And while it's good to know Liam has spoken so highly of me, I'd be more interested in hearing what he's had to say about my groom."

Liam didn't miss Jenna's word choice—*my groom*.

Ella didn't miss a beat. "He's been nothing but complimentary of the choices you and Mike have made for your wedding. Beyond that, he's said that your happiness is the most important thing in the world to him."

The tension around them fractured into a thousand pieces that the trade winds carried away.

Liam was dumbfounded, watching Mike and Jenna relax into each other as Jenna's smile morphed into the one reserved for friends and family—the *real* smile. Mike became engaging and, damn it all to hell, charming as well. Liam couldn't say what it was Ella had done, but her presence, her word choices, her approach—all of it had defused a situation that was fast devolving into something that would have made the papers.

The papers.

Jenna had been most clear about that—she didn't want news outlets carrying the story of her wedding or gossip rags featuring it on their covers. She'd been so worried about that one specific thing, and he'd nearly brought it down on her head.

He owed Jenna, at the very least, an apology. He stepped forward a fraction of a second after Mike took her hands and claimed her attention, face solemn.

"I owe you an apology, sweetheart. I let Liam bait me even after you asked me to keep my cool. I nearly caused a scene when I know you don't want anything to draw attention to us being here. I'm so damn sorry, baby. It won't happen again." He kissed her then, gently but thoroughly, before stepping away.

Flushed, Jenna smiled up at Mike. "Thanks, baby. I know he can be a lot to handle at times. He'll get better." The "or else" was implied. Heavily.

"I'm sure Mr. Baggett didn't intend to start a fight," Ella started, but Liam waved her off.

"No, Ella. Mike is right. I baited him. I'll not do it again."

Mike and Jenna nodded, but neither spoke.

Ella gestured toward the stairs that led to the resort's largest lawn and a raised garden that was framed in hedges and looked out over the ocean. "Let's head down to the garden, and we can discuss the rehearsal and ceremony."

Jenna and Mike started out ahead, Liam falling in step with Ella just behind them. "That was well done of you. Thanks."

She barely spared him a glance. "It was clear there was about to be bloodshed."

"Without a doubt."

"Why didn't you just apologize?" she asked. "It's the least you could do given that this is their big day."

"I beg your pardon," he snapped. "I bloody well did apologize."

"No, Liam. You didn't. You said you shouldn't have baited Mike."

"And?"

She sighed and shook her head, crossing her arms

under her breasts. "The words *I'm sorry* never passed your lips."

"She knows I meant it," he said, rationalizing his choice despite the voice in his ear that whispered Ella was right.

"It would have gone a long way with her, and him, to have heard those two words from you."

"I don't give a rat's ass what he thinks of me."

This time Ella laid a hand on his arm, forcing him to stop with her. "The thing is, Liam, this isn't about you or your decisions or your wants. This is about her—her future husband and the life they're about to build together."

The skin across Liam's shoulders grew tight. "He's not good enough for her."

"That's not your decision to make."

Her words, so softly delivered, set him back a step. "I want what's best for her."

"And you don't trust her to know what that is?" Ella countered.

"I've seen that man's true character, Ella. He has repeatedly talked over and around my sister. He has disrespected her in front of me, and I won't have it."

"How is what he's done so different from what you just did?"

"I love her!" he bit out.

Ella reached out and took one of Liam's hands, squeezing gently. "It would seem Mike does, too." She dropped his hand and then strode forward to catch up to the couple.

Liam stood there for several seconds, his mouth

hanging open like a fool's. Ella was absolutely right. He was no better than Mike. Liam had been presumptive, domineering, controlling and brash—all traits he'd criticized in the other man.

Could Ella be right? Could Jenna have found her miracle in this man who professed to love her? Could it be possible that he'd so severely underestimated Jenna's choices?

It seemed that he had.

Shaking off the stupor the truth had wrought in him, he strode toward the couple and their event coordinator. His lover. The woman who wasn't afraid to tell him the truth no matter the cost, and he vowed he'd make this right.

It dawned on him as he reached the steps to the garden that what they were about to encounter was as wrong as wrong could get. And he had no way to stop it.

CHAPTER THIRTEEN

ELLA WAS HALFWAY up the stairs when the scream hit her. She tripped up the last step and stumbled to a halt at the garden's back wall. Something pink darted left. Something darker pink darted right. And there, fifteen feet away, stood Hollywood's it girl, Jenna Williams, screaming as if an ax murderer was closing in. But it wasn't an ax murderer. It was…a peacock? No. It was a *pink* peacock.

Two.

Three.

Four pink peacocks ran amok, long tails flowing behind them.

And one, presumably the appropriately named cock, strutted toward Jenna, his red eyes sinister, his cotton candy–colored tail on full display, his head bobbing to and fro as if to mesmerize Jenna before slaying her.

Mike wrapped Jenna in his arms and looked about wildly.

Ella lurched forward as Liam crested the stairs and ran smack into her.

"What's going on?" she demanded.

"Where the hell did the peacocks come from?" Mike shouted, partly from obvious fury and partly to be heard above the bride's screaming and the birds' squawking.

Liam rushed past her and reached for Jenna, but Mike swung her up into his arms and carried her toward the nearest exit at a swift jog.

"Mike?" Ella called, following after them.

"She's terrified of birds, Ms. Montgomery," Mike bit out. "Actually diagnosed as ornithophobic. That's why the paperwork said 'Absolutely No Birds.' And why the hell did you dye them pink? Jenna is an animal activist, very vocal on animal rights and environmental preservation."

"I know. I didn't order the birds," Ella said, forcing herself to stand up straight and meet Mike's accusing stare.

Jenna peered up at her, tears having turned well-applied mascara into raccoon eyes. "Someone did, Ms. Montgomery, and there are only two people who would have. Liam, who knows I'm scared of birds, and you. I can't imagine Liam doing something like this when he knows I'm petrified of the things." She shuddered. "So who else would've done it if not you?"

"I don't know," Ella answered.

Looking around, she found Liam herding the last bird through the far exit and shutting the garden gate behind it. He turned and found them all staring. "They're contained, Jenna. The gate is locked.

They won't get out again. Mike, if you'd kindly remove my sister from the garden."

"I'm not leaving until I know who did this," Jenna said. "Liam wouldn't have."

"I have the paperwork here," Ella said. "Let me look at what your assistant filled out."

Mike consoled Jenna as Ella dug through her messenger bag. She'd left the paperwork in her bag last night, both copies, in fact—the original and the one with Liam's changes. But now the only one she could find was the one Jenna's assistant had originally sent over.

The groom said something soft in his future wife's ear, and she sagged against him, her sobs reduced to hiccuping little gasps. "Shh," he said gently. "I've got you. Deep breaths."

"I feel like such a fool," she said, voice muffled by his shirt. "Did anyone see me?"

Ella wanted to crawl into a hole and die. She hadn't ordered the peacocks, and certainly not *pink* peacocks, but she *had* ordered the flock of doves that were to be delivered tomorrow. Liam had made sure the order had been placed. She'd questioned him, referring to the "no birds" stipulation in the original paperwork, but he'd insisted his sister wanted the doves released. According to him, "no birds" meant she had wanted the area cleared of any indigenous animals—domesticated parrots, flocks of pelicans or whatever else might have been curated by the resort.

She'd done as he asked, but she'd kept the paperwork for reference.

Page after page, she flipped through the original paperwork. She finally came to the "Ceremonial Release Option," and there, in bold Sharpie next to the checkbox labeled "Birds," was the word *NO* in capital letters, underlined twice.

She wanted to vomit.

Instead, she grabbed her bag and dug through, determined—desperate—to find the copy Liam had provided, to redeem herself. But the copy he'd provided her wasn't there.

Mike must have been watching her, because he asked, "What's on the paperwork?"

Ella couldn't lie. God, she wanted to, but it went against everything she was.

"No birds," she answered, throat so dry she could've been labeled a fire hazard. She glanced over to where Liam stood. "I know there was something about a request for birds on the subsequent paperwork."

"Subsequent paperwork?" Mike asked.

Ella clarified. "The paperwork Liam, Mr. Baggett, provided."

"Liam didn't do it, Mike." Jenna looked up at him with doe eyes. "He wouldn't."

"Ms. Montgomery," Mike started, but Liam chose that moment to close the distance between them.

Liam reached out and gently touched Ella's arm, trying to gain her attention.

"Not now, Liam," she bit out.

"I'd like to see the paperwork."

"You've seen it plenty of times."

"Ella—"

"This is mine to fix, Liam. Somewhere, somehow, someone made a mistake. It appears that someone was me." She shrugged off Liam's hand and stepped toward Jenna. "I can only apologize profusely, Ms. Williams. I'll make this right and ensure there are no birds anywhere near the ceremony. You have my word."

"Why were they pink?" she asked, slipping into a hazy awareness. "I hate pink."

"I have no idea," Ella answered.

Jenna just looked at her, the accusation in her eyes unquestionable.

Ella's stomach was threatening a full-scale revolt. She swallowed several times before she was able to get her mouth to stop watering excessively and her eyes to stop tearing up. "I'm so sorry. We'll find out where the mistake was made. Perhaps it was for another wedding."

"Whatever the reason, I expect you to ensure nothing like this happens at the ceremony. I will not have our day destroyed by someone's mistake, no matter how innocent it allegedly was." Mike shifted his hold on Jenna. "I'm going to take her back to the room to clean up. We'll forgo the rest of the walk-through to give you time to make sure everything is in order. Guests begin arriving in the morning. Don't screw this up for us, Ms. Montgomery. If this goes well, it could make your career. If it goes poorly, it *will* ruin it. Don't make me regret hiring a relative unknown event coordinator."

And with that parting shot, Mike gently steered Jenna back toward the resort.

Liam laid a hand on Ella's arm. "I know—"

"No, Liam. *I* know. I know!" she shouted. She knew exactly who had ordered the peacocks. The same person who had encouraged her to include the dove release at the end of the ceremony. The only man who had the ability to authorize changes to the prewedding events. The man with the power to destroy her career without doing more than initialing changes he'd initiated on behalf of his sister. The only man she'd ever cared for so much that she'd overlooked changes she should have known better than to blindly accept.

Liam Baggett.

Liam had let Ella be, taking a walk along the beach to sort out the riot of emotions burning through him. He should have stepped up and taken responsibility for the bird debacle, but he hadn't. Planning on ruining the wedding had been one thing; seeing his plan come to fruition had been another.

When Jenna had experienced a full-blown panic attack this afternoon, Liam hadn't been able to make himself say the words. Accept blame. Look into his sister's eyes and tell her that he was the one who had scared her in the hopes her precious Mike would show his true colors.

Had he an ounce of chivalry, he'd have spoken up. But he hadn't. And he was disgusted with himself.

It had been seeing Ella step in and bear the brunt

of Mike's anger that gave his guilt a voice. Jenna might put up with that shit, but Liam wasn't going to allow Mike to treat Ella that way.

He'd stepped in, intent on clearing the issue up. But Ella had stopped him dead in his tracks. She shut him down, telling him, all of them, that she'd make it right. She'd fix the mistake, see the wedding through as promised and ensure there were no birds at the ceremony.

The least he could do was respect her wishes and let her save face by handling it as she saw fit.

He owed her that. That, and so much more.

He had to find a way to make it right for his sister and to salvage what lay between Ella and him. Part of his plan had failed in ways he hadn't been fully prepared for, but that didn't mean all was lost. There was still time to ensure Mike showed his true character before vows were exchanged. Liam would just have to be careful. He'd have to find a way to shield Ella as much as possible while still getting Mike to show Jenna he was the worst possible choice she could make. There was still the rehearsal and dinner. Time enough.

Standing on the bungalow's porch, his hand on the doorknob, Liam hesitated. Making the decision to go through the door and face Ella's anger was simple enough. It was her presumable disappointment in him that he didn't want to confront. So there he stood, the deep shade of early night settling around him, the winds stalling and the waves shushing. On the other side of the door, he heard Ella throwing things around with fervor, cursing his name with such creativity and thoroughness that it was clear she thought he and the devil himself were on a first-name basis.

With a deep breath, he turned the doorknob and stepped inside.

The one-bedroom suite was clean. As in, sparkling. No papers lay strewn about. No seating chart was tacked to the bulletin board. No computer with its portable printer sat on the desk. Nothing.

A shadow moved past the sliver of light that escaped through the bedroom door and door frame.

Ella.

Heart in his throat and pulse pounding out a heavy-metal drumbeat in his ears, he forced himself to knock.

She didn't answer, but he opened the door anyway.

Ella was packing. Or, in actuality, had already packed.

She let out a shout when she saw him. "You scared the shit out of me, Liam," she snapped, hand fluttering back and forth between her chest and throat like a hummingbird that wasn't sure where to land.

"I..." The word *sorry* hung up in his throat yet again. "You've packed."

"Brilliant observation." She shot him a bland look. "Next you'll tell me your London offices are at 221b Baker Street."

"Where are you going, Ella?" The question was

delivered with a quiet severity he managed only by keeping a fierce grip on his emotions—emotions that threatened to erupt in a bout of rage and desperation. She couldn't leave. If she left, he'd be forced to chase her down. His father's voice resonated through his head.

You're a Baggett, by God. You do not *lower yourself to such plebian behavior.*

"Ella?" he pressed when her silence broke through his father's posthumous rant.

"Away, Liam. I'm going away."

"Where? There aren't any rooms on the island."

"I've found a place."

"Where?"

She rounded on him then, all fury and fire. "Who the hell do you think you are, sabotaging my job and then demanding answers from me like I'm some bought-and-paid-for dinner date? Not to mention the fact that you stole my notes!"

"I didn't steal them," he ground out.

"What, you 'borrowed' them?" she asked, her air quotes exaggerated. "Couldn't keep up with all the shit you'd changed so you needed my paperwork to be in the right place at the right time to see this house of cards fall?"

"It wasn't like that." But nothing he could say would change her mind, and he knew it. Besides, part of her accusation stung with truth. Perhaps he'd wanted this more than he'd thought. "I don't want…" He tugged at the neck of his suddenly tight shirt.

"What, Liam? What is it you don't want so badly

that you'd destroy my career?" When he didn't answer right away, she shouted, "Tell me."

Something in Liam snapped, and the truth poured
out of him in a tsunami. Devastating. Unstoppable.
Catastrophic in force. "I don't want Jenna marrying
that son of a bitch, okay? She deserves better than
him. All he wants is her money, her fame—a key
to her house and her car and her heart. But what's
he giving her in return? What is it he brings to the
table, Ella? The answer is nothing. The man brings
nothing."

She stared at him, mouth slack with shock. "You're
standing in front of me telling me you truly believe
you're a better judge of what's best for your sister
than she is?"

"She's blinded by love, or what she thinks is love."

"Did you stop even once to think that maybe love
is *exactly* what she's found?"

"It's not possible."

"Why, Liam? Why couldn't she have fallen into
something beautiful and grand and promising? Tell
me. Convince me it's not possible."

"Because love isn't real, Ella!" The shouted words
echoed in the heart of who he was. "It's a figment
of imagination, something propagated by industries
like yours. You lie to people every day to get them
to buy in to the idea that there's this utopian life on
the other side of commitment where it's sunshine
and champagne every damn day, where people love
each other forever and no one ever leaves."

Ella looked so sad just then, standing there staring at him like she'd never seen him before. "You're wrong, Liam. So wrong. Love is a very real thing. And what I do isn't propagating a lie. It's celebrating a new beginning. It's rejoicing that you've finally found that one person who truly gets you. The person who always has your back. The one who will be there on Sunday morning so you don't have to do the crossword puzzle alone and when you need someone to hold back your hair because you're sick."

"So, if love is real, why is the divorce rate so high? Why are there a million country songs and rock ballads about heartache and loss? Why are there weekends with dads and visitations with moms for kids from divided households? Where's the power of love in these people's lives, Ella? Tell me, because I don't see it."

"It's right in front of you," she whispered. "People make bad choices sometimes, but—"

"Which is what I'm trying to prevent Jenna from doing," he said.

"Don't you get it? It's not your decision to make, Liam. Her life is not yours to micromanage."

"I promised our father I would make sure she was happy." Raking his hands through his hair, he spun away from her and stalked to the open patio doors. Beyond the railing lay the infinite sea, as dark at night as it was brilliant during the day. "I swore I would make sure Jenna was happy."

"Then trust her to make sure that happens and be there to help if she asks for it. But don't you dare take over her life and try to make it into your version of happy."

He didn't respond right away, just stood there staring out over the water.

"You don't get to choose for people, Liam. You don't get to live others' lives by proxy, to decide what's best for them under any given circumstance." The soles of her shoes tapped across the hardwood floor, the sound telling him she'd stopped somewhere nearby. "What did you see happening here, between us?"

There were a hundred things he wanted to say, each of them the truth, but like the apology that wouldn't come, neither would a single answer to her question.

"Did you seduce me so you could have free rein where this wedding was concerned, or did you seduce me because you wanted me?"

There was heartache in that question, and fury as well. What struck him the hardest was the sour note of regret she couldn't, or didn't bother to, hide.

So no more lies. No more deception. "Both."

She laughed, the sound brittle on the soft night air. "I can't believe I fell for you, let you use me like you did."

He rounded on her. "I didn't use you."

She looked up slowly as if she'd been stunned. "You did, and by your own admission. You seduced me. And I fell for it." She shook her head. "You must really think I'm a fool. I sure as hell do." She stepped away from him, and he moved to catch her when she swayed. She stumbled out of his reach and then froze, not looking at him when she spoke. "Touch me again, Liam Baggett, and I swear I will cause you a world of hurt."

Liam stepped back, and she shot him a look that would haunt him for the rest of his life. "I wouldn't hurt you, Ella."

She grabbed the handle of her bag and started for the door. Drawing parallel to him, she stopped and leaned in. "You already did."

And then she was gone.

CHAPTER FOURTEEN

ELLA REFUSED TO CRY. That man didn't deserve her tears any more than he deserved her forgiveness. He'd thrown her under the bus with so much force she'd nearly come out the other side. Had he apologized with an ounce of sincerity, she might have been able to forgive him. But hearing him admit that he'd seduced her not only for pleasure had wounded her pride. Not as much as it wounded her heart, though. Because as stupid as it was, she'd fallen for him.

She wandered the grounds for a while before collapsing onto an empty beach chaise. They were plentiful this late at night, but she craved one away from wandering beachgoers. Midnight strollers. Lovers. She'd lied to Liam when she told him she'd found a place to stay. There still wasn't a room available, but she'd be damned if she'd be dependent on his good will. Never again.

When dawn finally came, she made her way to the concierge's desk, asked them to stow her two bags and went to the dining room for breakfast. It was a quick trip through the buffet before Arvin called to inform her the first shuttle of guests had arrived and checked in to the block of rooms Liam had reserved under a fictitious party name. The whole thing had been set up under the guise of a family reunion. So far, it had worked.

Ella went to the event coordination desk and made sure the welcome bags for each guest were ready and labeled; she double-checked the contents and then went out to the docks to check on the boats reserved for parasailing.

At one o'clock, Ella confirmed all the guests had arrived and then had a member of Arvin's staff call each room and ask guests who had signed up for the excursion to meet her on the lawn behind the main dining room.

The guests trickled into the tent in twos and threes. Liam came somewhere in the middle, trying to speak to Ella. She avoided any conversation by saying, "I believe the bride is in that corner, Mr. Baggett. You'll want to see her, I'm sure." Then she focused on the guests behind him. Ella greeted each one, provided them with the courtesy towel, bottled water and sunscreen, and she explained that, after their excursion, there would be a champagne bar set up and in-room spa treatments available before the rehearsal dinner. Despite the fact she'd done it before, it was a bit intimidating to be mixing with Hollywood's elite. There was so much riding on this job. She had to get it right. From the positive responses coming from the group,

it seemed she had. It was just too soon to cash that
particular check, though.

They all went down to the docks, Mike and Jenna
walking with her. When they reached the power-
boats, Mike stopped short.

Jenna looked between the boat, her fiancé and
Ella. "What are we doing?"

"Parasailing?" Ella's response came out a timid
question.

Mike shot her a sharp look. "I thought we'd agreed
on diving."

Ella took a deep breath. "It was suggested that
more people would take part in parasailing, so the
event was changed."

Jenna stepped in close to Mike and took his free
hand in hers. "It will be okay. You don't have to do
this."

"Is there a problem?" Ella asked under her breath.

"Mike is, um…" Jenna glanced at her feet.

"I hate heights," he said between gritted teeth.

Oh. Shit.

Ella wanted to curl in on herself as much as she
wanted to explode with rage all over Liam. *He'd*
picked parasailing over horseback riding, and she'd
agreed. He'd done it again—thrown her to the wolves
and left her to be eaten alive.

She went into disaster intervention mode. Stepping back, she turned to the guests who were mill-
ing about, shooting curious glances their way. With a
broad grin, she said, "Jenna was torn between going
up with Mike on the first run, or going up with her

brother. Mike, being his typical gracious self, offered to let brother and sister go up first. And since we're an odd-numbered group, Mike has offered to man the ladder for everyone. After you land in the water at the end of your ride, an instructor will get you unhooked from the sail. You'll swim to the side of the boat and Mike will help you up the ladder if you need assistance." She beamed at Mike, maybe a little too overdone, but she beamed all the same. "Thank you, Mike, for being ever the gentleman."

A smattering of applause sounded.

Mike took a small bow.

Jenna nudged him aside and reached for Liam. "We're first!" She hauled her brother away as if the dock was on fire, shoving him into the first boat so hard he tripped and nearly fell in the water.

"Everyone else, pick your ride partner." Numb with anxiety, Ella moved like an automaton, helping people pair up and sorting them onto boats. Then she followed Mike onboard, fully expecting to get reamed out.

"Thank you," he said from the side of his mouth.

Ella shot him a speculative glance. "You're... welcome?"

"For not making a big deal about it *and* getting my ass out of that obligatory ride." He wiped actual sweat from his forehead. "You have no idea what that would have cost me."

"I didn't know."

His face darkened. "I'm sure you didn't." He waved her off when she started to apologize again. "Let's get through this and the rehearsal dinner, and we'll be golden. How bad can it actually be? As long as I come out of this married to that woman, it's all good."

Six hours later, as Mike was loaded into an ambulance, Ella realized exactly how bad it could be.

Liam had shown up at the rehearsal dinner late and taken his seat with a table of guests. When the appetizer came out and his plate was set before him, he'd shoved out of his chair and scanned the room. Eyes lighting on hers, he started toward Ella with long strides. She'd directed him back to his seat with a sharp point of her finger and a glare.

He'd kept coming.

So she'd jabbed her finger in the direction of his seat and mouthed the word *Now*.

Still, he kept coming.

Her stomach had twisted itself into a complex series of knots that tightened with every step Liam took toward her. Then he slipped his arm through Ella's and directed her to the back of the room, smiling as they went.

He leaned in, his lips brushing her ear, the move as sensual as his words were chilling. "Where are the scallops?"

"Don't worry, they're here. I had them added to the salmon croquette sauce because there weren't enough harvested to make them part of the main course."

"Ella, Mike hates shellfish. Absolutely abhors the things. Gags on them."

Everything after that happened in slow motion.

She turned toward Mike to find him choking and Jenna panicking. Someone shouted for a doctor. Another person rose and started toward him. Liam lifted his phone, dialed the front desk and requested emergency medical services in the dining room.

And Mike began to turn a weird puce color.

"Oh, God." She stumbled, and Liam caught her. "Liam, he doesn't hate shellfish. He's allergic."

"Oh, sweet hell."

She looked up at him, then, not sure what she'd find. He was so pale he appeared almost corpse-like.

The resort doctor rushed into the room moments later and, hauling a monster-size syringe out of his bag, stabbed Mike in the thigh. Seconds passed like minutes, hours, and then Mike took a ragged breath.

Sirens wailed, coming closer with every subsequent breath he took.

"Did you know?" she croaked out.

"I swear to you, I didn't. I intended to annoy him to pieces, but I didn't have a clue he was allergic. Only that he was a royal prick about not having them touch his food the first night I met him at dinner with Jenna."

Paramedics had Mike on a gurney and were wheeling him out before Ella was able to move. She rushed to the bride's table, where Liam was talking to Jenna in a low, calm voice.

Jenna caught sight of Ella and, with a tear-streaked face, said, "You served shellfish. Why? *Why?*" The last word was screamed, a demand for an unanswerable question.

Behind Ella, the crowd began to murmur.

"The why isn't important right now," Liam said. "We need to get you to Mike so you can be with him." Taking her by the arm, he steered her toward the exit at a brisk pace, not once looking back to where he'd left Ella...standing at the front of the room, under the weight of glares from people who believed she'd just poisoned the groom. What was worse, she couldn't remember if she'd made the change or if Liam had.

Regardless, Mike had suffered for the choice. Badly. And she'd never forgive herself.

Her career had been on life support, and Liam had just pulled the plug.

Liam stood in the corner of the hospital room and watched Jenna and Mike. Heads together and hands clasped, they whispered to each other and shared small, intimate kisses despite Mike's swollen face and lips. Hell, his swollen upper body. Even his fingers looked like sausages. His eyes were slits in his head. At least he was breathing.

And it was all because of the shellfish.

Liam stood quietly, hands in his pockets and chin to his chest. Damn, but that had been close. Mike had all but stopped breathing when the resort physician had arrived with an EpiPen. Mike had left his own in the hotel room.

God alone knew how guilty Liam felt. He'd known Mike didn't *like* scallops. When Liam had treated Mike and Jenna to a rather fancy dinner in London, the man had turned down the scallop appetizer. Liam had prodded him about being a burger-and-beer guy. Common. Mike had blown Liam off without mentioning that it was an allergy versus a preference. If he'd left Ella to do her job, it would have been fine. If he'd not insisted on poking at Mike until his temper exploded, this wouldn't have happened. If he'd only—

"Liam?"

He looked up and found Jenna focused on him. Mike had drifted off to sleep.

His little sister took a deep breath, stood and squared her shoulders. "I want you to fire the event coordinator."

"I'm not sure that's the best course of action."

Her brows winged up so far they nearly met her hairline. "Not the best course of action? How can you say that when she nearly killed my fiancé? Look at him, Liam." She tipped her head toward the sleeping man. "His oxygen saturation only just topped ninety. According to the doctor, it should be ninety-nine given the excellent shape he's in. I know you were involved in the peacock thing—" she held out her hand when he tried to interrupt "—don't bother denying it. But she knew I was scared of birds. It was on the original paperwork. The excursion was supposed to have been diving. It's what we picked. She changed that to parasailing. And we had specifically requested a native meal for the rehearsal and wedding dinners, listing things we wanted included. Shellfish wasn't on the list for a reason. And you don't serve something like that, let alone hide it in

a sauce, without knowing if someone is allergic."
Her voice had risen as she listed her complaints, and
Mike stirred beside her. "Shh, baby. Rest."

"Want to get married."

"And we will," she said softly, smoothing a hand
over his hair. "We will."

Liam had a difficult choice to make. He could respect Jenna's wishes and use Ella's termination as a
means of cutting ties with the woman. He could still
fire her but keep to his original plan and hire her to
coordinate several high-end functions, thus helping
her get things back on track. He could even leave
everything to his sister and let her terminate Ella,
keeping his hands out of it completely.

But he was the direct cause of everything that
had gone wrong. Ella had changed the dive excursion to parasailing because the changes Liam had insisted upon were eating into her profit margin. He'd
been directly responsible for the peacocks—*pink*
peacocks, at that. And the doves. And the changed
flowers, from the bride's bouquet to the groom's bou-
tonniere to the table toppers. And the revised seating
chart. And, worst of all, the addition of scallops to
the menu. While he wanted to deny it all, to affect
having no conscience, he couldn't. Not this time. Ella
had paid, and dearly, for his mistakes. He wouldn't
let her take the fall, again, for his screwups.

Regret bound his chest like a vise. And he knew
that whatever he was suffering, Ella had to be suffering a hundredfold. Her career's recovery had hinged
on the success of this job. People had seen what had

happened. Influential people. And they would talk. He might not be able to stop them, but he would do what he could to help her find her path forward.

If he could manage to salvage this, maybe he had a chance at getting her to forgive him.

Better luck betting the contents of my wallet on the afternoon races.

But he had to hope. It was all he had.

Then there was Jenna. And, more consequently, Mike, he acknowledged grudgingly. Watching them together in this intimate setting, he saw something between them he'd somehow missed before. They'd gotten together so quickly, had already been engaged when Jenna introduced him to Mike. Liam hadn't had the chance to observe them like this, to watch how the man tended to Jenna's every want, met her every need and cared for her without apology. Liam had been wrong about the man and his motives, and he'd have to admit it. Not just to Jenna, but to the man himself. So many apologies in front of him, the first of which would be hard, the last of which would be the hardest but also the most important.

Looking at Jenna, he struggled to find the right words. Liam blew out a hard breath, gave up what little semblance of control he had left and did what he'd never done before. He spoke from the heart. "Jenna, I've made a right mess of things."

"It's not your fault Ella nearly killed Mike."

Ever faithful, his little sister.

"Actually, it is." If he could just keep his voice

steady. "Your assistant provided her with your wish list. I have a copy of it on my computer."

Jenna just looked at him.

"I also have the digital copy as well as Ella's hard copy of that list with… Damn it." He raked his hands through his hair and grabbed fistfuls in frustration. This was proving even harder than he'd expected it would be.

"Leem, what's going on?" Jenna's skepticism was beginning to trump her faith in him, and witnessing the change devastated him.

Treat it like a bandage. Grab the edge and rip.

"I'm responsible for every change that was made to the original wedding plans." And he waited.

She stared at him, eyes wide. "You."

"Yes. Me." He blew out a breath. "I didn't believe Mike was the best choice for your husband, squid. You ran off and fell in love between Christmas and New Year, accepted a proposal without consideration and began planning a wedding by Easter. It was too fast. And my first impression of Mike was poor, to say the least."

"Your first impression trumps mine?" she wheezed. "What, he wasn't high enough on society's scale of 'Rich and Richer' for you? What about me, Liam? What about what I want? I told Ella precisely what my dream wedding would look like. It was her job to make that happen. Your only job was to be happy for me."

"Ella only did what I told her to do. She was operating in good faith and believed I was acting in your best interest as your proxy. I wasn't, and I own that."

"You *own* that?" she asked, voice deceptively calm. Her eyes? Not so calm. In them, a tempest raged, coming closer to the surface with every heartbeat. "How dare you, Liam. How dare you come in here to Mike's room, a room he wouldn't be in if it weren't for your callousness, your narcissistic belief you know what's right for everyone. How. Dare. You." She turned away from him and picked up Mike's hand. "Damn you, Liam. Your arrogance could have killed this man. Killed my heart. In turn, you would have killed me. You were okay with that?" Blond curls slid forward, curtaining her face, shielding her from him. "You aren't the man I thought you were. Please leave."

"Jenna—"

"Leave," Mike whispered, voice raspy. "We'll work out what's best for us and let you know where we go from here."

Liam swallowed the argument he'd been mounting, the words scraping his throat raw before plummeting into the depths of his belly.

He left.

CHAPTER FIFTEEN

ELLA DIDN'T BOTHER trying to sleep. There were no available flights off the island until the following afternoon, so she had time to kill and nowhere private to do so. She spent the first part of the night on a beach chaise again, but the resort's security patrol asked her to return to her room for her safety given that the height of the carnival was nearing. She couldn't argue with that, so she went to the hotel lobby, powered up her computer and opened her accounting file. No need to put off the truth of her financial situation. With a new spreadsheet, she began compiling a list of bills, a second sheet with a list of physical assets she could liquidate and a third sheet with a list of liquid assets. The last was the shortest list. She was broke, and it was only going to get worse before it got better.

Her eyes were heavy and she found herself bobbleheading as the hour hand slipped past two in the morning. No doubt she'd lost the job, and that meant she had nothing better to do. She was about to give in and lay her head on the table when someone slid a cup of coffee toward her.

"Brain juice," she whispered. Slurred? Whatever. She needed the caffeine like a newborn babe needed its mother's milk. Her hands shook as she lifted the cup to her mouth. Had she ever been this tired? She took a big sip.

"It's hot, Ella."

She spat the contents out. Yes, it was hot. But the warning was delivered with a British accent.

A *male* British accent.

Adrenaline crashed through her, and she started to shake even as her bleary vision cleared. Liam sat across from her, wiping coffee from his face. All the things she wanted to say rushed to the tip of her tongue and fought for their right to be the first words chosen, the first threat delivered, the first curse uttered. But instead of saying anything intelligible, she sputtered and tripped over her thoughts, managing single syllables.

"Not the greeting I expected, though not as bad as it could have been." Liam's words were muffled as he dragged his arm across his face and blinked a few times to clear the last of the coffee from his eyes.

"That you expected anything from me after all you've done tells me what a fool you really are." Ella gathered her personal flotsam, closed her computer and began shoving things into her bag.

"Ella, please." He settled a hand over hers.

Shock raced through that point of contact and up her arm. Heat followed, so intense it was nearly unbearable. She jerked away from him and knocked over the coffee cup and the saucer it sat in. Porcelain splintered on the tile floor and bled black as the still-hot brew seeped out of the mess in every direction. Shoving her chair back, she stepped around the mess and hoisted her messenger bag over her shoulder.

No matter what he'd done, seeing Liam hurt on a deep, personal level. But there were a couple of things she had to say or she'd never forgive herself. Steeling herself, she lifted her chin and met his dark gaze head-on. "It breaks my heart on a variety of levels that you lied to me, Liam, that you used me and proved yourself to be someone other than the man I thought I'd come to know."

"Ella," Liam interrupted.

But she was having none of it. "I'm. Not. Done." Her jaw was so tight she didn't know how she'd get the next words out, but they were burning a hole in her self-worth, and pride demanded she fling them out so she alone didn't have to bear the burden of their being. "You destroyed my career, Liam. You have made it impossible for me to go back to Los Angeles and get any type of respectable work in event planning. You screwed me—physically, mentally, emotionally and, above all, professionally. My only solace is that karma's a bitch, and her memory's infallible."

With that, she hoisted her bag higher and strode across the lobby, out the main doors and across the grass. She shook, an emotional tempest whipping her thoughts into a frenzy, the vortex dropping into her chest and battering her heart. She should've let him have it—*really* let him have it. She could've ripped him to shreds, could have left a tattered mess in her wake.

"Pretty to think so," she said to herself, kicking at a small coconut that had fallen on the path to the beach.

All night she'd been skirting the truth, coming close and then racing away. But when she'd stormed off, her heart aching with every beat and her eyes stinging with caustic tears, she'd realized that avoidance might work for others, but she wasn't programmed that way.

The truth? She wanted to hurt Liam, deliver a little tit for tat, but she couldn't. Because she'd fallen for him.

Sincerely.

Thoroughly.

Completely.

She stepped off the end of the path and onto the beach, feet sinking ankle deep into the soft white sand. The moon cast a silvery beam across the water. Waves rolled in and crashed against the shore.

Ella sighed. At least she had this last memory, the beauty of this place emblazoned on her mind.

"Ella."

Ella whipped around, fists clenched.

Keeping out of arm's reach, he pushed his hair off his forehead before shoving his hands in his pockets. "I want… I need to make this up to you."

"How? You think you can, what, demand others respect me after this? Maybe hire me despite the sheer fuckery this event turned into?" Her harsh laugh scraped her throat raw.

And wasn't it telling he wanted to fix the business

side of things while the personal side was far more devastating? How could he not know?

"I have connections, Ella. I can make people hire you."

"Make...people..." Against her will and despite her pride, her chin began to wobble. "Make them hire me. Buy my way into good graces with your financial backing."

"I didn't mean it that way."

"Then how did you mean it, Liam? Be very clear so I don't hear the wrong thing. Again."

"You're wildly talented. Look at all you did for my sister's wedding."

"I nearly killed the groom. That's a real résumé builder. How much money would it take to hide that little 'oops'?"

He looked out over the beach, his gaze fixed somewhere near the horizon. "I can't undo that, but I want you to know I can help you regain what was lost. I can arrange high-profile events, hire you to coordinate them, make sure there's media coverage and promote the rebuilding of your brand."

"And what about me, Liam? As an entrepreneur or, better, as a woman? What about my self-respect? My pride at having recovered from being screwed over the first time by my former business partner? My sense of self-worth that people desired my skills, my name on their registry, my vision for their perfect day? How do you propose to buy those back?" she demanded.

"I have resources you can't imagine. I have contacts with more power and influence than the combined social power of the entire guest list at that rehearsal dinner. I can pave the way for you to reclaim your social status and reassert your position as the elite event planner in more than just LA." He shifted his gaze to her and threw his hands in the air. "Why is this so hard for you to see?"

"Because what I see is you throwing your name and your influence and your money at a problem thinking you know the best way to fix it. Here's the thing, Liam. You might be able to buy my way back into society's good graces. You might even be able to save my business. But you can't *buy* my reputation. And if you can't buy that, you sure as hell can't buy my pride or my self-worth or my ethics. They were never for sale. Everything I did, I did because I thought it was the right thing to do. You broke that…" She paused and then thought, *What the hell*, and threw down the truth. He could do with it what he would. "You broke that, Liam, and you broke my heart."

With that, she turned and walked away from him. This time, he didn't follow.

Liam had always known where he belonged in the grand scheme of things, always knew just what he was supposed to do, who he was supposed to be, how he was supposed to act. From which fork to use at a formal dinner to the right putter on the golf course to the best wine to pair with steak, *he knew*. But just then, sitting on the beach in his suit pants and his tailored shirt with French cuffs and his polished wing tips, he had no clue what to do. He wouldn't have been surprised to look in the mirror and find a stranger staring back.

There were so many things he'd planned to say and do, so many ways he was going to make things right, and not a single one would come to pass. Not with Jenna and certainly not with Ella. Both women had made it clear that they were done with the whole debacle. They hadn't been talking entirely about the wedding, either. They'd been talking about Liam. They were done with *him*.

The image of Jenna's hurt but furious face flashed through his mind and was followed immediately by Ella. He remembered everything he'd said and done, from their initial meeting where he'd landed in her lap to the first time he'd kissed her to the first lie he'd told and his moment of conscience when he'd told her not to change the seating charts. Memory after memory flashed through his mind, the more personal ones—the scent of her perfume, the sound of his name sighed across her lips, the feel of her arching beneath his hand, her laugh, the way she looked when she slept—becoming rapid-fire kill shots that left him struggling to breathe. A single truth threaded its way through every interaction, every conversation and every moment he'd spent with her: the way she made him *feel*.

She'd made him doubt his cynicism and believe that, just maybe, finding his own happily-ever-after was possible.

He'd been such an ass.

"Oh, Leem," said a soft voice behind him. "What have you done?"

He whirled around and found Jenna standing there, the sun beginning to stain the darkness with dawn's light. Jenna, the sister he loved to the ends of the earth.

"Jenna. I'm so sorry." His voice broke on the last word, a word he couldn't remember offering to anyone before.

She crossed the sand and, in seconds, held him in her embrace. So huge, so all-encompassing for such a pixie of a woman. Arms tight around his waist and cheek against his chest, she spoke low but with undeniable fervor. "You really screwed up."

"You don't know the half of it."

"Ella?"

His entire body twitched in her embrace, but she didn't let go.

"I thought so." A smile lurked in her voice and he wanted to chastise her for relishing his defeat, but he'd earned her scorn. Then she surprised him by hugging him impossibly tighter. "You know, I still love the pudding out of you, but you *really* screwed up."

"I did," he admitted, breathing easier at her reassurance. "And with a self-righteous vigor reserved for few of my ilk."

She tilted her head back and considered him. "Your ilk?"

"I'm a capital ass, Jenna."

She smiled beatifically. "You so are."

Something in him—the fear he'd lost her—suddenly eased. She would forgive him. And somehow, some way, he would earn her trust as well as her respect again.

Jenna let him go and stepped back. "What happened?"

He'd always been there for his sister, always been her sounding board and confidant, but he'd never confided in her, thinking it was a show of weakness. Not anymore. So Liam did something he'd never done before: he told her everything. Too much, probably, if some of her reactions and the repeated "TMI" were any indication.

Jenna sat on the sand halfway through his story, listening and watching him pace. When he stopped speaking and went still, she popped back to her feet. "So, do you love her?"

He started to deny the emotion out of habit, but her stern look stopped him and he answered the only way he could. "I... How do I know? For sure, I mean."

"Nothing's guaranteed, Liam. Not even love. You have to take a chance."

"I deal in statistical probabilities and historical trends, not chance."

She punched him lightly on the shoulder. "You and that ilk thing. Cut your crap." She took both of his hands and stared up at him. "There are a hundred, a *thousand* questions I could ask you—does she make your breath come short? Do you relax, really relax, around her? Do you feel like you could tell her anything? Do you trust her? Do you love waking up to her face? Do you miss her the minute she begins to walk away? They're all valid, Liam, but there's only one question that really matters."

He waited.

"If she walks out of your life, walks out and never comes back, will you be a better man or a broken man?"

"Broken," he whispered.

"There's your answer." Jenna smiled, her true smile. "No matter what you think of Mike, I am crazy in love with that man. Your opinion—the world's opinion—will never change that for me. He's my One, capital *O*. I would give up everything for him, Liam, and he'd do the same for me. The beautiful thing, though? Love doesn't mean losing one thing to gain another. It's gaining something that enhances everything else in your life. There are compromises, yes," she said, one hand waving those invisible compromises off like they were a swarm of gnats. "But compromise isn't loss, either. It's just bending what you want to make it suit two lives instead of one. Only a fool would miss his shot at his one, Leem, and you're no fool."

He pulled her back in for a tight hug. "I've been exactly that."

"You've certainly been fool*ish*," she admonished, her words a bit warped as he had her face mashed into his chest. "But a fool? You're a Baggett, dear brother. Dad neither raised nor tolerated fools within his clan."

Only Jenna would call the elder Baggett "Dad." The thought made Liam smile, an action not at all common when remembering the old man. "Just so."

"Mike and I got married."

He stiffened. "Beg your pardon?"

"In the hospital. Ella showed up with a beautiful bridal bouquet, my dress, his tux jacket and the rings. I guess she got some guy named Arvin out of bed in the middle of the night and got our stuff together. She made my bouquet." Jenna pulled her phone out of her little handbag and showed Liam pictures. "She asked us if what we had was worth fighting for—no matter who fought against us." She looked up. "Ella so meant you, Liam."

"I got that." His tone was dry as dust.

"Just making sure you're keeping up. Anyway," she continued, "she asked us and we both said yes. She'd asked the doctor about Mike's possible release and they're keeping him for at least twenty-four hours of observation, so he wouldn't have been out in time for the wedding. So she said we should get married by the hospital chaplain and then show up, after they let Mike go, for the wedding dinner and share the good news that way." She grinned. "She repeated something Mike had said about how it couldn't be all that bad if he left here married to me, so she made it happen." Jenna sighed. "She's a total romantic, and the ceremony was beautiful and we had Mike's doctor give me away and the charge nurse was my maid of honor. It was lovely."

"You got married...in a hospital?" he choked out.

"Like you gave me any other option," she retorted. And he shut up.

"Don't let her go, Liam. Please. I'm going to tell everyone what happened and encourage my agency and my studio to use her for events. I'm going to ask my friends to use her. Whatever it takes, I want to help her get back on track. But most of all? I don't want you two to lose each other. Please."

Liam nodded, his vision watery with what he deemed gratitude. "Where is she?"

The sun had long since cleared the horizon and begun to warm the day. "I think she was going to catch the first available flight to the main island and head home from there." She glanced at her watch. "If you hurry—"

"I'll catch her," he said. He kissed Jenna's cheek. "I love you, Jen."

"And I you, Leem." She beamed up at him. "Go get your one."

CHAPTER SIXTEEN

ELLA STOOD IN line waiting to board the tiny puddle jumper for the first of four flights she'd take to get home. Professionally, she'd done what she could to pull a rabbit out of the hat and save the wedding. At first, Jenna had been unsure of Ella's plan to have them married at the hospital. Sure, it had been a long shot. *But no shot will make it if you don't take it.* Her dad's words had marched around inside Ella's head as she pulled things together and took the shuttle to the hospital. They hadn't even faltered at Jenna's reserved greeting. But when Mike had looked at Jenna, motioned her over and said, "Be my wife. Now and always," Ella had wanted to melt *and* pump a fist in the air.

The ceremony had been short but sweet, and it had been evident how in love the bride and groom were. Whatever came their way, they'd handle it. And provided Mike continued to improve, there would be one hell of a reception on the beach tonight. Thanks to Arvin, there would be no shellfish anywhere near the food, and he and his team would be following the original plans, save one thing. The bride and groom had thought it was kind of cool to have the sports drinks incorporated—despite their garish color. So those would stay, just not on the table. They'd be going home in everyone's swag bags.

The door to the plane opened, and the pilot stepped out onto the boarding ladder clipped to the side of the plane. "Good morning! This is flight one-nine-one-Alpha-Tango-Delta that will take you to the main island. It's a forty-minute trip from takeoff to touchdown. Welcome aboard."

Ella climbed the steps and shoved her suitcase in the small overhead bin. It barely fit, and she had to wrestle it into place. She'd probably never get the damn thing out. Figured. If she could just get home… She'd deal with the fallout there.

Her phone chimed, and she checked it, froze and blinked rapidly, trying to comprehend what she was seeing. It was a request from Jenna to coordinate her and Mike's reception in Hollywood. They'd decided to throw a big party once they were back from their honeymoon and sell the photos, with the proceeds going to their favorite environmental charity. A second email followed, this one from Jenna's studio, asking Ella to coordinate a small, intimate event where well-wishers from the studio could congratulate the bride and groom. The initial guest list of seventy-five people made Ella light-headed. The budget forced her to drop into her seat like her ass was made of granite.

Whatever was happening, it was like karma had

finally decided Ella deserved a little recognition and had upped the wattage to "spotlight." Jenna had sent the kindest thank-you note for their ceremony and said she hoped Ella would meet her for lunch to discuss the reception as soon as Jenna was back in town.

Ella tried to type a response, but her fingers shook so badly that what came out was something not even autocorrect could untangle. She tucked her phone away, determined to answer when the plane set down at the international concourse on the main island. She had a three-hour layover anyway. Plenty of time to get her nerves under control.

The door to the plane closed, the engines started and the noise echoed around inside the hollow pit in Ella's stomach. No matter how far Jenna's request went toward soothing Ella's fear she'd never work again, there was still the matter of Liam. The pain of losing him was far worse than she'd ever imagined it could be. It made little sense that she'd fallen for him so hard and fast. But it simply was what it was. She was sure she'd recover, but she'd have felt much better if she had a timeline. Right now it felt like it would be years before she could even stomach the idea of drinks with a stranger. She would simply have to fight her way back to her old self. Period.

"Even if it kills me a little bit each day," she murmured.

The plane taxied away from the tiny terminal, bouncing around as it crossed the cracked and broken asphalt that led to the slightly more even runway.

Ella closed her eyes and let her head rest against the seat back, the dull roar of the engines fueling a burgeoning headache. She was so tired. Maybe she'd be able to get some sleep, if not now then certainly on the next flight to Honolulu.

The engines powered down at the same time the pilot's voice came over the speaker system. "Ladies and gentlemen, there has been a slight delay in our departure. We'll be returning to the gate for a moment to resolve an outstanding issue and then we'll be on our way."

Grumbles and protests were soft, subtle.

Ella sat up, rubbing her temple. The plane came to a stop and the pilot emerged, opened the door and said something to someone outside.

"I'd come back for a piece of that pie," a woman murmured.

Something stirred in Ella's belly, something suspiciously similar to hope.

The pilot stepped back into the cockpit, leaving plenty of room for Liam to enter the cabin.

Ella stared at him, dumbfounded. "What do you think you're doing?"

He came toward her, movements lithe despite the cabin's tiny confines. "We're not done here, Ella."

"I am."

He stopped beside her seat, deep brown eyes meeting hers with an unfamiliar somberness. "If you really mean that, I'll get off this plane. I'd ask that you hear me out first."

Ella looked around. "Here?"

"Here," someone called out from farther back.

"Then here it is," Liam replied. "I'm an ass."

"News flash," Ella muttered. "You forgot a few adjectives, mostly *controlling, superior, vain, boorish, arrogant, egotistical, conceited, self-important.* Should I go on?"

"No need, seeing as I agree with everything you've said." Liam closed his eyes and took one deep breath, two, three, as he seemed to search for words. Finally, he opened his eyes and focused on her with an intensity that kept her silent. "It's become clear to me that I'm a rather self-righteous jackass who, until recently, operated on the assumption that I knew what was best for everyone." He held up a hand when she opened her mouth to respond. "Please. I'd like to get this out before I lose my nerve."

"You never lose your nerve," she whispered.

He traced a finger along her jaw. "I've never had something I was so scared to lose."

She couldn't speak, could only nod and pray that he didn't expect more from her.

"I have made mistakes in life, the most egregious ones this week. But if I let you leave this island without hearing how I feel about you—about *us*—it will be the biggest mistake I'll ever make. You see, I've always chosen duty over desire. It was the Baggett way. Emotions weren't a factor when one had to make a choice. Baggett men did what they were conditioned to do."

"Achieve the desired outcome at any cost." Ella

swallowed hard. "I remember this part of the program."

A smile teased one corner of his mouth. "I'm the boss, so I'm exercising my right to change the program."

Her head was spinning. This wasn't happening, wasn't real. It couldn't be. "You don't make yourself vulnerable, Liam. It's not who you are. You've said as much yourself."

"Words I'd take back if I could, but I can't. So, that leaves me with two choices."

"Which are?" she whispered, scared to death to hope.

"I can stay the course, or I can change. I can remain a closed-off, narcissistic, self-serving asshole, or I can open myself up to be the man I want to be—a man not quite so Baggett-like as my father would have preferred."

Change the course. A spark of hope flared in her heart and burned hot. "Why?"

"Because I'm still Baggett enough to do whatever is necessary to achieve the desired outcome. But a smart woman showed me that vulnerability is actually strength manifest. It takes a brutally strong person to put themselves out there, knowing they could be hurt, and yet still take the risk in pursuit of the reward."

"Sounds like a smart woman."

"She is. Smart, funny, loyal, brilliant, creative, sexy as hell. I could go on if you'd like."

She shook her head, the movement minute. "No. What I mean is, why now, Liam? Why me?"

"Jenna asked me the most profound question. 'If she walks out of your life, will you be a better man, Liam, or will you be a broken man?'"

Ella waited, not sure where Liam was going with the question. She knew—God help her, she *knew*—what she wanted, needed, to hear from Liam. But she wasn't going to put herself out there, refused to offer even a single word of encouragement that might change his authentic answer, the answer he had to come up with on his own if it was going to matter.

"I will be a broken man if you leave this island without me, Ella. I don't know how we'll make it work. But I know with absolute certainty that there is no obstacle so insurmountable that I can't conquer it with you."

With her. Not *for* her. "Sounds like a pretty intense partnership," she said quietly.

"I can only hope." He held out a hand. "I'm far from perfect. I'll make missteps. I'll stumble. I'll be an asshole of ridiculous proportions more often than not...but only until you've polished my roughest edges and helped me shape my vulnerability into strength."

She took his hand, and he pulled her to her feet.

"You are the only woman who has ever made me believe in love, Ella Montgomery."

"May it always be so." She smiled. "Unless we have daughters."

His eyes went comically wide. "God save us all. I

botched up having a little sister. Any daughter would be doomed…save for the fact she'd have you as her mother."

"Is she staying or going?" someone asked in a stage whisper. "I'm going to miss my connecting flight if she doesn't choose quickly."

Liam looked down at her. "What will it be, Ms. Montgomery? Will you stay?"

Ella took his face in her hands, rose to tiptoe and kissed the man who had won her heart.

Liam pulled her into a fierce hug. "Captain," he called out, "file your flight plan with one change. Your passenger count is minus one."

* * * * *

COMING SOON!

We really hope you enjoyed reading this book. If you're looking for more romance, be sure to head to the shops when new books are available on

Thursday 2nd May

To see which titles are coming soon, please visit

millsandboon.co.uk/nextmonth

Want even more
ROMANCE?

Join our bookclub today!

'Mills & Boon books, the perfect way to escape for an hour or so.'

Miss W. Dyer

'Excellent service, promptly delivered and very good subscription choices.'

Miss A. Pearson

'You get fantastic special offers and the chance to get books before they hit the shops'

Mrs V. Hall

Visit millsandbook.co.uk/Bookclub and save on brand new books.

MILLS & BOON

LET'S TALK
Romance

For exclusive extracts, competitions
and special offers, find us online:

f facebook.com/millsandboon

🐦 @MillsandBoon

📷 @MillsandBoonUK

Get in touch on 01413 063232

For all the latest titles coming soon, visit
millsandboon.co.uk/nextmonth